MOON OF
BITTER COLD

MOON OF
BITTER COLD

Frederick J. Chiaventone

A TOM DOHERTY ASSOCIATES BOOK
NEW YORK

This is a work of fiction. All the characters and events portrayed in this book are either products of the author's imagination or are used fictitiously.

MOON OF BITTER COLD

Copyright © 2002 by Frederick J. Chiaventone

A Forge Book
Published by Tom Doherty Associates, LLC
175 Fifth Avenue
New York, NY 10010

www.tor.com

Forge® is a registered trademark of Tom Doherty Associates, LLC.

ISBN: 0-765-34657-5

First edition: April 2002
First mass market edition: June 2003

Printed in the United States of America

0 9 8 7 6 5 4 3 2 1

For
Sharon, Owen, and Gabriel
and
Rosemary

Acknowledgments

As with any work of historical fiction, this has not been a solitary work but has been aided by countless people who gladly lent their time and expertise to its making. Therefore I would like to take this opportunity to extend my thanks to those who helped to make this story come alive. Thanks go to Dr. Jeff Prater of Sheridan, Wyoming, for his knowledge of frontier army mythology and to his wife, Dana, curator at the Trails End Museum in Sheridan, whose knowledge of the role of women on the frontier, their customs, courtesies, and influence is positively encyclopedic. Thanks also to Mr. Morton Reeber and J. Gehrig "Shadowcatcher" Fry for their assistance in helping me to grasp the complex business of wet plate photography. For their assistance in getting an inside look into Lakota internal politics, thanks go to Mr. Arthur Shortbull (Tatanka Ptcelele) and Dr. Leonard Bruguier, Director of American Indian Studies of the University of South Dakota. I wish to extend my gratitude to Paul and Skeeter McCarthy for their unerring support in this effort. Thanks also to Terry McGarry for her superb editing skills.

Thanks also to the staffs of the Frontier Army Museum and the Combined Arms Research Library at Fort Leavenworth, Kansas, for their unstinting and cheerful assistance in getting access to rather obscure documents and original artifacts. Thanks also to the staffs of the Fort Phil Kearny, Fort Stephen Watts Kearney, and Fort Laramie historic sites for their superb work in preserving bits of our past and allowing me access to same. Further thanks to Ms. Mary Ruth Peck and Mr. Joe Popper for their readings of my material and their priceless suggestions and comments on how to make the story better.

Thanks also to my great friends and fellow writers, Ralph Peters and Harold Coyle, who provided invaluable contributions to the end manuscript. And to Mr. Dan Carell, who trekked along the old Platte River Road and the site of Fort Phil Kearny with me and watched the herons in the pre-dawn hours at Fort Stephen Watts Kearney. Warmest thanks are reserved for Miss Connie Dover, a stunning songstress in her own right, for her invaluable help in tapping into the musical heritage of the American West and her incredible diligence in reading the drafts and providing her thoughts. And to Jeff Dover at Dover Graphics for his expertise in putting the whole thing together. Last but not least, my deepest thanks to my wife, Sharon, premier editor and my staunchest critic, who wants to make sure that everything is just so—this while raising two handsome young sons.

F. J. Chiaventone

Author's Note

Although it is one of the most compelling and tragic stories in American history, there is surprisingly little written about Red Cloud's War (1866–1868). Probably the best historical accounts are those penned by Dee Brown, *The Fetterman Massacre*, and by Margaret Carrington, *Ab' Sa' Ra' Ka: Home of the Crows*. For anyone who has actually walked the ground on which Fort Phil Kearny stood, or strolled on the windswept and desolate summit of Massacre Hill, it is difficult to imagine a more tragic and unnecessary episode. Eclipsed in our collective memory by the Battle of the Little Bighorn some ten years later, the disastrous Fetterman fight electrified a nation just beginning its long recovery from a ruinous Civil War. For many of the dispossessed and disillusioned survivors of that war the West provided a symbol of hope for new beginnings and a new way of life. Little thought was given to the fact that the lands viewed as balm for old wounds were already inhabited by a host of proud and combative peoples. As thousands of white Americans turned their eyes and hopes to the West, the Plains Indians reacted with alarm and indignation. With their homes and their way of life at risk, the Lakota, Cheyenne, and Arapaho were determined to resist. Two disparate cultures were set on a collision course and thus began one of the most savage protracted conflicts in America's history.

The prime mover in the events around which this novel is centered was a most unusual man. Still a controversial figure in Lakota history and politics, Red Cloud was not a man well-liked by his contemporaries. Pugnacious, ambitious, and abrasive, he had a talent for making enemies. It is thus even more surprising that he was able to surmount the myriad obstacles which mitigated against an effective confederation of the tribes inhabiting the area. The alliance which Red Cloud forged, while not a long-standing one, was strong enough to inflict a devastating defeat on the United States Army and force the United States government to sue for peace. Red Cloud's War was the only war in American history that was a clear-cut defeat for America and resulted in the only treaty in which the United States government yielded on every demand of the victor without some reciprocal concession. For Red Cloud, or, for that matter, any American Indian, this was a major accomplishment and one unequaled in our history.

It is interesting to note that after the Civil War, in the much reduced army that included the 18th Regiment of Infantry, men like Colonel Henry Carrington were assigned missions which parallel to an alarming degree the missions assigned to our forces in Kosovo and on the borders of Iraq prior to the current conflict. When I described the story of Colonel Henry Carrington and Fort Phil Kearny to a friend who had commanded the first U.S. armored brigade to enter Bosnia he nodded in sympathy and said, "We can only hope that somewhere out there we don't come up against another Red Cloud." Now, in the wake of the terrorist assaults on the World Trade Center in New York and the Pentagon in Virginia, and with our armed forces and those of our allies committed in Iraq it appears we are confronted with an adversary every bit as determined and dangerous.

Frederick J. Chiaventone
Weston, Missouri

As soldiers are sent to preserve the peace of the border and to prevent warfare, as much as to fight well if warfare becomes indispensable, it will be considered a very gross offense for a soldier to wrong or insult an Indian.

—Special orders issued by Colonel H. B. Carrington
Commander, 18th Infantry
13 June 1866

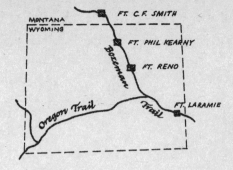

FT. C.F. SMITH

MONTANA
WYOMING

FT. PHIL KEARNY

Bozeman

FT. RENO

FT. LARAMIE

Oregon Trail

Trail

The Bozeman Trail
AND
Fort Phil Kearny
1866~1868

Bozeman Trail

FORT
PHIL KEARNY

Big Piney Creek

PILOT HILL

Prologue

Canwapegi wi
(Moon Of Calves Growing Black Hair)

Autumn 1865

The Powder River Country . . .

The young man lay stretched on the rock, gazing absently into the distance. The sun had heated the granite and he luxuriated in its warmth against his naked chest. He nestled his cheek against the rock. A breeze lifted up from the prairie below the precipice, enough to cool but not enough to chill. Below, the plains stretched and rolled off into eternity. Movement caught his eyes as a pronghorn antelope loped gracefully over to join its family. The young and females lay on their bellies in the lush grass while the older males stood off a few feet, their heads held high, ears twitching, scanning for the approach of predators.

HE HAD ALWAYS BEEN A WARRIOR. FROM HIS FIRST RAID AS a teenager he had found in battle a joy that eluded him in life. There was something magical, something *wakan*, about the feel of a strong, spirited horse under him, the animal's body heat gluing his thighs to its flanks, the sweat-slick roughness of the bow gripped in his left hand, the tickle of the feathered shaft caressed by the fingers of his right. Even now, in the silence of the mountains, he could feel the chill of the wind that would brush his face as he galloped into the chaos of battle. The rush of hot blood would pump through his veins and make his temples throb. Hoarseness would come from shrieking the war songs. That peculiar chill would run down his spine and quicken his flesh. Everything was more intense in battle—sounds, smells, taste, touch. It was unlike anything else a man could do. He liked women. He liked their smell, their taste, the feel of warm, willing flesh, but, compared with battle, they were so—ordinary. He had known women and he had known battle. The difference was that while he could remember and enjoy the thoughts of sharing a woman's blanket, such memories were invariably soft and indistinct. But the smallest detail of every single battle was seared into his memory. He could sense this in some of the older warriors—old men who could not remember the face of a wife dead ten winters but who recalled every streak of paint, every feather worn by an enemy killed long before. Battle was the truest of passions.

Every coup counted left a wonderful scar on the spirit. He had touched the enemy many times, but he most cherished those coups made when he felt no one else could see the touch. It was as if the act were too personal, too intimate to share with onlookers. It was always for himself and his enemy alone. He had the man's life, or his honor. He knew it, his enemy knew it, and that was all that mattered. Let the others brag and boast about their deeds; that held no interest for him. Why should he care if others knew it or not? He would remember the act, that was what mattered. He would take no scalps. Never. What use to him were such trophies? What was a man's hair compared with his life? To his honor? His courage?

The other warriors, especially the younger ones, found his behavior odd. They did not understand why he did this and he had no inclination to explain it. They could never understand how he felt and he did not care that they would not understand. And so he kept silent. To the other young braves he seemed distant and moody; a strange young man, they called him, and, with an inkling of fear, they avoided his company.

In reality it was he who avoided them, which was not the same thing. Perhaps it was his odd hair. It was so much lighter that some of them whispered that he was part white. But they dared not say it to his face. It was bad enough that his hair was light and that the ends curled up like a damned *wasichu*. He hated the whites for this. Not that this was their fault but he resented comparison to anyone. That he was different was his own doing. He needed no one else, white or Lakota, for that. Bad enough that he had been called *Ohinnya*, the Curly One, as a child. He would not be taunted with it. As a youth he had flown into a rage and thrashed anyone foolish enough to mock him. It was only when he had brought all of those captured ponies back from the Kiowa camp, and they had called him His-Horse-Is-In-Sight, that the other boys stopped mocking him. But it was the fight for the Arapaho's horses that changed his name forever.

Hoppo! What a fight! The Arapaho had hidden on that hilltop in the ring of boulders screaming and shooting and daring the Oglala to fight them. He hardly knew what he was doing when he charged out ahead of them all. His brother Little Hawk, his friend Hump, they could only stare as he drove his horse up the hill into the midst of the enemy. Three times he struck out and counted coup before the Arapaho knew what to do. His open hand was red and stinging from the faces of his enemies. He could recall the wide, horrified look as the enemy realized they had been struck, that this boy had taken their honor from them. His horse flew from the circle of stunned warriors, its nostrils flaring, mane flying, eyes wide. But he turned his mount around and crashed back into the enemy. This time he killed two of them before they could recover from their shock.

The other Oglala went wild. They shouted, they shrieked, they loosed a hundred arrows into the Arapaho as he turned his horse again and fled back to his friends. Hump and Little Hawk grinned and shrieked with joy and pride. His cousin Little Big Man just shook his head.

"I thought you were a dead man," Little Big Man said.

"Your horse must be crazy to carry you into the middle of those people."

Though the Arapaho had kept their horses, it was a great day for the Oglala. When the people feasted afterward all they could talk about was the daring young warrior who rode into the middle of the enemy twice and came out covered with glory. In front of the whole village his father had made a great show of retelling his son's exploits and calling all to hear his new name—*Taschunka Witko*, "His Horse Is Crazy." *Crazy Horse*. It was a good name.

He smiled, remembering those incidents. Such foolishness. None of that really mattered anymore. What the others thought, what they said, didn't concern him. He was different from them all and he cared nothing for their opinions. He heard the keening cry of a hawk and let his gaze drift upward. A red-tailed hawk soared and circled over the plains, wheeling in the endless sky. Crazy Horse thought back to the words of his friend Short Bull. Short Bull was a mystic, a young man of visions and dreams, thoughtful. He alone seemed to understand Crazy Horse's gift.

"Have you ever noticed," Short Bull had said to him one day, "how the hawk soars above the People?"

Crazy Horse thought it a foolish question and simply snorted.

"No, my friend," Short Bull insisted. "I mean this seriously. Have you truly watched how the hawk circles high above the People? He soars ever higher, farther from all humans and their troubles and ever closer to the sun. He soars alone, with maybe one smaller bird to give him counsel. But the higher he goes, the farther he is from the ground. When he passes across the sun, the larger is his shadow. I think that maybe you are like this. You try to take yourself farther away but I think you will see that your shadow will be a great one."

Short Bull's musings had startled him, and he often wondered if his friend somehow knew the future. He wondered if Short Bull was right and he, Crazy Horse, was destined to cast a great shadow over his nation. His eyes rose up again to follow the hawk's wheeling progress.

Maybe we're the same, brother, he thought. *We let the others scrabble in the dust while we wait for the right moment. When it is right, we swoop down and seize our prey and soar again to circle and wait for the next moment. A rabbit for you, honor for me. It's all one.*

He shut his eyes so tightly that he could hear the rush of his own blood in his ears and imagined himself as a hawk, wings outspread, circling above the plains and the mountains and looking down on the people who crowded together in their lodges, babbling in a language he no longer understood, or cared to understand, as his shadow raced across the plains.

The distant thunder opened his eyes again. The sky had darkened while he lay there dreaming. The eastern horizon blackened with the coming storm. That was odd. The storms seldom came from that direction. He watched as the clouds began to build, slowly at first, then boiling upward in great billows, white at their tops and deepening to indigo where they met the ground. The slanting rays of the sun still lit the earth ahead of the storm a blinding yellow. Flashes of light flickered in the approaching darkness as lightning reached down from the thunderheads to scratch at the prairie floor. Around him, the trees began to sway, their limbs bouncing and tops bending. The breeze built in intensity until the slender pines began to look like bows pulled taut for the hunt. The wind whispered as if to say, "Go now, the worst is yet to come."

Out on the plain, the pronghorns had begun their dash for shelter, the large males shepherding their families toward the protection of timbered slopes. The hawk had vanished as if he had been a dream. The storm arrived with a blast not of rain but ice. Small hailstones struck his face, leaving tiny red welts. A sudden flash of lightning streaked from the heavens, shattering an old tree that stood only a few feet away. The noise was stunning and the air seemed to flee from his lungs. One limb arced over him to strike the boulder and cartwheel, smoking into a small stream below him.

Crazy Horse slithered down the granite slope and snatched the blackened limb from the stream. As he pulled it from the water he saw that a small round pebble had been lodged in its splintered end. He worked the pebble free just as another bolt of lightning shattered the silence, nearly deafening him in his left ear.

Crazy Horse's heart pounded wildly. His skin tingled with the lashing of the hail and the electrical charge of the storm. This must be it! This must be the sign he had waited for. *Wakan Tanka* was speaking to him. Somehow he knew that his life was about to change. Grasping the pebble firmly in his fist, his cheeks still stinging from the hailstones, he raced down the mountainside. As he dashed between the trees and boulders it seemed that the Everywhere Spirit was telling him of a strange storm coming from the east. It was this storm that carried with it his destiny.

1

Istawikawazan
(Moon When The Eyes Are Sore)

March 1866

He is called *Waziya* and every year he comes from beyond the Grandmother's country, out of the land of the spirits. Cruel and frigid in his thick robes of buffalo fur, he sends his breath soaring over the Dakotas' granite peaks, down through the close-set pines and out onto the endless prairies beyond. Where *Waziya* walks he leaves in his wake an icy blanket of white silence. A powerful spirit, his breath is the north wind, which freezes and kills. He makes the mountains and prairies unbearably bright and drives his breath so hard that a man's eyes water and strain to see. The pronghorn and the elk huddle away from his passing. *Pte*, the buffalo, turns his heavy, bearded face from *Waziya*'s gaze. Even *Mato Hota'*, the bear, flees to his den rather than face *Waziya*'s ill humors. They know that *Waziya* is as unpredictable as he is cruel, and he was particularly cruel this year. Along the banks of the Powder River, deep in the sheltering pines, a small camp circle of the Brulé lay helpless under his assault, the snow swept high against the sides of the lodges, the smoke of their fires driven sideways from the darkened lodgepoles as it fled before the killing wind. And in one lodge a darkness was descending that could not be lifted and blown away into the forest beyond, even if that spirit had been willing to do this thing.

Within the smoke-blackened hides of that lodge, as *Waziya* swept out of the Grandmother's country and keened through the frozen landscape with a mournful sound, a numbing fear gripped *Sinté-Galeska*, the man the whites called Spotted Tail. It was almost as if the Everywhere Spirit himself was wailing at the condition of his child *Mni Aku Win*. Brings Back Water, for that was her name, almost but not quite a woman, who lay pale and trembling under the buffalo robes. He had placed her pallet to one side so that as people entered and left the lodge the sharp, wind-driven cold would not cause her any more discomfort. She was his true joy in life and to see her like this, her small frame wracked by the hacking spasms that sent her into convulsions and brought a bloodied foam to dribble from her lips, tore at his heart. When he looked at her he saw so much of her mother in her face. How he missed her.

Her mother had just been this age when he'd first seen her— seventeen and a great beauty. He had always had a great fondness for women, but her mother, she had been so different, so special. Her name was *Anpetu Otanin* and she was exactly as her name described her—Appearing Dream. It was as if she had appeared to him out of his dreams and their love had consumed him. He had had to fight to win her from Running Bear, who was favored by her parents. Spotted Tail had slain his rival but been terribly wounded by a wicked thrust from the man's lance, and Appearing Dream had nursed him back to health despite the horror of her parents. Afterward all agreed that theirs was a true love match, and this was ever more evident as the years went by. When the other men took more than one wife, Spotted Tail remained true only to Appearing Dream. There was, he would say to them, no other woman that he could see, or that he wanted to see. There was no other woman with whom he would share his robes.

When the coughing sickness took her from him he thought he would never smile again, but it was their daughter who saved him from his despair. Beautiful, mischievous, and with eyes that sparkled with curiosity and joy. It was no wonder that so many of the young men pursued her with such passion.

But she would have none of them. She was as independent and stubborn as Spotted Tail's own mother, Walks As She Thinks, and took delight in brushing the young men away. She took them no more seriously than one took the flies that buzzed around the stew pots in the summer.

"Don't bother me with your silliness," she would say to them with a laugh. "What do I want with a foolish boy like you? Someday I will marry a great warrior like my father with many horses and a fine wooden lodge where the wind will not seep through in the winter and freeze your eyes shut."

Spotted Tail had at first been amused and relieved by her easy dismissal of her callow suitors—he didn't want to lose her so soon. He knew he would miss not having her fussing about him—making sure that he ate properly, insisting that he wear heavy robes when he went out in the cold winters, scolding him for suggesting that she go a bit easier on her admirers. But this "Capitan" that she always brought up had begun to worry him. He had thought her Capitan was but another invention of her impish nature until he had seen her one day during a visit to the white man's Fort Laramie. She had wandered off. He had thought it was to look at the goods in the sutler's store, but when he took himself off to the river to be away from the incessant chattering of the white traders and the squaws and their boisterous children, he saw her there among the cottonwoods with a man. He had been stunned to see them together—Brings Back Water, his own daughter, the daughter of a great warrior and war chief, together with a white man, a *wasichu*. And a soldier at that! He had slipped unseen into the willows to watch them, the soldier, tall and erect, his uniform sparkling with brass, his daughter with her dark eyes looking adoringly up into the soldier's. The tall young man, wearing white gloves, had taken his daughter's hand and held it to his lips. Spotted Tail was speechless, his head swam to imagine what this might mean. How could she do this to him? How could she do this to her people? He had waited until they left Laramie before he brought up the subject with her, and they had had the worst, really the only, argument they had ever had between them.

"You cannot see this *wasichu*!" he had demanded. "I won't

allow it!" But she had remained unmoved by his anger.

"I will marry my Capitan when I am ready, Father," she retorted, her eyes flashing. "I will have no one else but him. Certainly not these foolish children who call themselves warriors." She stuck her chin defiantly into the air. And then, before he realized what he was doing, he struck her, for the first time in her life. His only child. His only love. And he regretted it immediately as the tears sprang to her eyes. "Go ahead and beat me if you wish," she'd said, sobbing. "But Mother would know what is in my heart. She knew what it was to listen to her heart rather than her parents' words. This, you of all people should know."

She could have said nothing which would have been better calculated to crush his resistance. He had looked into her eyes and seen her mother. He had seen what Appearing Dream's father must have seen when she rejected Running Bear and embraced his killer, healed his wounds, shared his blanket. Brings Back Water sat in a far corner of the lodge sobbing and Spotted Tail sat down heavily, his heart numb, his throat dry and tongue swollen, his head spinning. What had he done? What could he do? What, indeed, would Appearing Dream have said to him?

And now, what difference would it make? What did it matter?

Spotted Tail was distraught. Now, in the watches of the night, he sat, his brow creased by deep furrows, hunched over in the dim interior of the smoky lodge, watching his child, her delicate, round face all that protruded from under the buffalo robes, the smooth forehead glistening with sweat. In the orange glow of the central fire, which was the only source of light, the warrior listened hollow-eyed to the mumblings of the old medicine man. The *Pejuta Wicasa*[1] squinted as he dug in his bag for his charms and potions. But never before had his little girl been this sick, and nothing the medicine man did seemed to make any difference whatsoever. Although Spotted

---

[1] *Pejuta Wicasa*: A "medicine man," more properly a healer skilled in the use of natural potions, herbs, poultices, and such, and not to be confused with a *Wicasa Wakan*, or "holy man," who deals with visions and sacred issues.

Tail had not yet seen forty winters he was beginning to look much older. And now his daughter's illness had etched deeper the lines on his face and caused dark rings to form under his eyes, which were red from lack of sleep.

"What have you got in your *wozuta pejuta* to cure my daughter, old man?" Spotted Tail asked sardonically, nodding toward the leather bag in which the medicine man was rummaging. The old healer screwed up his lips and scowled at Spotted Tail.

"You know better than to ask, *Sinté-Galeska!*" the old man grumbled. "I have what your daughter needs and that is all you need to know. You must leave now. What must be done is between me and the Everywhere Spirit. You will only break the medicine if you remain."

The *Pejuta Wicasa* began tossing cedar chips into the fire, filling the interior of the lodge with a thick, aromatic smoke that assaulted the nostrils and made Spotted Tail's eyes begin to well with tears. The medicine man then picked up a small drum and began to beat a slow rhythm on it. He cast a disapproving glance at the girl's father. Spotted Tail grunted and turned toward the flap of the lodge. The healer stopped his drumming.

"*Sinté-Galeska,*" he said, his voice betraying an uncommon gentleness. "I will do everything in my power to heal your child." Spotted Tail did not reply but only cast a pained look at his daughter and pushed his way out into the snow and the darkness.

A dark shape looming in the swirls of snowflakes was waiting for him outside. It was his old friend Two Strike, a heavy buffalo robe wrapped around his shoulders to ward off the cold. He put his arm around Spotted Tail and led him gently away as the muffled sound of the small drum began again only to be drowned out by the howling of the wind in the creaking pines. Two Strike had never been a very smart man, but he was a fierce and skillful fighter and no man could claim a warmer and more loyal friend. Whatever Spotted Tail did, wherever he went, whatever ordeal he might face, he could depend on Two Strike's friendship and unquestioning support.

Two Strike's wife, who had been waiting for them in his

lodge, pushed tin cups of steaming soup at the two men, who took them in stiff fingers. Two Strike slurped his soup noisily, but his friend only sat and stared blankly in the direction from which they had just come.

"Try not to worry, old friend," Two Strike said gently. "He is doing everything he can for her."

"It's not enough," Spotted Tail grunted. "I know you won't approve but I've asked for the White Medicine Chief to come to help her."

Two Strike raised his eyebrows.

"Don't look at me so," Spotted Tail said. "She is my daughter and I will try anything and anyone who can possibly make her well. This coughing sickness is something which the *wasichu* brought with them and perhaps their medicine chief knows what to do to take it away." He paused for a moment and then, as if in explanation, said quietly, "She asked me to bring him here and the Black Robe, too."

Two Strike nodded slowly.

"I'm not questioning you," Two Strike said. "But I don't think you should expect the medicine chief to come soon. I've heard that the whites have many sick now too and I think he'll have to help them before he can come to see your daughter. Little Crow told me this when he came to tell us of the council at the fort. The white soldier chief Mah-nah-deer has sent out word for the chiefs to come to the fort when there is grass enough to feed the ponies." Two Strike shrugged and stared into his tin cup. "Maybe the Black Robe will come to us here but I don't think his medicine is any better than ours."

"If the medicine chief will not come," Spotted Tail said grimly, "then we'll go to him. He has many medicines there and perhaps it will take all of them to make her well."

Two Strike said nothing but glanced at his wife, who only shook her head. A chill ran down his spine and he gripped the tin cup even tighter as if trying to squeeze the last drop of warmth into his fingers. Brings Back Water was dying. He knew it, his wife knew it, and, Two Strike suspected, everyone in the camp knew the inevitable outcome of this illness. Everyone, that is, except her father.

*   *   *

WHATEVER THE *PEJUTA WICASA* DID, IT WAS, AS SPOTTED Tail had feared, not enough, and in the morning his daughter was still feverish. The coughing fits seemed to come more frequently and between the violent bouts of hacking her breath was more shallow and labored. He could wait no longer. The wind had died in the night and now, with a bright sun overhead, he pushed his small band into a frenzy of activity as they broke down the lodges and prepared for the long trip to Fort Laramie and whatever potions and charms the white medicine chief might have. He tried to supervise the women who prepared to move the wisp of a girl to the waiting horses, but Walks Among Clouds Woman chased him away with a scowl and an impatient wave of her hand.

So Spotted Tail stood motionless and feeling utterly helpless as Brings Back Water was carried tenderly to a waiting travois and placed on a thick cushion of buffalo robes. Other robes were piled over her and rawhide ropes used to fasten down their edges so that no breeze could sift in to chill the girl further. Two Strike tried to distract his friend by talking about the journey they were taking, suggesting where they might best be able to pitch their next camp, speculating on how long it would take them to reach the fort, wondering about the weather and how deep the snow might have fallen in the miles ahead. But to every comment Spotted Tail merely grunted in response and Two Strike knew that he might as well have been talking to the snow as about it.

The small procession moved doggedly south, pushing through drifted snow which was all too often crusted by frequent storms of sleet. Their moccasins and leggings were quickly shredded by the jagged edges of their own footprints. When they stopped to camp the men used their war clubs to break through the ice-plated streams to water the animals. Spotted Tail refused to ride his favorite pony but walked slowly alongside his daughter's travois, his hand grasping tightly one of the trailing poles as if he could somehow lessen the jolting motion of the litter. With every rasping cough that came from the bouncing travois his chest tightened as if *Gnas-kinyan*'s[2] hand of ice had reached in to try to squeeze the very life from his heart. The old warrior raged inwardly at his own helplessness. Why could he not protect her? If it were an enemy he could see he could smash his head with his club, wring the life from him with his bare hands. If the white "Capitan" had done this he could rip his scalp from his head. Tear his heart from his chest and eat it while it still beat! But this sickness, this invisible enemy! The bravest, the most skilled warrior in the world was helpless against his attack. He gagged on his own bile trying not to curse the Everywhere Spirit for allowing such enemies to prey on this world.

There was a faint murmuring from the small, heavily bundled form and the old warrior glanced over to see his daughter's lips moving weakly. He detected a slight movement under the buffalo robes and knew that she was fumbling with the little string of beads that she had been given by the Black Robe the summer before. She must be saying the prayers the Black Robe had taught her. Spotted Tail clenched his teeth together and fought to hold back the tears. Everything was changing too fast. The *wasichu* were making everything change and he felt powerless to do anything to stop them. He had tried to fight them and it had cost him a year of his life as a prisoner of the whites at their Fort Leavenworth.

Hosti! The things he had seen! Everywhere he had turned there were bluecoats and more bluecoats every day as they came and went to the great war that they fought among themselves. And however many came and went they were always followed by others as if there was no end to them. They seemed to spring from the very earth itself like the grass in the spring.

It was while at Fort Leavenworth that he had begun to have his doubts that the Lakota could ever stop them. Since then much had happened that seemed to confirm his worst fears. The whites had ended the great war and spring would bring

---

[2]*Gnaskinyan*: A malevolent spirit, sometimes called Crazy Buffalo or the Demon Buffalo and considered the most to be feared of the evil gods.

them in ever-increasing numbers through this country. In the times gone by, most had simply passed through and were gone. But this would not last forever. More and more would decide to stay, and the Lakota, if they could not drive them out, would have to find some way to live with them. But how could one even live with them? The Southern Cheyenne had tried and it had done them no good. Black Kettle had even put the white soldiers' flag over their camp and the Shiny-eyed Eagle Chief had tried to kill them all anyway[3]. White Antelope, one of the Cheyenne who believed that the whites were his friends, had been shot down while he tried to talk to the bluecoats and died singing his death song:

> *"Nothing lives forever . . . only the earth and the mountains . . ."*

The Cheyenne they called Left Hand too had died near the soldiers' flag believing that they were his friends. Sitting Bull the Hunkpapa and Dull Knife of the Northern Cheyenne did not believe that the white man was a friend and had tried to fight against the Star Chief Connor. But that too had been a disaster. It was all so confusing. It seemed that nothing they did was the right thing. When they fought the whites they lost. When they didn't fight the whites they were killed like buffalo calves and chased from their land. When they tried to do what the whites asked, somehow it was turned around on them and came out wrong. White Antelope and Left Hand had tried to

---

[3]A clear reference to the infamous Sand Creek Massacre of November 1864. With U.S. regular forces pulled away by the ongoing Civil War, Colorado (like many western territories) was left to handle its own security affairs. John Chivington, an ambitious and politically minded Methodist minister from Denver, got himself appointed as colonel of the Colorado Volunteer Militia and set out to rid the area of its Indian population. His attack on the peaceful village of Southern Cheyenne led by Black Kettle resulted in a terrible slaughter of innocents and loosed a frightful Indian war on the citizens of Colorado. Congressional investigations of the incident condemned Chivington's actions but the harm was already done.

live with the whites and what had it brought them?

Now his own daughter too had been touched by these strange
times. He wished that he had never taken her to Fort Laramie in
the first place. He wished that she had never seen her "Capitan."
But he could deny her nothing and when she had finally seen the
wondrous things the white men had her eyes had lit up like the
bright morning star. She was such a beautiful child that even
the *wasichu* could not help but fall in love with her and they had
given her many presents. She had become especially fond of the
Black Robe, the one the whites called Father O'Hara. O'Hara
was a man of Spotted Tail's own age with a kind face and who
spoke with the *wasichu's* Great Spirit. Brings Back Water had
spent hours talking with him and he had even come to visit their
camp afterward, always bringing with him sweet things for the
children to eat and always a special gift of some sort for Brings
Back Water. The girl had come to love the *wasichu* and all they
had given her in return were a few trinkets and now the coughing sickness.

His head hurt. It was so hard to know what to do next. He
was afraid to take her back among the whites but he was even
more afraid not to take her to them. What if the whites were
the only ones who knew how to make the coughing sickness
go away? But, in the end, the fact that she wanted him to take
her to them was what had decided him. What would he not
do for her? Even if it meant taking her back among the whites.
Even if it meant losing her to her "Capitan."

They were such a strange people. They were very clever in
some ways—the things they made out of metal were indeed
wonderful, especially their guns. But they brought so many
strange and not so wonderful things with them: the water that
made men crazy and strange sicknesses that killed the Lakota
quickly. To Spotted Tail perhaps one of the more disturbing of
these strange things was the idea of time. The whites always
talked about it when he was at their fort. "It is time to do this and
time to do that. What time is it? How much time do we have
left?" He had never thought much about it before—this thing
they called time. It had meant nothing to him. And yet now that
he was aware of time he felt oppressed by it. The days crept by.

The nights lasted forever. Every moment seemed to hang on him like the fog hangs on the river in the early morning—gray and wet and cold. Hiding the land. Hiding tomorrow. It closed in on him. Stole his breath. Stole his sleep. Before he had never known or needed this thing called time and now he could not escape it. He had too much of time and his daughter not enough of it. He wanted less and he wanted more. He mourned its passing. Dreaded its coming. A man could never know what evil this thing called time would bring with it.

It was just when the sun had risen for the fourth time in their journey that a familiar figure appeared coming out of the trees. At first it was nothing more than a small dark spot moving against the expanse of white. It could have been a small moose, an elk, perhaps even a lone buffalo. But it proved to be the Black Robe on his mule. It was a particularly noisy animal that made honking noises like a goose but it seemed that Father O'Hara rather enjoyed the animal's company. His skinny legs dangled far down the animal's flanks and he was bundled up in a heavy coat against the bitter cold, his breath trailing behind him like a small white cloud. Spotted Tail could almost smile to see that although the Black Robe was clearly a white man, the cold had turned the priest's nose and ears to a bright red color. In the cold months the *wasichu* seemed to be the real redskins in this country. The Black Robe, squinting against the glare of the snow, recognized Spotted Tail immediately and jammed his heels into the flanks of the mule, who brayed and scampered forward to meet the procession, clods of snow flying up from his hooves. As he came up to the travois the Black Robe flung himself down from his mount and rushed up to the anguished father.

"Spotted Tail," the white man said in the traditional Lakota greeting, "I see your face."

"I see your face, Black Robe," the Brulé said, glancing past the priest into the snowy forest beyond. "Have you brought the White Medicine Chief with you?"

The priest, who was at least a foot shorter than Spotted Tail, shook his head as he looked over at the man's child. The warrior examined the Black Robe's face and saw the concern registered in the man's eyes. Also, the little priest tried hard to use the Lakota's own tongue and even knew the strange little twists which the Brulé put on it. It usually amused Spotted Tail that the priest's most frequent mistakes were in using women's expressions—a fairly natural mistake for a white man to make, as they usually learned what they knew of the Lakota tongue from women. The irony that most amused Spotted Tail was that the Black Robe would not have learned from women in the same way as most whites. He knew the Black Robe did not take an interest in women that way. This man was so different from the other *wasichu* and Spotted Tail found himself wondering why, if the whites had to come, they couldn't all be more like this little Black Robe.

"No, friend. I have not brought the medicine chief," the priest said finally. "There are still many sick ones at the fort and he cannot leave them yet."

Father O'Hara moved to the side of the travois opposite the girl's father and, removing his heavy mitten with his teeth, placed a thin, white hand upon the child's head. He muttered something quietly and Spotted Tail knew that the man was offering a prayer to his Great Spirit for his little girl. After a moment the priest looked up from the girl.

"But the Eagle Chief, Colonel Maynardier," O'Hara said, "has commanded that the surgeon, uh, the medicine chief, make ready to receive your daughter and he has ordered that she will receive anything which is needful to make sure that she becomes well again."

Spotted Tail again looked deeply into the man's eyes and saw that he was saying only what he believed to be true. The Black Robe was very fond of Brings Back Water, that was no secret, and he must have ridden hard to bring this news to the Lakota. The fort was still over a day's march away and it was a brave white man who ventured alone into the snow at this time of year. The warrior nodded his acknowledgment to the Black Robe and turned his eyes back to the trail that stretched before them. They were coming down out of the hills now and there would be little to protect them from the winds that would surely come as the sun set. Soon they would have to find a place where they could shelter for the night.

THE SCOUTS LOCATED A PLACE OUT OF THE WIND AND THE women had hastily erected a lodge and carried the girl in out of the cold. As dusk was falling a light flurry of snow had begun to whirl about the small encampment and fires had been started to ward off the cold and to cook the evening meal. Father O'Hara, who had been concerned for Brings Back Water's health, was now a very depressed man. Even in the dimly lit interior of the lodge O'Hara could see that Brings Back Water's condition was deteriorating rapidly. Her breathing had become little more than a hollow rasping and blood trickled in a constant stream from a corner of her delicate lips. The girl drifted in and out of consciousness and beads of sweat stood out on her forehead as the priest dabbed gently at it with his own handkerchief. He mumbled prayers over and over in a low monotone and his fingers traced the pattern of small crosses on her forehead and lips.

"Should I go away, holy man?" Spotted Tail asked quietly.

O'Hara glanced up from his charge, a puzzled look in his eyes.

"Will my presence ruin your medicine for my child?" the warrior asked.

"Ahh," O'Hara said, and shook his head.

Now he understood. The Brulé's medicine men must insist on secrecy for their ministrations. He was angry for a moment before he thought of his own religion and reflected that few of his flock at Fort Laramie must understand the Latin phrases that he uttered at mass or at times like this. Perhaps there wasn't as much of a difference between himself and the most illiterate *Wicasa Wakan* after all. Black robes, white collars, and rosary beads or buffalo hides, feathers, and rattles—what difference did it all make in the end? This girl, this beautiful child, was dying. He had seen consumption before and knew that she was beyond any help in this world. Red prayers or white, it didn't matter, either would have the same effect— nothing. What good could he do her or her father now? What comfort could he bring to her or this strong old warrior whose only joy in the world was contained in this fragile vessel shivering under his pale hands? Was his God any better than Spotted Tail's *Wakan Tanka*? O'Hara closed his eyes tight and felt the tears burning as they slipped down his windburned cheeks.

"No, my friend," O'Hara said in a whisper. "You mustn't leave her now." The priest reached over and pulled Spotted Tail's arm to him and then placed the little girl's delicate fingers into her father's large hand, closing the man's fingers tightly around the child's.

Brings Back Water's eyes flickered open and she smiled weakly at Father O'Hara. She then turned to her father, whose ruddy face was already stained with tears.

"Atkuku," she whispered. "You will take me to the fort, Papa? It is such a wonderful place!"

"Yes, my heart." He choked the words out. "I will take you to wherever your heart wishes to be. I will give to you anything that your heart wishes to have. That which you wish, I wish. I will take you to your Capitan. You are my light and my heart. You . . ." The warrior could say no more, for his throat seemed to have closed up on him and his chest heaved violently as he grasped the tiny hand in his own rough paw.

"In Nomine Patri, et Filii, et Spiritus Sancti . . ." The Black Robe was chanting in his strange tongue again. Outside the snow whirled and skittered through the thinned trees and *Waziya* had begun to howl across the frigid plains beyond.

WITH THE DAWN THE SNOW HAD CHANGED OVER TO A CUTting storm of sleet driven by high winds. To move any further in these conditions would have been foolhardy even had Spotted Tail and his small band been inclined to do so. But they were not. The camp woke to hear the warrior singing a death song for his daughter, and Walks Among Clouds Woman and the other women soon took up his sorrowful keening. None truly noticed the weather, which, if anything, was more appropriate to their grief than had the sun broken through the dismal grayness of the day.

The little priest had remained by the girl and her father throughout the painful night, quietly administering last rites to the child, and then slipped from the lodge to leave the brokenhearted warrior with his child. O'Hara wandered away from the small encampment to allow the man his grief. It seemed to the small Irishman hard enough for the Brulé that his daughter had so willingly embraced the white man's religion. He didn't think his presence would serve any purpose beyond forcing the man to share his sorrow with a *wasichu*. O'Hara's bishop would probably not have approved of this solicitude but the little priest didn't care. The bishop was not here and would never deign to come here. O'Hara was determined to leave the man in peace.

It was Two Strike who noticed the Black Robe's absence and followed the priest's footprints, tracking him easily into a small stand of trees. He would fetch him back to the encampment before the man got himself lost. The warrior shook his head to find the little holy man sitting on a rock weeping into the face of the storm. He pushed through the snow to stand behind the man, then reached out and placed his hand on his shoulder.

"Black Robe," the warrior said, his voice straining to be heard above the wind. "Do you want to freeze to death out here? Come back to the camp and warm yourself. Another death will not help anything." Two Strike shook his head. "I have always thought that you whites were fools. I don't need you to prove this to me."

The priest nodded and trudged dutifully behind the Brulé as he led him back toward the others. They had not gone more than a few yards when Two Strike stopped suddenly and pulled the priest to a halt, holding his hand up for silence. The priest stood there dumbly, for the first time noticing that his feet had begun to grow numb with the cold. Two Strike appeared to be listening to something but all O'Hara could hear was the wind. A few moments passed before O'Hara recognized the source of Two Strike's interest. Off through the trees he could now hear the sharp jingling of metal and the faint creaking sounds of a wagon. A few minutes passed before the sounds came more distinctly to them and were joined by the

voices of men and the snorting of horses. O'Hara pushed past
the Brulé to see who was making the sounds. When the warrior tried to hold him back the priest removed the man's hand
gently from his sleeve.

"It's all right, Two Strike," he said quietly. "They're obviously whites and until we know who they are it's best that
they see me first. Even a nervous white man is less inclined
to shoot at a Black Robe."

The warrior nodded and let the priest move out toward the
trail, but he cast anxious glances back toward his camp. If
these whites meant trouble he would have to move quickly to
warn the others. He silently cursed his own foolishness for
having wandered away from the camp without bringing his
rifle along. But his fears were unfounded, for O'Hara quickly
recognized a small troop of soldiers from Fort Laramie and,
in the lead, their commander himself, Colonel Maynardier.

"Father O'Hara!" Maynardier called out. "I'm afraid the
surgeon is still taken up with the sick at Laramie but I've
brought an ambulance and a medical orderly along to have a
look at the girl." Maynardier would have said more but he
could tell from the look on O'Hara's face that he had come
too late. "Oh, dear" was all he could manage. But there was
no look of remonstrance on the priest's face.

"No, Colonel," O'Hara said, shaking his head. "You could
have come a week ago and brought all the surgeons in the
world with ye and it'd ha' been of no use anyway. It was
consumption and no hope whatever. I've not said anything to
her father on that score but I will explain it to him when he
has had time to mourn her. Knowing that you could not have
helped may not ease the pain but the fact that you even tried
cannot hurt you in his eyes. Come, we can at least provide
him escort to the fort."

The colonel hoped that O'Hara was right. He was under a
great deal of pressure from the people in Washington now that
the war in the east was over. Those treaties which had been
in effect with these tribes were worse than useless because
none of the tribes' war leaders had signed up for them. With
people starting to move west again, and likely in numbers far

greater than ever before, the chances of friction between them and these people were much more serious. If he was going to keep Washington happy he needed people like Spotted Tail and Red Cloud to come over to his side. He would also need to do something with Dull Knife and Black Horse. The Northern Cheyenne had not always had the best of relations with the Sioux and while some would think this an opportunity to be exploited Maynardier did not share this opinion. If the Sioux and Cheyenne clashed here it could easily involve whites and that would soon lead to a general Indian war. The colonel pinched the bridge of his nose as if he could force the throbbing in his head out through his nostrils.

That damned fanatic in Colorado had really complicated matters. Those militia hooligans butchering those people had done nothing but turn a generally peaceful band of Southern Cheyennes into a vengeful enemy. What an ugly business that had been. All the apologies and mea culpas in the world would not undo Sand Creek, would not bring back the dead men, women and children—or the dead trust. Christ, but that had been madness! And it was just more trouble for him. The Cheyenne in the Dakota Territory doubtless knew of the massacre of their cousins in Colorado. It would be a close thing to convince them that the meeting at Laramie was anything less than a ruse to lure them to the slaughter. Even now Newton Edmunds, the newly appointed "governor" of the Dakota Territory, and his commissioners were moving up the Missouri in hopes of holding a grand council at Fort Laramie. Maynardier had already sent couriers out to all the tribes, Sioux, Cheyenne, Arapaho, trying to convince their chiefs, and better yet, their war leaders, to come in to the talk. He knew some, like the recalcitrant young Hunkpapa, Sitting Bull, would refuse. Sand Creek was too fresh in their minds. But others, men like Red Cloud and Spotted Tail, might still be persuaded to attend. If an army escort for a dead girl and her father could help bring more of the tribes to the council, then so be it.

*   *   *

IN THE END, COLONEL MAYNARDIER DID MORE THAN PROVIDE
an escort. Something in Spotted Tail's demeanor touched the
colonel deeply, although if asked to explain it he could not.
Maybe it was the single tear that he had seen tracing down
the warrior's cheek that had done it. He didn't know. But
when the party finally reached Laramie he granted the bereaved warrior a most unusual request. Brings Back Water was
to be allowed to rest in the post cemetery. Maynardier personally supervised the erection of a traditional Sioux burial
scaffold, a stark spidery framework that towered incongru-
ously over the simple headboards of soldiers, wives, and in-
fants. Spotted Tail slew his daughter's favorite ponies. He
wrapped the tails tightly with strips of trade cloth and tied
them to the upright poles, the bright red streamers snapping
and dancing crazily in the cold wind like mad dogs straining
at their tethers.

And then it was time. Light flurries of snow swirled and eddied around the headboards, the names of the dead crusted over
with white crystals clinging to the cracked and weathered wood.
And, winding slowly up the hill from the buildings below came
a small group of people, Indians and soldiers together, bearing a
new offering for the land of the spirits. If the white dead objected to their newest member they said not a word but lay silent
beneath the frigid hillside listening to the muffled drums that
beat slowly to announce her coming. Soldiers, the small capes
of their blue greatcoats flapping in the wind, bore Brings Back
Water's blanket-wrapped coffin to the scaffold. Colonel Maynardier, standing alongside of Spotted Tail, stopped the soldiers
with a raised hand. He tugged off his heavy gauntlets and placed
them carefully on the top of the coffin.

"So that your daughter's hands shall not be cold on her
journey," he said to her father.

Spotted Tail nodded silently.

Maynardier laid a hand on Spotted Tail's arm. "My friend,"
he said quietly, "do you see our flag there at the fort? See how
there are red stripes and white together. The wind blows the flag
and it waves and the red stripes and the white are moved by it
but they are together and in peace. There is room for each and so

is there room here for us all, red and white, to live together in peace." For a moment the distraught father thought that this man was scolding him for his objection to Brings Back Water's love for a soldier, but it was quickly obvious, even to Spotted Tail, that Maynardier knew nothing of this. He had been speaking not as a soldier, or a white man, but only as a man.

The bearded soldiers, their ears and noses reddened by the cold, their breath billowing into the frigid air, struggled to lift the coffin into place far above the surrounding graves. The Lakota women, shrouded in heavy robes of buffalo fur, stood huddled to one side of the cemetery, unwilling to disturb the resident dead. They trilled and wailed a death song for their departed sister. Below the scaffold a party of soldiers pointed their rifles to the sky and fired a salute, the long dark barrels exploding with flame and smoke.

As a final gesture, Colonel Maynardier had arranged for the post's artillerymen to man one of the small mountain howitzers out on the parade ground. At the marking of each hour of the long night the gunner snatched the lanyard back and the small brass mouth roared, the hollow boom echoing over the windswept plains. It would, the colonel assured Spotted Tail, hold any evil spirits at bay. The warrior had said nothing but his eyes conveyed his thanks better than any interpreter could have rendered into speech.

But then, when the ceremonies were done, when the mourning party and the firing party had gone back to their barracks and their homes and their lodges, even as the night passed, as the new dawn approached and the moon dropped toward the horizon, a lone figure stood in the dusk, an arm wrapped tightly around one of the poles supporting the scaffold, a cheek pressed hard against it, his tall frame shuddering but not with the chill of the night. Spotted Tail, his heart broken, stood beneath his little girl and thought how queer it was. He had never thought that he would see the kindness that a white soldier had showed to him on this day—surely the blackest in his life. Never had he thought that the name his people gave to this month would have such a deep meaning. It was indeed for him, and would forever be, the Moon When The Eyes Are Sore.

2

Canwapto wi
(Moon When The Leaves Are Green)

May 1866

A soft breeze stirred the cottonwoods along the Platte and the rustling of the newly leafed trees competed briefly with the sounds of the bustling fort, which, for all its activity, was still but a tiny speck on the vast plains of the Nebraska Territory. Spring was late in coming this year and the sandhill cranes still gathered in their thousands on the plains around the isolated post, in no obvious hurry to follow their traditional migratory path. In the cottonwoods the owls blinked their disapproval of their ungainly cousins, wishing that the cranes would conclude their visit and hurry on to annoy other relatives. The cranes circled overhead, crackling their strange hoarse language, before swooping in to plant spindly legs in the rich prairie soil. The cranes' long necks uncoiled to snatch at the insects and frogs that skittered haplessly from between the newly sprouting grasses and then lifted as the birds swallowed their prey.

Margaret Carrington, gazing out through the open window of her kitchen on Officers' Row, was constantly amazed at how they were able to handle their large, ungainly gray bodies with such fluid grace. She had been surprised to see the willow-legged birds on the prairie, associating that sort of bird

in her mind more with marshes and ponds. Yet here they were
in uncountable numbers, stalking and strutting, weaving and
swallowing and preening their feathers as they prepared for
the next leg of their journey. The cranes worked the prairie
with single-minded diligence, apparently undisturbed by the
bustle and racket produced by the residents of Fort Stephen
Watts Kearney. The regimental band was drilling on the parade ground but, to Margaret's ear, not with the instruments
with which they were most comfortable. How she would have
enjoyed listening to a Schottische or a reel right now. Instead,
all she heard were the barked commands to "Load" and "Present!" And the crisp clicking and clacking sounds of steel on
steel as fingers more accustomed to trumpets and French horns
worked the breeches of the fancy new repeating rifles. Ah,
well, it shouldn't be too much longer and tonight, for sure,
there would be some music for the benefit of General Sherman.

Margaret used the back of her hand to brush a stray wisp
of hair from her face as she bent over the kitchen table, knead-
ing the dough with a vigor that shook the old table and flung
small clouds of flour into the air of the small room. She stifled
a cough that rose up from her lungs—likely too much flour.
It was only the breeze that wafted through the open window
that kept her from being covered in the fine white dust. She
rolled the dough into three long strips, which she braided into
a single loaf, and quickly transferred the whole to a baking
sheet. Wiping her hands on a towel, she reached into another
mixing bowl for another, denser ball of dough.

"Lawdy, Miss Marg'ret, you's making a terrible mess in
this house!"

"Oh, now, hush, George," Margaret shot back. "You just
get a bit more wood into that stove and I'll worry about the
mess."

"Yes'm," George chuckled. "I'll stick to stockin' and not
mind the messin'."

Margaret grinned at the large black man who bent to shove
more firewood into the stove that took up the largest portion
of the small kitchen's available space. A quick glance about

the place told her that George had not understated the situation. The kitchen was a shambles of mixing bowls, pans, knives, and foodstuffs, all in various phases of preparation. She blew an exasperated sigh from her lips and tossed her head to clear the errant lock of chestnut hair from where it dropped down across her eyes again. So much to do! She would have to see if Mrs. Wands would allow her to borrow Laura to help get the house better organized before the guests began to arrive. Margaret reached for a rolling pin and began to flatten the dough. She hoped the general liked peach pie, as peaches were about the only canned fruit they had left to them after the long winter months that had stretched into the early weeks of May this year. Well, he'd just have to be satisfied with what he got, she thought grimly.

At least they'd have plenty of food tonight. Of that she'd made sure. There would be a nice clam chowder followed by spiced beef pie, soda biscuits, a mayonnaise of chicken and celery, scalloped onions, and potato puffs. Then there would be a French loaf cake and peach pie along with fresh buttermilk and gallons of coffee to wash everything down. And, of course, there were the two magnums of Madame Clicquot's wonderful champagne that she had managed to set aside for this affair. That reminded her, Surgeon Horton had said that he and Lieutenant Brown would be providing some Bordeaux to accompany the meal. She would have to send George to fetch it along before she forgot completely.

Margaret slipped the worked dough expertly into its pan and filled it with the contents of a pair of canning jars labeled "peaches." A few deft slashes with a small knife produced enough strips of dough for her nimble fingers to weave a top crust, which she pinched firmly into position before sliding the whole assemblage into the oven. She stood upright, brushed her hair back from her face, and peered critically at the small repair that had been effected on the stovepipe near the flue.

The stovepipe had somehow developed a small crack the day before and there was simply not enough time to get a replacement before General Sherman arrived. Luckily Sergeant Bowers had happened by and been able to show Mrs.

Carrington an old Army trick for repairing such things in an emergency. Bowers had sifted through the fine wood ashes in the stove, mixing in a bit of clay and a pinch of salt, then adding small amounts of water until he had formed a heavy paste. The sergeant had then spooned the paste into the crack and molded it to form a small joint. Once the fire had been rekindled, the heat of the stove had quickly dried the paste to a rock hardness. Margaret smiled and silently blessed Sergeant Bowers and his fertile imagination. The patch seemed to be holding wonderfully and, with any luck, they'd be able to make it through this dinner party after all. In Margaret's opinion Sergeant Bowers had certainly earned the right to loaf a bit this afternoon, and every once in a while she could hear his voice raised to tease the members of the band as they went through the unfamiliar drills.

The band had recently been issued brand new Spencer carbines. They were squat, ugly little weapons but had the remarkable ability to fire seven shots without reloading. The musicians, shaking their heads, had picked up the odd-looking pieces and the ungainly leather cartridge boxes that held the tubular magazines used to reload the weapon quickly. Bandmaster Samuel Curry was thrilled with his new acquisitions and had been enthusiastically conducting loading drills all week, much to the disgust of his musician charges and the envy of the infantrymen. The former, still armed with the ungainly, muzzle-loading Springfields, were immediately jealous that the "beaters and bleaters" should have the luxury of using weapons that, if nothing else, were a great deal easier to load than their own rifles. When Sergeant Bowers complained that it was unfair, Curry had just laughed at the infantryman's ire.

"Ah, give it up, G. R.!" Curry retorted. "Your damned doughboys would just waste ammunition. Uncle Sam couldn't afford to hand these beauties out to your pirates. The lot of ye'd bankrupt the government inside of a month."

Margaret's husband, Henry, who commanded the regiment, had overheard the exchange and told her about it later that night.

"In a way, dear, Curry was not far from wrong," Henry said

as he shucked off his heavy tunic. "With the war over, the
Army is shrinking rapidly and the budget along with it. The
people are tired of war and the Army. Anything Congress can
do to save money is certain to be tried. It will cost millions
to rebuild the South and most of the nation's interest will be
focused there. If they think that they can save a few dollars
on ammunition, why, save them they will."

Margaret was puzzled by this logic and pressed the question
further.

"I don't understand," Margaret said quietly. "Surely the
Congress would want the few left to have the best equipment
and weapons which they can. We will after all be expected to
protect those who are moving. If there are enough of these
new weapons available that you can issue them to musicians
who will probably never use them, then why not simply give
them to your infantrymen instead?"

Henry shook his head, smiling. "You answered your own
question when you said that they would probably never use
them. A rifle not fired is a few cents not spent on the bullets.
Economy, my love. Oh, granted it's a false and foolish economy, but what other solution would you expect from a poli-
tician?"

Henry, in Margaret's opinion, was far too patient and decent
a man to put up with such silliness on the part of the fools in
Washington. Well, she would just have to have her say about
such things to General Sherman when he arrived. She'd wait
until he'd stuffed himself at her table before she confronted
him, but confront him she would. Maybe Sherman would be
able to make Congress see reason. The Army had become such
a political animal that she knew Henry dare not make a fuss.
Not that he would. A kinder, more gentle and modest man she
had never known. But she did not wear a uniform, and General
Sherman, as a gentleman, would be obliged to at least listen
politely to his hostess. She would only have to take care to
wait until Henry was out of earshot.

*   *   *

THE FLOORBOARDS CREAKED LIGHTLY AS WILLIAM TECUMSEH Sherman shoved his chair back from the table and stretched out long legs to cross his ankles casually under the dinner table. The general leaned back and allowed his lanky form to slump comfortably into the chair while he undid the buttons of his uniform frock coat and slid his fingers down into the pockets of his vest over his still-flat stomach. The general's reddish hair was cropped short and looked forever as though he had just run his slender fingers through it. Its wildness, combined with his craggy features, gave him a predatory appearance, which suited perfectly his reputation as one of the Army's fiercest and most implacable warriors. There was a satisfied silence as his fellow diners dabbed at lips with napkins and took small sips from crystal filled with water or wine, the table a snowy expanse of white linen, china, and silver. The silver winked as it was handled, reflecting the soft light of the candles that guttered fitfully in the silver candelabras that had belonged to Margaret's mother, and her mother before her.

"Mrs. Carrington," Sherman said earnestly, "that was truly the best, the finest repast I have enjoyed since I last dined at Delmonico's in New York. My compliments, madam, and to your husband, whose taste must be exceptional to find a woman who is not only beautiful but charming and a brilliant cook into the bargain."

Henry and Margaret Carrington exchanged smiles as the other officers and their wives gathered around the table echoed the general's compliments with "Hear, hear!," their wineglasses all raised in salute to Margaret, who fairly glowed in the praise and the soft candlelight. Margaret was glad that the dim light hid her blushing cheeks but couldn't help the broad smile that played on her full lips.

"You gentlemen are much too kind," Margaret demurred. "But were it not for the talents and generosity of Mrs. Wands, Mrs. Horton, and Mrs. Bisbee, you would, I fear, have dined on not much more than a few beans and a very anemic chicken." Margaret raised her wineglass in a salute to her fellow wives, who fluttered their eyelashes and beamed back at her. So many colonels' wives would have been content to sit back and bask in the general's praise without a nod to the junior wives who had truly made such an evening possible. This was not Margaret Carrington's style, and the wives gathered around her table returned her generosity with a loyalty and devotion that exceeded the norms even of the unusually close-knit society that was the frontier Army.

This fact was not lost on Sherman, who, although he had comparatively little knowledge of the society of women, recognized that the distaff side of the Army family could make all the difference in the world. He chewed thoughtfully on his lower lip, his head nodding almost imperceptibly as he put a silent stamp of approval on this small group. Where these people were headed, they would need all the mutual support and comfort they could muster.

Sherman glanced over at his host, Colonel Henry Carrington. The general wished he could take a reliable measure of the man, but Carrington was an enigma to him. Small in stature, with a sloping forehead, long black hair and beard, and soft, dark eyes, Carrington did not look much like a soldier, but rather more like a poet or scholar. Well, Sam Grant[1] had never looked much like a soldier either, for that matter. Looks were no measure of a man's abilities, as Lee had found to his sorrow. But Carrington was not a poet. In truth he had been a lawyer, Yale-educated and highly successful. He had even spent some time, it was said, as a secretary to the great Washington Irving. *Maybe that's where he comes by that scholarly cast*, Sherman mused. He knew that Carrington had never seen action, at least not outside the courtroom. During the war the man had served out his time as a recruiting officer and only nominally as commander of volunteer infantry. That worried Sherman some. Of course, the mere fact that the man was a good lawyer did not mean that he would necessarily make a

[1]Ulysses Simpson Grant, known to his friends as "Sam." Lieutenant general during the Civil War who had defeated Robert E. Lee and his Army of Northern Virginia. In July of 1866 he will be promoted to the newly created rank of General of the Army. Grant and Sherman are old friends.

bad soldier. Sherman had been a lawyer himself. The general suppressed a small smile, thinking of his one and only case back in Leavenworth City. His poor client hadn't had a chance. If it hadn't been for the war, Sherman thought wryly, he and Grant both would have either starved or gone mad. *Well*, he thought, *who's to say that we aren't mad at that?* Maybe Carrington would prove better at soldiering than Sherman had been at lawyering or Grant at clerking.

The general let his gaze wander about the table and took some solace in the fact that the other officers of the regiment had already "seen the elephant." Combat veterans all, they should more than make up for their colonel's inexperience. He hoped their skills would never be needed, for the 18th Infantry Regiment was not going into combat—at least that was not the intention of the War Department. Their job would not be to wage a war but to keep the peace. Now, with the South's rebellion at an end, there was a great movement of people to the West. They went to start fresh—to heal and forget old wounds, to build homes and farms, to start businesses, to make their fortunes, to make their lives over again. The 18th Infantry—Carrington and his colleagues—would go along to insure that these new emigrants could do these things in safety and security. It might not be the sort of work a soldier preferred—at least the average citizen might not think so—but it was, in Sherman's mind, one of the most fitting and worthwhile pursuits for an army. He, for one, had seen enough of war and it sickened him even to think of it. The things he had seen done to his fellow countrymen. The things he had done to contribute to their misery. The brutal acts of war.

They haunted his dreams, images of Atlanta and of the Shenandoah in flames, his old friends dead by the score, often not even recognizable through their horrible wounds. Men he had loved like brothers reduced to little more than fragments of meat and shattered bone. The hawk-faced soldier gritted his teeth, biting clean through a cigar that he did not even remember placing in his mouth.

"Gentlemen." Margaret Carrington's voice brought him back to the present. "We ladies will excuse ourselves to clear away some of this mess. Please feel free to enjoy your cigars and help yourselves to the port."

She smiled graciously at the general, who looked a little sheepish at having produced a cigar without so much as a "by your leave." Sherman and the other officers rose to their feet and nodded to the ladies, who began gathering in the plates and silver that littered the linen tablecloth. As they retreated into the kitchen, chatting gaily among themselves, Henry Carrington moved to the sideboard to produce a bottle of port and a few glasses. William Bisbee, the adjutant, dabbed his napkin at the corner of his mouth and whispered into the ear of the regimental quartermaster, Fred Brown. Lieutenant Brown chortled at the remark and ran his hand across his balding pate.

"Lieutenant Bisbee," Brown announced in mock distaste, "you shock me, sir! Why, I believe that any Indian worth his salt would be pleased and proud to decorate his lodge with what remains of this glorious head of hair! Do you impugn my locks, sir? Why, I should demand satisfaction!"

"Well, you're more likely to get it than any Indian is," Bisbee said with a grin. "Unless, of course, he don't mind working on his trophies from the bottom up!"

Bisbee reached out and tugged at Brown's heavy beard. This brought a roar of laughter from the other officers and even Sherman couldn't resist the smile that creased his leathery face. Bisbee, who with his wife and little boy shared a set of quarters with Brown, couldn't resist the temptation to tease his balding roommate.

Henry Carrington handed a small glass of port to the general and turned to his officers with a worried look.

"Gentlemen, please," he urged quietly. "Let's not upset the ladies with lurid tales of scalp-taking and butchery."

"Oh, it's all right, Henry," the general said easily as he held a candle under his cigar and puffed contentedly at it. "There'll be no scalping or other mischief for these boys to get into. Were it otherwise I would never have agreed to allow your wives to accompany this expedition." Sherman blew a large smoke ring and watched it hover heavily in the air before it dissolved into a light gray mist. He laid a hand on Carrington's shoulder and steered him gently toward the open hearth, where a small fire crackled against the cool of the drafty quarters. The general sipped at his port, then placed the glass on the mantel and slid both hands into the pockets of his vest, waiting as the other officers filled their glasses and came slowly to gather around him.

"This expedition," he began quietly, "is a great thing." The general tried consciously to keep his voice in a lower register, for he knew that when he forgot himself it would rise and sound crackly and a little feminine, not the sort of voice to inspire confidence. He began again,

"This expedition, gentlemen and ladies, is a great opportunity not only for you but for this country. The years of war and destruction are behind us and we should thank God for that." A muffled chorus of "Hear! Hear!" and "Amen!" came back to him.

"Now is the time to rebuild and to build anew. And not just homes and businesses, but lives as well. Colonel Carrington, in a way, I envy you your job. You will be a bit like a latter-day Moses, leading your people out into a wilderness that should prove to be a promised land. You have a good flock here." Sherman nodded at the assembled officers and at the few wives who had momentarily halted their chores to listen attentively to the guest of honor.

"I believe that this will be the beginning of a great adventure and a healing salve for the nation's wounds. You ladies," the general turned to regard the gathered wives with what he hoped looked like a benevolent gaze, "will help to pour oil on troubled waters and ease the transition from wilderness to civilization. This expedition would be unthinkable without your valued presence, your aid, your counsel, and your skills. I urge you to relish this opportunity. If you have not already done so, please keep the most detailed journals of your lives. Note with care the progress of this journey and the requirements of daily life, for these are the things of which dreams and history are built. Your children, your grandchildren, and indeed generations to come will never know how they came to enjoy the fruits of your labors unless you record these days for posterity.

They will thank you and so, I dare say, will your country. And to this end, I propose a toast to my gallant colleagues and their lovely wives. Your health and Godspeed!"

The general took his glass from the mantel and raised it in salute before taking a delicate sip and taking care not to drain it. There would be other toasts, he knew, and he'd best keep a fairly clear head for the moment. He hated to invoke those damned clichéd Biblical references but he had noted the numerous religious tracts that occupied Carrington's bookshelves and believed that this gave him some gauge of his host's interests. Judging from the slight glistening appearance of Carrington's eyes Sherman knew he had not guessed wrong.

Well, at least the man hadn't started blubbering outright—a maudlin commander was a disaster waiting to happen. Neither did he want a damned zealot. Look at the mischief that Bible-thumping madman from Kansas had precipitated. Sherman shook his head thinking of the fiery-eyed John Brown pushing the nation into the abyss of war. He thought also of the deranged Chivington. A fire-and-brimstone preacher turned colonel of the militia. With no regulars to control his misguided passions he and his Colorado Volunteers had butchered hundreds of people just for the color of their skin. With one stroke the maniacal preacher had turned peaceful Indians into bitter enemies—more damned bloody work for the regulars. Damn all fanatics!

Carrington raised his glass and the slight murmuring of the guests subsided. General Sherman held his breath slightly, waiting to hear what the man had to say. He'd soon know the sort of fellow he was dealing with. At least he had some decent wine and port on hand and even partook of it himself. That was a hopeful sign.

"Ladies and gentlemen," Carrington announced quietly, "General Sherman, sir. I give you all the Union. I propose a toast to these, by the grace of God, once more United States of America."

"The United States," the guests echoed with glasses raised.

William Tecumseh Sherman drained his glass and upended it on the mantel, breathing a sigh of relief. Not a religious zealot. Well, perhaps this would work out to the best after all. He hurled the butt of his cigar into the fire and reached into an inner pocket to withdraw another. Time to get down to business.

COLONEL HENRY CARRINGTON TURNED IN HIS SADDLE AND looked back with a sigh at the column that lay behind him. First in line were the nearly seven hundred infantrymen, many of them new recruits, broiling under the hot prairie sun as they toiled along in their heavy wool uniforms whose dark blue color had dulled to gray from the dust of the trail. Behind the infantry was a long line of wagons and domestic animals that stretched in a seemingly endless procession toward the horizon until it disappeared into the dust cloud raised by its own passing. While spring had been late in coming it made up for lost time by baking the travelers in an almost suffocating heat. The air was close and hummed with gnats, horseflies, and the ubiquitous mosquitoes. And then there were the fleas that gnawed endlessly at the movable feast. The fleas, it seemed, had a charter to afflict every portion of the body not exposed to the mosquitoes, so it was that most of the marchers were covered with angry red blotches along their ankles, behind their knees, and, most annoyingly, in their crotches. It made for uncomfortable days and restless nights in infested blankets. And then there was the condition of the road, such as it was, which was less of a highway than it was an oversized dirt washboard. Many had elected to walk alongside the wagons rather than endure the bone-rattling jolting and yawing of the heavy vehicles. Even Margaret had at one point confessed to having felt a bit seasick. It was a condition she thought ironic, considering that their constant companion, the Platte River, was hardly sufficient to float a canoe let alone a ship, even a small one.

Margaret, and everyone else it seemed, was fond of making jokes about the Platte River, whose course they had tried to parallel for most of the journey. It was an understandable temptation, for the Platte was the sorriest excuse for a river

that Henry Carrington had ever seen. It did not flow—it me-
andered, it wandered, it straggled and twisted and oozed
wherever it pleased. It spread itself out sometimes to nearly a
mile in width but to a depth of only a few inches. It split into
ten, twenty separate fingers, each wriggling its own way
through the sandbars, skirting around and seeping under fallen
limbs, catching on the brush and thickets, tickling its way under the feathery balls of tumbleweed, swirling off to rest in
brackish pools where it could raise its own little families of
mosquitoes. All along its length it zigged and zagged, twisted,
looped, turned back on itself and stretched itself thin. And
then, just when you thought you'd taken its measure, it
changed. It swelled and deepened and rushed by in a torrent
of eddies and whirlpools, and this normally just when you had
reached a point where it had to be crossed. It was as if the
Platte were a living thing, a watery Loki, a mischievous,
mocking little god of contrariness. It was brown and sludgy
with the tons of soil it carried in its aqueous grip, and you
could see why those who had preceded them had cursed the
Platte and said it was "too thick to drink and too thin to plow."
But for all its faults the Platte had some things to recommend
it. It was a constant source of water and lined by willow
and cottonwood. The cottonwood is a remarkably brittle tree
and is quick to divest itself of any and all dead limbs at the
slightest hint of a breeze. Thus they had at least never wanted
for firewood and the timber needed to effect numerous repairs
to the wagons. And the Platte did attract game. While not
enough to supply the needs of the entire column at all times,
at least enough to vary what would otherwise have been a
very monotonous diet, consisting largely of salt pork, beans,
and hardtack.

In some ways, Carrington thought, the Platte was a perfect
companion for the odd caravan that plodded alongside it.
However he might try to keep the column organized, it invariably stretched, straggled, and spread out in a most unaesthetic,
most unmilitary manner. Besides the wagons and their draft
teams there were over a thousand head of cattle clumping
along in their wake. And then there were the oxen, pigs, goats,

and even chickens whose coops were all too frequently jolted and bounced off of the wagons to set their feathered inmates clucking and pecking aimlessly about the landscape as soldiers scampered and tripped through the brush trying to round them up again. No wonder the officers had taken to calling it "Carrington's Overland Circus."

Carrington turned back to the front and squinted into the clear air ahead. Somewhere in the distance lay the town of Julesburg and nearby Fort Sedgewick. He would halt the column at Sedgewick for a short rest before attempting what he hoped would be the final crossing of the Platte. Then they would turn toward the northwest and Fort Laramie. The sun beat down mercilessly and the plains ahead shimmered and rolled in the waves of heat that radiated back upward. So it was that he almost didn't notice the return of the scouts until they were very nearly on top of him. The two men were taking their time coming in, their mounts plodding along at a leisurely pace. The smaller and younger of the men, Henry Williams, rode a sorrel roan, while his larger, and much older, companion favored a powerful mule of enormous proportions. The larger man was, in Carrington's estimation, the single most valuable man in the column, and not only because his pay of ten dollars a day was more than the colonel's own salary.

As the colonel well knew, Jim Bridger's value lay in his encyclopedic knowledge of this country—its flora, its fauna, its maddeningly capricious weather, and, most importantly, its inhabitants, both transplanted and native. The sixty-two-year-old Bridger was already a legend, not only here but back in the States. Tales of his exploits had been told for years, and Colonel Carrington had been both thrilled and secretly relieved to find that the old mountain man had been hired on as the guide for this expedition.

Carrington had been more than a little surprised upon first meeting the man, for Bridger looked nothing like what he might have imagined. Certainly he was tall and rangy, with a gaunt face that readily told of its years exposed to the elements. The man's gray-blue eyes had a hawklike, almost predatory clarity, but the rest of Bridger's aspect was ordinary. For all of his height, his shoulders tended to slump a bit and his clothes were simple, store-bought items that would not look out of place on a farmer: from the low-crowned slouch hat of gray felt to the sturdy, workmanlike shoes, there was nowhere a trace of the fringed buckskins or beaded moccasins that one would have expected of a mountain man and an adventurer of his reputation. Nor was Bridger averse to good company, and the colonel noted with surprise the animated pleasure that the old man seemed to take in frequent chats with Margaret. Polite to a fault, Bridger, with his gruff, uncultured tongue, would spend hours in rapt conversation with the colonel's beautiful and kindly spouse. He was also much taken by the Carringtons' children, and before they left Fort Kearney he had presented the boys with a nimble Indian pony, which was quickly dubbed Calico by Jimmy.

Margaret, both flattered and charmed by the scout's attention, returned the favor by acceding to Bridger's childlike desire to be read to. The old man, although illiterate, always carried with him a copy of the Bible and, while preparations were being made for the expedition, was delighted to find that another book, which he had ordered all the way from St. Louis, had arrived with the supply train that had also brought General Sherman. Henry had been surprised, and Margaret delighted, to find that the handsomely bound tome was a collection of Shakespeare's plays. And so it had become a fixture in the daily routine of life on the trail that, when camp had been established for the night, Jim Bridger would appear outside the Carringtons' ambulance bearing a book under his arm. He would stand silently by the wagon, his hat in his gnarled fingers, waiting for Margaret to glance his way.

"Oh, Major Bridger," Margaret would exclaim. "I see you have your Shakespeare by you! Would it be too much of an imposition if I asked if I might be able to read a passage or two aloud to my boys?"

"I'd be most pleased, ma'am," Bridger would venture shyly, "and, be it not too much trouble, I might lend an ear myself, if ye'd not mind. This child's become powerful fond of the old feller's stories."

Margaret would always agree happily and offer "Old Gabe," as he was known around camp, a cup of coffee and the use of one of their few remaining chairs while she went off to round up her children for the evening's entertainment. The burlesque, for such it was, had originated at Fort Kearney shortly after General Sherman's departure. Sergeant Bowers' mending job to the stove's flue, while ingenious, had proven imperfect and, on the morning following the general's departure, the Carringtons had been awakened not by the bugler but by the crackling roar of a fire. Despite the best efforts of the regiment, the flames soon reduced the Carringtons' quarters to a smoking ruin. A few items had been salvaged—such as the chair that Bridger was so often offered—but much of the family's belongings, including their small but cherished collection of books, had drifted across the Nebraska plains in a flurry of ashes, which winked sparks as they whirled and tumbled in the breezes that had fanned the fire to roaring life.

Afterward, Bridger had approached Mrs. Carrington and quietly offered to give her his two books to help replace the volumes she had lost. Margaret had gracefully declined but hinted that she would like very much to borrow the books from time to time—for the enlightenment of the children, as she put it.

"O brave new world, that hath such people in't!" Henry Carrington murmured softly as he watched Bridger guide his mule easily up the gentle slope toward him. Bridger exchanged a few words with his companion, and Williams touched his hat in acknowledgment of the colonel before he turned his horse off toward the rest of the column.

"Evenin', Colonel," Bridger said as his mule slowed to a stop and began to munch on the sparse grass. "Have ye fared well enough today?"

"Quite well, Major Bridger," Carrington responded. "Quite well indeed. Have you found us a place for the evening?"

Bridger reached back for a canteen, from which he took a long drink before wiping his mouth on his sleeve. "Better'n you might expect, Colonel. Figger if ye can keep a steady pace and no trouble, we'll hail Sedgewick 'bout sundown."

The colonel was visibly heartened at the news. If Julesburg and Sedgewick were as close as Bridger said, then they were truly within easy reach of Fort Laramie. What a blessed relief that would be. As they had rolled and jolted across the sun-baked plains, mile after dusty mile, the seemingly endless, sweat-soaked days had melted into mosquito-swarmed nights with a mind-numbing relentlessness. There had been times when Sherman's quip about Moses leading his people into the promised land had seemed to Carrington an ironic misstatement. The colonel had felt more like Moses leading his people through the desert for forty years. Now they were almost there. Ah yes, a blessed relief it would be.

JULESBURG, A HAPHAZARD COLLECTION OF RUDELY BUILT and sun-blistered clapboard and adobe structures, was a disappointment. Any hopes that Sedgewick might be a more pleasant stop were dashed by the appearance of that miserable post. Sedgewick was distinguished from Julesburg by the complete absence of any clapboard buildings. Here everything was of crumbling, sun-bleached adobe and an earthen parapet—a smooth, sloping wall of hard-packed dirt—that surrounded the entire post. As they trudged wearily past the front gate, Private William Murphy remarked sourly to his friend Frank Fessenden that if it weren't for the parapet, he would have mistaken the place for a prairie-dog village. Private Fessenden grimaced. The young band member had brought along his even younger, and very pregnant, bride, and it was beginning to look as if their first child would be born in this godforsaken place.

While the wagons were being arranged around the perimeter of the fort and the animals cared for, Colonel Carrington decided to pay a courtesy call on the post's commander, a pallid young man who looked older than his years and seemed glumly resigned to his position. Captain Frank Norris commanded the company of the 2nd Cavalry, which had drawn the unenviable duty of manning the adobe fort.

"It's a rum business, Colonel," Norris said quietly. "The Cheyenne burned Julesburg out last year and so here we are, the pride of the U.S. government, playing watchdog for a dozen shanties. I try to keep the men occupied with making improvements to the fort." Norris strolled alongside the colonel, waving his hands airily at the fresh patches in the buildings and the loopholed barricades which could be placed into every window at a moment's notice. "But there does not seem to be much point in it. Not even the Cheyenne are very much interested in Sedgewick these days. I doubt they'd waste what little effort it would take to touch fire to the place. Most of the men would rather be anywhere but here in this wilderness."

"Have you lost many of your men, Captain?" Carrington asked casually. Norris stopped walking and looked directly into the colonel's eyes.

"A few, Colonel," he said. "But probably not as you might expect. Indians are nowhere near as dangerous as boredom. It'll drive a man to desperation or insanity, sir." The captain stared evenly into Carrington's eyes, his jaw set and hard.

"Mark my words, Colonel. Your greatest enemy, I fear, will be boredom. You will lose more men to Mammon than to any arrow or hatchet." Carrington frowned at the reference.

"Mammon?"

"Greed, Colonel. Greed, avarice, gold fever." Norris went on. "Where you're headed it will be especially hard. The dispatches tell me you're to build new posts along the new Montana Road. The one they call the Bozeman Trail. Well, Colonel, do not let the gentlemen in Washington deceive you. They put it out that this Bozeman Trail is a new avenue for the homesteader and those bound for Oregon, but this is hardly true. Oh, you'll doubtless have a train or two that brings the farmer and his wife through, but most of the folks you'll be providing protection for will be single men, hard cases all. They'll not be looking for homes but for gold. The Bozeman was not laid out to cut through to Oregon, sir, it goes straight to Hell. Or Virginia City, which is the same thing in my view. Colonel, your charges will not be coming to build homes but to dig gold." Norris tossed his head toward Carrington's command, which was just settling into its encampment. "Keep busy 'em, sir. Rule them with an iron fist and work them hard.

If you can't keep their hands occupied, their feet will itch and
you'll be lucky to have half of your command left to you come
next summer."

Carrington swallowed hard. He was not an experienced
commander and Captain Norris had the look of a man who
knew of what he spoke. Carrington had never really worried
much about the Indians until he had seen the defenses that
Norris had erected at Sedgewick. Then he had assumed, as
had the other officers, that the walls were to ward off the fierce
tribesmen who had burned Julesburg. None had ever suspected
that there was a deeper reason for their existence. Carrington
was a religious man and Captain Norris' words haunted
him. How much more mortifying it would be to have lost his
command to sin rather than to battle. He had no intention of
fighting a war, but the thought of mass desertion terrified him.
Carrington looked out over the mass of blue-coated men,
sweating and laughing in the growing dusk. Perhaps it would
almost be better if the Indians were not as placid as he had
once hoped. He did not want any of his men to lose their lives
unnecessarily but neither did he want them to lose their souls.

Sometimes it seemed as if everything about this expedition,
everything about this country, was both more and less than it
appeared. The few Indians they'd met had been either friendly
or shy, while the settlers they'd come across were frequently
sullen and usurious. Carrington bristled to think of the ridic-
ulously high rent one place had charged them for a ramshackle
building in which the ladies could sleep for one night. Then,
yesterday they had been approached by a lone Indian who had
proclaimed himself a Cheyenne chief and announced indig-
nantly that one of the soldiers had stolen his rifle. A search
had turned up the missing weapon, which was quickly returned
to its owner. The Indian had indeed been telling the truth,
despite Bridger's sour looks. Carrington then had the regimental band play a small serenade for the aggrieved "chief,"
much to the man's delight, while Lieutenant Brown was left
to supervise the offending soldier's punishment. Afterward,
Bridger had quietly informed the colonel that the old Indian's
son had been the leader of the raid that destroyed Julesburg.

No, nothing it seemed was very simple in this wilderness. But the sudden appearance of Bridger and his assistant denied the colonel the luxury of further contemplating this contradictory country. The scout nodded to Captain Norris and turned quickly to Carrington.

"Colonel," Bridger said abruptly. "We've got a bit o' worrisome work ahead. That damned river's unpredictable as a blamed Sioux. Two days ago we'd ha' walked right acrost her but today she's on the rise and not a place in a week's march where we can cross any easier'n here . . . and that'll be a chore."

"How long do you estimate it will take us, Major?" Carrington asked, concern creasing his face. He had planned on this operation taking less than a day. Damn this country, it played the devil with a man's best-laid plans.

Bridger pushed his hat back on his head and rubbed dirty fingers across a stubbled chin, his left eye squinted as he cast a critical look around at the now scattered column.

"Well, sir," he said slowly, "I figger that if ye can get 'em organized fair and moving smart we may get 'em across in two, three days without too much lost."

"Lost? Lost what? Time?" Carrington demanded crossly.

"Things, Colonel. Mules, victuals, maybeso men," Bridger said matter-of-factly. "You don't cross the Platte when she's like she is without givin' up a few things. She's like one o' them ancient, jealous pagan gods, y'see. She'll have her tribute. That Shakespeare fella would say she'd hafta have her pound o' flesh. We'll just take 'er slow and maybe she'll be satisfied with a pound o' sugar or two instead. Yessir," Bridger concluded. "Two, three days and call ourselves flush."

The crossing of the Platte at Fort Sedgewick, as Carrington had rightly assumed, should normally have taken only a few hours, but the capricious river seemed to have taken the arrival of the expedition as an excuse to misbehave. The usually shallow, slow-moving Platte was swelled up over its banks and the rushing torrent churned, swirled, and gurgled as Carrington and his officers looked on. In desperation the colonel turned to Captain Tenedor Ten Eyck, a former surveyor and lumber-

man, for help. Ten Eyck quickly pressed several hundred of
the soldiers into service, most of whom were glad for the opportunity to do anything to break the monotony of the trail.

With much shouting and sweating they had restored an old
flatboat someone had located nearby and quickly converted it
into a sort of ferry in which they planned to haul the seemingly
endless string of mules, horses, wagons, and oxen across to
the far bank. Ten Eyck supervised the rigging of a double
cable run through an ingenious series of blocks and tackle to
span the nearly mile-wide Platte. With the flatboat rigged to
one end of the cable and dozens of mules and oxen straining
at the other, they finally got the makeshift ferry floated. But
even the flatboat was not proof against the river's vagaries.
No sooner would they get the boat out into the stream than it
would hang itself up on an unseen sandbank. With bulging
muscles and muttered curses the men would get the boat float-
ing free only to have it run aground again a few minutes later.
Even with every man and beast working at full capacity it
soon became clear that a single trip across the Platte and back
must consume nearly a full four hours. In his frustration Carrington ground his teeth and clenched his fists so tightly that
his short nails threatened to draw blood. But there was nothing
to be done. Ten Eyck and his men were doing everything
humanly possible and with such fierce determination that the
colonel felt that to say anything contrary would not only be
ungracious but, and more importantly to Carrington, un-
Christian.

MEANWHILE, UNDER THE DIRECTION OF MAJOR VAN VOAST
and the ever-energetic adjutant Lieutenant Phisterer, those soldiers not actively engaged in the crossing operations began
erecting the large hospital tents, joining them together to form
a large, covered area that closely resembled a structure more
suited for a church revival. As the final adjustments were being
made on the guy lines, other soldiers began setting up rows
of chairs and camp stools which had been collected from the
off-loaded wagons.

"What're we settin' up all these darn chairs for, Frank?" Private Murphy asked. "Is the old man going to host some sort o' revival meeting or some such?"

Fessenden carefully adjusted the camp stool he had just unfolded and squinted down the row of seats toward the front of the tent.

"Nope," he said easily. "Gonna have us a frolic."

"A what? A frolic? What kind of a frolic, Frank?"

"Minstrel show, for a start," Fessenden said happily, satisfied that the future occupant of this particular stool would have a good view of the performing area. "Gonna have us some music, and some singing, and I suspect we'll even have a bit of a theatrical performance."

"You're daft! No, you're not neither, are you?" Murphy decided as Fessenden, his immediate chores done, wandered off to check on his pregnant wife. Murphy watched his friend hurrying across the open prairie toward the small post hospital building and decided that he might as well tag along and say hello to the girl. It would also serve to take him out of the immediate vicinity of Sergeant Bowers, who, he knew, would be glad to find other employment for him.

THE EVENING'S ENTERTAINMENT WAS A GREAT SUCCESS. THE large hospital tents were lit by a hundred lamps and a small stage had been improvised by lashing planking together on top of the regiment's supply of nail kegs. To one side of the stage the regimental band, dressed in their finest uniforms for the occasion, played accompaniment to the amateur thespians, soldiers all, who had spent the afternoon devising a series of small skits and burlesque routines—some obviously borrowed from productions they had seen in the East. A few band members had gone to elaborate lengths to create their own ensemble of "minstrels," complete with cork-blackened faces and white gloves. These impromptu "darkies" played "Dixie" and "Massa's in de Cold, Cold Ground" to an appreciative audience who saw no contradiction in having just fought a brutal war to bring freedom to the very people they parodied with

such élan. That the Carringtons' manservant George seemed
genuinely delighted in the minstrels' antics only confirmed
their belief that their comrades were fine actors.

Colonel Carrington beamed proudly at his wife. He
squeezed her hand affectionately and craned his head to catch
a glimpse of Captain Norris, invited along with his soldiers to
enjoy the show, who was now roaring at the antics of a pair
of enlisted men. The two privates, hastily gotten up in "Indian
clothes," were waving small hatchets wildly in the air as they
led the rest of the regiment in their improvised version of
"That's What's the Matter," an old Stephen Foster favorite
from the war years. In this liberally adapted variation, the "rebels" had been replaced by their newest fascination.

> That's what's the matter
> The redskins have to scatter
> We're here to stay
> We can't go 'way
> And that's what's the matter.

The "Injun" privates mugged and capered across their precarious stage, much to the delight of their friends and fellow
soldiers, who quickly took up the chorus and roared it back
at them with obvious glee. The Carringtons were genuinely
amused and impressed that the soldiers had managed in so
short a time to incorporate virtually every recognizable malady
of travel into their verses. Mosquitoes, horseflies, buffalo
gnats, salt pork, beans, sunburn, fleas, rattlesnakes, thunder-
storms, dust, and even prodigal cattle and chickens had been
worked into the sometimes tortuous rhymes required by Mr.
Foster's original ditty. When the players had spent themselves
and the last guffaws had died to a quiet chortling and coughing, Henry Carrington nodded to Bandmaster Curry, who led
the band in a short fanfare to introduce the colonel of the
regiment. The audience grew quiet as Carrington stepped
lightly onto the stage and nodded to Curry before turning to
the audience.

"Gentlemen," Carrington began, "and most gentle and gra-

cious ladies who have blessed us with your presence this fine
evening and indeed throughout this perilous and trying journey. I thank you for attending this grand evening of entertainment and hope you will join me in applauding the efforts of
our most gallant players, comrades, and members in good
standing of Carrington's Overland Circus."

The crowd roared and clapped in a thunderous gale of appreciative hoots and whistles. Even the officers, and the few
ladies present, grinned at one another, nodding their approval
of the colonel's decision to poke a bit of fun at himself by
acknowledging the regiment's private joke on the expedition.
When the applause had begun to die down Henry Carrington
lifted his hands for attention. When all had grown silent the
colonel smiled at his followers.

"And I want to thank you, all of you, officers, men, gentle
ladies, children, teamsters, scouts, all of you: for your loyalty,
your devotion to duty, your cheerful demeanor in the face of
all adversity." Henry's eyes swept over the uplifted faces in
the dim glow of the lanterns, which were licking at the bottom
of their shallow reserves. He cleared his throat and fought
down the feeling of pride that welled up from his chest and
promised to choke off any further speech. "You," he went on,
"have done all that I have asked without murmur or complaint,
at least none that has reached my ears." There was a brief
twittering in the crowd and Henry smiled at his little joke.
"And for that I shall always be grateful." He paused. "There
is, as you well know, much yet to be done. And we must here
bid farewell to the officers and men of the 3rd Battalion who
will be taking over other of our forts in the Colorado Territory
and beyond. You will all be missed sorely. Godspeed and good
luck. All of us still have far to travel, and at the end of that
journey we face a great deal of hard labor. Forts must be built,
firewood cut for future warmth. What small gardens that can
be planted must be planted, hay must be cut and stored for
our animals. We must build shelter for ourselves and quickly
before the snows of winter catch us unprepared. But with your
strength and with God's grace and blessings we shall do all
of this and do it well. I ask you all to join me for just a moment

in asking God's continued blessing on our undertaking." The regiment rose as one, hats were lifted from heads and clutched in grimy fingers, and all stood silent among the chattering of the cicadas from the cottonwoods.

"Heavenly Father," Carrington began. "We ask your blessing and guidance in the long days ahead. Give us the courage and serenity to face whatever perils lie ahead of us. Bring us to our journey's end in safety and in health and deliver us from the wrath of the savages who inhabit the country in which we must dwell. Intercede for us in the councils of the red men and bring them to realize that we come into this country not in search of war but as harbingers of peace, progress, and prosperity. We ask all of this in your name. Amen."

The regiment echoed the colonel's amen as Carrington turned to Bandmaster Curry and nodded. As the colonel climbed down from the small stage the band struck up the gentle strains of "Good Night, Ladies," a traditional ending for an evening's festivities. As the music swam in the night breeze, soldiers made their way back to their tents as the officers said their good-nights to their fellows. Walking arm in arm toward their tent, the Carringtons were intercepted by Captain Norris, who saluted the colonel and bowed slightly to Margaret in his most formal manner.

"Ahh, Captain Norris." Henry said quietly, returning the salute. "I hope you found this evening's activities a pleasant diversion."

"None more so, Colonel," Norris replied, smiling. "I can't remember an evening I've enjoyed more in a great many years. Thank you for inviting myself and my men to join you for this very special night."

"It was our pleasure entirely, Captain," Margaret interjected. "I only wish that we could do more to lighten your burden here at this place. The evenings must be very long and lonely for you here so far from your homes and families."

Norris smiled. "Duty is often a harsh mistress, madam, but sometimes she is all we have."

Margaret detected the soft strains of Virginia in the captain's voice and from the faraway look in his eyes, she suspected that he was one of the many men, far too many, who had lost all in the great war. It made her heart ache for him, for the thousands like him who had nothing to go home to, no home left in all likelihood. If her guess was right, Norris was one of those southerners who had felt his loyalty lay with the Union and had found himself called upon to aid in the destruction of the land he loved, the killing and maiming of old friends and neighbors, perhaps of his own family. What a burden he must bear. She wondered if his family had disowned him, if he had been forced to watch as his home burned to a ruin. She felt warm tears begin to fill her eyes and reached out to lay her hand on his.

"We are all in your debt, sir," Margaret said softly. "May God be with you and bring you comfort."

Captain Norris bowed and lifted Margaret's hand to his lips while Henry Carrington stood by quietly. He was so proud of his wife. She was so kind, so gentle to all men, be they captain, colonel, private, or teamster. She always knew what to say to them and how precisely to say it. It was no wonder that so many men admired her so. She gathered admirers as easily, as effortlessly as most women gathered flowers. Through this entire journey westward she had borne every trial as if it were nothing at all. She watched over the children, inquired over the health and families of the men, prepared wonderful meals, read to the children and Old Gabe in the evenings. She treated the entire expedition as if it were no more trouble than a family picnic. And this did not go unnoticed by the men of the regiment, for always they were bringing her some little thing— a bouquet of wildflowers, a rabbit for dinner, an extra armload of firewood, a small willow basket filled with wild onions.

Had he been a jealous man he would have had ample excuse to indulge this emotion, but Henry Carrington was not a jealous man. Rather he was a grateful and appreciative husband. While he often found it difficult to express himself, the words he searched for all too frequently eluded his grasp, he was bound up by his love for this gentle woman. Sometimes, when he looked at her in the evenings, and he loved to watch her when she was preoccupied with something else, his eyes

soaked in her every movement. The way her fingers closed on
the stem of a flower. How gracefully she bent her head to
smell the flower's fragrance. He loved the gentle curve of her
neck, the soft slope of her shoulders, the errant wisps of chestnut hair that escaped their confining bun. She seemed such a
delicate and frail creature and yet he knew that her heart was
greater, stronger than that of many a general he had known.
He watched as Captain Norris turned and disappeared into the
darkness, then put his arm around Margaret's shoulders and
pulled her close to him. He felt her nestle her head into his
chest and heard her sigh. In the emptiness of the prairie night
they stood together and listened to the buzzing of the cicadas
in the sheltering cottonwoods.

3

Wipazuka was'hte wi
(Moon When The Berries Are Ripe)

June 1866

Mahkpia-Luta, the man the whites called Red Cloud, was in a particularly foul mood, a condition which his wife Pretty Owl found had become more common of late. The Oglala had about had his fill of this nonsense with the white man and desired above all else that he never again see another *wasichu* or even hear that hated word uttered in his presence. He had seen forty-five winters and should be considered *Tezi Tanka*, a Big Belly. In the normal scheme of things, he would be quit of most of his responsibilities to the clan, free to enjoy life, to rest on the reputation of a warrior who had proven himself. Free to hunt when he pleased. Grow fat if he pleased. But these damned whites would ruin it all. Here the Lakota had taken the best hunting grounds he had ever known from the Crow, land rich in deer, buffalo, antelope, and bear. Mountains whose slopes were covered with the finest lodgepoles he had ever seen. Valleys that were lush with chokecherries, berries, and wild onions and the sweet grass that fattened the ponies and scented the air wonderfully. It was truly a paradise and now it was all threatened by these bearded fools whose breath stank of liquor and whose repulsive bodies were covered with hair. These pale, inferior creatures who frightened off the game with their noise and their stink. They swarmed over this country like maggots on a carcass.

What bothered him perhaps most of all was that he should have seen it coming. The *wasichu* had not just sprung from the earth overnight, they had been coming for more than twenty winters now. At first there had been just a few of them—hunters and trappers and those who came to trade with the Lakota. He had himself rather gotten used to them and, in many ways, come to depend on them for things—for their good knives, the iron which made better points for arrows, pots for cooking, needles for sewing, guns and the bullets to feed them. In many ways the whites were handy to have nearby, and when you didn't smell them, you could almost forget that they were even there. As a young man Red Cloud had enjoyed his visits to their Fort Laramie. It was such an interesting place and he found the whites a very curious people. He had been amused by how they lived and dressed. At least that was how it used to be. For too long the Lakota had ignored them. It was convenient to pretend they weren't there until you needed something and this had been fairly easy to do when the whites stayed around their Fort Laramie. But now you couldn't leave your own lodge without coming across one of them. He should have seen it happening but he'd been too busy.

Red Cloud ground his teeth and glanced down in surprise to see that, with an involuntary twitch of his fists, he had snapped in two the arrow he was fletching. *Has!* He was so angry he couldn't see straight, couldn't concentrate on anything. His sleep was full of dreams and his head throbbed. Even his stomach was giving him trouble of late.

Pretty Owl looked up from her work, a frown creasing her otherwise smooth forehead. This morning she had stretched out a fresh deerhide, pegged it securely in the grass, and was now scraping away the flesh and sinew with a blade lashed into an elk's antler. It was hard work; sweat ran freely down her back, and her fingers were slick with the blood and brain tissue that would make the hide softer and more pliable. She wanted another child and intended that this hide would make a cradleboard for the baby, which she hoped they would have before the grass began to grow the following year. Her husband was not too old for this and it was something she had dearly hoped for these many moons now. Their only son reached nearly to her waist now and it was time that he had a younger brother or sister. She looked up from the stretched hide and saw that the boy was playing happily with his small bow, launching tiny arrows toward a sun-bleached deer skull.

Her husband's distraction did not bode well. Too many times he had come home in a sour mood, clutching his stomach or pinching the bridge of his nose and snarling at every little thing. His appetites were as unpredictable as his moods. Sometimes he would gorge himself with food and fall into a deep, rumbling sleep, his snoring loud enough to frighten the ponies. At other times he would simply pick at his supper distractedly, throw it aside, and then roll himself into his robes only to toss and turn throughout the night grinding his teeth and passing wind. In either state, it seemed that the last thing he desired was her company and this was just not natural. He was prone to odd compulsions, wandering off at all hours, going off to hunt and leaving behind his weapons. This business with the arrows was a good example. Usually the making of arrows was reserved for the winter, when it was easier to find the straightest shafts and there was little else to do outside of the lodge. She looked at his fooling about with the arrows now as an excuse not to talk to her.

Several times she had gone to see her friend White Cow Sees and asked for her advice on how to deal with Red Cloud. White Cow's husband, Black Elk[1], was the clan's *Wicasa Wakan* and a friend to Red Cloud as well, so Pretty Owl hoped that her friend might have heard something from her husband that could help her understand how to deal with the unrest in her own lodge. White Cow Sees was very sympathetic and gladly lent an ear to her complaints but admitted that she had

---

[1] **Black Elk** (*Hehaka Sapa*): Not to be confused with the famous Black Elk of "Black Elk Speaks," although this was, in fact his father. The younger Black Elk would have been about three years old at this time.

never taken much interest in the politics of the clan and suspected that that was where the trouble really lay.

"Yun!" Pretty Owl exclaimed, throwing her hands in the
air. "Politics! What should politics have to do with children?"
she demanded. "And if politics is the root of this problem what
can I possibly do about it? Must I watch him slump and sulk
around the lodge forever?"

"Politics, woman," a man's voice said in a low tone, "has
everything to do with children."

Pretty Owl and White Cow Sees looked up suddenly to see
Black Elk pushing his way under the rolled-up sides of the
lodge. They had not expected him to return so soon and wondered just how much of the conversation he had overheard.
The holy man walked past Pretty Owl and dropped heavily to
the buffalo robes on the other side of the central fire pit, easing
himself onto the woven willow backrest that faced the lodge's
entrance. White Cow Sees looked anxiously at her friend, then
rose and left the lodge briefly to fetch her husband a tin cup,
which she filled with coffee. Black Elk had become particularly fond of the white man's drink, which they called *Pejuta
Sapa*, "black medicine." White Cow Sees thought he drank far
too much of it, but her friends just laughed and some even
joked that her husband should change his name from *Hehaka
Sapa* to *Wicasa Pejuta Sapa* or Black Medicine Man. Handing
the cup to her husband, the older woman quietly took her place
next to Pretty Owl on the women's side of the lodge[2]. Black
Elk sat quietly sipping his coffee and waving absently at the
flies that buzzed around the cup; he had also become very
fond of sugar and tended to put far too much of it in his coffee.
For a few moments he said nothing but only sat looking
closely at Pretty Owl, pursing his lips as if thinking of how
to phrase what he had to say to her.

"Pretty Owl," he said finally, "let me tell you something

---

[2]**"women's side"**: The typical Oglala Lakota lodge had very specific places
assigned for articles and people. The entrance always faced to the east with
the place of honor directly opposite the lodge opening (or *tiyopa*). The men's
side of the lodge was located on the south, the women's side on the north.

about men and politics and children. Sometimes you women think that men are more interested in their politics than they are in their children, but you are wrong. I think that it is only because of their children that men take any interest in politics." The holy man smiled at the quizzical look on his visitor's face.

"Oh, certainly," he went on, "there are some fools who care only about themselves, but I'm not talking about them. They are only interested in politics insofar as it reflects their own image and makes it bigger. But most men, I think, would care nothing about politics if they did not worry about their children. They want the young ones to be able to enjoy what they enjoyed and they argue among themselves when they see that there is something that could change the dreams they have for the little ones. This is what is bothering your man. It is not that he is not interested in having more children. If anything, he is too interested. He worries about the future."

Pretty Owl tilted her head and frowned, surprised by his words. She had never considered such a thing and wondered if she had been judging her husband too harshly. But then, if what Black Elk said was right, if her husband was worried about what the future held for his children, then why was he avoiding the one thing which would guarantee that they should come into the world? It just didn't make sense. She opened her mouth to ask this question, but Black Elk held up his hand.

"Wait, woman," he said quietly, "you don't know the whole of it as yet. I will now tell you a little something about your husband that you perhaps don't know very well. We *Oglala Oyate* are not as our name would have you think. We are not one people. There are many different groups of us and we do not always get along. Now, this is no secret, you will say, but you don't know why this should have anything to do with children. Be patient."

Pretty Owl sat back on her heels and listened intently, now very interested in what her friend's husband had to say. White Cow Sees, who had lived with Black Elk for many years, just rolled her eyes and busied herself with beading a pair of moccasins. She recognized this tone of voice and associated it with long, drawn-out tales that seemed to go on forever. Black Elk caught a glimpse of her expression and shot a glare at her, but she replied with a smile and continued to ply the needle and sinew with deft fingers.

"Many years ago," Black Elk continued, "there were two *itancan* among the Oglala who were terrible rivals. It was over twenty winters ago when these two leaders had a great feud and it was the whites who brought it to the final confrontation. These two men were Bull Bear and Old Smoke and they disliked each other for reasons which I do not remember and which were probably foolish little things to begin with anyway. I remember that Bull Bear was a very vain man and he was hard to like.

"At that time there were several white traders that we used to go to see because they were the first ones to bring us things like blankets and these beads my wife is using and other useful things like iron kettles and guns. But not only did they give us such things as this *Pejuta Sapa*, which is a very good drink, but they also gave us the water that makes men crazy. I remember that Bull Bear and Old Smoke were quarreling about some petty thing and the *wasichu* laughed to see them shouting and gave them more of the crazy water to drink and urged them to fight each other. These white men are very strange people and they fight with each other all the time. Old Smoke would not fight Bull Bear even though his horse had been cut by the man. But he did not forget and neither did his friends and relations. The next year, I think it was during the Drying Grass Moon, Bull Bear came to Old Smoke's camp when it was near the traders' Fort John. Again, the whites gave away much of the crazy water and there was a scuffle among the younger men. When Bull Bear tried to stop the fighting, a young man shot him dead on the spot. This young brave who killed him was Old Smoke's nephew. Your husband."

Pretty Owl felt her mouth drop open a little. She knew nothing of this affair and certainly not that her husband had killed one of their own people, and a chief at that. She bit her lip and rubbed her fingers across her forehead. What else had her husband not told her about and how did this affect her? Still it all did not make any sense.

"That," Black Elk said, "was the end of the quarrel between these two but it was not the end of the fight. The two leaders' friends and relations were in a terrible state and a great fight broke out immediately. There was much shooting and seven other Oglala were killed by their own people. One of those killed was Yellow Lodge, who was your husband's brother. Ever since that day our two *tiyospaye* have been, if not enemies, at least not friends. There is still a lot of anger to this day and we are divided now into two camps. Old Smoke leads our camp and we are the Smoke people, while Old Man Afraid Of His Horses[3] leads the other, the Bear people. Old Man Afraid still holds Red Cloud responsible for this fight even though it was his own friend Bull Bear who started all the trouble when he cut Old Smoke's horse and called him *Wagluhe*—one who picks up the scraps of his betters." Black Elk stopped and handed his empty cup to his wife, who took it and left the lodge for more coffee. Her husband sat regarding the young woman, whose brow was furrowed with thought and whose eyes seemed to have drifted off as if she were looking at a man she thought she knew but whose name she could not remember. If anything she seemed more confused than before she came.

"But," Pretty Owl asked finally, "what does this have to do with why my husband will not lie with me and make another child?"

White Cow Sees, coming back with the full cup, winced silently, amazed that her friend would bring up such a delicate subject and, at the same time, give her husband any more reason to go on yammering about old feuds. Her husband dearly loved to hear himself talk. Black Elk shot a frown at his wife, who was shaking her head. He took the cup from her and turned to regard the younger woman. After a moment he gave Pretty Owl a patient smile.

"You see," Black Elk said, "Red Cloud knows that Old Man

[3] Afraid Of His Horses was not, as the name implies, a man fearful of animals, but a fierce warrior. A more literal translation of the name would be "He is so fierce that the sight of his horses makes the enemy afraid."

Afraid Of His Horses dislikes him, which would not be that bad but Red Cloud is older now and he thinks that maybe Old Man Afraid is right. When he was young, your husband was blind to the mischief of the white traders. Many of us are like that today. We are blinded by the things that they bring and we see the whites as lesser, foolish beings. We take the things they have that are useful to us but we do not see them as very important. We think of them like we do the grass that feeds our ponies and we do not consider that they are human beings. This is a dangerous thing for now they are becoming like the grass—every spring there are more and more of them. Now Red Cloud thinks that maybe because he has remained blind through all these winters that it his fault that we quarrel among ourselves while the whites grow ever more numerous all around us. And this is partially his fault because he fired the shot that made all the trouble so bad and he never considered that it was the whites who helped to bring the trouble on in the first place." Black Elk paused but kept one hand raised to fend off Pretty Owl's inevitable question.

"So," he went on, "your husband thinks, what can he offer to your children when his own actions have allowed the *wasichu* to become so powerful that the child may not have this place as a home. I see you shake your head but this is how men think. There are four virtues that a Lakota should have. He should be brave, he should be generous, he should always be truthful, and he should beget children. Your husband has all of these virtues in plenty but one. If he is to be whole, he must do this last thing and you are the one who must convince him that he must do this."

If Pretty Owl had been puzzled before by Black Elk's explanations she was now thoroughly confused. How did he expect her to accomplish this? Hadn't she already employed every stratagem she knew to try to lure her husband to her robes? What influence could she possibly have over his politics and how could that help her to achieve her goal of another child? She glanced at her friend White Cow Sees, wondering if she too was confused by her husband's explanation of things. To her surprise she saw that her friend, rather than shaking her head in sympathy, was nodding gravely at her. So she too thought that what Black Elk said was right? It was all so confusing. What did they expect her to do? Before she could give voice to her questions, the holy man leaned forward and placed a hand on her knee.

"Listen well, woman," he said quietly. "There is only one thing which stands between you and your desire for another child and it is the same thing which keeps your husband from fulfilling his obligations as a man. This is politics and, whatever you may have thought, this is a thing which you can influence. Some men will say that this is not a woman's place to become involved in such things but this is nonsense." White Cow Sees looked up suddenly at this remark. While normally she would only pretend to listen to his ramblings she now was very much interested in what he had to say. White Cow Sees wondered, can two people live together for so long and still surprise each other?

"You must remember," Black Elk went on, "that the seven sacred rites of the Lakota were given to us by the White Buffalo Calf Woman. Anyone who says that a woman is of no influence is a fool. It is the woman who owns the lodge. It is the woman who makes things in camp run smoothly. It is the woman who convinces the man that what he is doing is right or wrong. So, you must assert your influence in this matter. We still worry about our petty squabbles and the whites come in ever greater numbers while we fight among ourselves. And your husband is right, this is his fault. You must tell him this. He must find a way to mend the wounds we have given ourselves and only then will we be strong enough to stop the *wasichu* from coming into this country. And only then will you have your child." The medicine man sipped at his coffee quietly and watched his guest over the rim of the cup. Finally Pretty Owl nodded.

"Very well, Black Elk," she said, her chin set firmly and jaw muscles tightening. "If this is what it takes, I will do it. But I want you to remember someday, when the winter count is made, that this was the year when a woman saved the Lakota." As she left the lodge she could hear White Cow Sees talking behind her.

"What wonderful advice you give, my husband," White Cow was cooing. "Would you like me to get you a little more coffee?" Black Elk was looking at his wife as if he was stunned by her question.

JIM BRIDGER LEANED AGAINST THE TOP RAIL OF THE SMALL corral and sipped pensively at a cup of coffee. Looking off to the east, he could watch the large dust cloud that so clearly marked the progress of Carrington's Overland Circus as the column moved inexorably toward the spot he had chosen for the evening's camp. He had reasoned with the colonel that if he did not want to antagonize the Indians at Fort Laramie, it would be best that he put the bulk of the regiment into a secure encampment a few miles distant. Out of sight might not be out of mind for an Indian, but then out of sight was frequently just good enough. Judging from the rate at which the dust cloud was moving he calculated that he had another two hours before the first wagons rolled into sight. Enough time to get a decent meal out of Jules and maybe a short nap before he had to play wet nurse to the soldiers again.

Not that they were all bad. He found, much to his own surprise, that he'd gotten rather fond of the colonel. A decent man, Carrington. Not a frontiersman, probably not even a great soldier either for that matter, but then Bridger had never been much of a judge of soldiers. But Carrington was a decent man. A reasonable man. He had a lot of common sense and he knew what he didn't know and wasn't afraid to ask questions about things. And he wasn't too proud to take a man's advice. When Bridger had warned about letting folks wander too far off from the column, the colonel had clamped right down on the practice the same day. The soldiers hadn't liked it and more than one of the officers had looked a bit peeved about the orders themselves, but they hadn't lost a single man to an Indian yet and that was something. It had taken a bit of sand for the colonel to shut down the young bucks who were so full of themselves as war heroes that they resented the end the old man had put to their hunting days. Thought they could handle any Indians fool enough to try to take them on. Well, they'd soon see how wrong they were. Indians were not like these paper-collared soldiers—as they'd find to their sorrow.

"Gabe, you want s'more coffee?"

Bridger turned to see Jules Coffee, the owner of this small spread, wander over from the cabin, a large, fire-blackened pot gripped in his huge paw. Jules was an old friend, a former fellow trapper and scout who still did a bit of work now and again for the soldiers at Fort Laramie, which was located a few miles farther west. Jules had taken a Sioux woman as a wife and spoke several of the local dialects with easy assurance. Thus Jules found that his services were frequently in demand and the pay, while not extravagant, was sufficient to supplement his modest needs.

"Dern, Jules," Bridger drawled, "there ain't nought *but* Coffee 'round this lodge."

He waved his tin cup at the four Coffee children, who were scampering about the small yard in front of the cabin. Bridger's joke was well timed, for Jules came close to tripping over four-year-old Evangeline just at that moment. The girl's father dodged the tyke quickly and barely managed to get the fire-blackened coffeepot swung far enough away to avoid spilling any on her. Evangeline, oblivious of her close call, leaped to her feet and scrambled over to throw herself against Bridger's legs.

The old man smiled and reached down to tousle her hair with arthritic fingers. He liked children. That too rather surprised him. After all the years he had spent either by himself or in the company of men, he had never much thought about children, and yet now, now that he had seen more than sixty winters, he found himself thinking about what it would be like to have a family of his own. Well, maybe that wasn't exactly it. He had been married before, three times in fact. Once to a Flathead, once to a Ute, and once to a Snake, and had outlived all of them. He had several children of his own by his late wives but had never taken much interest in them. When their mothers died he had simply shipped them back East to attend school. He guessed that this wasn't exactly the same thing as having a family.

The thought of raising children had never before appealed to him. There had always been too much to do. Too many beaver to trap. Too many bear to hunt. Too much new country to see to be tied down with little ones. There had always been too much open country. Why give it up for one small cabin on one tiny piece of ground covered by the same small patch of sky every day? And now he found himself wondering if maybe he'd made a mistake or two. Just what was it that he had maybe missed over all these years? Jules Coffee, for all of the strength in his huge, callused paws, handled those "childers" as if they were the most delicate of flowers and seemed almost to glow in their presence. Bridger wondered why it was that he had never noticed this before.

He wondered if this new awareness had sprung from his contact with the colonel's wife and the comfort he had found in the presence of that gentle woman and her bright young sons, gathered around the fire in the evenings, listening to her recite the words of that Shakespeare fellow. What a comfort those evenings had been. He thought about those nights. His fingers unconsciously stroked Evangeline's hair as he thought about his own children. Where were they now? What did they look like? Would he even know them if he met them on the trail? All those years gone by. All those years. It was a strange sensation and it very much took him aback. Oh, to be a young buck again. To have all of this country left to see. To have all of those evenings left to sit by a fire in the company of a good wife and loving children. Was that the reason he had become so fond of Colonel Carrington? The colonel seemed to both know and appreciate what he had. Did he perhaps envy the man? Did he see himself in the colonel's eyes or did he merely wish to see himself reflected in the eyes of Margaret Carrington?

Bridger closed his eyes and tried to banish the thoughts from his mind. *What a damn fool I am*, he thought, *letting myself start worrying about all such nonsense at such an age.*

He knew full well that given that time over again he'd likely
have done it all the same anyway and it was foolish to think
otherwise. He opened his eyes again and looked to the east,
squinting against the glare of the bright sunlight. His eyes were
failing and he knew it. Time was catching up with him and
this would probably be the last time that he would be able to
ply his trade as a guide and a scout. A scout who couldn't see
wasn't worth a tinker's damn to anyone. Well, he would make
a good show of this last effort, that was about all he could do.
He watched the slowly approaching dust cloud and it warmed
him to think that it marked the spot where Margaret Carrington
and her boys would be. The colonel was a lucky man to have
so fine a woman. The old scout rubbed his rheumy eyes and
tried to hear Margaret's voice, rising and falling in soft, breathless melody as she read to him and the boys. Bridger raised
the tin cup in salute to the horizon and made a silent toast to
his commander and new friend.

"I'm more bound to ye than yer fellows," he thought, imperfectly recalling a line from one of the plays he had grown
so fond of, *"for they be but lightly rewarded."* He could not
recall the name of the play but perhaps this was a good thing.[4]

STANDING ELK HAD BEEN WATCHING THE APPROACHING DUST
cloud for many hours now. From the rate at which it moved
the old warrior knew that it could be made by only one
thing—wagons. More *wasichu* were coming. Sometimes it
seemed like every day that dawned brought with it another
white man. You would think that, as many whites as had come
through this country already, there must surely be no more left
anywhere else, but still they came. Spotted Tail had said to
him that however many they had seen was as nothing to the
numbers of them that were left in their big villages to the east.
Spotted Tail was fond of saying that "they are as many as
there are blades of grass." Standing Elk had always found that
a little hard to believe.

[4]The play was *Love's Labour's Lost*.

TuwakakeŠa! Impossible! he had thought, and yet still they came. Maybe his old friend was telling the truth after all. It still seemed a hard thing to imagine. He looked at the grass-covered prairie and tried to think of how long it would take him to count every blade of grass that he saw just in this one place and shook his head at the enormity of it all. Where did they all come from? It was a wonder.

This group of whites could only be headed for the big council at the fort. If this were true then it was a very good possibility that they would have a great many gifts with them. If they were going to the council then they would probably be easy to approach and talk to. It would not be such a bad thing to talk to these people before they arrived at the fort. If they were bringing presents there would be quite a scramble at the fort as everyone crowded around trying to get something from them. Standing Elk smiled to think of the scene. When they wanted something the *wasichu* could be very generous with their things. They would give you just about anything you wanted. He decided that he would wait a little while. He would wait and see if it looked like they were going to camp before they got to the fort. The whites were always easier to approach if they were stopped. They were less inclined to think that you were going to attack them and it was easier to get close to them without one of the more nervous ones trying to shoot at you. If they stopped before they got to the fort he would go and see them and talk to their chief. Maybe he would get a few more gifts and better gifts than if he waited to take his chances with everyone else.

Standing Elk's mouth watered as he thought of the taste of the *Pejuta Sapa*, especially when it was mixed with *Ca-ÑhaÑpi*, the sweet, white sand that the *wasichu* had in large sacks. The Brulé was glad that he had brought his pipe with him today, thinking about how he would use it to make a large show with the white chief and convince him that he was an important man and deserving of gifts. It was hard not to laugh when you thought how simple the whites were. It was so easy to fool them.

*   *   *

HENRY WILLIAMS LAID A HAND ON BRIDGER'S SHOULDER AND
nodded off to the north. The old scout squinted into the distance and grunted as his eyes focused on the dark shape that
was working its way slowly down the lightly wooded slope
toward the encampment.

"Another Cheyenne, Gabe?" Williams asked. Bridger
shaded his eyes with his hand and watched closely for another
few moments.

"Nope," he said finally. "He be Sioux for sure. Ye can tell
that by the way he wears his hair. Cain't tell much else from
here but I'm thinkin' we'll know plenty soon enough. You go
git the colonel and tell him we're gonna have a little parley.
Give him a chance to practice his skills for the big palaver
over at Laramie."

Williams turned to leave but Bridger took hold of his sleeve
and stopped him short.

"No, hold up a second, Henry. Believe I'll get the colonel,
you just go and get Stead up here. We'll want him to do the
talkin'. And fer God's sake see the man's sober. We ain't been
standing still all that long yet but I hear it don't take him long
neither."

Williams nodded and started off after Jack Stead, who was
being paid, far too much in Bridger's opinion, as the interpreter for the expedition. Bridger knew the man spoke Pawnee
pretty well but that had so far been of damned little use. His
abilities with the Sioux lingo were yet to be seen. Stead had
fought alongside the Pawnee against the Sioux and the Sioux
hated him with a passion. That could be a problem. Another
thing that worried Bridger was the fact that he had never found
out which Sioux clan Stead had learned the language from. It
might make a difference. Most whites figured that if a fellow
spoke any Sioux at all that was good enough. What they never
gave much thought to was the fact that the Sioux weren't any
more a damned big happy family than the whites were themselves. It galled him to think that any fellow who understood
why it was that Southerners hated Yankees couldn't figure out

that a Hunkpapa might have no cess with an Oglala. All too
often a fella who had lived a piece with a clan and learned
the lingo from 'em brought that clan's prejudices with him to
the council fire. The fact that Stead had fought against these
people was one more reason to be cautious. If the man was
on the peck he might deliberately flub a couple of things.
Made for all sorts of damned mischief. Bridger didn't speak
but a few words of Sioux himself and he hoped that Stead
was up to the task. He'd have to figure out a way to run a bit
of a bluff to see if he could get Stead's best out of him.

Bridger glanced back up the hill and watched the lone figure
guiding his pony down the hillside. Maybe this fellow's appearance was a lucky stroke. Not only would a little parley
give the colonel a chance to practice his talking skills but it
would also give Bridger a chance to watch Stead in action
before they got to Laramie. Jules Coffee had mentioned that
the commander at Laramie was expecting Stead to have a hand
in the translating at the conference when he arrived. A little
test now might save a whole heap of trouble later.

A SMALL CIRCLE OF OFFICERS AND WIVES HOVERED AT A RE-
spectful distance, some leaning against the wheels of an Army
ambulance, all straining to hear what was being said a few
yards away. Following Bridger's careful instructions, Henry
Carrington had directed that a small grassy area be cleared of
all debris—twigs, a few rocks, and a rather sluggish rattlesnake—and a blanket laid out on the ground. Nearby a fire
had been kindled and a large pot of coffee put on to boil.
Lieutenant Brown had been assigned to gather up a few
items as gifts—some coffee, a small sack of sugar, a large
butcher knife, and some tobacco—all of which were placed
on the blanket and then lightly covered by folding a corner of
the blanket over them. Bridger had watched the placement
of the blanket and then reached down into the folds and artfully tugged on a plug of tobacco so that its twisted end peeked
seductively from under its blue wool wrapping.

"Gittin' an Injun's attention, Colonel." Bridger said, "is a bit like gittin' a beaver to step in yore steel. Y'hafta make sure that ye put jest enough medicine on yer stick an' place it jest right or ye'll catch yerself nary but a sneeze an' rheumatiz."

Henry Carrington watched this little operation with interest and smiled at the delicacy with which Bridger fixed what he called "Sioux bait." Then everyone but the colonel, Jack Stead, and Jim Bridger was instructed to keep back from the small council site. Ostensibly this was so that the colonel and the Indian visitor could discuss important matters in privacy. In reality it was so that Bridger could concentrate fully on what was being said and gauge the accuracy with which Stead translated.

The lone Sioux, within a hundred yards of the camp, had begun to guide his pony forward with a measured zigzag motion which, Bridger explained to the colonel, indicated that his intentions were peaceful.

"Not that he need do it," Bridger added laconically. "He'd be a damn fool to try any devilment with a train this size. 'Sides, he wants to be sure nobody feels edgy 'nough to try to put a ball in 'im. But mostly he's jest puttin' a shine on it."

Bringing his pony to a halt, the lone warrior held up his hand palm outward and announced that he was Standing Elk, a Brulé chief, and that he had come to parley with the Little White Chief. He pointed at Carrington, the colonel's full dress uniform having given him the correct impression as to who was in charge in this small group. Bridger answered the warrior in the Sioux's own language, to the surprise of both Standing Elk and Jack Stead, and invited the Indian to join them for a smoke and some coffee. Bridger noticed that the warrior's eye had been immediately drawn to the folded blanket lying in the grass. Standing Elk nodded his head and slipped easily from the pony's back, leaving the animal to graze contentedly a few yards away. He was a tall man, probably in his late forties, with a powerful build, and he moved with an easy, catlike grace. His face was broad and somewhat creased and he had long, thick black hair, braided loosely and decorated by a single eagle feather placed at a slant at the back of his head.

"A chief," Carrington exclaimed, impressed by his visitor's introduction.

"Don't be swoggled, Colonel," Bridger said quietly. "I'm thinkin' he's about as much a chief as you are President. It don't mean the same thing out here. Oh, he could be a war leader of a great many bucks I s'pose, but I rather doubt it. A bit past his prime for that business. More like he's chief of a few lodges, a *tiyospaye*. Them're folks who're intermarried or accustomed to hunt or travel together, which is probably more like the band he heads up."

The colonel screwed up his face for a moment as if perturbed about being deceived.

"No, Colonel," Bridger cautioned, "it don't do to disregard him entire. For all we know he could well be some big war chief I never heard of. Now, like I said, I'm thinkin' he ain't, but it don't hurt to treat 'im like a chief. Just so's you don't expect to get too much out of the deal. What we may get is some information that might prove useful later and that alone'll be worth the plug an' palaver."

Carrington nodded and, as a smile spread across his face, he moved forward to greet his guest. When all had been comfortably seated on the blanket, Standing Elk produced his pipe from the buckskin bag that was slung casually across his shoulder. After introductions had been made and the pipe shared around the small circle of men, Bridger produced tin cups and turned to fill them from the large coffeepot. He handed these around to Carrington and Standing Elk, keeping one for himself and consciously not giving a cup to Stead, who looked at Bridger with a squint. A small sack of sugar had been placed casually on the blanket and Standing Elk reached into this and pulled out a fistful, which he quickly tasted before dumping it into his mug. Bridger, who took no sugar in his coffee, could almost feel his teeth aching at the thought of all that sweetness.

Stead, having not been offered coffee, understood immediately that he was being tested by Bridger and resolved that he would prove himself worthy of the scout's trust. Thus he translated every word as best he could and even commented on nuances of the language to try to convey to the colonel, and Bridger, that he understood the nonverbal messages that Standing Elk was sending. He was, much to Bridger's surprise, exceedingly good at his job, and after a few minutes it seemed as if Carrington was conversing directly with the Brulé warrior. Even Bridger quietly acknowledged that this was a mark of Stead's skill as a translator.

"Where are you going?" Standing Elk said finally.

"We're going to Fort Laramie, Chief," Carrington answered. "We will attend the great council with your people and then I will take my soldiers further to guard the great road which goes to the Montana Territory." There was a moment's pause as Stead explained what the colonel meant by Montana Territory.

"Yes," the Brulé said, nodding. "The Powder River country. There are many people gathering at the fort for the big talk between the white chiefs and the Lakota and their friends. Already many of the people have set up their lodges and spend much time at the fort. Not everyone is there yet but many are coming to hear what the whites will have to say to them. Many of the Lakota who are coming live in that country where you are going."

"Will the great chiefs all be there?" Carrington asked casually.

Standing Elk gulped his coffee down eagerly. He smacked his lips and motioned toward the coffeepot with the empty cup.

"*Kaiyakic 'uya!*" the Brulé grunted.

Bridger took the cup to refill it and Standing Elk turned back to Carrington as Jack Stead translated his answer.

"Many of the people who live in this country you are going to are coming to the council but not all of them. The fighting men in that country have not come to Laramie and you will have to fight them. They do not want to give you the road that you will be going on." Standing Elk shrugged. "They will not sell their hunting grounds to the white man for a road. If you want to keep the road you will have to fight them. And you will have to whip them."

Carrington looked across at Bridger, a worried look crossing his face. Bridger maintained an impassive look but a slight shift in his eyes indicated to the colonel that they would talk later about his concerns. For now, the old mountain man simply offered more coffee to the Brulé, who seemed not at all concerned by his statement that implied an impending war.

"These warriors who want to fight you," the Brulé said as he gulped down more coffee, "they are mostly Minneconjou and Oglala. There is a man called Red Cloud who talks most about fighting. He is *Itesica* and a lot of the younger men follow him now."

"Itesica?" Carrington looked to Bridger who simply shrugged his shoulders.

"It means Bad Faces. It's a clan, Colonel," Jack Stead put in. "Well, actually less of a clan than a group of fellas who think alike. Kind of like a small political splinter group in the Republicans or Democrats. Well, that ain't exactly accurate, I guess they're more like the Know-Nothings.[5] These Bad Faces probably started out as a sort of warrior society in the Oglalas and then started attracting other braves who shared their feelings about fighting us. I'd bet that most of 'em are the younger bucks full of piss and vinegar, if you'll pardon the expression, Colonel. These young braves'll do near about anything to get themselves into a good fight."

Bridger pursed his lips but nodded curtly to Carrington. It seemed to him that Stead's explanation was about as good a definition as they were likely to get. The old scout was impressed. Stead was doing a much better job of this than he had thought possible and he was wondering if maybe he'd got the fellow wrong before. He resolved that he must be more careful about jumping to conclusions about people in the future. Out here a man needed to know what he could expect of the men he worked with. Gossip was a foolish old man's sub-

---

[5]"Know-Nothings:" A short-lived but energetic political party (1853–1857) with origins in a secret society of "nativists." These were primarily urban Protestants who feared the political activism and job competition from an influx of Catholic immigrants (largely Irish).

stitute for using his own God-given common sense and instincts. He'd damn sure not do that again.

"I am going to Laramie to this council," Standing Elk said as if no one else had been talking. "It will be a fine time and most of the chiefs will be there. I will touch the pen and so will Spotted Tail. But these others, these Bad Faces," the Brulé shook his head, "they will not give up the road unless you whip them."

"THAT'S A GOOD HORSE YOU HAVE. HIS EYES ARE SOFT BUT his ears hear everything."

"I don't need you to tell me what a good horse I have, Red Cloud." The young warrior glanced up from his horse's hoof on which he was checking the condition of the quick, his face clouded over with ill-disguised distaste. "When a man hears you compliment his choice of horses, he would do well to watch them closely."

Red Cloud's fists tensed involuntarily at this remark but he fought down the impulse to respond in kind. This man was difficult to talk to, almost as bad as his father. The feud had lasted long enough and now there were more important things to be done. He almost choked at the thought of working with these people but he was in need of their help. He thought of what Pretty Owl had said to him.

"If you can't bring yourself to make peace with Old Man Afraid Of His Horses," she had said firmly, "then you must do it with his son." Her words had caused the gorge to rise in his throat but then she had pointed to their son, who was sleeping peacefully in his father's robes. "Look at a him," she'd urged. "If you can't make peace with our own people, what will happen to your son? Will you leave it to him to deal with the whites? Will Young Man Afraid try to kill your son? Will he try to take this land from him? Will you go to these *wasichu* and say 'You cannot take this land from my *tiyospaye*, I alone, the great Red Cloud, will stop you'? Is that what you'll do? This is stupidity. You might as well hand a gun to your son right now." He had looked up to see the tears start from her eyes.

It was as close as Pretty Owl had ever come to making him feel shame. He had looked long at the sleeping child. Listened to his breathing. Watched the gentle rise and fall of his little chest and heard his quiet sighs as he snuggled deeper into his father's robes. What would be left for him if the whites kept coming? Would this child ever have a child of his own? He reached out and slid one of his large fingers into the tiny fist and felt it tighten as a slight smile flickered across the sleeping boy's face. Suddenly he had had no trouble making his decision. So he had come to seek out his enemy's son, Young Man Afraid Of His Horses, and to do what had to be done.

"Whatever you may have heard, Young Man Afraid Of His Horses, you know that I do not steal the horses of a Lakota, or a Shyela." Red Cloud paused as the younger warrior stood and turned to face him. "Crow, Shoshone, Winnebago are another matter. Their horses are good enough and they are careless with them. But the *wasichu* horses are the ones that I want."

Young Man Afraid Of His Horses snorted derisively.

"Then you don't know as much about horses as I thought, Red Cloud. The *wasichu* animals are less than worthless. They are bigger and can carry more but only for a little while. The *wasichu* spoil them by feeding them grain and if they do not have it they quickly grow weak and die. I think you have been drinking their crazy water, like your father. You like the whites so much that you want to be like them."

Red Cloud's fists tightened again, his fingernails tearing open the flesh of his palms; his eyes narrowed with rage and his lips grew tight and twisted. His father, Lone Man, had indeed died of drinking the white man's whiskey, this was no secret, but the younger man's insult was too close to the truth in other ways as well. Despite his father's death Red Cloud had once had some very close relations with the whites and in years past had been friendly with the old trader John Richards and several officers at Fort Laramie. Young Man Afraid Of His Horses turned his back and pretended to examine his horse's ass, lifting the tail carefully and glancing at the dock. A grin flitted across his face as he enjoyed this last bit of theater and imagined Red Cloud's face contorted with rage. He reached up and slapped the animal's rump.

"This horse," Man Afraid said idly, as if his previous comments were of no import, "is like the wind and hungers for battle. I need no saddle to ride him and when the winter comes he will eat the bark of the young trees and still carry me into war when the whites' horses are good for nothing but to make into stew and . . ." He looked up and stopped abruptly, surprised to see that Red Cloud's face was creased by a smile. It had taken a supreme effort from the older man but this Man Afraid would never know.

"I hope that the Lakota will never be that hungry, Man Afraid," Red Cloud said quietly.

Young Man Afraid Of His Horses looked at him curiously. "You didn't come here to talk about horses, I see," he said.

"No, not about horses."

Red Cloud locked his eyes on Young Man Afraid's and then moved slowly along the side of the horse, running his hand along the animal's smooth back, his thumb and forefinger cradling the animal's spine the way a man does when he checks to see that a horse's vertebrae are not pinched. The horse nickered softly and flicked his tail to shoo off the flies. Young Man Afraid's brow furrowed, his hand tightening on his mount's halter. He looked up at Red Cloud and their eyes met for a moment, each seeing a question forming in the other's gaze but neither willing to be the first to break the uneasy silence. Red Cloud turned and walked down the slight slope to stop along the bank of the river, where he stood with his back to the younger warrior. Young Man Afraid hesitated for a moment, then moved down to join him, his horse trailing along easily. Red Cloud's gaze seemed to be fixed on a point on the mountains that lay in the distance. Young Man Afraid, puzzled, tried to discern what had drawn the older man's attention, then turned to study the man's profile.

"I am going to this council at Fort Laramie, Man Afraid. Are you going along?"

"You know that the *wasichu* have nothing to say that I want to hear, Red Cloud," Man Afraid said with heat, "but I should not be surprised that you have decided to go."

"That's what I expected to hear you say," Red Cloud said, stifling the urge to strike the man. Man Afraid looked at him puzzled. What sort of game was Red Cloud playing with him? What did all of this mean?

"It means," Red Cloud said, seeing the question forming on Man Afraid's face, "that you share my feelings about these *wasichu* and that we have at least one thing in common. Something that we can talk about. I am going for the same reason that you don't want to go." Red Cloud turned and looked the other man in the eye.

"I know we've not been friends, Man Afraid. There are old feuds, bad blood between your *tiyospaye* and mine. A lot of this is my own doing. Don't misunderstand what I say. I am not sorry for anything that I have done. It would not change anything, and what was done then has made us who we are today. This cannot be changed and it is foolish to dwell on it. What has happened in the past has happened. I don't care to think about it anymore. Only what happens tomorrow and the next day can be changed. But what will happen tomorrow is something that I do think about."

Man Afraid said nothing but it was clear that Red Cloud had his attention. His horse sneezed behind him and nuzzled his shoulder gently.

"It's time," Red Cloud said quietly, "that we left the old quarrels in the past. We scowl at each other and bicker and make noises and all the while these white thieves are taking this country away from us. And they do it under our noses. They come with their sweet words and their gifts and they fool the Big Bellies into touching the pen. And in a few moons what do we find? That their words were all lies and their gifts nothing more than their leavings . . . things that mean no more to them than dung means to the buffalo who drops it. Then they show us their talking papers and say that the Big Bellies gave them our land, as if anyone can give our mother away. You think that I haven't seen all of this and maybe I was blinded for a time by their things. But I'm not stupid. I can see how very dangerous these people have become."

This was a side of Red Cloud that Young Man Afraid Of His Horses had never seen before. He knew that Red Cloud mocked the old men who went to the fort to talk to the *wasichu*, that he despised the men who hung around the white man's fort looking for scraps and begging the crazy water. But he had always discounted it. He wondered if the feud between his father, Old Man Afraid Of His Horses, and Red Cloud's clan stood in the way of his taking anything that Red Cloud said seriously. He had never particularly liked the man. For all his skill as a warrior, and it was considerable, there was a brutal hardness and a slyness to Red Cloud which made him a hard man to trust. But there was something about his manner today that fascinated him. Man Afraid sat down on the bank of the river and picked up a stick. Something was happening here that puzzled him and this made him uncomfortable. He snapped the stick in two and hurled it into the water. The pieces disappeared so quickly that even the splashes to mark their passing were gone before they could rise into the air, carried away by the rushing torrent.

The whites will come rushing through this country like the rivers when they are swollen by snow melting in the mountains. "That stick," Red Cloud said, "could be the Lakota. We could be swallowed up and washed away without a ripple. If we do nothing you can be sure that this will happen."

"If this is how you feel," Man Afraid ventured, "then why do you say you are going to go to this council at Fort Laramie? If you don't mean to touch the pen, then why go at all?"

Red Cloud sat down beside the younger warrior and looked him in the eye, his jaw muscles tightening. "I go to stop others from giving this land away." He paused. "And I think that you are the man to help me to do this. I am just one man and while I will fight these people forever it is not enough for one man, or one clan to try to do it all. If we two clans of the Oglala can't work out our differences, if only for a short while, there is no hope of our ever keeping this land. But, if we who have been enemies can work together, who is to say that we cannot bring more of the people together? And if we can do this," he waved his hand at the surrounding countryside, "then we can keep this."

Young Man Afraid Of His Horses thought for a moment, then rose slowly to his feet, gazing at the distant mountains whose peaks, even in the heat of the summer, were still wrapped in a blanket of snow. He glanced back at the rushing torrent and considered Red Cloud's words.

"*Hetchetu!*" Man Afraid said. "Whatever our differences," he said quietly, "I will put them aside . . . for now. Until the *wasichu* are driven out of this country. I will not fight against you."

Red Cloud nodded. "That's good enough. Until the *wasichu* are driven out." The two men eyed each other warily. There was still no love lost between them, but for now there were other, more dangerous enemies to attend to.

MARGARET CARRINGTON WAS HAVING DIFFICULTY CONCEAL-ing her excitement and delight at the prospect of today's visit to Fort Laramie. She had managed to convince her husband that the four-mile trip into Laramie would be perfectly safe and that she, along with the wives of Surgeon Horton and Lieutenant Bisbee, had endured such privation along the march that they all deserved a well-earned day of diversion at this last outpost of civilization. The colonel blustered and coughed his way through a catalogue of objections, but when Jim Bridger appeared and allowed that there would be no harm in it Henry Carrington had finally relented and one of the regiment's ambulances was made available for the ladies' use that day.

"Now, Margaret," Carrington said with mock strictness. "You're to wait no longer than thirty minutes after my departure to get the ladies organized and be on your way. And pay close attention to Sergeant Bowers. I'll give him instructions that at the first inkling of trouble he's to spirit you back here and no delay. I insist that you have a small escort, and whatever happens, Bowers is in full charge from the time you leave this encampment until you arrive at Laramie. Is that perfectly clear?"

"Of course, dear," Margaret said solemnly, then grinned and stood on tiptoes to plant a kiss on his cheek. "We'll be fine, Henry, and thank you. The ladies do so need some recreation after all we've asked of them on this trip."

"Well, of course they do, and if Old Gabe says it's all right I don't suppose I have a leg to stand on, do I?"

Margaret threw her arms around Henry to give him a hug. With her chin nestled on her husband's shoulder she managed a wink at Jim Bridger, who had already mounted his mule and was waiting for the colonel to join him for their trip to Fort Laramie. Old Gabe smiled down at her and touched his fingers to the brim of his hat.

"Colonel," Bridger said, "we're burnin' daylight an' this child's got a powerful hankerin' for something cool to drink. Something you don't have to wait for the mud to settle out of."

Henry Carrington gave his wife a final peck on the cheek and turned to swing up into the saddle. An orderly handed the reins up to him and he tugged gently on them to turn toward the west and Fort Laramie. As Bridger and the colonel began to move off, Major Van Voast fell in behind them, signaling to his officers to begin moving a sizable column of infantry-men in the same direction. These were members of the 1st Battalion of the regiment, most of them recruits, destined to relieve the volunteers at the fort.

MARGARET WATCHED AS THE COLUMN OF MEN SWUNG OFF into the distance. A number of supply wagons followed in their wake, large sandy-colored clouds of dust marking their progress. Although the sun had risen only an hour before, the day promised to be a hot one and she wanted to be off to Laramie before the heat became unbearable. As the colonel and Bridger disappeared beyond a rise in the ground she turned and hurried off to gather up her friends, who were as eager as she to indulge in an outing.

Sergeant Bowers already had the ambulance hitched up and escort detail assembled. Now he leaned casually against the wheel of the wagon, sipping at a mug of coffee and smiling to himself as he anticipated the day's activities. His messmates had chided him about playing nursemaid to the Colonel's Lady and her friends, but Bowers had taken their ribbing in silence. *Let 'em squawk*, he thought. It was a short enough jog into the fort and once he'd got Mrs. Carrington and the other ladies unloaded he would pretty much be on his own for several hours. He'd overheard Bridger and the colonel talking the night before and knew that Bullock and Ward, the post sutlers, had a pretty decent little operation going—complete with a small cantina. It was just what the doctor ordered—a comfortable chair out of the sun, a blanket-covered table, a deck of cards, and a nice long bar fully stocked with cold beer. Well, he'd just have to see what he could do to help reduce Bullock and Ward's liquid inventory. Bowers caught sight of Margaret Carrington as she hurried by in search of her friends. He doffed his hat and smiled.

Bless you, darlin', he thought as Margaret waved and disappeared around the corner of a wagon.

THE WHEELS OF THE AMBULANCE HISSED THROUGH THE shallow crossing, throwing up water that streaked the layers of dust caked onto the vehicle's sides, the stiff springs jolting the occupants roughly from side to side and bouncing a squeal out of a startled Lucy Bisbee. Lucy snatched at her hat which was sliding down her nose and then nearly poked Margaret in the eye with her elbow as the ambulance hit yet another rut concealed by the slow moving water.

"Oh, Margaret," Lucy gasped. "Are you all right? I'm so sorry. I didn't see that one coming. It's easy to see why the soldiers call this thing an avalanche."

But Margaret hardly heard Lucy's pleadings. She was enjoying the brief illusion of coolness provided by the shade of the cottonwoods that reached over the Laramie River. The heat of the mid-June day had burst open the cottonwoods' seedpods and thousands of cottonlike bits of fluff floated and swirled listlessly in the air. It reminded Margaret of an early snowfall in Ohio and she found herself longing for the coolness that winter would bring.

"Oh, I'm sorry, Lucy, what were you saying? I was just looking at that. Isn't that an odd sight?" She pointed off toward a gently sloping hill and what was obviously the post cemetery. In the midst of the simple, whitewashed headboards stood an odd frame of poles lashed together and supporting a blanket-wrapped bundle. She could not know that this was the resting place of Spotted Tail's daughter. Tattered strips of cloth, faded to a dull sandy color, fluttered in the slight breeze. "Doesn't that look like one of those Indian burial scaffolds?"

"I wouldn't know, Margaret," Lucy said. "I've never actually ever seen one. But I can't imagine that they would put one in the post cemetery."

"Yes, that is strange, isn't it?" Margaret sighed and shook her head. What an odd place this country must be, she thought, where two cultures so very different could intermingle so closely that even their dead shared the land together. "But then," she said half to herself, "this is a very strange country."

The ambulance hit another rut and shuddered as the horses strained to pull it up the far bank of the ford. Margaret, Lucy, and their companion, Surgeon Horton's wife, Sallie, held tightly to anything that seemed immovable and stared out at the scene that was unfolding before them. A fringe of cottonwoods marked the course of the river they had just crossed, and along its banks, as far as they could see, stretched a mass of Indian lodges. It was like nothing they had ever seen before and they were amazed to see the hundreds of buffalo-hide tipis in such close proximity to Fort Laramie which, Lucy observed with some evident anxiety, was not enclosed by a stockade.

"My goodness," Lucy exclaimed in a breathless whisper, "what if there was an uprising? Wherever would we go? Where could we hide?"

Sallie Horton shuddered and her face seemed to drain of color. "We'd be at the mercy of these savages," she whispered. "How horrid!"

Margaret's lips tightened into a small smile as she reached out and patted the hands of her companions. "Now, ladies," she said quietly. "Let's not get ourselves all worked up over absolutely nothing at all. I rather suspect that there is no stockade because there has never been need of a stockade and I sincerely doubt that the colonel would even have considered letting us visit the fort if he had even an inkling of danger to us." She grinned mischievously. "You both know what a terrible worrier he is."

The other women looked at each other a bit sheepishly, for Margaret was obviously correct in her assumptions, which seemed to be borne out by the pastoral scene. From this distance Fort Laramie and its surrounding Indian encampment looked positively sleepy. In every direction all was calm and eerily quiet. Hundreds of horses wandered loose, grazing from the already browned and close-cropped grass; Indian children splashed playfully in the river while their mothers busied themselves with the myriad domestic chores required to keep a village going in so inhospitable an environment. The lodges glowed tan in the warm light, their sides rolled up in the heat. And everywhere there were knots of people moving in slow motion in the intense heat. The surrounding hills rolled off into the distance, a sea of sun-scorched grass.

Fort Laramie, for the large size of its garrison, and its supposed importance, disappointed the ladies upon closer inspection. The parade ground was a barren expanse of hard-packed dirt. What little paint there was in evidence on the surrounding buildings was peeling and faded, a number of roofs were in sore need of repair, and the decorative "gingerbread" on many of the quarters showed gaps where bits had simply rotted away. Most of the quarters were nicely designed with railed porches, but many were missing spindles, kicked away by careless boots. There were also a number of squat adobe buildings, rough-hewn cottonwood logs protruding from under their roofs, which served various roles as bakery, blacksmith shop, post sutler's, and guardhouse. And everywhere were the mementos of bored and listless troopers—names, initials, dates, and crude sketches, gouged, scratched, and carved by count-

less pocketknives and bayonets into every available surface. It
was, Margaret thought, a fairly shabby affair.

The ambulance crawled across the crowded parade ground
to roll to a stop in front of the commanding officer's quarters,
where Sergeant Bowers leaped down from the mule seat to
assist the ladies from the wagon as a young private held the
horses steady and gawked at the passing parade.

MARGARET PAUSED TO DRINK IN THE ENTIRE SCENE, HER
head turning slowly as her brain registered the diverse humanity that milled and mingled among the weathered and dilapidated buildings. Hundreds of Indians and whites in every
state of dress and undress wandered through the fort. It overwhelmed the senses. She saw Indian men, women, and children, a mass of sun-bronzed skin, some smeared with brightly
colored paints, long, glossy black hair, braided or loose, fes-
tooned with feathers, wrapped in strips of trade cloth or bits
of fur. And moving easily among the Indians were scores of
trappers, traders, soldiers, and civilians, in every imaginable
costume, their skin burned brown and many half covered by
beards. Blond hair, cropped close and bristling. Brown hair
matted and curling over darkened, sweat-stained collars of cot-
ton or elkhide. Hundreds of bodies were draped in everything
from breechclouts to blankets, and over all was a buzzing chatter of twenty different dialects, all unintelligible to her. Here
and there a familiar speech pattern slipped into her ears. The
slow drawl of the South. The nasal twang and clipped phrases
of New England. And then there were snatches of conversation
which were barely recognizable, garbled and twisted by the
accents of Ireland, France, Scotland, Germany, and who
knew how many other nations. They talked, argued, sang,
whistled, hummed, smoked, drank, cursed, chewed, spat, swatted, sweated, and scratched. And the competing smells were
overpowering: sweat, grease, leather, woodsmoke, horses, hay,
manure, sage, and tobacco. Swarms of flies and buffalo gnats
buzzed, bothered, and bit at their leisure. Lucy and Sallie stood

just behind Margaret, peering openmouthed over her shoulder at the moving mass of people.

"Mrs. Carrington, ma'am." Sergeant Bowers stood at attention, bowing slightly from the waist. "If you'd like to do some shopping, ma'am, Mr. Bullock and Mr. Ward have a general store just across the parade ground there." He pointed across the parade ground toward a low adobe building that they had passed on their way into the fort. "I would have stopped the ambulance there, ma'am, but, as you can see, it's just chockablock with Injuns an' I thought the ladies might wish to pay a visit to Colonel Maynardier's missus and maybe freshen up a bit afore taking the plunge." He jerked a thumb over his shoulder at the crowd.

Margaret looked up at him. "Why, Sergeant Bowers, what a considerate gesture," she said with a bright smile. "We should indeed do just that and I thank you for your courtesy."

Bowers blushed and touched his cap with his fingers in salute.

"Now, Sergeant," she went on in a whisper. "I think we'll be just fine from here. Why don't you and your men try to enjoy yourselves for a while. I'm sure you're all quite thirsty from the trip and I know the colonel wouldn't mind if you availed yourselves of a little refreshment."

"Why, thank you, ma'am," Bowers said with a smile. "But if you should need anything . . ."

"Well," Margaret interrupted, "then I should just have to look for you. Now, let me see," she lifted one finger and placed it thoughtfully on her chin. "I believe the enlisted men's cantina should be fairly easy to find. I think I saw it as we passed in. You wouldn't mind if I asked that either you or one of your men remain somewhere in that vicinity for an hour or two, would you?"

Bowers broke into a wide grin. "Why not at all, ma'am," he said. "It would be my, I mean, uh, our pleasure to be at your service, ma'am."

"Well then," Margaret said. "We're all settled. Come along, Mrs. Bisbee, Mrs. Horton, let's pay our compliments to Mrs. Maynardier and then get on to a bit of shopping."

Margaret turned and climbed easily up the steps to the commanding officer's quarters with Lucy and Sallie talking quietly among themselves and following along behind. The three women stopped briefly on the porch to check each other's appearance, brushing a stray hair into place, setting the angle of a hat, plucking away a random bit of cottonwood fluff. Margaret glanced toward the parade ground again and wondered about the curious arrangement of benches just below the commanding officer's quarters. They were set in a sort of large bower constructed of roughly trimmed saplings lashed together with hemp and the whole roofed loosely with cottonwood boughs wilting rapidly in the heat and bright sun. Set up at the end closest to the quarters was a low platform that reminded her of the makeshift stage that had been improvised for the minstrel show. This, she concluded, was to be the focal point of the council, and she decided that she would have to make sure that they finished their shopping in time to secure themselves a comfortable seat on the porch. While they wouldn't be the "Ironclad Minstrels," the performers slated to appear on this stage were sure to be a fascinating ensemble. The minstrel show had provided farce and now they would have drama. Margaret found herself wondering how Mr. Shakespeare would describe the impending play. She felt a cough rising up in her chest and hoped it would not be quite so dusty where they were headed.

Oh, for a muse of fire, she thought, *that would ascend the highest heaven of invention. A kingdom for a stage, princes to act, monarchs to attend the swelling scene*. And oh, what a scene this should be. She found she could hardly wait for the play to begin.

The rough wooden benches filled quickly with men who wandered in from various points of the fort in time to attend the day's main event. Large barrels of water with hooked handle ladles dangling over the sides had been set out at intervals along the edges of the imperfectly shaded bower. There was a shuffling and scraping, and the drone of discordant voices as tribesmen nudged past each other, seeking out friends and fellow clan members with whom they could talk as the council unfolded. Blue-coated Army officers, their dark uniforms freshly brushed and already soaked with sweat, glistening with brass and bullion donned for the occasion, leaned casually against the bower's uprights. Some of the older men dabbed frequently at their foreheads with handkerchiefs pulled from woolen cuffs.

Standing alongside the small stage, Jack Stead was talking quietly with Jim Bridger. Stead was a bit nervous anticipating the role he was to play in the coming discussions but Bridger, who had consciously sought out his company since the session with Standing Elk, was quick to reassure the interpreter.

"Look here, son," Bridger whispered. "There's not another man-jack here who can do as fair a job as ye can. You just cozy on up to Colonel Carrington and see he gets as good a story from this palaver as ye can give. Most of these paper-collar soldiers and shiny-suit civilians'll be cleared out o'here in a few days and devil take the hindmost. But the colonel, he's the one going to be held accountable for how these devils behave, so he's the one you gotta stick with."

"I've been wondering, Major," Stead ventured. "Seein' as how you speak Lakota, how come you didn't handle that palaver with Standin' Elk?"

Bridger grinned broadly, wrapped a sinewy arm around Stead's shoulders, and pulled him close.

"Jack, my boy," Bridger whispered confidentially, "this nigger kin speak about enough Sioux to get some young squaw's husband itchin' to take my scalp. I could no more a talked turkey with Mr. Standin' Elk than I coulda talked with Kublai Khan." Stead frowned, incredulous.

"I savvy Crow an' Blackfeet," Bridger chuckled. "Do pretty fair with sign and got a bit o' Ute and Snake from my wives, rest their souls, but that's about the long an' square of it. But I know a bit about men an' I could see from his face that Standin' Elk thought you savvied his lingo purty dern good. I figger if it's good enough for him it'll suit me right down to the ground. You're a steadfast man, Jack, an' I depend on ye to do what ye do."

He glanced across the small stage to see Colonel Carrington

nodding to an Indian whom Stead immediately recognized as
Standing Elk. The Sioux was in the company of another warrior, about the same age but noticeably taller and, to Stead's
eye, a much more impressive figure. Where Standing Elk
might or might not have been a chief, it seemed fairly obvious
that the man with him was a figure of considerable stature and
authority.

"Who's that fella, Major?" Stead asked, nodding in the direction of Standing Elk's companion. It was *Sinté-Galeska*,
who had but three months earlier brought his dead daughter
to this place.

"That gentleman is called Shan-tag-galisk, Mr. Interpreter,"
a strange, deep voice put in from over Bridger's shoulder.
"That was his daughter's burial scaffold you might have seen
as you came in across the Laramie."

Stead looked up to see a large black man with a handsome,
broad face smiling at him, a meaty hand resting easily on
Bridger's shoulder.

"You have a queer definition of gentleman, Medicine Calf,"
Bridger said with a wry grin. "But then I knowed you to put
a shine on the facts a tad here an' there to suit yore tastes, ye
old scoundrel."

The man Bridger called "Medicine Calf" was dressed from
head to foot in a suit of buckskins, beaded and quilled in the
fashion of the Crow, his hair worn in long braids and wrapped
in otter skin. It was immediately apparent to Stead that these
two men had a long history. Bridger introduced the newcomer.

"Jack Stead," Bridger said, "this here is Jim Beckwourth.
He is a braggart and a scoundrel who somehow manages not
to get himself kilt or lost too often, which does amaze me
somethin' fierce."

Beckwourth stuck out a large, callused hand and took
Stead's in a grip which quickly made Jack wince. For a man
of Beckwourth's obvious age he was an incredible specimen,
broad-shouldered and muscular with a face that was open and
nearly free of wrinkles beyond the laugh creases around his
eyes. He had a smile that sparkled and revealed strong even
teeth that Stead and Bridger both might envy. Beckwourth's

eyes, however, seemed to Stead to be hazel in color, an odd thing to see in a black man.

"I am plumb struck they ain't yet raised yer har, Medicine Calf."

Beckwourth flashed a dazzling smile at Bridger.

"I have hair and to spare, Big Throat," Beckwourth said, flicking his long fingers at a pair of scalplocks that dangled loosely from his ornate buckskins. "The bucks who raised this crop have no further use for it.

"You seem a bit confused, Mr. Interpreter," Beckwourth said easily. "I will enlighten you. My late father, you see, was Sir Jennings Beckwith, and I thus had the benefit of rather a better education than my friend Bridger here. So you needn't be put off by my unusually dulcet tones. I changed the name to Beckwourth to distance myself somewhat from papa. You know in what low regard the Irish are held out here and I cared not to deal with that stigma. Thankfully my people among the Crow tend not to be so small-minded as folks back in Virginia and Missouri. They are rather a depressing lot, the graybacks. Most of them, you see, were thrown out of Kentucky. This might give one a rather higher opinion of Kentuckians than they deserve. The Crow have made me a war chief and accord me considerably more respect than I might expect from the War Department, despite my many and valuable services to them. I saved a general from drowning once you know. I am at your service, sir."[6] Beckwourth made an exaggerated bow, sweeping his powerful arm in a great arc.

[6]James Beckwourth (nee Beckwith) (1800–1866) was indeed the son of a minor Irish aristocrat, Sir Jennings Beckwith, and a slave woman. A trapper and mountain man of great renown, Beckwourth had helped initiate the famous Green River Rendezvous and his career included service with the American Fur Company, a stint in the Seminole and the Mexican Wars, and an uncertain involvement in the Sand Creek Massacre in Colorado. Adopted by the Crow Indians, he did have considerable status among them, but his claim of war chief may be apocryphal. The general he claimed to have saved from drowning was William Ashley, who led the Rocky Mountain supply expedition to trappers (1824–1826). General Ashley, however, denied in his diaries that it was Beckwourth who rescued him from the Green River in 1825.

"Oh, uh," Stead began, taken aback by Beckwourth's monologue.

"Well, sir," Beckwourth said, seemingly without pause. "This nigger has made an enemy or two among our red brethren here. They're even now likely debating who among them shall have first go at my resplendent mane of hair, a trophy any buck would be proud to display. So if you will excuse me, I shall repair to a less public place for the moment. It was a pleasure, sir." Beckwourth nodded solemnly to Stead, shot a wink at Bridger, and melted back into the crowd. Stead's eyes followed the retreating figure with an admixture of wonder and disbelief.

"A Crow war chief?" he muttered.

"Well," Bridger snorted shaking his head, "there be more rooster than Crow in Beckwourth if you ask me. Though he crows loud enough about himself to beat all."

"Is that a fact?" Stead asked.

"I cain't never be sure," Bridger said, shaking his head, "what a thing that man says has anythin' whatever to do with a fact. He's a muzzle-loadin' daisy, he is. But if you loved a liar, you could just hug that man to death."

Out of the corner of his eye Bridger caught sight of a bright flash accompanied by a muffled *whump*. A small cloud of white smoke boiled up over the crowd. His first thought was that some fool had "flashed a pan" and he gritted his teeth at the idiocy that would allow someone to fool about with a musket in this volatile mix of people. Several of the Indians he noticed were either alarmed or scowling and reaching under their blankets—he assumed for weapons they had concealed in disregard to the rules laid down by Colonel Maynardier. Contrary buggers they were. He wouldn't trust 'em as far as he could comfortably spit. As the smoke cleared away Bridger caught a glimpse of the author of the mischief, a soberly dressed young man with shoulder-length blond hair and a face that he doubted yet had need for a razor. Bridger had seen the man wandering about the fort earlier. He was always pushing a strange little handcart in front of him and Bridger thought he looked for all the world like a Mormon.[7] The fellow was now holding a small tray over his head, grinning like a cat and waving his other hand at a group of officers and Indians who were packed tightly together on the steps of Colonel Maynardier's headquarters building. Between the "Mormon" and the steps was a large box camera perched precariously upon a tripod of bamboo poles and draped with a black hood.

A Mormon and a photographer to boot, Bridger concluded, and spat. Bad cess to the lot of 'em. Damned nuisances they were. Always poking their damned foolish heads where they were least wanted—like mice in the manger. The problem with Indians was that they were as high-strung and unpredictable as some horses. *Damn fool gets to popping off his flashpowder*, thought Bridger, *and he's like as not to start a damned stampede among them red devils*. From the looks the man was getting Bridger figured that a couple of the younger braves had already set their minds on acquiring the shadow catcher's pretty yellow hair.

"Mr. Glover!"

Bridger recognized Colonel Maynardier's gravelly and exasperated voice. The colonel had rushed down the steps of the building and confronted the photographer. "Would you please try to give some warning to the rest of us when you're about to make your plates. I have tried to explain to you the delicacy one must use when dealing with the natives. A great many of them very much fear the camera. They consider it very big medicine and capable of stealing their souls. This can only breed difficulties where we need not have them."

---

[7]Bridger's assumption was probably based on Glover's use of a photographers' handcart. Called the "perambulator dark tent," this was an ingenious mobile darkroom mounted on a wheelbarrow-type frame which carried all of the equipment and chemicals needed for field photography. When opened up it provided a fully functional, if cramped, darkroom in which to process collodion wet-plate photographs. This apparatus was very popular for its compact portability and fully loaded weighed between 60 and 100 pounds. Some variations of the "perambulator" looked much like the handcarts used by Mormon "handcart companies" in their westward movement between 1856–1860.

"I'm sorry, sir," the photographer stammered out. "I didn't realize that . . ."

"What you didn't realize, Mr. Glover, is of no concern to me, sir." Colonel Maynardier had planted himself directly in front of the camera, his arms akimbo, jaw thrust forward, and the veins of his temples pulsing visibly. "When I give you instructions on how to go about doing something I do not expect you to weigh my comments against your momentary passions and disregard them. I have sound reasons for dictating how and under what conditions your plates may be made and they are not, I assure you, frivolous. I will do anything in my power to assist your efforts but I warn you, sir, that if you deviate from my guidance in future I will place you under arrest and there will be no more photographs of this conference taken under any circumstances. Have I made myself clear, sir?"

Ridgway Glover, his face a deep crimson, stood with head bowed as the post commander upbraided him for his absentminded breach of the colonel's instructions. Maynardier concluded by putting Glover in the care of Jim Beckwourth, who was to advise him of which Indians did not object to having their pictures taken and where these images could be taken without causing a general uproar among the other conferees. Beckwourth as a keeper for a photographer. That, Bridger thought with an inward chuckle, was just perfect. Knowing Beckwourth, not another photo would be taken of this conference without Beckwourth's toothy grin flashing out for all posterity to see. The man was a pure glutton for notoriety and would sooner miss a meal than a chance to get in the newspapers. Bridger looked on with growing sense of glee as Beckwourth placed a heavy arm around the photographer's narrow shoulders and led him off whispering into the fellow's ear. Bridger noted the wide-eyed look which was spreading over Glover's face and could see that Beckwourth was thoroughly enjoying his new role of wet-nurse. Well, if anyone deserved Beckwourth's ministrations it was a greenhorn-by-God-photographer.

* * *

MORMON PHOTOGRAPHERS AND LARGE BLACK IRISHMEN NOT-
withstanding, what posterity might have gained from the conference looked to Bridger like a lost opportunity. Negotiations
had been nerve-wrackingly slow. After the almost intermina-
ble smoking of pipes and self-serving, high-flown introductory
statements of the principals—and it was a near-run thing as
to whether the damned Sioux or the damned Washington politicians were the windier of the lot—the talks had begun to
come around to the central issue of the day. This, as Bridger
rightly concluded, was whether the Sioux and their friends
were about to trade away access to the Bozeman Trail.

Fort Laramie stood square on the route of the old Oregon
Trail, which Bridger himself had opened in 1841. It was tense
enough business running emigrants bound for the west coast
through the Sioux's country, but when John Bozeman had decided to blaze a spur north from Laramie to the Powder River
and the newly discovered gold fields in Virginia City things
began to get considerably worse. The prospectors and specu-
lators greatly appreciated the shortcut but the Sioux and Arapaho who lived in this country had just about had their fill. The
Bozeman Trail, known variously as the Montana Road and the
Virginia City Road, ran not only to the gold fields but directly
through what the Sioux and Arapaho considered their premier
hunting grounds. This, Bridger knew, spelled trouble. Now
that the talks had finally come around to the business of the
trail, just how bad this trouble might be quickly became apparent. In the hot, still air of the late afternoon a dull murmuring began among the Indians and the atmosphere fairly
crackled with tension.

MARGARET CARRINGTON HAD QUICKLY TIRED OF SHOPPING.
Bullock and Ward's wares were not nearly as enticing as she
had hoped. In addition, the small store was packed with a
heaving mass of Indians and frontiersmen, all shockingly aromatic in the close quarters of the adobe building and, it
seemed to her, all jabbering away at the top of their lungs.
The press of bodies and cacophony of voices was unbearably

disorienting. Margaret felt she could hardly move three steps without tripping over a naked Indian child scuffling through the peanut shells and cracker crumbs which littered the rough, wide-planked floor. She pushed her way through the door and out into the open air. The glare reflected from the packed earth was blinding and the heat overwhelming. Margaret drew a deep breath and felt her head begin to swim. She leaned against the adobe wall of the sutler's to let her head clear, then made her way slowly across the open expanse to the head-quarters building, where the conference was already in session.

It wasn't long before the heat and sonorous droning of each successive speaker proved nearly as trying as Bullock and Ward's, and with an unanticipated feeling of weariness Margaret finally sought sanctuary in the ambulance that had brought her to Laramie. With the canvas window blinds pulled down against the fierce sun and nestled into the relative comfort of the canvas-covered seats, she began to yawn in the warm stillness of the wagon. The monotonous buzzing of insects and human voices contributed to the fluttering of her eyelids and soon she was napping peacefully in the vehicle's dim interior. A sudden shouting and commotion outside snapped her awake and she looked about her, bewildered.

Under the now wilted bower that shielded the conferees from the sun, a sad-faced and solemn Spotted Tail was making a reasoned appeal to all to maintain their calm when Colonel Carrington was introduced as the "soldier chief who will take care of all who use, hunt, or live alongside the new road." Carrington, seated comfortably in a ladder-back chair, nodded to Spotted Tail and began to speak.

"It is my greatest wish," Carrington said, "that we shall be able to make this into a great union of our two peoples. This country, my friends, is your home and we respect your wishes that it shall be safeguarded from all who would despoil it and rob you of your livelihood and heritage. These forts that we shall build, I assure you, will . . ."

Jim Bridger leaned casually against the side of the head-quarters building a few feet behind the commissioners and strained to hear what his friend was saying. But neither

Bridger nor anyone else for that matter could hear the remainder of Carrington's statement, drowned out as it was by
the ugly mutterings in the assembled warriors. Lakota, Cheyenne, and Arapaho alike began to gesticulate angrily, their
voices raised in dissent. Shouts of *"Tula!"* and *"Hon!"*[8] echoed across the parade ground and there was a great rustling
and jostling about in the tightly packed crowd. Colonel Maynardier cast a worried glance at a puzzled Carrington. Jack
Stead bent over between them and whispered urgently in their
ears. The commissioners, looking visibly pale and sweating
profusely in their dark suits, tugged anxiously at collars that
suddenly seemed too tight. A number of them cast worried
eyes about to count silently the number of troops who were
within easy reach and carefully noting those who were obviously armed. At least one member of the commission felt his
bowels begin to grumble uncomfortably and feared that he
would not get off of the platform without soiling himself.

Bridger's hands tensed into tightly balled fists as his eyes
swept the crowd, looking to identify those most likely to give
physical vent to their emotions. Every itch scratched under a
blanket could as easily be a knife or revolver fingered in anger
and frustration. He had seen such situations before and he
knew that it took but one miscalculation to turn a harsh word
into bloodshed. Thank God the fort was full of many of the
warriors' families, he thought grimly. The closer their women
and children were, the more circumspect the older men would
be and they, he hoped, would help to keep the younger braves
in check. Bridger felt a brush against his arm and glanced over
to see a nervous young soldier fidgeting with the catch on his
cartridge box. The old scout reached out quietly and placed a
viselike grip around the youngster's forearm.

"You leave 'er be, son," he whispered calmly, his eyes still
on the crowd. "If'n you see me reach for a smoke wagon then
you can git nervous. Til then you just behave yourself and
you'll likely keep your hair where it is."

The young private swallowed hard and nodded uneasily, an

---

[8] *"Tula!"* Shame! *"Hon!"* Don't give me that!

overlarge drop of sweat running down the bridge of his nose to plop silently onto the dusty boards at his feet. He was about to question the old scout more closely but Bridger was focused on a middle-aged warrior with a powerful form and a prominent Roman nose. Rising to his feet, the Indian towered over his peers and fairly exuded charisma. The large warrior held up his hands and drew the attention of all the other braves and the particular interest of Spotted Tail.

"I will not hear any more of these lies," Red Cloud growled.

"You have not let the soldier chief say what he has to say yet, Red Cloud," Spotted Tail scolded. "How can you expect that any good will come of your discourtesy to this man?"

"Discourtesy!" Red Cloud snapped. "You make me laugh, old man! Courtesy has nothing to do with anything that has happened here today. These men"—he spat out the words, waving his fist contemptuously toward the commissioners—"tell us that they are our friends, our protectors, and our hosts. This is a lie, I tell you! They are not protectors of anyone but themselves and their greed. They are not our friends and if anyone is a host here it is the Lakota! This is our country and it is only by our good wishes that these people have been allowed to live here." A chorus of approving grunts met his remarks.

"*Sehans, Tokaska!*"[9] Young Man Afraid Of His Horses yelled.

"*Eces!* No!" Spotted Tail exclaimed, his hand raised for silence. "You know that we have long ago all agreed that this place was to be allowed for this fort and for the whites to live peaceably among us."

"We are not talking about this fort, old man," Red Cloud interrupted. "You know as well as I do that these people did not come to talk about this fort. That is not why we are here. These people are not satisfied with what they have here but will build more forts. We did not object to their Holy Road but that is not enough for them. They will take what we have left to us and leave us begging their scraps. They will push their new road through the Powder River country and with it

[9]"*Sehans, Tokaska!*" Most certainly, there is something said!

they will push out the game and the Lakota!" Bridger was impressed by the man's height. He stood well over six feet and his frame seemed even more substantial than it had first appeared. The crowd waited patiently as Red Cloud turned to address them in a body.

"These men treat us as children. They come and offer us presents and say they wish only to travel through this country. But they think that we are foolish children and that they have already taken this country by conquest. They will strip this country like wolves and buzzards strip a carcass until there is no scrap of flesh left on the bones of the Lakota. Will you stand by and do nothing while these thieves steal the very food from your children's mouths?"

The angry rumbling and mutterings rose again. Henry Carrington, feeling obliged to do something, stood to try to bring some sense of calm back to the proceedings, which were growing more tense with each passing moment. He raised his hands, palms outward, and spoke in what he hoped was a soothing and reasonable tone.

"The forts along this road," he began, meaning to explain how they were meant as much to protect Indian rights as those of white travelers, but was cut off in midsentence by a livid Young Man Afraid Of His Horses. The Lakota stood trembling with anger, his face distorted with rage, and pointed a finger directly at Carrington.

"You try to build one more fort in this country, Little White Chief," Young Man Afraid said through gritted teeth, "and in two moons you will not have a hoof left!"

Carrington felt the color drain from his face and his stomach contract into a tight ball. He had never been physically threatened by anyone and it was a strangely disorienting experience. Jack Stead, sensing his employer's discomfiture, placed a hand gently on the colonel's sleeve and whispered urgently. *"Easy, sir. Stay calm, don't react."* The colonel nodded and sat down heavily as Young Man Afraid shot a quick glance at Red Cloud and received a curt approving nod in reply. The latter took his cue as Young Man Afraid looked smugly about him at his friends and resumed his seat on a rough wooden bench.

Red Cloud threw his arms out wide in a dramatic gesture indicating that the other warriors should look about themselves.

"You see what these people have done?" he began in a low tone. "Look about you, my brothers. Every day that passes brings yet another ten white men into this country. They say that they wish only to pass through our lands on their way to the great water in the west. But do they all go to this land they speak of? No, I tell you. If ten men come here," he said spreading the fingers of his outstretched hands, "five remain behind when the others go on." He held up his right hand with the fingers still fanned outward. "But these five men who stay are like this." Red Cloud curled the fingers into a fist. "They make a fist that they will use to strike us! How many fists must you see before you wake up and see that our enemies are among us and stronger than the Lakota. Stronger than the Shyela. Stronger than the Arapaho. Stronger than all of our peoples together." There was a renewed muttering of assent.

"*Hon! Tokaska!*" came the guttural voices. "What he says is true." A slight smile flitted across Red Cloud's face. He knew he had hit a number of exposed nerves. He turned to face the peace commissioners and again leveled a finger at Colonel Carrington. "These whites come to us with presents from the Great Father," Red Cloud said, his voice dripping with sarcasm, "and say they want our permission to build a road. But, at the same time they send their Little White Chief and his soldiers to steal this road before a Lakota says yes or no!" The crowd exploded in anger. Hundreds of warriors began shouting and shaking their fists at the commissioners.

Spotted Tail saw that things were going very badly and his first thought was of placating the incensed men and trying to bring some semblance of order and dignity back to the proceedings. But, as he attempted to rise, Standing Elk placed a restraining hand on Spotted Tail's arm, shaking his head slightly. Two Strike, sitting to Spotted Tail's left, glanced around with a puzzled look on his face, searching for a clue to how he should react. He rather liked what Red Cloud had to say and felt like joining in the general shouting—the man certainly had a way of speaking that was convincing—but Two Strike was torn be-

tween his acceptance of Red Cloud's words and his loyalty to
Spotted Tail. When he looked at his friend he could see an almost unutterable sadness in Spotted Tail's eyes and immediately decided in his friend's favor. He would stay by his friend,
whatever his feelings toward the whites.

Colonel Maynardier decided that things had gone quite far
enough for one day. To prolong the meetings any further in
this atmosphere could only lead to hotter tempers. He would
not tolerate bloodshed on his post and was not about to take
the blame for igniting a general Indian war. Maynardier stood
and raised his hands for silence just as Red Cloud and Young
Man Afraid, not wishing to lose the dramatic impact of their
rhetoric, stormed from the conference bower with a number
of the younger braves hastening to follow them. Maynardier
shouted to make himself heard above the tumult.

"Red Cloud is right," Maynardier said, hoping to throw the
malcontents off balance. "We have done all that can be done today. There is much that must be considered and that must be
done when all are rested and have had time to reflect on what
has been said. To talk any further today is only to have our judgment clouded by hot words and rash statements. We have gifts
and much food which we gladly share with our brothers. Let us
leave off this talking for tonight and gather again in the morning
to see what wisdom sleep can lend our efforts."

Several of the older warriors who had remained behind nodded solemnly. The civilian peace commissioners, who had been
sweating profusely, breathed a collective sigh of relief at the apparent cooling of tempers. Red Cloud himself, who had stopped
a few feet away from the conference bower to observe the impact of his performance, could not hear the colonel's words.
From the reactions of the warriors who remained Red Cloud
saw that Maynardier seemed to be cooling things off. The warrior stood stock-still and glowered, not at Maynardier or the civilian commissioners, but at Carrington, the "Little Soldier
Chief" who had just brought more soldiers into the country.

Maynardier finished his speech by thanking the warriors for
their courtesy and great good sense. Those who had remained
began to drift off in twos and threes to their lodges and favored

haunts around the post. As the conference began to break up Spotted Tail pushed past the restraining arm of Standing Elk and moved purposefully toward Red Cloud. Two Strike and Standing Elk hesitated for a moment and then hurried to catch up with their friend, fearful that there would be a confrontation with Red Cloud's faction. The trio came to within a few feet of a knot of young braves jostling about Red Cloud and Young Man Afraid Of His Horses and congratulating them on their boldness in confronting the *wasichu*. The young men grew silent and stood uneasily aside as Spotted Tail stepped directly in front of a very smug Red Cloud. The two men towered above the other warriors and the air fairly crackled with electricity. Young Man Afraid Of His Horses hunched his shoulders slightly the way a man on horseback does when a storm boils up suddenly on the open plains and he expects lightning to strike at any moment.

"What did you think you were doing, Red Cloud," Spotted Tail asked slowly, his rage barely concealed. "What were you trying to do by making statements like that? Did you want to stir up more trouble between us and the whites? Why'd you come to this place if all you will talk of is war?"

Red Cloud did not reply but looked disdainfully at the older warrior, a slight smile on his face.

"You think to make a great name for yourself, Red Cloud," the older man went on, his voice in a hoarse whisper but his eyes blazing with an intense inner light. "You want to be a great man among the Oglala. You want to be the savior of the Lakota. You and your Bad Faces'll do anything even if it means starting a war right here and now with all of our women and children sitting here under the guns of the *wasichu*! You don't care who gets killed as long as your deeds are the ones painted on the Winter Count. But I will ask you something, you who wish to be a great one, and you should think hard about your answer to me, for I have more scars of battle than you have fleas in your blankets and I know a fool when I see his face. What good'll your bragging do when there's no one left to make the Winter Count? Who'll tell of your deeds when every Lakota is dead and their bones scattered by the wolves?"

Red Cloud's face flushed with anger but he held his tongue. Spotted Tail turned on Young Man Afraid, the other warriors shrinking back from eyes that seemed to shoot off sparks of soul-burning anger.

"And you," Spotted Tail snapped. "Do you enjoy being Red Cloud's pet dog? Do you like barking and nipping at the blue-coats when he snaps his fingers? You should know what happens to pet dogs when a hard winter comes. This great man will not shrink from placing you in his wife's stew pot. And you, you foolish young men," he said, rounding on the gathered braves. "Think before you follow these men down the Black Road, for that is the road to sadness and death. There is no glory in dead wives and starving children whose wailing in the night will bring even the coyote to tears. You may think that this is nonsense but you have not yet seen how these whites will make war. They don't fight like we fight. You may kill ten of them today but tomorrow a hundred more will come after them and they will not be satisfied with the scalps of a few foolish young men. They will slaughter the buffalo so that our families will starve. They will kill our ponies. They will burn our lodges. They will be like a great fire on the prairie. They will destroy everything and leave only blackened earth and ashes behind."

Red Cloud was tempted to denounce the older man, to hold him up to ridicule in front of the others, but in the distance he could see the tattered and faded strips of cloth that dangled limply from the burial scaffold of Spotted Tail's daughter, and the sight made him pause. The man had lost his daughter to the *wasichus'* sickness and their god. He was a broken man but he was also still a respected war chief. He had the sympathy and the ear of too many people to risk offending him. A confrontation now, Red Cloud knew, would not help his cause. There had to be a better way to deal with this man. He knew he must bide his time but it was hard to fight down the anger that he felt welling up inside of him, tainting his tongue with the sour taste of bile. He watched impassively as Spotted Tail turned on his heel and strode off. Standing Elk and Two Strike remained behind a moment to add their warning stares

at the now silent young warriors before turning to join their
friend as he crossed the parade ground heading for his lodge
across the river. As the three older men disappeared into the
crowd that choked the fort's open space, the younger warriors
began once more to grumble among themselves.

"Hunhunhe Onsila," Red Cloud said quietly, at which
Young Man Afraid Of His Horses frowned and tilted his head
to the side.

"Why do you say that, Red Cloud?" Man Afraid asked,
puzzled. "Why do you say the old fool's to be pitied?"

Red Cloud shook his head and spoke loudly enough for the
other warriors to hear him plainly.

"His eyes are blinded by grief," Red Cloud said shaking his
head sadly. "You have to remember that when he speaks against
war it is not the warrior speaking but the man whose wife and
daughter are dead. How can you hate a man who has seen what
he has seen? He has become one of the older ones whom it is
now our job to protect." He turned to the assembled younger
braves and raised his hand for their attention. "Let no one speak
ill of *Sinté-Galeska*. He has borne enough for any man. I hate
his words but I respect the man and so should you all." The
younger men listened and he could see their heads nodding silently. Even Young Man Afraid Of His Horses seemed favorably impressed by this unexpected display of largess.

Good, Red Cloud thought. *That was well said.* Rather than
confront the older man he had acted the part of a generous
man. After confronting the whites he'd dealt with his most
influential rival in a way that could only make him look good.
It took some of the sting out of Spotted Tail's insults but the
anger still burned. He had to fight it. No, he would not fight
it. Better to turn it against a worthy target—the *wasichu*.

COLONEL HENRY CARRINGTON WAS FRUSTRATED. HE HAD
never expected anything like this. Everything General Sherman and Colonel Maynardier had told him had led him to
believe that this whole business about the road had already
been settled with the tribes and that his attendance at the con-

ference was merely a formality—an extension of courtesy to him as the new commander of the district. It was all very disconcerting and it made his stomach queasy to think that they had come so close to open violence here at a peace conference. He walked slowly toward the ambulance in which he had been told Margaret was waiting for him, his head filled with conflicting ideas as he tried to determine exactly how and where everything had started to go wrong during the talks. Maybe if he could isolate the problem he could figure a way to patch things up in the morning.

"That Red Cloud need be watched close, Colonel." Bridger's harsh voice brought him back to the present.

"Oh, Major Bridger," Carrington said, looking up at his friend. "I don't know. He certainly was a presence today though. That much I will allow him."

"Ye'd do better, Colonel, to allow him a ball from that smoke wagon," Bridger said with a slight edge to his voice and a nod at the holstered pistol on Carrington's hip. "He means a fight and a fight we'll have afore all's said and done. I allow there be many a poor lad here today what won't be with us when the grass comes up next spring and Red Cloud'll be the reason why."

Carrington considered Bridger's words carefully for a moment, his eyes fixed on Bridger's unflinching gaze.

"I hope for once that you are mistaken, Major," he said quietly. "I know the Bible says that 'there will be wars and rumors of wars' but it also says that 'they will beat their swords into plowshares.' If I may be so bold as to interpret the Lord's words I believe he would want us to beat not only our swords but pistols and tomahawks into plowshares as well. I can only say that I will do my very best to see that there is no war in this country."

Bridger screwed up his face and spat a stream of tobacco juice into the dust.

"Well, Colonel," he said, "I have been wrong afore and hope to be so again. But I don't think it'll be on the score of Red Cloud." He touched his fingers to the brim of his hat in a sort of half-salute and turned to stalk off across the parade ground toward Bullock and Ward's store. Carrington watched the retreating figure of Bridger and found himself hoping desperately that his friend was wrong in his assessment of this Red Cloud fellow. Margaret's shrill warning startled him from his thoughts.

"Henry!" Margaret called out, a touch of panic in her voice. "Watch out!"

Henry Carrington turned to see Red Cloud standing within a few feet of him and it was unnerving to think that the man had moved so close with no sound whatever. The warrior had been looking closely at Carrington's horse Grey Eagle, which was tethered to a rail next to the headquarters building. It was clear that the Sioux liked the look of the horse, perhaps a bit too much, for there was a glint in the man's eyes that warned of mischief. Their eyes locked and Carrington felt his insides quiver at the look which came from his antagonist. If ever he had seen a look of pure hate, this was it, and it sent a chill running down his spine. Those eyes! They pierced a man to his very soul with their intensity. As he watched, Carrington could see the muscles of the warrior's face tense suddenly, contorting his visage into a mask worthy of Hieronymus Bosch's demons. For one bone-chilling moment the colonel felt that he was staring into the pit of Hell itself. Red Cloud's hand tightened on his beaded knife sheath and he shifted his stance as if to move toward Carrington. Henry fought back the impulse to step backward but let his hand drop to his side and quietly unbuttoned the flap of his holster.

A horrified Margaret froze, her hand to her mouth, her heart beating wildly in her chest as the two men stood locked in each other's gaze. It was as if time had stopped. She could feel the blood pounding in her ears and she shivered as if the sun had been suddenly extinguished. And then, without warning, the moment passed. The warrior's face relaxed to an impassive, unreadable countenance, transformed in an instant as if a schoolboy had simply wiped the chalked scribblings from his slate. The warrior turned and moved past Carrington without a sound. But the colonel felt, as the man shimmered past him, that Death itself had brushed his sleeve.

4

Canpasapa wi
(Moon When The Chokecherries Are Black)

July 1866

Jim Bridger tipped back his battered slouch hat and used the sleeve of his shirt to wipe the sweat from his eyes. The heat of the day was as bad as he could recall having experienced. He had never much minded the heat in the past but this was almost more than a man could bear. Lieutenant Phisterer had ridden up to the colonel a few minutes earlier and observed that the mercury registered above 106 already and it was still fairly early in the day. The worse thing about the heat, Bridger thought, was that it made a man sluggish, fogged his brain. Heat made a man careless. A hot climate changed a man for the worse. It made bad soldiers of Mexicans and addlepated fanatics of Mormons. He didn't care much for either breed. He'd had his share of problems with both[1] and allowed how

[1]Bridger's problems with Mormons dated back to August 1853 when the xenophobically militant Danite faction had destroyed Bridger's ferry and trading post on the Green River, killing several of Bridger's associates in the process. A long-running feud between Brigham Young and Bridger ended in June 1857 when Bridger, as an army scout, led Colonel Albert Sidney Johnston and Lieutenant Colonel Philip St. George Cooke into Salt Lake City as the U.S. Government used the army to suppress Mormon attacks on gentile wagon trains and bring Utah under U.S. jurisdiction.

the Mormons deserved the unwelcome attentions of the Apaches and the United States Army both. It was different for Indians. Devils were comfortable in Hell and Indians were comfortable in the heat and, as far as Bridger was concerned, there was little difference between them—except that you could put a ball in an Indian and hope for a good result. He squinted and blinked against the glare as he scanned the surrounding countryside, his practiced eyes traversing incessantly from left to right, rotating upward and down behind slitted lids as they picked out every detail of the arid landscape. He took special care to study the ground within a hundred yards of him, for that, he knew, was the place of greatest peril. Inattention and arrogance had done for more men than he could rightly remember. The novice watched the horizon hoping to spot trouble from afar when in fact the area most dangerous to him was there in plain sight. Death lurked always within arrow flight and the distance a man could cover in one spring. It was not the war party on the skyline that would kill you, it was the solitary buck crouched behind a clump of sage or lying quietly in a buffalo wallow with dust heaped over himself. If a man kept his eyes on the horizon he might never have a chance to cock his piece before one of those devils buried a willow shaft in his chest or sank a hatchet into his brainpan.

Bridger would rather have pushed on well ahead of the column toward the mountains to scout for a suitable location for this fort, but he felt obliged to stay particularly close to the colonel today. Something didn't seem quite right. He could feel it in his bones and couldn't bring himself to leave Carrington and his boys to fend for themselves out here. The sandy and rock-strewn ground they had traversed from Fort Laramie was much the same as they'd endured for weeks. Monotonously flat and dry as a bone, it was dangerously deceptive. Without warning the traveler would come upon a yawning dry wash or coulee, the banks steep and crumbling and the bottom wide and strewn with sand, gravel, and deadwood. A thunderstorm a hundred miles away could drown a man unaware in seconds while he scratched at a dry streambed for water. Bridger knew ten men drowned for every one that was scalped. A coulee could also hide a sizable war party until it was too late to notice. Scattered here and there on the landscape were crazily propped towers of red rock, their tops often wider than their bases. Centuries of wind-driven sand and water had chewed these into fantastic shapes. Welcome landmarks for the traveler, they were also fraught with menace for what they could conceal. Bridger did not doubt for an instant that many of these rock formations had been employed by Sioux scouts throughout their route of march. While riding ahead of the column he had on more than one occasion skirted around one of these towers only to find the unmistakable tracks of unshod ponies and scourings at their bases. They were being watched.

Bridger's mule nickered and rubbed his muzzle up against a sagebush to shoo away a horsefly. What poor grass had grown here had long since disappeared under the hooves and beards of the buffalo and the remainder had burned to brittle stubble by the summer heat. Now stunted sage and cactus seemed to be the only vegetation these barren wastes would support, and all baked under a merciless sun with not even a whisper of a breeze for relief.

Poor country for grazing, Bridger thought, and found himself glancing at the mountains in the distance, longing for the coolness of an upland meadow—good grass and water for his mule, shade and maybe a chance to make meat. A plump young elk cow would be just the thing to make a man's mouth water. The very thought angered him, for he took it as a sign of frailty. The heat had made his mind wander and that could be the most deadly of mistakes. Seconds later he ground his yellowed, painful teeth in disgust as the faintest trace of dust smudged the horizon. He cursed his own carelessness and told himself he should have seen it earlier but for the distraction of his own meandering thoughts.

"An old dog will tarry sniffin' scat, and never see the mountain cat," he muttered in disgust. There were people coming in up ahead. He studied the slight dust cloud for a few moments and quickly determined that whoever was raising it was not white. Too heavy for game, which in this heat would be moving in smaller groups. Too faint and irregular for infantry or cavalry. Indians. Had to be. He wheeled his mule about and trotted back the half mile that separated him from the head of the column.

"COLONEL," BRIDGER SAID AS HE REINED UP IN FRONT OF Carrington. "I believe we ought call a short halt here and throw a few of your folks out as skirmishers. And, if you'd oblige, I think we ought keep the stock in close for a bit."

A frown clouded Carrington's face at this suggestion. He was eager to cover as much ground as was possible, a goal he thought Bridger shared, and was annoyed that the scout would suggest such a thing when it appeared they were making such good progress.

"Injuns comin' in, Colonel," Bridger explained quickly. "I shoulda told ye a bit earlier but calculate we've time enough to ready ourselves." The truth was that Bridger didn't want to admit his own weakness. He rationalized the lie by telling himself that Carrington's confidence need not be shaken by allowing the demon of doubt to creep into his thoughts. If the colonel could not depend on his scout he was a lost man. Carrington, who did not detect the lie, nodded and held up his hand to halt the column. Captain Ten Eyck and Lieutenant Phisterer came forward at a trot.

"Gentlemen," Carrington said calmly to his officers. "Major Bridger informs me that we shall be entertaining guests shortly and I wish that we shall be prepared to receive them as befits their intentions. Bring in the stock and form square with the wagons as per my standing instructions. I will instruct Captain Haymond to deploy a company as skirmishers but all hands will be on the *qui vive* for the duration. Their intentions may be benign and I intend that we shall be hospitable. But the better prepared we are for a fight the more we shall ensure that this interlude is a peaceful one."

Bridger smiled at the colonel's comments. He was always amused by the flowery way these soldiers talked to each other and made everything seem so nice and genteel. In a way they

were as windy as Indians who took an hour to say "good
morning, we've come to beg for coffee." The old scout
thought it was funny to hear the colonel announce the arrival
of a pack of Indians as if he were a Methodist preacher urging
his congregation to be nice to visiting Baptists.

Ten Eyck and Phisterer saluted and wheeled their horses to
rejoin the column. In moments voices rang out above a low
curtain of dust as teams were whipped up and wagons jockeyed carefully into a defensive position shaped a bit like a
hollow square into the center of which were driven the domestic livestock. Carrington had specified how this maneuver
was to be accomplished and the teamsters had become quite
adept at forming square with a minimum of fuss. Captain
Henry Haymond trotted up for instructions. Since Carrington
had assumed the duties as the commander of the entire Mountain District, actual command of the 2nd Battalion had automatically devolved to Haymond.

"Colonel," Haymond said simply with a sharp salute, which
Carrington returned with a flourish.

"Henry," Carrington said quietly. "Major Bridger says that
we've got some Indians coming in soon. We do not yet know
their intentions but we should be prepared against any, um,
irregularities." Haymond nodded silently—a veteran soldier,
he was not given to idle chatter. "I want it made very clear
that hostilities are not the order of the day." Haymond shot a
quick look at Bridger and back at the colonel, who went on
quickly, "I wish that we should appear ready for trouble but
not provoke an exchange of fire, if you take my meaning."

"Perfectly, sir," Haymond said. "If you've no objection,
Colonel, perhaps Major Bridger would be good enough to advise me on how best to place the men. I've little experience
with Indians and will defer to his counsel."

Bridger raised an eyebrow and immediately thought better
of Haymond for his request. *A sensible man*, he thought. *He
mayn't know much about this country yet but he knows enough
to know what he don't know*. The 2nd Battalion likely had a
fine commander here, a man who was not about to risk a fight
where one could be avoided. A smart man. The scout nodded

his agreement to Carrington and eased his mule into position alongside the captain. Haymond saluted his commanding officer and then turned to Bridger, who quickly outlined where he thought the men should be posted and how they should react upon the arrival of the visitors.

Bridger, as much as anyone else, and perhaps more so, was surprised by the composition of the party that rode into camp a few minutes later. It was a very curious column of men who walked their horses leisurely into the midst of Carrington's position. Indians they were indeed, but they were not what he or the colonel had expected.

Winnebago! Bridger thought. *These bucks're a long way from home.* The Winnebago were originally from Wisconsin. Bridger knew they'd been moved about a bit after the Sioux uprising in Minnesota[2] but last he'd heard they were all living at the Omaha Reservation in Nebraska Territory. That there was no love lost between them and their Sioux cousins was no secret—in fact they were bitter enemies—but it seemed a far piece to come just to settle old scores.

Strongly muscled, bare legs with feet encased in moccasins dangled along their horses' flanks but from the waist up each warrior was clad in the dark blue, yellow-piped shell jackets issued to Union cavalry during the late war. Every jacket was unbuttoned and bronzed chests displayed necklaces of elk teeth, shells, or the claws of grizzly bears, depending upon the wearer's tastes. From many a pierced ear depended multiple

[2]Minnesota Uprising: In August and September of 1862 the Santee Sioux of Minnesota staged a major uprising against their immigrant neighbors. A tragic affair brought on largely through the combined factors of an unresponsive government, a bad harvest, insensitive officials, and hotheaded young Sioux warriors. It was a short but bloody business resulting in the wholesale slaughter of some 800 civilians by rampaging Sioux war parties. It was especially regrettable in that white-Indian relations had been relatively good beforehand. Government reaction was swift and brutal and resulted not only in a chastisement of the guilty parties but exile of a number of noninvolved tribes as well—including the blameless Winnebago. Terrified by the great loss of life and suddenness of the uprising, settlers all but abandoned the territory, and it remained sparsely populated for many years afterward.

dangles of copper that twisted and chimed with the movement of the horses and their riders. Every face was streaked with paint, predominantly red and black. A few wore odd-looking bands of skunk fur around their ankles.[3] Their hair was twisted into thick braids and each wore an arresting headpiece, which Bridger described as a "roach," a thick, bristling brush of stiffened deer hair dyed a bright red. These reminded Captain Haymond of the Mohican scalplocks described by Fenimore Cooper or perhaps the crests one would expect to see on the helmet of a Greek hoplite. Each man sat easily in an old Grimsley saddle of prewar issue and carried a cavalry-issue Sharps carbine. Captain Haymond noted with silent approval that both saddles and weapons were clearly very well maintained.

The Indian in the lead of the column was an imposing figure with particularly well muscled legs and a face that might have been hacked from granite. A pale, ragged scar began at his left temple and ran down the side of his face to slip under the curve of his jaw. A crescent moon of hammered silver dangled from his left ear and flashed in the sunlight, drawing attention to the scar. A black handprint was painted directly on the man's face. His eyes were cold and deadly as a snake's. The whole effect lent his countenance an especially fierce and unnerving aspect. The scar-faced veteran also wore the stripes of a sergeant on his sleeves. He reined in his horse to stop directly in front of Carrington and Bridger, who sat their mounts calmly a hundred paces beyond the hastily formed defensive perimeter and just a few paces ahead of the line of armed pickets. The scar-faced man raised his hand to halt the men who followed him and then gave Carrington a casual salute, much to the colonel's surprise.

"We hear you are coming, Colonel," the scar-faced Indian said in amazingly clear English. "I am Takes The Horse and these people are with me. We are Winnebago and have made war for the Great Father. Now they tell us your war with the graycoats is over and we are to go home.

"Throat-cutters are the enemy," Takes The Horse explained.

[3]Skunk-fur anklets indicated that the wearer had touched a dead enemy.

"They make things bad for us. Their relatives kill many whites by the big rivers to the East. They make the white men angry at all Indians. Many of our people lose their homes because of them. Now we make war on the throat-cutters. We will make war with you. We'll kill many throat-cutters with you."

This last statement was accompanied by a casual flick at a scalp tied to his saddlebow and a wicked grin. Captain Haymond, who was sitting his horse to Carrington's right, observed this act with interest and leaned out of his saddle to confer with his commander.

"This is an interesting development, sir," Haymond said quietly. "I can't see that it would do any harm to have a few additional allies out here. Especially in light of the threats which that Red Cloud made at Laramie. Besides, it appears they're as well-heeled as our own men, if not better." He glanced at the Sharps carbine in Takes The Horse's hand.

Carrington's head nodded slightly, his lips pursed in thought, as his eyes wandered up and down the ranks of the Winnebago scouts, taking their measure and considering what would be the best response, what would be the prudent thing to do. They were a hard-looking lot. More than one scar was in evidence among the fierce-looking warriors and every braided lock of hair sported feathers notched to tell of personal exploits in battle, a code he had learned from his conversations with Bridger. Most of their saddlebows were adorned with human hair, and every pony bore the handprints of its rider in red or black paint, signifying an enemy wounded or killed. These were not green troops but seasoned veterans. Captain Haymond had a point. The command was woefully short of experience with Indians. The supplies he had expected to acquire at Fort Laramie had not materialized. Maynardier had barely enough ammunition for his own garrison and no stocks of rifles to replace the aging and in many cases nonfunctional Springfields that the 18th carried. The bacon and flour had been badly infested by mice. Carrington and his officers had then watched in frustration as hundreds of warriors rode off to their camps on the Powder River trailing packhorses laden with sacks of coffee and sugar, bolts of calico, and kegs of gunpowder—all the gifts of a government that denied the same supplies to its own soldiers. It often appeared to Carrington that he was to be left on his own out here. It was maddening.

He turned and motioned for Lieutenant Brown to join him. Fred Brown, as the acting quartermaster, would know how the command might contract for the services of these men and, as Brown had acquired considerable knowledge of the Pawnee scouts while at Kearny, might also know how such organizations should be handled.

Bridger interrupted, shaking his head. "I know what ye're thinking, Colonel, but I would not do it. I know how ye might be tempted to enlist these Winnebago but I have to tell ye that it is a poor bargain." Carrington frowned at Bridger's remark.

"I find that odd coming from you, Major," he said, puzzled. "I should think you would welcome the extra eyes and ears that these men might provide. It would certainly ease the burden placed on you. If it's the money you are concerned about, please be assured that our engaging these gentlemen would in no way diminish your value to the command."

"That's not my worry, Colonel." Bridger waved one hand carelessly as if brushing away a fly. "I'm thinkin' we'll have to fight the damned Sioux sooner or later come what may. But that's neither here nor there. You hope not to have a war and that is a fine ambition, but if you use these men a war you will have. The Sioux are madder'n hornets as it is and they'll take any excuse to say you made 'em fight ye. If we take up with their blood enemies they will say 'there you are, they've come fer a fight, let's away at 'em' and that is that. Now, like I say, I figger we'll have to fight the Sioux anyhow but if we hire on these Winnebago we'll certain sure have to fight 'em now. To be honest, Colonel, I hazard that your boys ain't yet ready to take 'em on. That's all I'll say on the matter."

Lieutenant Brown rode up and halted his horse a respectful distance from the conferring men. He sat his horse quietly and waited for further instructions. Henry Carrington looked hard at Bridger as he considered the man's words. The old scout was right in what he'd said and the colonel was embarrassed that he had not seen the truth of it until Bridger's comment.

He could feel the color rising to his ears. The frustrations at Laramie and the strain of the long march had preyed upon him during the journey and disturbed his sleep at night. They had served to undermine his self-confidence. To employ these Winnebago would be no more than to take counsel of his own fears and that would be a mistake. It could be a fatal mistake. Red Cloud would see it as an overtly hostile act. A war would be unavoidable and it would be his own fault.

"Of course you're right, Major Bridger," Carrington said a bit sheepishly. "Our mission here is to preserve the peace and not provoke a war. I thank you for reminding me of my duty, sir. I should have seen the consequences more clearly." Carrington turned to the Winnebago leader and shook his head.

"Sergeant Takes The Horse. I am sure your men are great warriors and the best scouts that I could hope to have but I am unable to use you. I thank you for your offer and for your service to the Great Father in Washington, but there is nothing I can do about this. I wish you a good journey to your homes and your families."

Takes The Horse grunted and shrugged. It didn't really matter to him if the bluecoats wanted his help or not. He and his warriors could stay here and kill Sioux or go home, wherever that home might be now. Even when they left this place he could not be sure that they would be able to find their families. Whether he stayed here or kept moving toward the sunrise made little difference in the end. Well, let the bluecoats do what they wanted, there was a long journey ahead and he did not doubt that there would be ample opportunity to take a few more scalps from the Sioux on the way.

"You give us tobacco and coffee," Takes The Horse said as he gazed levelly into Carrington's eyes.

The colonel was momentarily taken aback, but nodded and turned to Lieutenant Brown, who understood what needed to be done. The Indians passed slowly through a line of pickets, seeming to take no notice of the men who stood with rifles at half-cock cradled casually under their arms but with slitted eyes trained on the mounted party. Brown led the Indians to a freight wagon and supervised the issue of the requested items, and in a few minutes twists of tobacco and small burlap sacks of coffee beans had been handed up to each of the riders. When Takes The Horse was satisfied he gave Carrington a cursory nod and waved his fellow warriors ahead. All eyes followed the ghostly party as it moved silently past the column and vanished into the distance.

Margaret Carrington, Sallie Horton, and Lucy Bisbee watched breathlessly from behind an ambulance as the Indians passed. They had by now seen hundreds of Indians—Pawnee at Fort Kearney, Sioux, Cheyenne, and Arapaho at Fort Laramie—but, unlike these Winnebago, none had been dressed and painted for war. The fierce appearance of these warrior-scouts was a revelation, and the women shuddered at the raw savagery that seemed to ripple beneath the surface of their visitors. More dreadful yet were the scalps strung across their saddles and brushing at the warriors' thighs, looking for all the world like so many slaughtered rabbits carried home for the stew pot. For a moment it was hard to imagine that these Indians were friendly or even that they were quite human. Indeed, if these were counted among friends how horrible must enemies look in battle. Like demons loosed upon the earth. Lucy Bisbee, hands clasped in front of her mouth, whispered a prayer under her breath. As far as she was concerned they could not get to Fort Reno fast enough.

FORT RENO WAS NOT MUCH OF A FORT. MUCH THE SAME dimensions of Fort Sedgewick, it too was a ramshackle collection of crumbling adobe buildings roofed over with cottonwood timbers and sod. The shabby headquarters building and officers' quarters were the only frame structures in evidence. The civil war had made tremendous demands on the nation's resources and virtually every frontier outpost was left to languish and make do as best it could. To Carrington's eyes Reno appeared in even worse shape than Laramie and Sedgewick and he wondered if the fact that the garrison at Reno was composed of paroled rebels had earned it the particular indifference of the War Department.

Captain George Bailey, who commanded the two companies of the 5th U.S. Volunteers, stationed at Reno, saw the arrival of Carrington's command much as a Baptist preacher might view the Second Coming. From the look in Bailey's eyes as he enthusiastically pumped Carrington's hand the colonel half expected to hear a shouted "Hallelujah!" rather than the more customary "At your service, sir." Bailey's enthusiasm was short-lived. The young officer was crestfallen to hear that Carrington had no instructions to relieve the volunteers so that they might be mustered out to return home. The colonel looked on with true empathy as Bailey's shoulders slumped and the light in his eyes faded like the embers of a campfire gone dead in a winter rain.

"I'm terribly sorry, Captain Bailey," Carrington said as gently as he could manage, "but I have no demobilization orders for the Volunteers. Until instructed by headquarters, and as commander of the Mountain District, your organization is now under my command." Carrington cleared his throat, almost embarrassed to further crush Bailey's spirits. Well, it must be said.

"I am afraid, Captain," Carrington went on, "that I am however authorized, indeed required, to avail the Mountain District of whatever supplies have been stockpiled here at Fort Reno. If you would be good enough to direct Lieutenant Brown to your quartermaster, he will conduct an inspection and make known our requirements. We are especially in need of munitions as Fort Laramie had not yet received the allocation promised me by General Sherman."

Bailey sighed and dropped his head with a shrug. What else, he thought bitterly, could he possibly expect from an ungrateful War Department? He waved a hand listlessly in the direction of the post warehouse.

"I'll escort Lieutenant Brown myself, sir. Munitions there are, but probably not in the quantities which you require. As to rations, sir, you are of course, welcome to take whatever you wish, although I would not inflict the government's culinary largess on my worst enemy. I'll see to it directly. In the meantime, Colonel, may I offer you and the ladies accompanying your party what little hospitality my poor quarters may afford?"

Carrington replied with a sad smile. "You are too kind, Captain Bailey. It is a hard task you've been asked to do out here and I sincerely regret any further burden which I must impose on you."

Bailey smiled wanly, shook his head, and coughed out a hollow laugh. "Not at all, Colonel. It's you who have the hard task ahead. We're not yet relieved but our job here is nearly done and we'll be away if not today then soon. Whatever stocks you draw relieves me of the responsibility to maintain and account for them and tells me I'm that much closer to going home." His remarks had a bittersweet edge to them. "Home. That's a word I use most loosely. I for one will not be sorry to leave this wilderness." He glanced at the dilapidated barracks. "It's a rare man in this command who has a home left to return to and, when mustered out, more of them will likely go north rather than south. They'll head for the goldfields and a new start." Bailey looked off to the north at the jagged peaks of the Bighorns, their edges softened by distance and dulled to a blue-gray smear on the horizon. "We've had no trouble to speak of with the Indians thus far, Colonel, but I fear that this is about to change. There are three emigrant trains camped but a few miles from here, all headed north. Headed for the goldfields."

"Three trains?" Carrington asked, incredulous. "Headed north?"

"Yes sir, Colonel," Bailey said, "it's already begun. And it will, I'm afraid, only get worse. Ever since the war ended in the East we've seen a steady increase in the traffic passing through this country."

"Have you had any trouble with the Indians as a result?"

"We've been fortunate in our relations with the local tribes thus far, Colonel. They've continued to trade with French Pete and have generally left the emigrants alone. In most cases the train bosses are smart enough to distribute coffee, tobacco, calico, trinkets, and such, which suffices to buy safe passage. I have urged every civilian train which passes through here to

refrain from distributing spirits among the tribes—however **much they ask for it.** Oh, the odd cow or horse has disappeared and we've had a few minor incidents but nothing serious, yet."

"That's an odd way of putting it, Captain," Carrington said uneasily. "It's as if you expect this to change drastically. Is there something you are not telling me?"

Bailey drew in a deep breath and sucked on his teeth as he considered his answer. His mouth was screwed up as if he'd just taken a large bite of a lemon.

"You might find this less than convincing," Bailey said, "but French Pete's squaw says that the Sioux are starting to make ugly noises."

Carrington held up his hand. "Who is this French Pete you keep referring to, Captain Bailey? Is he some sort of a scout or a trapper?"

Bailey smiled. "Not hardly, sir. Oh, he likely started out as a trapper but he's a trader or has been as long as we've been here. He supplies the tribes with the usual things, knives, blankets, calico, beads, and such, in exchange for pelts and robes. You may have come across him as you came up sir, he's usually set up within a few miles of here. Has a partner named Arrison and a Sioux wife. His real name is Pierre Gazzous or Louis Gazeau or some such name but everyone calls him 'French Pete.' Now, if Pete was to tell me something about the Sioux I would have to discount much of it but his wife seems, if not overly intelligent, at least possessed of uncommon good sense."

"Ah yes," Carrington said, his brow furrowed by the memory. "I recall now he had rather an extemporaneous establishment."

Carrington had not been overly impressed by French Pete's rustic version of a sutler's store, a few boards thrown across nail kegs and draped with shoddy trade goods, a few jars of preserves, tinned sardines, and rotgut whiskey. An unctuous man, the rumpled Gazzous had a shifty look in his eyes, and had been particularly solicitous towards Margaret and the other ladies. He had even made a gift of a young pet antelope to Surgeon Horton's wife. Although Bridger seemed to converse with French Pete easily enough, something about the man left Carrington with an uncomfortable feeling, and for the colonel the little camp had an oppressive atmosphere.

"I thought him a somewhat unsavory frontier type."

"A typical frontier type, sir. And there are more like him moving into this country every day. He's not the most intelligent of men and thinks that because he has a Sioux wife that he's invulnerable. His wife is not so sanguine. I imagine she hears quite a bit from her relatives and has suggested on several occasions that Fort Reno needed a trading post within the garrison. I have discouraged the notion."

"Liquor?"

Bailey nodded.

"The men are easily enough tempted to go astray and I dare not risk putting too large a supply of cheerwater and popskull at their disposal. If you've already met Gazzous then I expect that he is even now plying his trade among the trains camped nearby. I believe, sir, you've not heard the last of French Pete."

MARGARET CARRINGTON WAS MOMENTARILY STARTLED BY the rustling noise outside her tent and gasped to see a small furry nose push its way through the tent flap at about knee height. The gasp was replaced by a small smile as the nose was followed by two large, soft brown eyes belonging to Star, the young antelope which French Pete had presented to Sallie Horton. Margaret reached into a small traveling case near her cot and fished a slice of dried apple out of a small jar of treats she kept handy for the boys. Henry had been up and gone for nearly an hour already and the boys were still fast asleep in their blankets and buffalo robe nestled snugly in one corner of the tent. She didn't think the boys would object to a judicious use of their treat cache.

"Here, Star," she whispered, letting the antelope nibble it delicately and feeling the soft wetness of the nose on her open palm. "Have a bit of a treat and then we had best take you back to Sallie before she misses you."

As Star withdrew from the tent Margaret peeked through the flap at the new day. It was still an hour before sunup but already the valley was flooded with a soft rosy light. She wrapped her dressing gown more tightly around her shoulders and stepped lightly out into the crisp morning air, closed her eyes, and took a deep breath. It was heavenly. The air was redolent of sweet grass and pine and the light, sweet fragrance of plum blossoms. It was glorious. She felt the cool moistness of the rich grass beneath her bare feet and opened her eyes to gaze up at the towering face of Cloud Peak. The minaret of snow-clad granite soared thousands of feet above her and was bathed in a pink glow, as if the mountain could already see the sun's disk from his lofty height. What a beautiful country they had entered. It hardly seemed possible.

The column had left Fort Reno in burning heat and trudged the endless miles across a sunbaked wasteland for nearly a week—although with the mercury hovering at 106 degrees it seemed an eternity—before crossing over a small rise just beyond the branching of a pair of streams called Crazy Woman Fork. What an odd and strangely melancholy name it had seemed at the time and Margaret wondered what poor soul had inspired the name. Had she been driven completely mad by the seemingly endless wasteland that preceded? Had the mountain coolness come a day too late? It was a sad thing to consider for the transformation in the country seemed magical.

As they crossed over Crazy Woman Fork it was as if a whole new world opened up before them. The air became wonderfully cool, and sweet, burnt grass and pale, brittle sage gave way to thick mountain meadows. Grass so thick in places that you waded through it like a swimmer in the ocean's surf. Everywhere the grass was dotted with myriad colors as wildflowers swayed gently in cool mountain breezes to dodge the bees which hovered and swooped in legions. Hillsides were black with forests of pine and ash and to the west the Bighorn Mountains thrust against a sky of brilliant azure as if they held the very heavens aloft on their rugged, snow-dusted shoulders. She didn't know how the soldiers saw this country but Margaret felt that this, if ever there was one, was a true Paradise.

Henry Carrington was more impressed by the lay of the land and the availability of resources. Clear, fresh streams jumping with trout coursed down from the mountains and a small, level plateau, rich in grass and close to the water sources, afforded wide vistas of the surrounding country. The plateau was also somewhat sheltered by nearby ridges, which would help to break the winter wind. Wood for construction and fuel could be felled easily from hillsides but a few miles distant. The forests were also rich with game, which would provide a nice supplement to the rather bland Army rations. This, he thought, was the ideal spot to build his headquarters.

Margaret was delighted. Though they would likely spend many weeks living under canvas, Henry assured her that before the winter came they would all be snug and warm in solid quarters that they would begin building almost immediately. *Yes*, Margaret thought, *this will be a good place to call home*.

The day of their arrival, Margaret and Sallie had had a bit of a shock. As the men were busied setting up the camp—erecting tents, unloading needed equipment, pacing off the dimensions of the new fort, driving stakes and banderols to mark boundaries—Margaret and Sallie set up their camp stools near the rushing creek that Old Gabe had called the Little Piney. As they sat and chatted and drank in the scenery, Sallie's shawl slipped from her shoulders. Bending to retrieve it from the lush grass, she leapt up with a shriek. Margaret was up in a flash and the two women were horrified to find that a rattlesnake had slipped through the grass to coil up directly beneath their camp stools. The ubiquitous Jim Bridger appeared seemingly from nowhere and rushed to their assistance. He dispatched the reptile with a quick blow from the butt of his rifle and flung the limp remains into the stream, where they disappeared into the roiling water.

"Never fear, ladies," he said easily. "It's only God's way of remindin' us of the fickleness of nature. Even Paradise, I hear tell, had a serpent in the garden. That rattler will be of no danger to anyone now but I allow as he is the least of our worries here. Not every serpent has a rattle to give warning and some go on two legs."

Bridger reached into the leather bag he called his possibles sack, which he habitually carried slung across his shoulder. He fumbled about for a bit and pulled out a small pistol which Margaret recognized as a five-barreled pepperbox. He handed it to her.

"I have seen you use your husband's piece to dispatch a snake back at Kearney so I doubt not that you can use this little geegaw with no trouble, ma'am. I have not had need of it in many a year and would be obliged if you would keep it for me."

Margaret hesitated a moment but reached out and took the weapon with easy grace in long, delicate fingers. This man was a puzzle to her, but there was no mistaking his tender regard for her family. She noticed the slight trembling of his outstretched hand. She would not wound his pride for the world.

"Why, thank you, Major Bridger," she said sweetly. "I do not think that I shall ever have recourse to it with such gallant gentlemen as yourself to look out for us. But, I shall keep it with me as a small assurance. Against the serpents in our garden."

Bridger blushed at her compliment but managed a small smile and a nod to both ladies before he turned on his heel and strode off to rejoin his friend Williams, who was just bringing their mounts around for the two men.

"The serpent in the garden," Sallie said, and shuddered as she glanced quickly at the stream that had swallowed the rattlesnake. Margaret had said nothing but hefted the small weapon in her hand, the worn smoothness of the grips and the coolness of the steel seeming to generate its own electrical charge, and knew that Bridger had not been referring to rattlesnakes.

Now, gazing on the face of Cloud Peak, Margaret dismissed the incident with a slight smile. She wiggled her toes in the wet grass and delighted at the sensation, which reminded her of her days as a child when she could run barefoot and splash in the little streams near her home. She sighed to think that as "the Colonel's Lady" she could no longer indulge in such frolics and envied her sleeping children. Star now stood cropping contentedly at the grass nearby. *Well*, Margaret thought, *I'd best return her to Sallie before she's missed*. She slipped back into the tent and quickly began to dress. She glanced at the small camp stool that served as a bedside table and saw the oiled smoothness of Bridger's pistol. Its very presence was somehow jarring and she wrapped the weapon in a handkerchief before slipping it deep into the recesses of her traveling case.

PIERRE GAZZEAU — OR FRENCH PETE, AS HE HAD COME TO BE known to all—was rubbing his hands together in anticipation of the coming season. He had not expected so many emigrants so soon after the war. He had anticipated a great rush to the goldfields but not quite so quickly and cursed himself and his partner for having been unprepared to make as much of a profit as was obviously there to be made from the travelers. Not one to dwell on past mistakes, he had quickly put his disappointment behind him and determined to make the best of things. If he didn't have enough merchandise to realize a healthy profit from the whites he would shift focus and trade with the tribes.

Although it was still high summer it would not be long before the snows started to fly and the newly arrived whites would be clamoring for furs and buffalo robes against the fierce winter storms. Gazzeau and his partner Henry Arrison determined that they would do better to start laying in a supply of these necessities rather than squeeze the odd greenback out of strapped prospectors. Let them get established in the goldfields and make a few strikes and then, when *Waziya* made his annual appearance, beaver pelts, wolf, bear, and coyote furs, and buffalo robes would bring top dollar from the shivering newcomers. Thus, having tarried for a day or two with the trains camped near Fort Reno, Gazzeau's party quickly packed up their wares and headed deeper into the Powder River country in search of new customers and more pricey merchandise.

"Goddamnit, Pete," Dowaire spat angrily, "why the hell are we stoppin' here? The damned goldfields ain't but a few days off and we're stuck out here in the middle of goddamned nowhere at all chawin' the fat and watching you play plug-a-plew⁴ with a bunch of damned savages!" Dowaire was one of several men in Gazzeau's employ and anxious to move north as quickly as possible.

"Haw there, *mon ami*!" Gazzeau grinned at his companion. "You want the goldfields, *non*? Well, you listen to me then an' I tell you somethin' make you a rich man quicker'n scratching the damned dirt ever do." Gazzeau stooped to adjust a board on nail kegs that would serve as his store counter in the coming weeks. His Sioux wife, Goes Slow, had turned the children loose to play in a nearby creek, and she was now pulling sacks of merchandise and strings of beads out of the wagons and arranging them artfully on the rough counter space.

"How many 'omesteaders and 'unters you figure we see in those trains we been visitin' this last week, eh?" Gazzeau went on as he stacked tins of sardines into a small pyramid. "Ten, fifteen maybe? These people are like you, Dowaire, they don' want to work they want to strike it rich quick. *N'est-ce pas?*" Gazzeau straightened up and tapped the side of his head with a grimy finger.

"They think they dip into any damn river up north and they go home rich men in a few weeks. They got the gold fever an' this I tell you true, when the fever hit you don' know nothin' else. *Enfant de grace!* They think they fool around with their pie pans an' picks a few weeks an' that's all but that ain't how it'll work." Gazzeau wagged his finger in Dowaire's face.

"A few of 'em strike it rich and they be just enough to keep the rest of 'em there an' more comin' every day. They will splash and dig and curse and 'ope and pay no attention to the

⁴Plug-a-plew: An archaic reference to the fur trade in which a "plug" of tobacco could be traded for a "plew" or beaver pelt. Plew was derived from the French Canadian term *pelu*, meaning hairy.

weather till it's too damned late an' then they gotta stay here
for the winter." Gazzeau chuckled and shook his head. "And
they will be cold! *Mon Dieu!* When the cold she comes hard
they spend ever' damned copper an' nugget to keep warm an'
we gonna be there to keep 'em warm. One buffalo robe be
worth a month diggin' gold when the snow comes, my friend."
Gazzeau turned and slapped Goes Slow on the rump. He
grinned at Dowaire and spread his arms out wide.

"*Ici, mon ami!* These are the real goldfields all around you.
These mountains they are full of gold walking on four legs.
You don't 'ave to splash in the water or swing a pick until
your nose bleeds. You give out a few plugs of tobacco, beads,
a knife or two, splash a little whiskey on the groun' an' the
Sioux an' Cheyenne they will just lay gold in your hand! You
want to work like a damn *sans coulotte* you go on ahead. I
won't stop you—that's more money for me and Henri to
share. *Allons!* Go ahead!"

Dowaire looked over at Moss and Arrison, who had been
listening to Gazzeau's little speech and were grinning like
weasels in a henhouse. He took a deep breath and, shaking
his head, made his way to one of the wagons, where he began
to unload small iron kettles and a case of skinning knives.

"Goddamnit, Moss!" he shouted over his shoulder. "I ain't
gonna unload the whole shitaree by my own damn self. Haul
your lazy carcass over here and grab out some of this here
calico for the ladies. An' don't drop it in the dirt. This here's
a quality operation we got going and I'll not have you cutting
into our profits."

BLACK HORSE WATCHED THE SOLDIERS HOIST THEIR FLAG TO
the top of the lodgepole that stood in the center of the little
plateau between the forks of the Piney and wondered if this
were some version of the white man's Sundance ceremony.
From his position on a small rise several hundred yards away
the soldiers looked like prairie dogs with blue fur. He liked
listening to the strange music the whites made with their horns

and drums and was amazed by the explosions they made with their wagon guns.

Several of the little blue prairie dogs had stood in front of the others, holding up their hands and apparently making long speeches to them and these were probably their *Wicasa Wakan* appealing to the whites' Everywhere Spirit for their ceremonies. Dull Knife, who crouched by his side, was slightly younger than him and had seen more of the whites than Black Horse. Though Dull Knife did not seem very impressed by them, Black Horse was still curious. The Cheyenne had watched the long march of the bluecoats since they had left Fort Reno and begun to move ever deeper into the Bighorn country. For a while it looked like they would not stop until they reached the Tongue or the Yellowstone but just two sleeps before they had stopped here in this valley. Now they were setting up their little canvas lodges and everywhere they had driven posts into the ground around which they had tied strips of cloth. Already the hillsides were ringing with the sound of their axes as the soldiers hacked at the huge pines that covered the mountains a few miles from the new fort. Black Horse thought it a little foolish—first the white trappers had come and taken nearly all the beaver from the streams and now the white soldiers were here to do the work the beavers no longer did. There was something mystical about the way things worked, but he didn't say anything about this thought to Dull Knife, who would have thought him a bit crazy.

"We will go to talk to them tomorrow, Dull Knife," he said quietly. "I am interested in these wagon guns and I want to see the things they make music with up close. It may be some powerful medicine that they have to be able to make such noises."

"Hunh," Dull Knife grunted. "They are only men, Black Horse. The wagon gun is big medicine but the bluecoats have to touch it to make it work properly. It's not like the lightning that the Everywhere Spirit uses to fire the prairies or to strike down trees. And I don't like the noise they make with their horns. You say it's interesting music but it just sounds like noise to me."

"Bah!" Black Horse said with a little grin. "You are so cynical about such things. You wear your age like a shabby blanket. What is there that surprises you anymore, Dull Knife?"

"I'll be surprised if these long knives have anything good to say to us. This Little White Chief who sent us the talking paper through the Frenchman says sweet things but our cousins did not have any luck with the white men. Many of them are dead now and those who are left are fighting them to the South. You know the Medicine Calf is with these whites. He was at Sand Creek and where he goes trouble and war follow."

Black Horse raised his eyebrows. He had heard of Beckwourth's involvement with the Sand Creek fight but did not know that he was now here with the long knives. Black Kettle had trusted Medicine Calf and the whites had slaughtered his people. Now Black Kettle was in disgrace, while Leg In The Water and Little Robe led the survivors in a war of vengeance. They had chased Beckwourth away when he came to offer them peace and now he was here. The Crow had made him a chief and the Cheyenne had no argument with the Crow. Now Black Horse began to think hard about what he would say to the long knives when he met with them. He did not want a fight with the whites and he did not want a fight with the Lakota. Nor did he want to be caught between the Lakota and the Crow. This was a delicate situation, more delicate than he had first imagined. If the whites had come to take this country from the Lakota, perhaps the Crow would help the whites to fight against them. If the Crow and the whites fought together against the Lakota—who had been too busy fighting among themselves to do much to oppose the whites—then it seemed that there was no real doubt as to who would win. Black Horse sighed and held his head. He was tired of war. Maybe it appealed to younger men like Dull Knife but he had long since had his fill of it.

"They say," Dull Knife said casually, "that Red Cloud is making a peace among the tribes here. He wants the Arapaho

to join a united Lakota nation to drive the whites out of this
country. Crazy Horse, the Hunkpatila, joined with the Dog
Soldiers when they raided Julesburg and he made many friends
among Medicine Arrow's people. Two Moons is said to be
very friendly with him now too and may be persuaded to join
the Lakota's war."

Black Horse looked curiously at his friend. "Is that so?"

"So it would seem."

Black Horse knew Two Moons and did not doubt that he
would take any opportunity to fight. Two Moons was a noisy
man and told everyone that he was more important than he
really was. He would probably convince the Lakota that all of
the Cheyenne would follow him in a war against the whites.
This would not be true but the Lakota would believe him anyway and would take this as a sign that they could win. Then
it would be a war. Sooner or later it would come. Now the
only thing to do was to figure out how best to survive it. He
would have to wait and see what the whites had to say tomorrow and he would look at their strength. Then he would
choose.

FRENCH PETE WAS GENUINELY PLEASED TO SEE THE CHEY-
enne who rode into his small camp. The sun was just slipping
behind the mountains and Goes Slow had only just started to
prepare dinner for the camp. Joe Donaldson, a teamster not
yet old enough to use a razor, had left one of the emigrant
trains to join up with Gazzeau's and was busily gathering more
firewood when Black Horse and Dull Knife rode into the clearing followed by a dozen other Cheyenne all dressed in their
finest clothes. Joe had never seen an Indian in full fig before
and he was greatly impressed. These were fine-looking men
when they set their minds to cleaning up.

"Joseph," Gazzeau shouted, "don' just stand there gawking.
You go 'aul over a couple more 'aunches of that venison Dowaire kilt today. *Venez vite! Va le chercher*. We have the
guests and they'll be 'ongry, I'll wager."

Gazzeau liked the Cheyenne, Black Horse especially. His

people had been good customers and the robes they had
brought in for trade were all first quality. If he could maintain
a good relationship with Black Horse and his tribe, which was
near to two hundred lodges, his fortune was made. Gazzeau
noticed that the warriors in Black Horse's party were all toting
government-issue grain sacks, which he guessed were filled
with coffee, tobacco, bacon, and sugar. So, Black Horse had
met with Carrington after all and apparently come away with
gifts. This might be a good sign. The Cheyenne did not seem
much interested in Gazzeau's merchandise, which he had already covered with tarpaulins for the evening. Normally he
would expect them to at least steal a peek under the heavy
canvas but they seemed preoccupied and more than a little
uneasy. Well, you could never tell with Indians. There were
times when he simply gave up trying to fathom his own wife.
Goes Slow was subject to unusual moods and talked of her
dreams as if they were somehow miraculous visions from God.
He shrugged. Goes Slow would keep him and the children fed
and Black Horse would put money in his pocket and that was
all he felt he needed to understand. There was simply no point
in looking under the plate that his dinner was on.

"Well, my friend Black Horse!" Gazzeau raised his hand in
greeting. "It is good to see you again! Come join me for dinner
and a smoke. We do no business this evening. It is a time for
friends to enjoy good food and good talk."

Black Horse returned the greeting. He liked this Frenchman
and was always pleased when he heard a white man able to
use the Cheyenne tongue as well as this man could. Black
Horse did not care for the Frenchman's liquor but his other
trade goods were always good quality and his dealings with
the Cheyenne had always been fair. Gazzeau did not treat them
like children as so many of the other traders did. He glanced
over at Goes Slow, who was busily slicing large chunks of
venison and pitching them into an oversized kettle which Joe
Donaldson had helped her erect over a large fire. The boy was
a pleasant youth but Black Horse was always astonished to
see how white men seemed to go out of their way to help
women to do their work. Such a strange people. They had

wagon guns which could shatter boulders like they were nuts
from farther away than you could shoot an arrow and yet they
would gather wood and fetch kettles for a woman. He decided
that he would never understand these people. Goes Slow
looked up from her kettle and Black Horse thought he saw
fear in her eyes and he wondered if she knew what was in his
mind even before he had said a thing. She was a strange
woman—even for a Lakota. Her husband always laughed and
made jokes about the things she said to him about her dreams
but Black Horse was not so sure how funny he would think
them when they had talked a little longer. There would be
time enough for talk after dinner.

"AHH, MY FRIEND," GAZZEAU SAID AS HE POKED A STICK INTO
the fire to fetch a light for his pipe, "too much you worry
about these Lakota. Red Cloud is the 'ot 'ead and everybody
know it. *Non?* It is Spotted Tail who is the real power among
those people and 'e 'as touched the pen at Fort Laramie. There
will be no war 'ere. The Crow don't want a war and the Arapaho don't want a war and the Cheyenne don't want a war.
The only one who wants a war is Red Cloud and some of his
Bad Faces. They are but a few lodges and they 'ave never
been able to get along even with their own relations. He'll
never get a good war started 'ere, 'e's just a loudmouth and
a dreamer. Now, what 'appened when you go to see the Little
White Chief at Reno? I'm anxious to 'ear about your visit."

Black Horse breathed in deeply and let forth a loud belch.
Goes Slow had made a very good stew and everyone had eaten
their fill. He could feel himself starting to get a little sleepy
and wondered if maybe Gazzeau was right about Red Cloud.
It was a warm and pleasant night, his belly was full, and it
was comfortable to sit here in the dim light of a summer evening listening to the chirping of crickets and watching the odd
spark drift through the pines beyond the light of the small fire.
Dull Knife was examining Henry Arrison's new rifle with
great interest while Joe Donaldson was playing at some sort
of game with Moss and Dowaire. Maybe the Frenchman was

right. Maybe he worried about things too much.

"I like the soldiers' Little White Chief," Black Horse said finally. "He seems like a good man and he does not want a war here. He said that he will do everything he can to keep the peace on this new road they are making. He showed me a great many things like their wagon guns. I told him that Red Cloud was dangerous and that he wanted to drive the whites from this place but he just smiled and pointed to this wagon gun and said that Red Cloud's medicine was not more powerful than his. Oh, that is truly *wakan*! I wonder how they can make it shoot twice. It must be very big medicine. Do you know how this thing works?"

"Not well, *mon frere*," Gazzeau said with a shake of his head. "I know that she is like the very large fusil but 'ow they make the bullet explode after they shoot 'er," he shrugged, "is more than I can tell. Prob'ly they put gunpowder in the bullet but 'ow it does not explode when the gun she is fired is *wakan*. Now, go on, tell me more about your talk with the soldiers."

"Hunh, there is not much more to tell you. The Little White Chief gave us all pieces of the paper that talks so other whites will not shoot at us and he said that he will help the Cheyenne if they come and ask him. He also gave us as much to eat as we wanted and made presents to everyone who was with me. I told the Little White Chief that when the young men come back from hunting I will send him one hundred warriors to help fight the Lakota but," Black Horse shrugged, "he said that he would not need them. He said he has enough long knives and wagon guns to fight Red Cloud but he didn't think he would even need them. I hope he is right about that."

The horses began to snort and shy at their picket line, their ears twitching and nostrils wide. The men gathered in camp stopped what they were doing and listened carefully as the animals nickered and pawed nervously at the ground, their heads tugging at the lines that secured them. The forest seemed suddenly to have become deathly silent. Even the cicadas had stopped their insistent chattering. For a few moments there was no sound but the light crackle of the small fire and then there was a call of an owl which was quickly answered by another.

Black Horse and the other Cheyenne knew that this was not an owl and they all peered into the surrounding blackness of the trees. Almost immediately Red Cloud appeared in the midst of the encampment surrounded by more than two dozen warriors all dressed for battle. None of the new arrivals got down from their horses. Gazzeau stood and held up his hand in greeting.

"*Cannako, Mahkpiya-Luta!*" he said in a loud voice. "You are welcome 'ere. Will you smoke with us and 'ave someting to eat?"

Red Cloud ignored the Frenchman and glared down at Black Horse, who stood and returned the look without any trace of fear or anxiety.

"*Hes!*" Red Cloud spat out at the older Cheyenne. "Well, Shyela, what did the *wasichu* tell you? What do they want from you people?"

Black Horse, although deeply offended by the Lakota's condescending tone, did not appear ruffled by this summary interrogation. He immediately determined that he did not like this man's manners. Red Cloud had been greeted in his own language and offered hospitality by Gazzeau. Instead of responding in kind he ignored his host and was rude to the Frenchman's guests.

"Lakota, the whites want nothing from us," Black Horse said quietly. He knew Red Cloud's name but decided that he would not give him the satisfaction of being recognized. "The whites were very courteous and here we are on our way to our lodges having a visit with our friend. What do you care what the white men say to us? I don't know you and I don't answer questions about things that are not your concern."

Red Cloud snarled and quirted his horse sharply to keep the animal from shifting under him. Black Horse was amused to see that the man was angered by his remark.

"Then tell me this, old man," Red Cloud said through gritted teeth. "Are the soldiers going back to the Powder River?"

"They are leaving that fort. Lakota, but they are not going to the Powder River. They are going north, to the Tongue. They are going to build more forts in this country. Are you expecting a visit from your white friends? If you welcome them as this man has welcomed you perhaps they will not return your hospitality so discourteously as you have returned his."

Red Cloud fought down his irritation. He wanted the Cheyenne to join him in this war but this old man was trying his patience severely. That the man seemed unconcerned about the whites moving into this country only fueled his anger with him. His horse backed again and Red Cloud dug in his heels to force the animal forward.

"What did the whites give you to make you their friends, Cheyenne?"

Black Horse raised his tin mug and took a long sip of coffee. "I do not recall saying that they were our friends. But they gave us presents. Coffee, bacon, sugar, tobacco, and all we could eat. They were good hosts . . . and we were good guests. We did not abuse their hospitality as some younger, less wise people might do." Black Horse looked around at the other Lakota and then looked off into the surrounding darkness. "I'll tell you this, Lakota. You have taken this land from the Crow because they would not take half and give you peace with the other half. Now the whites are here and they want to share this land but you are like the Crow and will not share it. If they want it badly enough they will take it with their long knives and their wagon guns. But I will not be like the Crow. I will take the white man's hand and what he gives us rather than fight him and lose all."

Red Cloud leaned over toward Black Horse and stared down at him. "The whites," he hissed, "are liars and thieves! They want everything and they'll take it if we let them. Well, I won't let them. We'll fight the whites for every blade of grass and every lodgepole and if we have to we'll die where our fathers' bones are."

"For you," Black Horse replied under his breath, "that would be under a barrel of the white man's crazy water."

Red Cloud exploded. Before anyone could move he jerked his unstrung bow from the case slung across his back and swung it with a vengeance. The wooden arc flashed in the firelight as it sliced through the air and caught Black Horse a stunning blow on the side of his head. The old warrior staggered under the blow as the rest of Red Cloud's party took their leader's cue and began to beat the dismounted Cheyenne mercilessly with their weapons. The night air was filled with their whoops and a slapping, thumping sound as they flailed about them, their horses wheeling in the dust. The Cheyenne ducked and weaved to avoid the blows but none escaped without a bruise, welt, or bloody cut. Red Cloud held his bow high in the air and roared to the heavens in a voice which echoed through the pines.

Then, as suddenly as they had come, the Lakota vanished into the night, leaving the Cheyenne bruised and aching and burning with the humiliation of the act. Dull Knife, in particular, was beside himself with rage and shame. No man had ever done such a thing to him and lived. Gazzeau and his fellow whites stood or sat frozen in the places they had occupied when the Lakota first appeared. They had escaped unharmed. It was almost as if the Lakota had refused even to recognize their presence. Henry Arrison was tight-lipped, while Joe Donaldson was noticeably pale and trembling. Gazzeau seemed only to be baffled. He stood staring vacantly into the darkness into which Red Cloud had vanished.

"Friend," Black Horse said to him as he wiped a smear of blood back from a small gash on his forehead, "this Lakota is touched with madness. He will make a great trouble soon. I am taking my people and we are going away from here now. We are going to the mountains and we are staying away from this man. If you are wise, you will go to the white man's fort before the sun rises again. Your woman is a Lakota but I have seen what is in Red Cloud's eyes. He will not stop at murdering his relatives. Are you listening to me? We are going now and you should go too. If you wait even another sleep it will be your last in this world."

"Eh?" Gazzeau still seemed somewhat puzzled by the events he had witnessed. "I will think on what you say, Black Horse." His eyes were still fixed on the darkness. "I surely will think about it."

Black Horse and his companions quickly gathered up their few belongings and in minutes all that remained to betray their presence was the echoing sound of their horses' hooves as they rode off toward the mountains. A few moments more and this sound too faded into silence. Henry Arrison walked slowly across the clearing to join French Pete, who was now staring idly into the embers of the campfire.

"Pete," Arrison said quietly. "I'm thinkin' we need to haul outta here purty damn quick. What Black Horse was saying made a hell of a lot of sense to me. That damn Red Cloud is trouble sure."

Gazzeau stared into the fire for another few seconds then looked up at his friend. "*Sacre Dieu, mon ami*, it's a hard thing. I don' know why the Sioux would want to 'arm us but with them you never know what they thinkin'. I s'pose you right. We go to Reno first thing tomorrow."

"I'd feel one hell of a lot better if we pulled stakes right now, Pete. I got a powerful bad feelin' 'bout them redskins."

"*Oui*, I know what you say Henri, but I ask you. If they want to kill us, why we still 'ave our scalps now, eh? *D'accord*, we go back to Reno but it's damned late now an' if they mean to kill us tonight we already be dead, *non*?"

Arrison screwed up his lips and snorted down a deep breath. "Well, I s'pose."

"Me too, Henri. We go on to Reno tomorrow. We be up an' movin' before first light, *n'est-ce pas*? I think we all right for tonight an' the lightnin' she don' strike us twice in this place for a few hours."

The partners turned to explain the plan to their companions, who readily agreed that Fort Reno would be a much more comfortable place to be for a while anyway. Joe Donaldson wanted to leave immediately but the others were inclined to agree with French Pete's reasoning that they'd have a few hours' grace and could at least salvage what merchandise and furs they had in stock. Arrison suggested that Donaldson was welcome to head out by himself if he was so inclined and no hard feelings but the youngster had no desire to set off into the forest by himself not knowing if the Sioux were out there waiting for him in the darkness. The men, casting anxious glances over their shoulders, worked hurriedly heaving kettles and kegs into wagon beds and rolling the small canvas tents into bundles which were tossed in on top of the sardines and trade axes. Within an hour everything was packed up, if not neatly, at least securely, and the men dropped exhausted to the ground to catch an hour or two of sleep under the beds of the heavily laden wagons. French Pete was the last man to crawl under a blanket and he lay near the still-warm embers of the fire staring up at the vast dark emptiness of space and listening to the mournful hoot of an owl calling to its mate as sleep finally closed in on him.

CAPTAIN HENRY HAYMOND ADJUSTED THE CRIMSON SASH that he had bound tightly around his waist and reached down to pick up his sword belt, which he had slung across the back of the folding chair in his tent. As the Officer of the Day he was obliged to wear the sash and sword, which he considered a great nuisance. The tassels thunked and slapped against his thigh and tangled annoyingly with the sword knot and scabbard. Haymond was forever fidgeting with the sword, which, in his opinion, was good for nothing but tripping the wearer if he was in a hurry. He strapped on the belt, flipped open the holster, and withdrew his heavy revolver. He quickly checked it to insure that the loads were properly seated and that the small percussion caps were fitted tightly onto the nipples of each chamber save the one directly under the hammer. No sense in risking an accidental discharge. Satisfied, he dropped the weapon back into its holster, buckled the flap and reached for the sword which was icy cold from the chill of the night just passed.

Haymond was about to slip the ornate, and in his view useless, weapon into its leather frog when the loud report of a gunshot rang through the sleepy encampment. The captain heaved the sword onto his cot and ducked through the tent flap forgetting his kepi in his haste. Outside pandemonium reigned. Just to the south of the main encampment, in the area which Colonel Carrington had designated for corrals, there was a great tumult and a roiling cloud of dust as a large number of the command's mules and several horses were being driven headlong across the Little Piney by a handful of Indians. The south end of the camp was a bedlam of shouts and curses punctuated by the pop-popping of gunshots and the shrill yelping of the raiding warriors. In addition to the sentries, who had evidently been caught napping by the raid, scores of men were rushing to the scene in various states of undress—some shoeless, others with braces trailing in the grass behind them, but all carrying some kind of weapon, if not a rifle then a pitchfork, a bayonet, an ax, and in one case a broken beer bottle. As Haymond watched in consternation the herd was driven in a circuit around to the west of the encampment and then off to the north along the Sullivant Hills, trailing dust in their wake.

Private John Ryan, who had been assigned as Haymond's orderly, came racing up to the captain's tent. He was mounted on a well-muscled Morgan and leading the captain's mare, already saddled and with a Spencer carbine slung over the saddlebow. Ryan reined the horses to a halt and waited wordlessly as Haymond launched himself into the saddle and gathered the reins up in his left hand while at the same time slipping the carbine sling over his shoulder. Without a word the two spurred their mounts into pursuit. Behind them Lieutenant Bisbee had already begun to gather up the command's cavalry detachment. The corrals were a blur of men jockeying horses into line and swinging saddles onto the backs of the excited animals who pranced and shied away as their riders cursed and flailed with a tangle of halters, reins, cinches, and stirrup leathers flying every which way.

"Goddamn them!" Henry Haymond cursed under his breath as he and Ryan galloped along on the ridges trying to keep the raiders in sight. Somehow the Indians had managed to slip through his picket lines, something which the rebels had never been able to accomplish, and Haymond was both mortified and enraged. Someone's head would roll for this debacle. Haymond dug his spurs deeper into the horse's flanks and raced forward, his right hand gripping the stock of the carbine slung at his side and his teeth gritted in anger. Beside him Private Ryan leaned forward in the saddle and slipped the reins between his teeth as he brought his Spencer up with both hands and worked the lever to jack a cartridge into the weapon's breech. Ryan was desperate for a shot at one of those painted devils. While he'd seldom had much use for "shoulder straps," he liked and respected the captain and had served with him throughout the last two years of the rebellion. He'd be damned if he'd let some savage sully the "old man's" reputation by running off the stock. Just let one of those scamps come within range and he'd tend him for sure.

Within minutes a number of men had managed to form a party in pursuit of the raiders and Captain Haymond. But, despite their best efforts, it was a bedraggled-looking affair. The men in various states of undress on reluctant mounts had been slow in getting out of the camp, charging off not in a body but in small groups of two and three at a time. As a result, what should have looked like an organized body of cavalry in hot pursuit of the enemy had more the appearance of a badly bungled horse race at a church picnic. Haymond glanced back over his shoulder to see his men scattered across the hillsides and stretching in a ragged line all the way back to the Little Piney. From his vantage point he could still see the herd headed off to the north and noticed that the clear trail of hoofprints should prove no great feat to track. A cold shiver slipped down Haymond's spine and he reined in his horse, reaching out to pull Ryan to a halt alongside. Something was not quite right. He could not put his finger on what bothered him but something told him to wait for the rest of the pursuit party to come up.

The first few troopers had no sooner begun to arrive when one of them tumbled abruptly from the saddle, an arrow transfixed through his neck. A shrill war cry screeched out and was immediately joined by scores of other voices shrieking and whooping from the cover of boulders and scrub in almost every direction. Haymond formed his small command into a defensive circle and ordered the men from their horses to return fire. *A trap!* Haymond thought suddenly. *They lured us out here and mean to ambush us.* He tossed his Spencer to one of the men who he noticed had brought along a muzzle-loader and yanked his revolver from its holster. "Steady men," he yelled. "Wait and mark your targets. Don't waste a shot, there'll be reinforcements along presently." Haymond sent a ball into a small bush that had moved slightly and hoped like hell that he was right.

Lieutenant William Bisbee ground his teeth in frustration. Whatever they were supposed to be doing, he felt that they were making a terrible hash of it. He'd watched Haymond's small group straggle out after the herd and then had set about trying to get a relief company organized. It took him less than half an hour but seemed to him an eternity. The camp was in an uproar with Carrington dashing hither and yon ordering people about and getting the tarpaulins pulled off the artillery. As if artillery would be any good at all against a couple of young bucks who were probably already halfway to the Tongue with the command's mules in tow. The last time Bisbee'd seen anything so discouraging had been at Murfreesboro when Forrest's cavalry had made monkeys of the lot of them. This was Carrington's fault, the damned pompous little lawyer. He'd made the teamsters crazy having them rearrange the corrals three times before they were neat enough for him and far enough away from the camp that he didn't have to endure the smell of manure. Now they were strung out all over creation trying to snatch the mules back from a couple of little savages. In Bisbee's view the new commander of the Mountain District was a damned noncombatant, paper-collared Jonah who couldn't organize a game of euchre in a dog tent.

Before an hour had elapsed Bisbee was galloping north along the Bozeman Road with a tightly organized company of fifty men close behind him. They could hear the echoing reports of Spencers and at least one Colt's revolver, which told Bisbee that Haymond had run into somebody up ahead. A few minutes of hard riding brought them into sight of Haymond's party and at the same time flushed a covey of Sioux warriors—most of them armed with bows, although one or two of the bucks had trade muskets. Haymond, who had pushed his group into a small position among a jumble of large boulders, was visibly relieved by Bisbee's arrival. Haymond sprang into the saddle and took up the pursuit with Bisbee's column fast on his heels. The mounted men scrambled along the hillsides, the horses' hooves dislodging rocks and churning up large clods of earth as they hurried along after the raiders. Bisbee figured they had covered a good fifteen miles in a running fight which took them over Lodge Trail Ridge and splashing through Peno Creek at a dead run. Finally, as the nimble Indians disappeared into the landscape, even Haymond was convinced of the futility of pushing on any farther. He held up his hand and brought the command to a halt.

"Goddamnit all to Hell!" Haymond spat.

He looked around and took stock of what the morning's exertions had produced. A few yards behind the tail of the column one trooper was leading three mules and a roan mare—all that was left of the stolen herd, and one of the mules had come up lame. He turned to Bisbee, whose face was pinched with anger.

"Any losses, Lieutenant?"

"Two dead, sir," Bisbee said quietly. "And three wounded that I know of. Donovan's been hit twice. A musket ball in the shoulder and an arrow in his left leg. Murphy's lashed him to his saddle but he needs tending pretty quick."

"Two dead," Haymond said, shaking his head. "For three lousy mules and a damned mare. It's a poor bargain we've made." Bisbee nodded, his jaw muscles bulging with tension.

"I won't lose another man for naught, Will," Haymond went on, tight-lipped. He glanced at the surrounding forest and wheeled his horse toward the Bozeman Road. "Let's get out of this damned forest as quickly as possible. Turn 'em about and we'll fall back on the Montana Road to lick our wounds. But I'll be damned if I'll let 'em catch me asleep again."

Bisbee saluted and the command swung around to file out through the pines to the dusty trail that led back toward the encampment. As the troopers climbed out onto the road Haymond reorganized the command and ordered several men out to serve as flankers on the return march. He didn't intend to be surprised again and so this duty went only to men he knew had served in the rebellion. Even then he checked each man to insure that he had chambered a round in his carbine. He'd not lose another man today if he could help it. With Haymond and Bisbee in the lead the company trotted easily along the wide trail with every head swiveling left and right and every man, except those supporting their wounded comrades, gripping his weapon tightly. As they rounded a bend the road dipped down into a swale where it crossed over Peno Creek. As the column splashed through the rushing current and clambered up the opposite bank, a slight movement just off of the road ahead caught Captain Haymond's eye. The command closed up as Haymond brought it to a halt. He nodded to Bisbee and waved for two sergeants to join them. Both officers drew their revolvers from their holsters, then, leaving the command at an uneasy rest, moved cautiously through the trees to investigate.

The movement that had caught Haymond's attention was a flapping piece of canvas from the battered remains of a wagon. Three other wagons, bristling with arrows and missing chunks, were scattered nearby amid a clutter of tinned sardines, shattered jars of fruit, broken nail kegs, and scattered horseshoes. Shredded bolts of calico and gingham fabric had been unraveled and dragged off into the trees where, snagged on deadfall and brush, they twisted and fluttered like the strands of an oversized, multicolored spider's web. The remains of three small tents were similarly abused and their contents strewn haphazardly throughout a small clearing and the surrounding pines. There was a strangled retching sound behind him and Bisbee turned to see a visibly pale Sergeant Delaney hunched over in his saddle with vomit streaming down his horse's withers.

"Delaney! What the hell do you . . . oh, good God in Heaven!"

Bisbee could feel himself go light-headed, and for a moment the forest seemed to swim around him. His face was successively flushed and drained of blood, leaving his entire scalp tingling as if pricked by a thousand small pins. He was suddenly drenched with a cold sweat and the evil taste of bile welled up around the base of his tongue. He'd never in his life seen such a thing. In all the battles he'd fought, Hoover's Gap, Lookout Mountain, Corinth, with all of their carnage of shattered corpses and clotted pools of blood, never had he seen a human being handled in such a fashion. At first he thought that this was the body of a woman until he noticed that the beardless man's genitals had been sliced away and stuffed into his gaping mouth. The man's body cavity had been slashed open and a fire built inside. The corpse's entrails had been yanked from within and strewn like a string of sausage on the surrounding evergreens, draped over lower limbs like ghastly Christmas ornaments. That Lieutenant Bisbee did not recognize the man was not a judgment on his memory, for Joe Donaldson's own mother would not have known her son's battered corpse. Bisbee fought to hold down the meager contents of his stomach and was glad that he had barely had time to manage a few sips of coffee before the mules had been run off.

Donaldson had not died alone. As Haymond and Bisbee picked their way through the wreckage they discovered the remains of five other men. At least, they had once been men, for now one would be hard-pressed to differentiate between what had been left strewn across the forest floor and inexpertly butchered hogs. At least three of the five had been taken alive and Bisbee could not even begin to fathom the horror which had accompanied their last moments on earth. One man's skull had been split from crown to lip, the brain scooped out and smashed on a nearby rock. Bisbee wondered if this had been done largely for the benefit of those of his comrades who were still alive at the time. This was the work of fiends. The lieutenant had no idea who these men were but no one, he decided, should have had to suffer as they must have done.

"William!" Haymond called out from across the clearing.

Bisbee looked over at his commander, a small trickle of bile slipping from his half-open mouth. God, how he wanted to throw up, but he knew it would be bad form in front of the sergeants. He clenched his teeth, forcing his tongue against the roof of his mouth, and nudged his horse, which picked its way gingerly through the wreckage of the camp. Haymond was staring down at one of the corpses. Haymond nodded at the man.

"That was French Pete," he said quietly. "I recognize those moccasins. I admired them once and he said that he'd have his squaw sew some up for me. He was not a bad fellow. God, how they've done for him."

Bisbee just nodded, afraid that if he tried to say anything it would just come out as vomit. Haymond noticed his friend's pallid features, reached into his saddlebags, and produced a flask. He screwed the cap off and took a swig, then handed it to Bisbee without comment. Bisbee took the flask in shaking hands and tipped it back, the raw taste of the brandy searing his throat but cutting through the taste of the bile. He shuddered and shook his head.

"Wonder where his squaw is?" Bisbee handed the flask back to the captain.

"Don't know," Haymond said, his eyes scanning through the surrounding trees. "There were several children too. Orphans now, I suspect. If they lived."

"You think they've killed them too?"

"Don't know for sure, Will, but anyone who could do this is capable of any outrage. We'll have some of the men search through the brush to see if they're still here. I want you to throw out a picket line around this spot. Let them see this charnel house first. It'll keep them alert. Set the rest of the troop to salvaging what they can. I'll be damned if I'll let the savages come back at leisure to pick over what remains. We'll load the goods and wounded into the wagons and take the dead back for a Christian burial." Haymond waved at the tendrils of calico. "There's enough of that about for winding sheets. I noticed half a cask of popskull under that dog tent. Share out what's left among the boys but not more'n a gill each. It'll steady their nerve for what's ahead but without anyone bringing back a brick. Whoever did this has not been gone long, the wolves have not been at their work yet. The only beasts capable of this walk on two legs."

Bisbee nodded and wheeled his horse to rejoin the rest of the command, but Haymond remained in place surveying the surrounding forest. They were out there somewhere, the beasts, he could feel them watching him, and his gorge rose as he imagined them gloating over their bloody handiwork. Damn this country! And damn Carrington.

AWFUL DAMNED COUNTRY THEY HAVE OUT HERE, RIDGWAY Glover was thinking. Dry, dusty, and mostly flat as a billiard table. The dust was especially vexing for what it did to his equipment. It seemed that no matter how tightly he wrapped everything the damned dust seemed always to somehow find a chink in the armor and sift into the worst possible places. He had spent nearly all of his savings getting his camera and the supplies he needed this far and if he didn't do something about the dust it would all be just so much deadweight and he would be bankrupted.

Anthony and Company, it seemed to Glover, were awfully proud of the photographic supplies in which they traded, and their prices reflected it. They were, of course, used to doing business with such people as Brady and Gardner, for whom funds were not really a problem, but fellows like Glover were at a distinct disadvantage for capital outlay. If it hadn't been for his old boss Tim O'Sullivan vouching for him he could never have afforded the cost of this expedition. It was amazing the material you needed to do this work properly—collodion, alcohol, silver nitrate, iron sulphate, potassium cyanide, ether, not to mention the camera itself, with tripod, lenses, focusing cloth, and plates. It was no wonder he had no money left to buy a wagon in which to transport everything. If O'Sullivan hadn't let him have the old pram he would have truly been in a stick. It was O'Sullivan who had then marched him into the offices of *Frank Leslie's Illustrated Weekly* and demanded that the publisher cough up the funds for Glover's passage west. This demand, to Glover's surprise, was quickly accepted.

O'Sullivan was one of the best photographers in the business and Glover knew that Brady, who was half blind, had often put his own name on views taken by O'Sullivan and Gardner. O'Sullivan, a generous and easygoing New Yorker, did not seem to mind.

"Oh, Mathew's a good fellow for all his pride," O'Sullivan had said. "He taught Alex and me a good many tricks and I'll not begrudge him a picture or two. Now, let's say we get you started out West. You'll have to work fast, boyo, for I've a notion to come out and snatch a view or two myself next year."

Now, having come this far, it was almost maddening to think that it could all be undone by a little dust. It was not until the second day out of Laramie that Mrs. Wands kindly suggested that she take Glover's plates and camera body and sew them up in some oilskin that her husband had acquired at the fort. Lieutenant Alexander Wands was of a scientific bent, fancying himself an ethnographer, although he'd probably not have known the meaning of the word. Fascinated by Glover's camera, he readily agreed to the sacrifice. He extracted a promise that Glover would produce some first-rate portraits of himself and the family and handed over the oilskin with a flourish.

"Science, Mr. Glover," he'd said with a confidential grin, "is the new God of the nineteenth century. I have hopes that your little magic box will be at the forefront of scientific research. Why, just think of the things you'll be able to record with that machine! You know, these aborigines out here are a dying breed, I think, and it would be a shame to have them all pass from the earth without any trace. I suspect it's up to people like you and myself to make some sort of record of these vanishing tribes."

Ridgway Glover was immediately won over by the generous and obviously well-read lieutenant who, it turned out, shared a great many of Glover's interests. The two of them could often be seen locked in conversation about subjects that ranged from botany to chemistry and from photography to *The Origin of Species*, a copy of which Glover had purchased in Philadelphia and packed up with his photographic supplies. Glover was particularly fascinated by Darwin's theories on natural selection and wondered if there might be parallels to be found among the human animal. He once confided to Wands that he thought it was just possible that the country where they were going might harbor some mysterious lost tribe that could provide fodder for a new theory on human evolution. This brought the conversation around to the old story that a race of fair-haired, Gaelic-speaking Indians lurked somewhere in the interior of the country. This, of course, spun into a discussion of Captain Lewis' expedition with Captain Clark. They had also hoped to come across some evidence of this "lost tribe." First Lieutenant George Templeton, commander of the small party, was intrigued by the discussions that engrossed Glover and Wands. Mrs. Wands was not quite so amused. After six days on the trail, she was beginning to feel a bit neglected by her distracted husband.

"I'm beginning to wish I'd never stitched up those skins for Mr. Glover," she complained to Lieutenant Templeton. "If I hadn't, he'd be spending all of his time fussing over his precious plates and lenses and maybe, just maybe, Alexander would be a bit more help with Bobby!"

At age four, Bobby Wands was more than a handful for his long-suffering mother. A source of endless, impish energy, he was forever leaping about in the cramped space of the wagon and had already tumbled out into the dust twice. Amused by his mother's obvious distraction, the officers in the small party had all taken turns helping out with the youngster. Lieutenant George Templeton, who at the time was cradling young Bobby in the saddle in front of him, ruffled the sleeping boy's hair.

MARY WANDS GAZED AT BOBBY'S PEACEFUL FACE AS HE rested gently in the large officer's arms. She could see her own husband reflected in the boy's features and glanced off to see Alex laughing at something Glover had said as the two trudged along beside lieutenants Daniels and Bradley a few yards ahead. There were only four saddle horses for the detachment, so the men took turns riding them. Wands and

Glover were hiking along with improvised walking sticks, scuffing their boots through the dust and kicking up rocks as they went. For a moment they looked for all the world like a pair of schoolboys off to play hooky, and Mary relented. *George is right*, she thought. *They'll have plenty of work to do soon enough, I'll not begrudge them a little fun now.*

If anything, Lieutenant Templeton envied the other lieutenants their meager responsibilities on this march. As the senior officer present it was Templeton's lot to command the small party which was traveling to join the 18th Infantry at the new fort. From what he had heard, it was not much more than a collection of tents and a few stakes driven into the ground. In addition to the two ambulances carrying Mrs. Wands and Private Fessenden's wife—who had finally been delivered of a fine baby girl—nine freight wagons hauled an amazing collection of supplies destined to make life at the new post more comfortable and civilized. Packed tightly into the beds of the wagons along with the officers' baggage were cases of iron hinges and brass doorknobs, window latches, brass screws, padlocks and sash weights, candles and lamp oil. In addition there were two cases of replacement locks for Springfield rifles, ten cases of ammunition for those rifles, and the few surplus medical supplies that could be squeezed out of the stores at forts Laramie and Reno. These consisted largely of rolls of lint, a dozen bottles of quinine, some sulfur, and a few jars of carbolic acid.

Surgeon Hines, who was accompanying the group, was outraged by the scarcity of medical supplies and equipment and declared that if the Army had its way it would have as soon contracted witch doctors as surgeons. Chaplain White, also headed to take up his new post with the 18th Regiment, sympathized with the irate surgeon and offered a prayer that future medical services would be restricted to washing off the bruised knees of the children who had accompanied their parents. Bobby Wands kept Surgeon Hines busy with an assortment of cuts, scratches, and abrasions, and once gave Hines the opportunity to use smelling salts on the boy's mother when Bobby managed to drive a bayonet through his shoe, narrowly missing his toes but sending Mrs. Wands into a swoon.

Including the chaplain, the surgeon, Mrs. Wands with her son Bobby and her black servant Laura, Mrs. Fessenden and her baby, the young lieutenants, and Glover, Templeton was responsible for the safety and welfare of thirty-four people, mainly teamsters and a ten-man escort of green troops. Although an insignificantly small group compared with the units he had commanded in the recent war, he would have preferred a battalion of "galvanized Yankees" to this troublesome little detail. It wasn't so much that his wards were deliberately difficult or insubordinate, it was just that they were such . . . amateurs. It was like herding cats.

The teamsters were unimpressed by any rank. They did their jobs well enough but it was painfully evident that their efforts were motivated by Uncle Sam's dollars rather than his officers' authority. Between Mrs. Wands' vapors over Bobby's antics, and the squalling of Private Fessenden's new baby, the impromptu sermons of Chaplain White at every halt, and Surgeon Hines' railing at the penurious nature of the Army staff, Templeton felt sure that he would be driven mad long before they joined Carrington at the site of his new fort. When one of the teamsters mentioned that they would reach Crazy Woman Fork by noon, Templeton thought sardonically that the creek might well be renamed Crazy Lieutenant Fork by the time his party reached it.

As the day warmed to an uncomfortable degree, with the dust rising in the rutted trail. Glover removed his hat to reveal his bright blond hair and Templeton thought it looked for all the world like a lemon bouncing along levitated on a cloud of dust. This amusing thought soon had Templeton thinking of lemonade and baseball games and the hundred other places he would rather be at this particular moment. He was brought out of his reverie only by the sudden appearance of Lieutenant Daniels, who had trotted back from the head of the column and wheeled in alongside of him.

"Crazy Woman Fork should be just ahead a mile or so, sir," Napoleon Daniels said eagerly. "I'd like to volunteer to scout out a decent spot for nooning. Bradley's spotted some buffalo up ahead and it might make for a grand lunch treat and a bit of sport, too." The fresh-faced youngster had been enduring a merciless ribbing from his colleagues for his namesake's military abilities, and "Boney" Daniels was overly eager to establish his reputation as a soldier. Templeton understood the lad's sensitivity about his name but was not about to send him out alone even if the only Indians they had seen thus far were a few squaws who had tried to bargain for Fessenden's baby girl.

"Tell you what, Mr. Daniels. That sounds like a capital idea. But, if you wouldn't mind the company, I think I'd like to come along as well. I've had my fill of baby-sitting and dust eating for the time."

Templeton winked at the young lieutenant and saw that it had the desired effect, for Daniels returned a conspiratorial grin. Daniels didn't need to know his commander's real reason for coming along. Templeton turned to Mrs. Wands' ambulance and managed to pass the sleeping Bobby to her without waking him, then nodded to Daniels, and the two officers spurred their mounts toward the head of the column. In a few seconds they had trotted past Lieutenant Wands and Glover, who were so engaged in their conversation that they barely noticed the passage of the mounted men. They were about due for a halt and had heard about Bradley's sighting of buffalo. It was close enough to lunch that they assumed that Templeton was off to find a pleasant stream as a rally point for a picnic and hunt. Wands had already retrieved his new Henry repeating rifle from the ambulance in anticipation of a bit of fun. Daniels waved as he trotted past.

"I say, Glover," Alexander Wands was saying as he slipped cartridges into his rifle, "what do you intend to photograph out here anyway? Assuming, of course, that our aboriginal friends don't share your enthusiasm for the magic box?"

Glover waved his straw boater absently at the passing Daniels, tapped it gently back onto his head, and slipped one hand into his vest pocket as he gazed around them. "Well, Wands, I should hope to get some interesting stereoscopic views of the mountains," he said after a few steps. "The Bighorns aren't much farther, I don't suppose. Then we'll be out of this damned dust and I can get to work in earnest."

Glover, now at ease about the safety of his equipment, was once again invigorated by the challenges that lay ahead.

He was finally coming within reach of his goal. Initially concerned that he hadn't been able to purchase a full-size photographer's wagon, he found that the "pram" was surprisingly adequate for his purposes. Rather than push the cart around for long distances he had been able to secure a small space in the bed of a freight wagon into which he and one other man were able to easily lift the compact apparatus. Whenever he was camped they could roll the cart out, erect the dark tent, and complete the whole photographic process in its confines. The quarters were cramped but not much more so than the wagons Gardner and O'Sullivan had been using throughout the war. Luckily he had a slight build and was able to work with ease in spaces most men would find restrictive. After a few tries he discovered that even in his cramped quarters he could indeed accomplish the intricate process involved in coating his glass plates by feel, provided he arranged his chemicals just so. In fact, once he had gotten fairly comfortable with his spartan arrangements he found the process remarkably simple.

In the final analysis it was not hostile Indians, rattlesnakes, rutted trails, or clumsy teamsters but the climate which had thus far proved his greatest enemy. Unprepared for the dry heat of Fort Laramie, most of his exposures of the peace conference were disastrous. With the mercury registering 103 degrees his collodion had became overheated. Then the alcohol bath accelerated the evaporation process to the point where his views came out covered with irregular-sized bubbles. Where he had expected to see the stern visages of the assembled commissioners and Indians he was left with what appeared to be a family portrait of moon-faced cats dressed in polka-dotted frock coats and blankets. But now, as they moved farther into the hills, he could feel the first inklings of cool breezes wafting out of the mountains ahead, and he was eager to be approaching country where he could concentrate more on his subjects than on his chemicals. What he really wanted was another shot

at capturing the likenesses of men like Spotted Tail and the
charismatic Red Cloud.

As the wagons churned through the sandy soil of a slight de-
pression the surrounding landscape erupted. A firestorm of arrows and bullets ripped through the column. Horses and mules
bucked and screamed in their traces, men swore and cursed,
their heads ducking instinctively between hunched shoulders.
The noise was deafening.

"Indians!"

The ambush caught the party by surprise. But the men who
had been readying their rifles for buffalo were ready with a
return volley, which they sent crashing into the surrounding
brush. Glover was stunned to see Lieutenant Bradley rush past
him followed by a dozen men all yelling at the top of their
lungs and firing blindly into the dust raised by their attackers.
Lieutenant Wands, too, was yelping and yipping and working
the lever of his Henry rifle as fast as he could. Behind them the
teamsters had lashed the mules and horses into a trot and the
wagons were dragged lurching uphill after Bradley.

Lieutenant Bradley saw that the countryside was alive with
Indians screaming and shooting at the column. Furtive,
bronzed figures seemed to flit behind every boulder and clump
of sagebrush; flashes of faces painted in red and yellow streaks
bobbed up to send feathered shafts whirring toward the wagons or to disappear behind the flash and puff of gunsmoke.
Reaching higher, more defensible ground, Bradley wheeled his
horse to the rear, shouting instructions to the teamsters.
Hunched in his saddle and waving his pistol, he guided the
wagons into position to form a hasty perimeter. Those not
actively involved in the operation had tumbled out of the wagons and worked rifles and pistols with feverish haste. Mrs.
Wands, known to faint if her impish son displayed so much
as a spider bite, had stashed her toddler under a seat in the
ambulance and was busily pounding home loads in a Colt's
revolver, looking more like a seasoned trooper than a fretting
mother. A quick glance around showed Lieutenant Bradley
that despite the sudden nature of the assault none of his fellow
travelers had been struck by the firestorm of missiles. Most of

the arrows had plunged harmlessly into the dust or were lodged firmly in the sides of the wagons. Bradley's thoughts turned to lieutenants Daniels and Templeton just as a riderless horse burst out of the brush. A cavalry saddle had slipped around to hang under its belly and the hooded stirrups bounced crazily in the dust as the horse careered into the camp. Arrows were sticking out of the animal's neck and flanks; its nostrils were flared and its eyes wide with terror as one of the teamsters snatched at its reins and pulled the horse deeper into the ring of wagons. Bradley recognized it as the mare Boney Daniels had been riding. Moments later a hatless Lieutenant Templeton raced headlong toward the column, his horse lathered and his pistol used as a quirt to urge the mount on. Two arrows protruded from the animal's haunches and a third shaft was lodged deeply in Templeton's back. The lieutenant's ashen face was covered with blood as he spurred the mount over a wagon tongue and into the perimeter. He swayed in the saddle, gasping, "Daniels, oh my God. Indians!" Templeton slipped from the saddle just as Surgeon Hines and Chaplain White raced over to catch him.

"Alex," Bradley yelled, "looks like you're now senior man present." Lieutenant Wands squeezed off another shot with his rifle, then turned and walked calmly over to his friend.

"Well, hell's bells, Jimmy," he said. "It's a fine time to get regulation on me!"

Bradley grinned at Wands and saluted. "Your orders, sir?"

Alexander Wands quickly took stock of the situation. Templeton was out of action, Daniels was missing, and two of the mules had been so badly wounded that they were useless. The Indians, whoever they were, were not very good shots, but there was too much brush to provide cover for them. Sooner or later they'd be able to work in more closely and their shots would begin to tell. They had to move. A few hundreds yards away Wands noticed a small rise. It was treeless and exposed but there was very little to conceal attackers. They'd have to make a run for it.

"All right, Jimmy," Wands said, pointing his finger at the rise. "We're heading for that knob over there. Lieutenant Skin-

ner and I will take the advance guard. You take five of the
men and form a rear guard and hold these devils off as long
as you can but don't fall behind more than fifty yards. If they
split us up we're done for. Mr. Marr!" Wands called to one
of the civilians traveling with the party. "I understand, sir, you
were a captain with the Missouri Volunteers during the war."

"True, sir."

"Excellent." Wands clapped a hand on Marr's shoulder.
"Skinner and I are taking the advance while Bradley here
guards our rear. We're going to push onto that rise over there
and form a square. Can you form a flying column with some
of the riflemen to take the flanks as we go? We'll be moving
fast, sir. Things could get dicey."

"My pleasure, sir. When do we go?"

"As soon as you've picked your men. Can we be ready in
three minutes?"

Marr nodded.

"All right then," Wands said finally.

Minutes later the column had reached its goal under heavy
pressure from all sides. The most precarious moments had
been at the crossing of Crazy Woman Fork when the Sioux
had tried to cut them off. Marr, armed like Wands with a
Henry repeater, had killed the two lead warriors and broken
their charge, giving the column just enough time to close up
on the bald hilltop. It was, Wands thought, a worthwhile risk
as the new ground provided good fields of fire and was soft
enough to allow the men to dig shallow rifle pits. Wands began
once more to take stock of the situation. Surgeon Hines had
managed to get the arrow out of Templeton's back. The man
would live but he was effectively lost for this action. Daniels
was still missing and Wands had to assume the worst. It was
hard to swallow and he found himself regretting that he had
ever ribbed Boney about his name. Now it looked like Napoleon Daniels had met his Waterloo without ever having fired
a shot in anger.

Luckily, no one else had yet been injured. They had sufficient food to last them a week and more than enough ammunition, but their supply of water was dangerously low and

this exposed hilltop afforded no protection whatever from a
merciless sun. Wands began to calculate how far it was to Fort
Reno and whether they could get a messenger through to the
current commander, Captain Proctor, requesting a relief party.
A sudden whirring caused Wands to duck as a score of arrows
rained into the position, followed immediately by the yelps of
men hit by some of the missiles. Three men were injured, one
of them Chaplain White, who seemed more insulted than hurt
by his wound.

"Damned rascals!" the chaplain roared in his deepest fire-
and-brimstone voice. "I'll have their hides for this. This was
a perfectly good frock and now look at it. Ruined, by thunder!
I'll not stand for it!"

A slash across his upper arm was spreading a blackened
patch of blood into the fabric of his coat. Another flight of
arrows arced overhead and thunked into the dust of the perimeter, one of the shafts finding the rump of a mule, which
brayed loudly in protest. All attention was drawn to a small
ravine from which the attack seemed to have come and White
spotted a slight movement behind one of the bushes that
sprouted at the base of the draw.

"Come on, Fuller," White said to a young private who was
standing nearby. "With your permission, Lieutenant Wands,
Fuller and I will flush those birds before they do any more
mischief to my clothing."

Wands considered the chaplain's offer for a moment and
quickly decided that if allowed to remain in the ravine the
Indians could indeed be a serious threat to the command. He
nodded and motioned for Mr. Marr and one of the teamsters
to join him in providing a covering fire for the effort. White
and Fuller hopped over a wagon tongue, dropped into a
crouch, and raced headlong down the ravine to disappear into
the dust and scrub. Seconds later a ripple of gunshots rattled
out of the scrub, and moments later White and Fuller reappeared, both of them grinning broadly. Chaplin White's right
hand and face were blackened from gunpowder, and he was
cursing loudly at the pistol in his hand.

"Damned 'knuckler' went off all at once. All seven barrels,

by God," he declaimed, "Knocked me flat on my back. I've a
mind to write Mr. Reid and complain about his infernal device.
'My Friend,' indeed. A man hardly needs enemies with such
friends. But at least there are two good Indians down there
now, by God." White, apparently unaware of Lieutenant
Wands and the others, addressed his comments to the pistol
in his hand.

"The rest of 'em scattered, sir," Fuller added quietly, a pair
of fingers raised in a casual salute and his eyes rolling heavenward.

Wands nodded. It seemed somehow odd that Chaplain
White, so anxious to save the souls of the men and women in
his own flock, appeared to take great delight in killing men,
but then perhaps that was exactly how he viewed the situation,
looking at the Indians as little more than wolves in the fold.
Well, Wands concluded, he'd much rather a fighting parson
than one who simply took up space consuming Army rations
and terrifying the children on Sundays. He turned to survey
the rest of the party and caught sight of something else he
could not quite fathom.

Ridgway Glover had somehow managed to manhandle his
cart out of the wagon and set up his miniature darkroom. Now
he was busily engaged in taking photographs! In the confusion
of the fight Wands had quite forgotten about his odd friend
and was relieved to see that he'd not been killed outright. At
the same time he was baffled to see the man fiddling with his
camera, which he had erected on its tripod and was busily
feeding with slide after slide as he exposed plates to the battle
unfolding around him. Wands could not imagine how the fellow had managed to set up his complete apparatus, prepare
plates for his work, and then go about taking photographs as
Sioux arrows rained down on them and mounted warriors went
screaming past firing muskets into the defenders' midst. One
feathered shaft had even embedded itself in the side of the
small handcart. Glover seemed delighted with the entire affair
and oblivious of the danger, humming happily to himself as
he ducked his head under the focusing cloth and composed
yet another view. What sort of a command had Templeton left

him with? A parson who killed Indians and lectured pistols, and a photographer who wandered about talking to himself and trying to take pictures of the Indians who were trying to kill them. It was too much.

"Goddamnit, Glover!" Wands exploded.

Glover's left hand snaked out from under the black cloth and waved furiously as if to ward off any interference as he lined up the perfect view.

"Ridgway, get out from under that damned cloth this instant, you fool. This is serious business we're about here."

There was a soft click and Glover emerged from under the black hood blinking in the bright light and looking for all the world like a nearsighted turtle.

"Alexander, old man!" Glover enthused, "This is just first-rate. I'll be the only man in America. In the world, I should say, to have actually taken views of an Indian attack. Eastern papers will go wild for these plates. I hope the beggars weren't moving too quickly, the shutter on this beast is infernally slow and I'm afraid it might just develop as a bit of a blur beyond the wagons. I wonder if the blasted collodion isn't too hot again. Well, we can only hope on that score. This is all just too rare an opportunity to waste worrying about things like that. We'll just have to shoot as many as we can and hope something comes out in the wash. Well, would you look at that. One of the beggars damn near ruined my cart with an arrow. That'll make an interesting souvenir." Glover rattled on, half to himself, in a steady stream of commentary in which he fussed over exposures, shutter speeds, and dust and a number of things that were clearly more interesting to him than the intentions of the Sioux warriors who had surrounded the small detachment and continued to fire into it.

Wands rolled his eyes heavenward as if he had now seen everything. He reached into one of the wagon beds and snatched up a loaded rifle, then stalked over to his eccentric friend and grabbed him roughly by the shoulder. Glover looked up blinking and bewildered as Wands shoved the rifle into the his hands.

"Damnit, Ridgway," he shouted, "that's enough! If you're

so keen to shoot Indians you're a hell of a lot more use to me if you use a Springfield instead of a damned camera!"

Wands glared at his friend and marched off to rejoin the fight as Glover stood and looked dumbfounded at the rifle in his hands. Lieutenant Bradley, who was watching the little scene, thought Wands might as well have handed a sextant to an aborigine and asked him to compute the angle of the sun.

The afternoon dragged on as the Sioux lurked in the sage and scrub yelping war cries and firing into the defenders huddled behind their wagons and in shallow pits. The acrid taste of sulfur cloyed at every throat and stung the nostrils. Every face was smeared with black streaks of gunpowder and their clothes reeked of gunsmoke and sweat. As the hours crept by in the searing heat, water supplies dwindled away and the thirst became nearly unbearable. Mrs. Wands and Mrs. Fessenden had put themselves to tending the wounded once Surgeon Hines had done what he could to staunch the bleeding and extract arrow heads or badly deformed bullets. George Templeton, the arrowhead removed from his back and out of danger for the moment, drifted in and out of consciousness in the bed of a freight wagon. From time to time he would sit bolt upright and call out "Strike two!" or "Ball!" before sinking back into the blankets while one of the women mopped at his forehead and whispered soothing words into his ear.

Ridgway Glover, hunkered down under one of the freight wagons and working his Springfield with gritted teeth, was sulking after a bitter argument with Hines. The surgeon, who was already in a fit over the lack of useful medical supplies, had broken into Glover's stores and helped himself to the photographer's precious stores of collodion and ether—the latter to assist in minor surgery and the former because it made a superb dressing for the men's wounds.

"Just send your bill along to Congress, Glover, and steer out of my path. I've serious work to attend to here," Hines had said brusquely as he bent over a teamster and tried to get a loop of wire fished over the point of an arrow embedded in the man's thigh. "If you've a further complaint then I'd register it with those devils out there in the scrub. Now get out of my light. There, that's got it. Grit your teeth there, Amos, we'll have this free in a moment."

Mrs. Wands, in a blood-spattered apron, was not overly fond of Glover at the moment. Kneeling in the dust next to the surgeon she squeezed the wounded teamster's hand and glowered up at the photographer. Glover saw that he was wasting time with his protests. No one was interested in his concerns. Trailing the butt of his rifle in the dust, he slunk back to his position and comforted himself by blasting every bush that shifted in the fervent hope that there was an Indian or a Congressman concealed behind it.

In the late afternoon Alexander Wands organized a party of volunteers and made a mad rush down to the creek to fill a few canteens while "Captain" Marr and Chaplain White staged a diversion to keep the Sioux busy. The plan worked and with some water to restore their strength several wounded men dragged themselves back onto the firing line in time to drive off two charges of mounted warriors who thought that a final rush would collapse the last shred of resistance. A dozen warriors, some dead, others wounded, were left sprawled in the dust by these attempts, but they managed to kill a sergeant and put three other men into Surgeon Hines' care.

"This is getting to be a bad business, Mr. Wands," Marr said quietly.

"You're right, Captain," Wands agreed. "I am almost reluctant to suggest it but if we're not relieved we may be forced to do something rash." He glanced over at the two young women who were tending to a young private desperately wounded in the last assault.

Marr took Wands' meaning. If they were overrun by the savages the outcome for any survivors was too horrible to contemplate. The women especially, they had heard, would suffer outrages which did not bear thinking about. This could not be allowed. Chaplain White did not agree.

"It's an abomination before God! I'll not let you kill our own people like that."

"Keep your voice down, damnit!" Wands whispered fiercely. "What the hell would you have us do, Parson? I'm talking about my own wife and child here, too, man! Do you think I want to do this? But I'd sooner kill them myself before I'd let them fall into the hands of those devils out there. What kind of mercy should we expect from them?"

White grew silent for a space. He could see the pain in the man's eyes and knew that he'd been unfair with Wands. The lieutenant only wanted to spare his family the tortures which would surely be theirs if the Sioux won this fight. But there must be something else that could be done. "*I shall be exalted among the heathen,*" White thought as he wracked his brain for a solution.

"See here, Wands," he ventured. "Do you think we can hold 'em off for another day?"

Wands thought about it for a moment. He looked across at Marr, who shrugged his shoulders but gave a short nod. They had plenty of ammunition still, and now they had enough water to last a few more hours. If the men stayed low, made every shot count. He nodded to White.

"We might do, Parson. It'll be hot, but not impossible. What have you got in mind?"

"Well," White said leaning forward, "Fort Reno's not too far back down the trail. It's taken us three days to get this far with the wagons but a determined man on horseback could be there and back with a relief party in, say, twelve hours if he's a good horse under him."

"Take mine, Chaplain," Marr broke in. "Billy's a real goer. And take my pistol, too." He tugged the pepperbox out of White's grip and pressed a Colt's into the chaplain's powder-blackened hand. "Your damned toy will just spook Billy, if it don't go off and kill 'im outright when you climb in the saddle."

Private Wallace, who had been listening to the men discuss their plan, shoved himself forward.

"I'll go too, sir," Wallace said quickly. "We'll have a better chance of one of us getting through. Besides, if an Injun's gonna get me anyway, I'd just as soon it was standing up as holed up like a damned gopher. Oh, beg pardon, Parson."

"All right, Wallace," Wands said, amused that the youngster

would worry about swearing in front of a parson who could hold his own with a sailor in an argument. "You take my horse, son, and here's my pistol as well. Make sure you check your loads before you head out, there'll be no time to reload once you're away. God be with you, gentlemen."

The two men nodded and headed off to get the horses ready. Wands turned to peer out over one of the wagon beds and saw a lone figure in the distance hopping and waving his hands in the air. Wands picked up a pair of binoculars that had been tossed onto the wagon seat and focused them on the figure. It was a Sioux warrior, face streaked with black and yellow paint and naked but for a loin cloth and a dark blue jacket. The sun winked off of the jacket's brass buttons as the warrior danced about wildly and swung a hatchet in circles over his head. Wands recognized the cut of an officer's coat and knew instantly that Lieutenant Daniels would not be coming back. Wands reached out to a young private who was about to reload his Springfield and took the weapon from the man's grasp. Keeping his gaze fixed on the Indian cavorting in Daniels' jacket he reached into the private's cartridge box and withdrew a pair of paper cartridges. The first he ripped open with his teeth, spitting the soft lead bullet into the dirt as he poured the powder charge into the weapon. He ripped open the second cartridge and dumped in the powder, but this time he pushed the bullet into the muzzle after it and pounded all home with the ramrod. Wands snatched out the ramrod and tossed it to the private.

"Bastard thinks he's out of range, does he," Wands muttered. He slipped a cap onto the rifle's nipple and tugged the hammer to full cock. In one smooth movement he brought the rifle to his shoulder, squinted down the barrel, and squeezed the trigger. The blast was nearly deafening but as the gunsmoke cleared he could see the man in Daniels' jacket flopping in the dust like a grounded fish. "Dance to that tune, you son of a bitch!" Wands spat as he shoved the weapon back into the private's hands and stalked off to wait for sunset.

* * *

PRIVATE JOHN PETERS SQUINTED OFF INTO THE GATHERING darkness and brought his Springfield to half-cock. Before he could raise the piece to his shoulder, Lieutenant Wands put his hand on the barrel and pushed it gently down.

"Hold on a moment, Peters," Wands said quietly. Since the sun had begun to sink behind the mountains, the fire from the Indians had slackened and finally sputtered out, and, as dusk settled over the beleaguered party, the cicadas resumed chattering from a grove of cottonwoods down near the creek. Wands saw the dark figure moving toward them but something about it made him hesitate. He cupped his hands around his mouth and shouted out.

"Halt! Who comes there? Are you friend or foe?" The figure stopped suddenly.

"Wagh!" came a laconic reply, "What's your guess, soldier boy?"

Wands breathed a deep sigh of relief and Private Peters lowered his weapon with shaky hands, horrified that he'd come near to shooting a white man.

"Who are you?" Wands shouted back. "Advance friend and be recognized."

"I am Jim Bridger," a voice called out of the gloom. "But I doubt ye'll recognize me as we ain't been introduced."

Wands grinned at the reply and was delighted to see a large party of men coming up behind the old scout. Two companies of infantry destined for Fort Reno with an empty supply train were coming down the trail under the command of Captain Burrowes. This explained the sudden disappearance of their attackers, who had quietly melted away into the gathering darkness. Burrowes and his detachment were just coming down from Phil Kearny on a routine mission and had no idea that Wands and his people had been under attack. They had just happened to come along at the right moment and were surprised at the enthusiastic welcome when a chorus of cheering greeted their arrival.

Alexander Wands, a large smile on his face, saluted Bridger as the old scout passed into the camp. The lieutenant felt an instant relief of tension rolling down through his body like the rushing torrent of a rain-swelled creek. In a matter of a few seconds he had been transported from the depths of utter hopelessness to a feeling of relief and elation that bordered on giddiness. His head swam and his knees buckled slightly with the enormity of the moment. Wands reached out and put his hand on the iron rim of a wagon wheel to support himself.

"That was a close one, Peters," he whispered. "We damn near did for the Sioux what the rebs did for us when they shot old Stonewall at Chancellorsville."[5] The young private didn't reply, and Wands looked over to see that Peters had fainted dead away.

[5]General Thomas J. "Stonewall" Jackson (1824–1863): An aggressive and intelligent general, he fought magnificently at First Manassas (Bull Run), Front Royal, Winchester, Antietam, and Second Manassas. During the Battle of Chancellorsville of May 1863 Jackson was conducting a night reconnaissance when he was mistaken for the enemy and shot by one of his own sentries and died on May 10, 1863.

5

Wasuton wi
(Moon When Feathers Are Shed)

August 1866

An irregular, hollow chunking sound echoed and reverberated through the great pines that grew in thick confusion on the rocky slopes. The noise of axes all but drowned out the continuous roar of Peno Creek, which, except for the bellowing of elk and calls of birds, should have been the only sound to break the silence of these mountains. At odd intervals the chunking ceased, only to be followed by a labored creaking, a loud crack, and the whooshing thump of a tree as it toppled to crash among its fellows. A short spell would follow in which the voices of white men could be heard chattering in their strange tongue and laughing as if they enjoyed the labor of ripping apart the forests.

"Hunh." Crazy Horse spat into the dirt near where he was lying. "They will do the same to the buffalo as they do to the trees. They will slash and cut and kill them until nothing is left for us. If we don't fight them now there will be so little game left that we will not have the strength to fight them."

Dull Knife got up slowly and turned to start back toward where they had tethered the horses. Crazy Horse just glanced up for a moment but went back to watching the skittering flashes of blue and white as below them the soldiers, working in their shirt sleeves, continued to hack away at the tall pines. American Horse, who was crouched down next to Crazy Horse, looked over at his friend and then got up to follow the Cheyenne over the slight rise to the horses.

"Where are you going, Dull Knife?" he asked as he caught up to his friend.

"I've seen enough, brother."

"So, are you going to join us in this war?" American Horse asked eagerly. "How many warriors do you think you can bring with you?" The Lakota hurried alongside, casting glances back over his shoulder at Crazy Horse and at the lumber camp at the base of the slope. Dull Knife suddenly stopped short and American Horse stumbled into him, his arrows clattering together in their quiver as the younger warrior caught himself up. As the two men extricated themselves Dull Knife looked into his friend's eyes.

"Listen to me, American Horse," he said finally. "I'm not getting involved in this fight and I think you know why. No, don't interrupt, I'm going to tell you something. This nonsense you're spouting about trees and buffalo is just that, nonsense. It sounds more like something that Red Cloud would say and I have no time for his blustering. If you think that I will go to war because Red Cloud says so, you are very wrong."

American Horse had forgotten about the incident at French Pete's camp. The anger that shone now in Dull Knife's eyes brought the affair sharply into focus for a moment and he drew back. Dull Knife was a proud man, a great warrior, and never had a man counted coup on him and lived. If Dull Knife, Black Horse, and the others had been armed at the time, he felt sure, the incident would have only ended in great bloodshed. Red Cloud had made a serious error in that exchange. He'd let his pride and temper get the better of him and come close to making deadly enemies of a fierce tribe of warriors. The younger man's face clouded over as he thought about how he might overcome Dull Knife's reservations about the coming war. They really needed the Cheyenne and Arapaho if they were going to do this thing right.

He looked back toward where Crazy Horse still lay watch-

ing the *wasichu* and the thought of Red Cloud's ineptitude
made him suddenly very angry. *Has!* He hated having to clean
up the messes Red Cloud left in his wake. The man was sometimes impossible, like a bull buffalo whose eyesight was failing. He charged at every noise and damaged even his own
breed. It had been a near thing even getting Crazy Horse to
join up with this plan after the incident with Black Buffalo
Woman.[1] It was proving harder than he had imagined to get
the various tribes to join in their cause. Petty bickering and
backstabbing among the peoples had become so bad and gone
on so long that it was impossible to get anyone to trust anyone
else. Red Cloud had made more than his share of enemies.
How they'd ever manage to smooth things out long enough to
be able to fight a war was sometimes beyond him. He breathed
out loudly in exasperation and turned to Dull Knife, who had
been watching him closely.

"Look, my brother," he said in a lowered, reasoning tone,
"I know this is difficult for you. Red Cloud is a hard man to
endure, he is so full of himself. But, in this case I believe what
he counsels is the right thing to do. The only thing we can
do. If we don't fight the *wasichu* now, when can we fight
them? How can we hope to keep this country for ourselves
and our children if we let these thieves tear it up as they are
doing now right in front of our eyes?" He paused and raised
his hands in a gesture of entreaty.

"Join us in this fight, Dull Knife. It is not only for us Lakota
that we would make war on these whites but for the Arapaho
and the Cheyenne and all of the peoples who have lived on
this land since the beginning times. Look at Crazy Horse. He,

---

[1]Black Buffalo Woman was Crazy Horse's great love, and a niece of Red
Cloud. Red Cloud apparently did not approve of the match and, while Crazy
Horse was away from the tribe, arranged a marriage between Black Buffalo
Woman and a man named No Water. Crazy Horse, returning to discover that
his love had been married off, was enraged. There was a lot of bad blood
between all parties afterward. In later years Crazy Horse and Black Buffalo
Woman would have an illicit affair, which ended with Crazy Horse being
shot and badly wounded by No Water.

of all people, should have no love for Red Cloud, and he doesn't, but he does have a great love for the people. He knows that he must put aside his quarrel with one man so that many shall be helped in this struggle."

Dull Knife, who had listened patiently to his friend, reached out and touched him gently on the arm.

"Look, American Horse," he said patiently. "I know what you're trying to do here. Believe me, I would as soon fight alongside you and Crazy Horse as any of my own young men. You are great warriors and you have both ridden with the Cheyenne in our fights against the whites. I honor you as a warrior. But I will not fight Red Cloud's war for him." Dull Knife shook his head slowly.

"I have a bad feeling about this war, American Horse. I am not a young man anymore and I will tell you a few things that I have noticed and maybe you will understand why I am taking this stand. You claim the whites will destroy the buffalo and all the trees and perhaps you are right—they seem to be industrious in some things. But they are not alone in this. I myself have seen our cousins the Blackfeet kill more buffalo in a single day than they could eat in a year, taking just the tongue and the hump and trading the hides to the whites. Yes, it is the whites who buy these hides but Indians who have done the killing." He threw up his hands. "And this land we are standing on now is land we took from the Crows not so long ago. Will this war help them to get this land back, too? I do not think so." He paused for a moment. "Unless, of course, they join with the whites and ride against us.

"It isn't just the whites," Dull Knife went on in a pained voice, "who are making things hard for us. We are making things hard for ourselves. I do not know if you heard what Spotted Tail said to Red Cloud at Fort Laramie, but some of what he was saying makes sense. We may have to fight these people someday. I may have to fight them myself but I do not know if we can win. Red Cloud says, 'Let us make peace among ourselves and war against the whites,' but I ask you, what is it that he really wants? Peace among all of the tribes? Do you believe that when this war is over, if you win, that

things will be any better between all of us here? What does
Red Cloud care if the Cheyenne or Arapaho are killed in this
fight? What does he care if Hunkpapa or Sans Arc are killed?
Do you think he will mourn if his new friend Young Man
Afraid Of His Horses dies from the bullet of a wagon gun?
How many tears will he shed if his old enemies die fighting
this new enemy?" Dull Knife shook his head again. "No, old
friend, I will not fight Red Cloud's war for him. Perhaps we
will fight alongside each other again sometime." He smiled.
"I would enjoy that. But it will not be because Red Cloud says
we should."

American Horse was silent. He didn't know quite what to
say to Dull Knife, who had spoken to him not in anger but as
a father speaks to a beloved son. What if he was right? What
if Red Cloud's war on the whites was only a part of his plan?
What if this war was a way to allow the whites to kill his old
rivals while he gained battle honors at the same time? Red
Cloud was a crafty man, he knew. But could he be so petty?
American Horse found that hard to accept. And yet, behind
him, the axes of the whites still rang endlessly in the forests,
and every day more trains of wagons moved along the road.
The dust clouds had indeed become so thick in places that the
trees alongside the road appeared to be covered in dirty snow.
American Horse stood, not seeing his old friend, his mouth
open in thought. Everything had seemed so clear to him before
and now he was just not sure what was right. War had always
seemed to be a fairly simple thing. You fought to steal horses.
To gain honor. To protect your family. Now there was more
to it. Nothing anymore, it seemed, was as it had been.

"This one thing I will do for you, American Horse," Dull
Knife said finally as he slipped onto the back of his pony and
gathered the halter rope into his fist. "I will not try to keep
the other men from joining you. Many of them probably will.
Crazy Wolf, Dives Backwards, Two Moons, these men will
probably help you with this fight. I will not. I am taking my
people as far from here as I can for a while. The whites cannot
tell the difference between you and me and they give us talking papers to show to their people so they will not shoot at

us but how can you get close enough for them to look at the paper before they shoot you? Even if we do not join you they will think that we are with you and kill us anyway. I have started to move my people up into the mountains. Perhaps the *Mai yun* will help you win a great victory over these *wasichu*. But if they do not, then you come to my lodge and you will always be welcome." He raised his hand in salute, turned his pony away, and began the long trek toward his waiting people.

American Horse watched as his old friend disappeared into the forest and listened to the crash of another pine as it fell under the swinging axes.

HENRY BEEBE CARRINGTON HEARD THE CHUNKING OF AXES and gazed out from under the flap of the tent. The new fort, which was to be named in honor of General Phil Kearny, was taking shape nicely. The stands of trees at the pinery some six miles from the construction site were yielding beautiful long planks of smooth, fragrant pine. The steam sawmill was in operation and spitting out boards and beams with a screeching buzz which began at first light and lasted until it became too dim to safely operate the massive blades. Already a stout stockade of pine logs had been erected to mark off the perimeter of the fort. While the fort was not yet completed, it gave one a feeling of security to see the sharpened posts set snugly together to form a barrier eight foot high between the 18th Regiment and the surrounding country.

As some of the men continued to work on the stockade, others had already begun the construction of the buildings that would be necessary to a smooth administration of the Mountain District—warehouses, a headquarters building, barracks, blacksmith shop, armory, a powder magazine—and with luck and hard work they should be able to have livable quarters for all by the time the first snows began to fall. In the meantime most everyone was living in army tents—Sibley's and wedges—arranged neatly around the central parade ground, which had been mowed short and posted with signs warning all to KEEP OFF THE GRASS. Laramie's parade had been so

trampled by daily traffic that it was little more than a dust
bowl. While some of the men grumbled about it, Carrington
felt sure that they would thank him later for insuring that the
fort's interior would be a restful green island in an ocean of
dust. It would be a place to play croquet and baseball, to enjoy
regimental band concerts, to picnic. A place where the children
could play in safety while their mothers looked on from the
shaded comfort of surrounding porches. A cool breeze stirred
the flap, billowing out the tent's sides like the sails of a small
ship and filling the interior with the heavenly scent of freshly
mown grass, a welcome change from the stuffy odor of moldy
canvas everyone had grown to resent over the long weeks
preceding.

Carrington listened for a moment to the singsong of hand-
saws rip-ripping through pine, the banging of hammers, the
businesslike chattering of work parties as they set timbers,
raised beams, sighted down plumb lines, and tapped tenon and
mortise expertly into place. He got up from the folding camp
stool and pushed out from under the canvas to survey his domain. This work, he had found, much to his surprise, was
immensely satisfying, and he sometimes wondered if he would
have been more comfortable as an architect or city planner
than as a soldier. Carrington glanced up at the tiny dots that
stood silhouetted against the sky on Pilot Hill—sentries looking for anything out of the ordinary—then turned to peer at
the towering mass of Cloud Peak as the snow-covered mass
of stone was thrown into shadow from a passing cloud. For a
moment it was as if a similar cloud had passed over Carrington's spirit, for he was reminded of the enormity of the task
in front of him. There was so much work to be done, and there
were so few men available.

Sometimes it all but overwhelmed him. There were few officers left on whom he could now depend. Captain Haymond
and Lieutenant Phisterer, two of his old stalwarts, had been
transferred out by the War Department with no replacements
provided. It seemed so capricious. Pulled off for recruiting
duty, of all things! Captains Burrowes and Kinney had been
sent north to establish yet another fort some ninety miles away.

Lieutenant Daniels had been killed before he could even report for duty. As it was, they had become so shorthanded that everyone was required to serve in two or three different capacities. Captain Ten Eyck shuffled over to stand beside his commander, a document held loosely in his hand.

"Are you sure you want to say this precisely in this manner, Colonel?" Ten Eyck asked suspiciously. "I'm afraid that General Cooke may see this as a hard criticism of his command and take it rather badly. Might even see it as a personal attack."

"Tenedor," Carrington said with exasperation, "there is nothing personal about anything in this letter. It is a plain statement of the facts. What do you expect me to say to the man, all's well, don't bother about us, we're doing just famously? It would be a despicable lie and a disservice to these men out here." The colonel was trying to keep his voice down, but it was evident from the sudden quiet inside the large tent that the small staff was straining to overhear what the two officers were discussing. Carrington noticed the hush and suggested loudly to Ten Eyck that the two of them do a quick inspection tour of the fort. The last thing he wanted was to let slip any discouraging thoughts in front of the youngsters drafted for staff duty. Soldiers, he knew, were terrible gossips and any sensitive information would leak through the whole fort. Out of the tent and strolling alongside the uprights of the nearly completed stockade, the colonel waited until they were safely out of earshot of the soldiers. They had passed out through a gap in the southern end of the works and paused between the partially built commissary warehouse and the wagon park on Little Piney Creek.

"This is a terribly distressing situation we have here, Tenedor," Carrington said, removing his hat and running his fingers through his hair. He waved the hat in the direction of the fort. "The fact that we have to build this stockade should be evidence enough of that. Perhaps if General Cooke would consent to a tour of inspection he would readily see the state we're in. We're woefully short of officers and have already had to commit more than a third of the command to duties at Reno and to build the new fort up on the Big Horn." Carrington replaced his hat, held out his hands and began counting out the points on his fingers.

"In addition, we have escort duty for the emigrant trains as well as our own supply and wood trains, couriers to run, timber to cut, buildings to erect before the snow comes, animals to herd, hay to cut, corrals to build. We're all working night and day as it is and there's no relief in sight." The colonel threw up his hands. "Where does it all end, Tenedor? Under normal conditions we might manage this despite the strain on men and animals but, as you know, that's not the entire extent of the problem."

Ten Eyck looked off and up at the pickets atop Pilot Hill. The dark figures moved slowly against the skyline but the signal flag was nowhere to be seen. That was a good sign. All was quiet for now. His eyes drifted back down the slope to rest on the patch of ground near the base of Pilot Hill where fresh patches of turned earth were everywhere in evidence among the grass and wildflowers. There, just across the creek, more than a score of men had already been laid to rest. All had met violent, sometimes horrifying ends. Chaplain White had been a busy man since his arrival. First it was Henry Arrison, French Pete's partner, and a teamster named Burns. They were not long alone. Since their arrival here not a week had passed without some poor soul being carried solemnly through the lush grass of the bottoms and across the Little Piney to this rock-strewn and windswept slope. A pair of luckless miners had joined them just this past week. Ten Eyck hoped that God, at least, knew who all of these men were, for he certainly could not swear to their identities. In some cases the names scratched on the simple headboards were little better than guesses. The image of Lieutenant Daniels' butchered corpse still haunted his dreams, and even here, within a few steps of the stockade, with scores of heavily armed men within shouting distance, Ten Eyck suddenly felt exposed and vulnerable. An involuntary shudder rippled through his body. Supplies, ammunition, replacements. They were in need of all these things, to be sure, but what Tenedor Ten Eyck most wanted at that moment was a good strong drink.

MARGARET CARRINGTON GATHERED UP HER APRON AND USED it to open the door of the small oven that had been painstakingly assembled in their tent. After the disastrous fire in their quarters in Nebraska she was taking no chances and had insisted that special care was taken in making sure that the stove was placed on solidly packed earth, perfectly level, and with the stovepipe tight and without a single leak. A large space had been cleared from around the stove and everything of a flammable nature moved well away from it. Two leather buckets—one filled with sand, the other with water—were always kept close at hand.

The sweet scent of gingerbread wafted from the oven, and she pulled a small sheet of cookies out, slipped a fresh sheet in, and moved the finished batch to a table behind the tent. A light breeze sprang up and carried the odor of gingerbread off toward Laundress Row, where she knew Jimmy and Bobby, along with Bobby Wands, had taken Sallie Horton's pet antelope off for a visit to Mrs. Wands' servant Laura and Captain Ten Eyck's maid, whom everyone called Black Susan. George had followed the boys, saying that he'd keep them out of mischief, but Margaret suspected that he was more interested in Black Susan. It was likely that George hoped that the occasion of a visit by the colonel's boys would evince a motherly urge in Susan to feed the youngsters some of her famous pie, and he might profit by his presence.

Margaret slid the cookies off onto a towel laid out on the table, then straightened up and looked up at Cloud Peak towering above her. Sunlight flashed and sparkled on the snow-clad crags, which clawed at an intense blue sky. The sight never failed to take her breath away. Such incredibly beautiful country! Below the ever-present snowfields the mountainsides were black with forests. Majestic elk could be seen grazing peacefully in the verdant meadows. Below them the hillsides and valleys were lush and radiant. Wildflowers of blue, yel-

low, and purple waved and danced above thick grassy swards
and chokecherries, plums, and blackberries grew in profusion.
It looked and smelled, she thought, as close to Heaven as she
had ever experienced and it was painful to think how dangerously unlike Heaven this country really was. She could never
seem to reconcile the beauty of the country with the utter
savagery of the people who inhabited it. Nature could be so
cruelly deceptive. But that, it seemed to Margaret, was true of
almost everything in life. That which seemed to promise the
greatest joys so often brought one the deepest sorrows. She
thought of her children and how her pregnancies had been so
filled with hope and delight. Yet four of her children had been
taken from her in their earliest years, laid in their tiny graves
by what had seemed the simplest of maladies at the outset.
She thanked God that Jimmy and Bobby had been spared,
although they too, had been threatened by chills and fever.
Each time, as she mopped their brows through the watches of
the long nights, she had felt her stomach tighten and the old
griefs well up in her throat, certain that she could not bear
another loss so great. As she watched, a lone eagle soaring
above caught the current of a breeze and lifted effortlessly up
and away to disappear in the glare of the snowfields. Suddenly
Margaret felt a great emptiness and she doubted her strength
to turn and walk back to the tent.

In the course of their long journey she had learned, much
to her sorrow, that few of the officers under Henry held him
in very high esteem. While he had served honorably and well
as a colonel during the rebellion, his duties had excluded him
from the battlefield. Most of the men he commanded, however,
had been tested in the fire of battle and they wore their old
wounds, their memories of dead friends and shattered bodies,
like the robes and vestments of a fraternity. Theirs was a society more secret and exclusive than the Freemasons, and he
who had not shared their rites of passage, not been initiated
by the shedding of blood, was neither welcome nor worthy of
regard. It hurt her to see how some of the officers afforded
more respect to a common teamster than to their commander.
They had not displayed their contempt openly, refused to obey

orders, or indulged in any manifestations of insubordination. But she could sense it. She could hear the slight hesitancy in their voices and in their whispers when the colonel could not hear them. He was not one of them.

Why was it, she wondered, that the thing one desired most ardently so often proved so disastrous? She could see it now in Henry. He had so wanted this position. He had so long desired to be a professional soldier, a leader of men and a man who could help to shape history. Now that he had achieved that goal it seemed that the world conspired to destroy him. The supplies he had been promised had never been available. The Indians were not agreeable, as he had been assured. Instead they raided the livestock, murdered their couriers, butchered young officers from ambush. The letters he wrote, the reports he submitted to Washington and Omaha, were ignored. The officers he needed were reassigned. And still he was expected to do the job he had been given. In the space of a few weeks she had watched in compassionate and loving silence as his hairs began to show gray, the wrinkles on his brow became ever more deeply etched, and dark circles formed under his eyes. She had lain next to him in the coolness of their flimsy canvas home listening as he tossed and mumbled in troubled sleep. She had watched him through half-closed eyes as he rose before dawn every morning and slipped out of the tent as if by his diligence alone he could forestall whatever disaster lurked in the predawn gloom. Always she waited until he had left before she allowed herself the useless luxury of tears. She had never seen him so alone, so friendless.

But she knew him for what he was. Her husband was a decent and intelligent man, a leader who cared deeply for his soldiers, who wept secretly in their tent when a man was buried. Henry Carrington did not want to fight a war, but he was determined to accomplish the task he had been given. If it meant fighting, then that, too, he would do with every ounce of strength he possessed. He was not like Grant, who had sent so many thousands to needless deaths at Cold Harbor, the Wilderness, and Petersburg. Her husband believed in victory but would not sacrifice the lives of his men needlessly to attain it. He had laid down strict rules for engaging the enemy, though the reckless young firebrands saw his caution as timidity. He had the wisdom to recognize Jim Bridger's as the voice of experience in this wild country and it was Bridger to whom Henry listened, from whom he learned. Margaret's gaze drifted across the wall of mountains that loomed above her and wondered where in that wilderness Bridger was now. Henry had sent him north to accompany Burrowes and Kinney, and she hoped this mission would not keep him long from Henry's side. Henry needed Bridger by him. Captain Ten Eyck was a good man, loyal to a fault and a good friend to the colonel, but Henry could never accept the subordinate officer as a peer. And Tenedor had become a bit too fond of the bottle of late. Margaret and Henry were themselves not abstainers, but it had become evident to them both that Ten Eyck was becoming immoderate. It made him a poor choice of confidant in a situation that grew ever more perilous. Jim Bridger, safely beyond the exigencies of the Army, was the only man who could fill this role. He was not, Margaret admitted, an educated man. Hardly the sort of man with whom Henry, who had been President Lincoln's bodyguard, who had worked for the great Washington Irving, was accustomed to consorting. But Bridger, in his own rough, unpolished way, was as much a gentleman and as good a man as any Margaret had ever known. He was easily more honest than most of the politicians in Washington and as knowledgeable in his own field as her own father was in his.[2] Jim Bridger was in Margaret's estimation the only man on whom Henry could depend. The only man on whom he could safely depend. She missed him terribly. Not for her own sake but for Henry's.

[2]Margaret Sullivant Carrington was from an unusually distinguished family. Her grandfather established the town which became Columbus, Ohio, while her father was the founder of Ohio State University. Numbered among her relations were General Irvin McDowell, Chief Justice Marshall, and President James Madison.

6

Canwapegi wi
(Moon When The Leaves Turn Brown)

September 1866

The first snow of the season spread a light dusting of white along the slopes of the Bighorns and settled on the wild roses that nestled shivering in their tangled thickets alongside clear-rushing freshets. The north wind slipped over the mountains, rushed headlong through the pines, and slid down into the valley of the Pineys to whisper its chill warning of heavier snows to come. Along Goose Creek and beyond the Bozeman Trail the tall grass so lush and green a week before had ripened and faded. It rolled and churned in deep amber swells like a restless, golden sea. Small clouds of insects floated idly above the grasses and drifted with each breeze that rippled through the bobbing seedheads. Against a brilliant azure dome a lone hawk rode a rising column of air, spiraling upward in ever-widening circles as soft, white puffs of cloud glided lazily across the boundless sky, paused, tumbled onto their brothers, melted, re-formed, and slid toward the gently curved horizon.

Leviticus Carter leaned forward in the saddle and crossed his wrists over the pommel. There was fresh snow in the mountains. He could smell it on the breeze. It hadn't gotten this far down yet but it wouldn't be long and then any thoughts of cutting hay would be wishful thinking. Carter watched with satisfaction as the mowing machines cut wide swaths through the grassy plain. It was a fine deal getting this contract to supply hay to Fort Phil Kearny. Not as wildly profitable as a gold strike but a darn sight more certain. Carter chewed on a stem of grass and nodded, listening to the chinking of chains, the creak of harness, and the whirring of the machines' blades as teams of mules drew them steadily along. The smell of fresh-cut hay was as welcome to him as the smell of coffee on a cold morning. The mowers looked to him like the paddlewheels of riverboats churning up a river of gold. The men were in good spirits with the sun shining brightly and a pleasant wisp of a breeze to cool them as they labored in the fields. It had been an especially productive day. The mowing machines had functioned well with but one minor breakdown to slow progress. With any luck, and if the weather held like it had, they would finish off this section in a couple of days and could then move everything farther down toward Lake De Smet and start on that business there. At $168 per ton he would prefer to get as much hay in as possible before it dried completely and required more work to achieve the same weight. His right hand moved as of its own accord to wave away a persistent horsefly, then settled back onto its mate.

As he watched, one of the mowing machines lurched suddenly. There was the distinctive shivering crack of splintering wood and the high-pitched screech of rending metal as the machine ground to a halt near the top of a small rise. *Damn!* Carter thought as he trotted over to find out what the damage was. Carter slid out of the saddle and sauntered up to see what Edwards could tell him.

Frank Edwards, the bullwhacker operating the mower, had acted quickly and reined the mules in before much damage was done, but a quick look showed that a pair of struts had swung down just far enough to gouge into the earth and bend them into an unusable shape.

"Damned bolt's sheared off on the running gear, Levi," Edwards said matter-of-factly. "Ain't too bad yet. I figger Jose might could make us a new one an' straighten out them struts 'nough to get on with it."

Carter nodded as Edwards unhitched the team and led them off a few yards for a short break. A few minutes later Carter and Jose stretched out in the grass on their backs and peered up at the apparatus to see how it could be repaired. Jose, a grizzled man in his fifties with a filthy leather apron and a noticeable stutter, scratched his chin thoughtfully as he squinted up at the mangled metal struts, a dirty hand shielding his eyes against the brilliant sun. The effort scrunched up his face into a snaggletoothed smile and folded deep creases into the leathery skin at the corners of his eyes.

"Well, Levi," Jose drawled, "I mostly b-believe I can f-fix 'er if we can get a couple of the b-boys to haul 'er on up to the f-f-forge up yonder. We can cut us a new spar quick enough f-for the one that's splintered. Got a spare b-b-bolt. Couple of swats with a hammer an' she'll be runnin' again right as two-two-two r-rabbits."

Carter squinted up at the sun then glanced at the shadows that were beginning to lengthen around them and calculated that to haul the machine up the hill to their temporary corral would take more men than he could spare for the moment.

"All right, Jose," Carter said as he struggled to his feet and used his hat to dust himself off. "But I think what we'll do is let the boys finish up what they can today and when we break off for dinner we'll put everyone's shoulder to it and bring it up with us then. Figure you'll have enough light to work by if we call it quits by six of the clock?"

Jose didn't reply for a moment, and Carter was about to restate the question when he noticed that the blacksmith was not looking at him or the mower but was staring past him at the distant hills, his hooded eyes straining hard at something.

"Jose?"

"G-g-goddamnit, Levi," Jose said, scrambling to his feet. "The hell with the mower and dinner too. B-b-best call the boys in now and d-do it quick."

Carter wheeled around in time to catch a glimpse of the faint glimmer that had so caught Jose's attention. It was a small thing, little more than a flash of light reflected off a shiny surface on a hillside a half mile away, but Leviticus Carter knew enough to know that it meant trouble. Jose was already on his mule and moving at a trot toward the corral of freight wagons that had been parked in a tight circle on the top of a small hill. Frank Edwards quickly followed Jose's lead and was urging his team toward the corral, using his hat as a quirt. Carter didn't hesitate but swung into the saddle and yanked his revolver from its holster. He stuck the weapon into the air and squeezed off two quick shots just as Jose reached the corral and began frantically ringing the dinner triangle.

Everywhere work stopped in an instant as the mowers leapt from their machines to unhitch teams and scrambled up onto the backs of the offside lead mules. Every man had a weapon in his hand and was banging it on his mount's flanks to urge the teams back to the safety of the corral. The six large mowing machines were abandoned as everywhere men scurried back toward their hilltop camp. Satisfied that no one had been left behind, Carter wheeled his horse and galloped to the camp himself. That flash might be nothing at all but to ignore it was to court disaster.

Carter had no sooner slid from the back of his mount when his worst fears were confirmed. Peering out toward the hillside from which the flash had come, he now saw masses of mounted warriors spilling out along the edge of the forest. They began to fan out across the open plains and charge headlong toward his tiny corral with spearpoints and gun barrels glinting in the slanting rays of the sun. A cloud of dust rose up behind the oncoming hordes. There must be hundreds of them. Carter glanced around at his workers. He had eighty men. They were all well armed and already spread out behind the circled freight wagons awaiting the coming fight. Most of them, Carter knew, had served in the war. There were few greenhorns in his crew. But it would get hot, damn hot before long. He thumbed back the hammer of his Colt's and looked to see that the caps were firmly seated on each nipple.

"Stand fast, boys," he bellowed. "Hold your fire until you can pick your man out from the rest, then tend him proper. Make sure you keep your heads down. Aim low, boys, aim low!" A few moments later they could feel the earth begin to shake with the thunder of hooves pounding toward them. Carter noticed a small tinkling sound and looked up to see a lantern suspended on a wagon bow bouncing and vibrating as the trembling spread up from the ground. "Steady now!" A rattle of clicks rolled around the corral as hammers were brought to full cock. The riders were momentarily obscured by a wall of dust, churned up by racing hooves, moving inexorably across the prairie. Wild yips and screams floated above the dust.

"Steady, now! Fire away, boys! Give 'em hell!" The corral erupted in a sheet of flame and smoke as a torrent of riders swept up and around the trembling wagons like a rogue wave crashing around a rock jetty. The noise of battle rose to a crescendo as gunfire mingled with the frenzied yelps of warrors and the shouts of desperate men. The warriors surged past in a blur of horseflesh and fluttering feathers, spitting bullets and arrows into the small camp as they passed. The thundering diminished; dust and gunsmoke swirled through the wagon spokes and around men, mules and horses. Ramrods rattled against metal as powder and ball were rammed home. Hammers clicked back and trembling fingers slipped the tiny copper caps onto powder-blackened nipples. Curses mixed with coughs as the acrid smoke clawed at throats parched and raw. The earth again began to shake and hammers clicked back to full cock.

"South side, boys! Steady now, here they come again!" The world grew black with smoke and noise and the riders swept back past their prey, screaming and shooting as they came. Jose flinched as a feathered shaft thunked into the water keg he was leaning against. He whirled about and sent a ball into the curtain of dust from which the arrow had come, cursing his luck and the fact that two dollars a day hardly seemed enough for this kind of work.

BY THE TIME THE SUN SETTLED BEHIND THE MOUNTAINS LEviticus Carter had realized that the breeze that cleared the smoke from each assault was blowing steadily from the northwest. It meant that it carried with it not only the smoke but the sound of the fight—away from Fort Phil Kearny and support. They were on their own. Two of his people were already dead and a third so badly wounded that he doubted the man would see the rising of the sun. If the wind held steady, it was a sure bet that no one could know of their situation unless someone could carry the word back. He was equally sure that without help there would be a sight more of his people killed tomorrow. Someone would have to try to make a dash for it, but as scared as his men appeared he doubted any would be bold enough to try it. Even if they did manage to hold out against the Sioux, Carter mused darkly, they were losing valuable time. Six of his machines were already wrecked and with the cutting season drawing rapidly to a close every minute they delayed was money from his hay-cutting contract lost. He was damned if he'd let the Sioux cost him any more than they already had. Carter strode into the center of the corral and placed his hands on his hips.

"Boys," he announced in a gruff roar. "I'll pay a full five hundred dollars to the man who'll sell out for Kearny and bring a few of the boys up to help. Any takers?"

The blacksmith, wiry, near-toothless Jose, wiped his overlarge hands on his apron, sauntered up to Carter, and spat into the dirt between his boots. He stripped off his apron, tossed it aside, and held out a grimy hand.

"By G-God, Levi!" Jose stuttered. "I mostly expect I c-c-could paddle my own canoe fer a b-b-b-brick that size! Lemme have yer pistol and stand away, sir." Carter nodded, slipped the revolver into the blacksmith's belt, and took Jose's extended hand in both of his.

"Well, good luck to you, Jose," Carter said with a grim smile. "Wait'll it comes full dark before you go and you'll have every penny from me with thanks."

"Well, g-g-good luck be d-damned, Levi," Jose said. "I'd rather a g-g-good horse if you d-don't mind." Several of the men laughed at this, fear and nervous tension making the weakest of jibes hilarious.

"Fair enough, Jose," Carter said. "You take my mare. Lay down and let her have her head and she'll win you through.

She likes nothing better than to poke through the rubbish behind Liz Wheatley's cookhouse. God help the buck who tries
to stay 'er from that."

LIEUTENANT JOHN ADAIR WAS AS RELIEVED TO SEE LEVITI-
cus Carter's people as they were him. The blacksmith, Jose,
had come into Fort Phil Kearny after midnight, having taken
a full four hours to travel seven miles, so heavy with Indians
was the intervening ground. The nervous sentries would almost certainly have shot at him, but Jose was firing his revolver into the air and yelling at the top of his lungs as he
galloped the final hundred yards into the post. He had had
several narrow scrapes with small groups of warriors behind
him and was desperate to insure that the gate to the stockade
was open. Luckily the sentries recognized him. While Levi
Carter's proffered fee had seemed almost too good to be true
when made, Jose had quickly concluded that he had earned
every damn cent of it and more. Jose also made a silent oath
to himself never to volunteer again for such a job, cash money
or no. What hair the Sioux didn't get, he decided, would soon
be purely white with the worry of it. Fortunately the discharge
of Levi's borrowed revolver as he rode into the fort had had
the desired effect, and a large knot of soldiers in various states
of undress were awaiting his arrival just inside the stockade.
   Colonel Carrington, who had taken care to don his tunic
and boots, was just buckling on his own revolver when Jose
was ushered in to his presence in the headquarters tent. Carrington listened politely as Jose spelled out Carter's situation,
then turned to issue instructions to Lieutenant Adair, who happened to be the duty officer for the evening. It had taken a bit
longer than he wanted for Adair to assemble the relief party.
But men are never at their best in the wee hours of the morning, especially when saddling horses by lantern light, slipping
bridles over twitching, stubborn ears, and trying to work small
buckles with fumbling, sleep-stiffened fingers. The corral was
the stage for a surrealistic play in which actors yawned,
coughed, and cursed, blew stuffed noses out through their fin-

gers, and wiped the residue on rough coat sleeves. Horses snorted and stamped, their steamy breath mingling with that of the soldiers. The cold night air was filled with a cacophony of noise—the jingling of curb chains and bits, the scuffling of boots, and the dull slap of cinch straps and stirrup leathers against warm horseflesh. Wooden stirrups clunked together as saddles were slung over blanketed mounts. By the time the detail was assembled and moving away from the fort the night was melting into a formless, misty gray and a thin aura of light that blurred the distinction between pink and orange revealed in silhouette the irregular black mass of the eastern horizon.

As his detachment moved across the plain, Lieutenant Adair could now see some of the mowers waving their hats with joy at their appearance. For miles around the plain had been consumed by fire, small tendrils of smoke still spiraling lazily into the morning mist. A huge, red-orange disk of a sun had erupted from the blackened plain, giving the illusion that it had scorched off the earth as it rose. Now Adair could see the remains of the mowing machines—charred skeletons that had first been splintered by hatchets before being heaped with hay and set aflame. But what most arrested his attention were the riders scattering along the surrounding ridgelines. Splashed with light by the newly risen sun, they stood out in stark relief against the black hillsides, hundreds of nearly nude warriors on horseback cantering and waving weapons in the air. Flashes of light glinted off of naked steel. Feathers danced crazily in the slight breeze, which carried with it the faint echoes of taunts and jeers. Adair felt the hairs on the back of his neck rise, and his stomach twisted behind the pistol belt cinched securely around his waist.

Since they had arrived, in July, the lieutenant had lost count of the times they had ridden out against the Sioux. But this was somehow different. Usually the Sioux were like phantoms. They huddled along the roadsides waiting for the lone rider, the unwary courier, the careless prospector and his partner. They lurked in small bands just beyond the light of the campfires of the wood parties waiting for the logger who walked a few paces too far out to drop his trousers. In predawn hours they would slip in among the horses and cattle, cutting them out and driving them off into the hills, whooping and yipping as they went.

Always the Army gave chase. With too few men and too few horses they careened over the rugged terrain, always too far behind. But still they would doggedly pursue the enemy, throwing leaden balls and curses after the Indians until, miles later, the horses slowed to an unsteady walk, breathing heavily, foam dripping from their muzzles and oozing out from under sweat-soaked saddle blankets. And always it seemed the reward was the same. They recovered a lame mule and passed a winded horse collapsed into the brush. They retrieved the ripped remains of their comrades, left to look less like men than inexpertly butchered meat buzzing with flies, mouths open wide in silent screams, eyes staring sightless into the void. Then came the long, dispiriting ride home, with sore backs, wounded friends, and shattered hopes. It was enough to drive any man to madness. You wanted to lash out and kill something, anything. And now this.

Lieutenant Adair cast an uneasy glance over his shoulder at the men who followed him across the blackened plain. He had forty men with him but only nine were mounted, the rest being wedged tightly into army freight wagons. The men, a few of whose faces had taken on the pale, greenish cast so common among novice sailors, clutched at the rough sides of the wagons and swayed to absorb the shock as the ungainly vehicles lurched and jolted along the uneven ground. Scanning the horizon, Adair counted hundreds of warriors and felt his bowels rumble in protest. Never had he seen so many of them gathered in one place. He felt his mouth go suddenly dry and wanted nothing so badly as to be within that tiny corral of wagons silhouetted on the top of the small hill just ahead of him. He tugged open the flap of his holster to slip the heavy revolver out into his grasp and was comforted by the weight of it. If they had delayed but another hour the Sioux would have seen them coming up miles back. It would have been nothing for the Indians to slip in between them and the mowers just back of the last rise. Adair swallowed hard. It didn't bear thinking of.

YOUNG MAN AFRAID OF HIS HORSES SAT COMFORTABLY ON the back of his pony. He had slipped his right leg over the animal's back and was leaning forward, his elbow resting on his knee and his chin cradled in his palm. It was odd to watch the bluecoats coming up across the prairie. From this distance they appeared so small and insignificant, it seemed like one man could race down among them and crush them like so many ants. He wondered if they had actually managed to kill any of them the day before. It had been such a confusing scene it was hard to tell if you actually hit anything. He liked to think that at least a few of his arrows had gone home. The very thought was as satisfying as a good meal would be to a hungry man. He looked up to see Crazy Horse trotting easily up the slope, the mummified remains of a red-tailed hawk bouncing in his loose hair, his body dotted with paint to represent hailstones.

"*Haiye*, Crazy Horse!" he exclaimed. "Did you see us give those *wasichu* a whipping?"

Crazy Horse eased up alongside of him and looked down at the line of soldiers who were just moving into the circle of the mowers' wagons below. His lips tightened for a moment and Man Afraid could see the muscles of his jaw twitching.

"I was too busy to watch your people," Crazy Horse said without looking at Man Afraid. "It looks to me like there are quite a few of the whites left down there. I don't see any dead men scattered around their little wagon fort. How many exactly did you kill?"

"Well, I don't know exactly. A few of them, I'm sure. We also burned their wagons that cut the grass and stole many of their mules. *Hehehe!* It's been a bad day for them, I can tell you that. How did your people fare?"

"About the same," Crazy Horse grunted without much enthusiasm. "Two of the soldiers were struck but I can't say that they were killed. We ran off a number of their mules and Low

Dog's party stampeded a small herd of buffalo through their cattle and ran them off into the hills. Red Leaf is supposed to be stealing more of their animals at the fort right now." He shrugged. "It's something, I guess."

"Something, you guess! *Makteka!*" Man Afraid doubled over laughing and shaking his head. "You're a sour one, I'll tell you. We ram a stick up the *wasichu onze* and you say 'I'll bet that tickles!' That's good! Hah!"

Crazy Horse didn't say anything but sat watching the small camp below them as Man Afraid slapped at his thigh in appreciation of his own cleverness. Below them the whites scurried about inside the small corral, the soldiers spreading out among the grass cutters and shoving their rifle barrels out over the beds of the wagons. Some of them were digging holes in the ground like gophers and he knew that they would lie down in these holes to shoot. Crazy Horse looked over at Man Afraid and wondered if the man was smart enough not to venture another assault on the whites when they had had a chance to ready themselves. To attack them in that position would be foolish as nothing could come of it but the deaths of good warriors for no reason. As he was mulling this over another thought occurred to him.

"Man Afraid," he said, half-distracted, "what is different about the whites this time? Have you noticed anything?"

"Aside from the fact that we didn't kill all of them? I don't know, what are you trying to ask?"

"You know how every time we fight them the soldiers come out from the fort to give chase, right? And always they ride horses."

"Not very well they don't." Man Afraid snorted, still enjoying his little joke. "Some of them bounce up and down so badly they look like a beaver trying to mount a rabbit. What of it?"

"Didn't you see how the soldiers came this time?" Crazy Horse went on trying to make his point, although sometimes he despaired of explaining anything to Man Afraid. It was annoying how thick the man seemed sometimes. "A few of

them are riding their horses but most are in the wagons. Do
you see what this means?"

"What," Man Afraid laughed, "that their butts are too sore
to ride horses anymore?"

Crazy Horse fought down the temptation to shove Man
Afraid off of his pony. As far as he was concerned war was
a serious thing. *Wakan* was the best way he could describe it,
and he found that he had come to resent men like Man Afraid
and his friends, who treated war as a great sport with no more
significance than a game of hoops. Sometimes the thought of
having to share battle alongside such louts made him feel
tainted, and often he felt compelled after a fight to go off into
the mountains alone to cleanse himself. He gritted his teeth
and tried to concentrate on the subject at hand.

"No, no, no!" he insisted. "It means two things. First, it
means that you can depend on the soldiers always trying to
save other whites no matter how many of us there are. Second,
it means that their animals are getting weaker. Their horses
are used to eating corn and there is little or no corn for them
at the fort. That's why these people are out here cutting the
grass—to feed their horses in the winter. Our ponies grow
weaker in the winter but the *wasichu* horses will always be
weaker still."

"What?"

Man Afraid stared at Crazy Horse, a blank look of puzzle-
ment on his face. So what was this strange Hunkpatila trying
to tell him? So the whites always sent soldiers. So the soldiers'
horses were weak. Now that they had destroyed the grass-
cutting machines and burned off the grass their horses would
have even less to eat in the winter. It didn't take a *Wicasa
Wakan* to see that. He shook his head. The tales about Crazy
Horse must be true. He was a very strange man. Man Afraid
shook his head and slipped astride his pony. He looked again
at Crazy Horse, who seemed not even to see him anymore,
then nudged his pony with his heel. Crazy Horse was dreaming again and Man Afraid decided he had better things to do.
He headed the pony toward a group of his friends who were
flashing their buttocks at the whites and yelling insults. Let

this strange man brood about whatever it was that he brooded about. Young Man Afraid Of His Horses concluded that would rather join his friends and have a little fun.

As Man Afraid's pony picked its way down the hillside, Crazy Horse continued to study the whites below him. There was something to be learned here. If they had seen the blue-coats coming out from the fort earlier they could have killed all of them with hardly any trouble at all. But once they let them get into a small group, especially if they had wagons to hide behind or time to dig holes, then it was a different story. He turned these thoughts over in his mind and decided that he would discuss them with Hump and American Horse. He wasn't certain but it seemed possible that there might be a way to turn the soldiers' style of fighting against them and win a great victory. If a man would hunt the antelope or the bear he must know his prey intimately. He must know where his prey hunts and what he eats. He must know when he moves and how. Where he lives and how he fights. How the female protects her young. A good hunter must see the world through the eyes of his prey. If a man did not know his animal prey his family would surely starve. If a man did not understand his human enemy his family might well be de-stroyed. War was more than a foolish game.

The hollow chattering of laughter drifted uphill with the breeze and he looked down to see Young Man Afraid Of His Horses standing on the back of his pony. Man Afraid was bent over double and flapping the tail of his breechclout in the air to expose his buttocks to the whites. A small puff of dust spurted up on the hillside well below Man Afraid and his friends followed by the faint boom of a rifle from down below. For a fleeting moment Crazy Horse found himself almost wishing that one of the bluecoats had a rifle which would shoot far enough to put a bullet in Man Afraid's buttocks. It would serve the fool right.

IN THE DIM, GRAY HALF-LIGHT OF DAWN, RIDGWAY GLOVER knelt in a springy bed of fallen pine needles, the warmth of his knees melting away the frost that ever more frequently formed in tiny crystals during the night watches. A wafer-thin blanket of snow had fallen during the night, but the air had been so still that it filtered down in nearly a straight line from the clouds and left huge dark rings of pine needles directly beneath the trees. As soon as the sun peeked over the mountains, what little snow there was would vanish like a dream. Despite the damp cold his agile fingers moved rapidly over every interior surface of his odd-looking portable darkroom. The weak light was no impediment, as Glover had replayed this ritual countless times and, at need, could do it in perfect darkness by touch alone. His fingertips glided effortlessly across every carefully packed item of the pram, checking the stoppers in bottles of chemicals, twisting the small brass tabs that swiveled to lock various components into place. They tightened the brass-buckled leather straps that secured the virgin plates in their assigned slots. They slid across the smooth, oiled surfaces of rosewood and mahogany. He pressed gently to insure that the tiny band-metal leaf springs retained just the proper tension on compartment lids and tested the brass clasps that served to lock the compartments shut. Everything was secure. He was ready to go.

Glover had an ambitious plan of views that he wanted to take over the next day or two. There were a number of officers at the fort whose likenesses he wanted to capture around the newly completed stockade and the nearly finished officers' quarters. If done right, a few such views could bring a pretty penny from the papers back East. The grim aftermath of the war had left the Eastern public in a sour, despairing mood, and his friends back at the *Philadelphia Photographer* had written that there was a perfect hunger for anything that spoke to the public of new frontiers and fresh starts in an untamed and unsullied wilderness. It had also occurred to him that, if the photographs came out well, most of the officers would be happy to add a few double eagles to his coffers for a good *carte de visite* or two. But this plan required that he manhandle the wheelbarrow-like photographer's cart over some fairly rugged ground in getting back to the fort. The last thing he wanted was for something to jar loose and rattle about the interior of the pram or, worse yet, for the cyanide solution or glacial acetic acid to spill over and contaminate the whole shooting match. As it was his stocks of chemicals were about used up and it would likely be October before the additional supplies he had ordered came up with a train of medical stores that had been shipped out of Fort Kearney in Nebraska. Thus whatever chemicals and plates he had remaining would have to be handled with special care.

Glover knew he was in a bit of a stick. His funds had quickly run out soon after his arrival at Fort Phil Kearny and it was only through the good offices of Colonel Carrington and Alex Wands that he had been able to get a job working with the loggers in the pinery. For a man of his wiry frame he was remarkably strong and found that swinging an ax came naturally. In addition to making enough money to keep himself and to replenish his dwindling supplies, Glover found to his surprise that he actually enjoyed the work. He also enjoyed the rough company of the men in the two wood camps that supplied the building needs of the fort.

With his easy ways and wry sense of humor, Ridgway Glover made friends easily, and he didn't mind being the subject of much good-natured ribbing. He had earned a reputation as a bit of an eccentric. Intelligent and well read, he had spent some wonderful evenings in the company of Henry Carrington discussing natural science and philosophy. But he also had a common touch, unprepossessing and a bit naive, which endeared him to nearly all of the soldiers and civilians he had come in contact with. Generous with what little money he had, he was an eager and uncritical companion who always had a ready smile and a kind word. He was a good listener when his mind wasn't drifting off on a tangent. He was given to dreamy, vacant looks and could frequently be seen tripping over his own feet or bumping into things, so preoccupied was he with otherworldly thoughts.

"He's a babe-in-the-woods," Baldy Brown had once said to J. B. Gregory.

"True enough, Mr. Brown," Gregory replied. "But the genuine article and no shine to 'im."

Brown had nodded in agreement. Glover was a likable fellow and had, in effect, been adopted by many of the men, who looked at him almost like a pet or a child, a source of fond amusement, but in serious need of looking after.

The two wood camps where Glover had found his current employment were located about six miles west of the fort in a thick stand of timber bounded by North and South Piney Creeks and Spring Creek in such a way that the men took to calling the place Piney Island. With its ramrod-straight pines reaching toward the sky one hundred feet up, the "island" took on the appearance of an open-air cathedral. It was, to Glover's critical eye, a primordial paradise whose effect was not lessened by the hum of activity that announced the arrival of civilization in this arboreal wilderness. Glover particularly enjoyed his stay at the camps in the early mornings. The mist still hung wraithlike in the majestic pines and he could listen to the sounds that had filled this place for uncounted centuries, the breathless rushing of snow-fed creeks as they crashed and bubbled over moss-smooth stones, and the tentative whistling of birds as they ruffled up their sleep-matted feathers and prepared to begin the endless quest for insects. Countless squirrels skittered recklessly up and down the rough-barked pines, chattering loudly at each other in the fierce competition for pine nuts to see them through the coming winter. All too soon the scents of pine tar and dew were joined by the aromas of woodsmoke, of boiling coffee and bacon curling in heavy, cast-iron skillets. The chatter of squirrels was then masked by the deep-throated mumblings of men roused from hard-earned sleep and the chinking of tin cups against fire-blackened coffeepots. In an hour these domestic clatterings would in their turn be replaced by the rhythmic chunking of axes and the chuff-chuffing of J. B. Gregory's steam sawmill, which had recently been moved up to the pinery.

For some odd reason Glover found himself mesmerized by the shimmering disk of the huge sawblade as it buzzed and screeched through thousands of feet of lumber each day. Sawdust billowed out from the whirring blade in a dull, golden cloud to settle on the forest floor like gilded snow through which the sawyers waded in their heavy boots. His photographer's eye composed this view and that and tried to determine how odd it would look if done during the heat of the day. The sawyers would appear to be laboring in new-fallen snow in their shirtsleeves. Sawdust clung to every exposed surface and the pungent, sweet smell of bleeding pine permeated the atmosphere.

"Way-hey, Brigham! Headin' out for Deseret today?"

Glover looked up to see Gregory himself grinning down at him, a tin mug of coffee gripped in his huge paw. The fact that Glover's pram resembled the Mormons' favored handcarts had earned him the nickname "Brigham Young," which newly promoted Corporal Fessenden, who had befriended Glover, implied was done as much to irk Jim Bridger as to have the mickey out of Glover.

"Good morning, J. B.," Glover replied brightly. "Thought I might get a few last views of the 'shoulder straps' before the snow settles in for the winter. Once my new supplies get up I suspect I will have more than enough opportunity to go snow-blind around here."

"That's the fact, Ridgway," Gregory said, holding the mug up before his nose to bask in the scented steam. "I think I might hold off for another day though, were I you. The blame Sioux been giving Carrington one hell of a fit the last day or so and it would not do to bet against their hand. It being Sunday the colonel's given us the day off and we'll not be sending any wagons back into Kearny today. I for sure would feel better if you spent another day here with us coffee coolers and head on in tomorrow."

Glover just smiled and shook his head. "Things to do, J. B. Things to do. Look at that sky, won't you. We'll surely have a good snow tonight and I'll play hell pushing this damned cart through that or, if it warms afterward, through the mud which will surely be all that's left of the Wood Road."

"Oh, pushing be damned, Glover, ye addlepated idiot," Gregory laughed. "We'll just heave your silly cart into one of

the wagons and ye can ride along like a gentleman and not
even get your boots mucky. That pretty blond hair of yours is
just too large a temptation to Red Cloud's bucks right now.
Long as you've let it get I swear they'll be happy to trim it
for you."

"J. B., you're starting to sound like little Frank Fessenden
worrying about my hair. I tell you this lovely handcart is as
good as a policy with New York Life. The Sioux will take
one look at it and give me a wide berth figuring me for a
Mormon."

"Well, if you'd have said moron, Ridgway, I'd not argue
for that'd sure be my judgment. Around these parts when it
comes to hair, them'll take who have the power and them'll
keep who can. I sure as hell hope you can keep." Gregory
shook his head. "Damned shame about Sam Curry ain't it?"

Glover's mention of Fessenden, the young trumpeter, had
put Gregory in mind of the regiment's bandmaster, Sergeant
Curry, who had suddenly sickened and died only days before
the attack on Levi Carter's hay cutters.

"The hell of the thing is that so far he's the only man we've
buried who ain't been served to Kingdom by the damned
Sioux. I tell you, Ridgway, it's a near thing wandering about
loose out here." Gregory shuddered. "Too damned chilly this
morning. Come on, Brigham, I need some more coffee if I'm
going to enjoy my day of rest."

Gregory headed toward one of the two blockhouses that had
been built for defense against Sioux raiding parties. About a
mile to the south, at the other end of the island, or the "lower
cutting" as it was called, a similar set of blockhouses provided
a refuge for the loggers at that camp. By now most all of the
loggers and the soldiers at the "upper cutting," detailed to provide both labor and defense, had gathered around the cook
fires, where a leisurely Sunday breakfast was simmering. A
small cloud of steam from their warm breath hung over the
group of men, who huddled in their greatcoats and stamped
their feet against the cold. This week out Company H had
supplied the guard detail and Gregory knew that the detail
commander, First Sergeant Alexander Smith, was on good

terms with Lieutenant Baldy Brown, who, as regimental quartermaster, had managed to slip his friend Smith a couple of sacks of ground cornmeal to augment his detail's rations. Gregory was curious to see to what use the cornmeal would be put and was hoping for a a steaming slab of cornbread to go with his coffee. Much to Gregory's disappointment, Private Patrick Smith, who had drawn the short straw as detail cook this week, was in the midst of turning this welcome contraband into a form of mush for the morning's repast. Judging from the ribbing Private Smith was getting from some of the other soldiers, he was making rather a bad effort at it. There was a jangling babble of critical voices urging Smith to "Squash that damned lump there, son, what're you tryin' to do? Make up a damned baseball for this afternoon's game?" and "Hey Paddy, where the hell's the cornmeal? That looks more like damned sawdust than grits, boy. Lemme have that paddle for a minute and I'll show you how to stand and deliver!" There was a crash of hoarse laughter and several of the men began humming the tune to Stephen Foster's "Hard Times" while Corporal Phillips warbled the corrupted lyrics:

> But to groans and to murmurs
> There has come a sudden hush,
> Our frail forms are fainting at the door;
> We are choking now on horse feed
> That Paddy says is mush,
> Oh, hardtack come again once more!

At the chorus the rest of the raucous breakfast crowd joined in with a will:

> It's the dying wail of the starving
> Hardtack, hardtack, come again once more;
> You were old and very wormy, but we pass
> your failings o'er.
> Oh, hardtack come again once more!

Private Smith's ears reddened and he hunched scowling over the bubbling pot of mush, using the paddle to swat at the fingers of his colleagues who were dipping into the mush to sample it.

"Awww, ye're all a bunch o' croakers," Paddy Smith growled. "I shoulda used sawdust instead o' cornmeal. It'd serve y'all up proper an' more'n ye deserve. G'wan, Phillips, git yer grubby digits outta my porridge!"

The sound of a dull thwack against the kettle rim punctuated Private Smith's swipe at Corporal Phillips' fingers, while some of the other soldiers guffawed and others helped themselves to another mug of coffee, which was as indispensable to the soldier's routine as sleep.

"Reach me a can o' Lewis,[1] J. B. This swill needs a touch of light."

Gregory handed the small tin to First Sergeant Smith and looked up to see Glover, his preparations completed, making his way casually across the clearing, shoulders hunched over, his hands stuck deep into his pockets and the corduroy collar of his jacket turned up against the chill. A wisp of mist drifted across the cutting, all but obscuring the photographer for a moment and lending him the appearance of a disembodied spirit. Glover plowed heedlessly through the damp curtain, a dreamy look on his face with his blond locks trailing limply over his shoulders. Gregory raised his coffee mug in salute and managed to catch Glover's attention. The photographer grinned and waved back. Gregory was oddly concerned about Glover and determined to convince the man to remain in camp one more night. He liked the man but sometimes despaired of talking sense to him. Glover was so wrapped up in his plates and his thoughts that he often seemed oblivious of his surroundings.

*   *   *

[1]"Lewis": A favorite among soldiers, and a rare treat in their coffee, was the tinned, condensed milk available from the Lewis or Borden companies. On the frontier this could cost as much as a dollar a tin and was thus an unusual extravagance.

THINGS HAD LOOKED A BIT TIGHT TO BRIDGER WHEN HE'D left Phil Kearny, but he'd had no reason to believe that this was at all unusual for this country. The Indians were generally always up to some devilment or other, and for the most part it was simply a matter of keeping your eyes skinned and well out of their way. The Sioux had always been a bit more troublesome than most, but then they didn't much get along with anyone. Crow, Shoshone, Arapaho, Winnebago, hell, it seemed like there was hardly a tribe out here that didn't have some old bone to pick with those fellows. And that, Bridger had thought, was pretty much what Henry Carrington's boys were up against. Weren't anything odd about that. Or so he had thought until he'd spent a few weeks among the Crow who made their camps along the Tongue. Iron Shirt, a distinguished old fellow whom Bridger had known for many years, had acted the host to the old friend he called Big Throat and made him welcome in his own lodge.

"Nope," he said half to himself, "things don't look so good as I thought."

"Your eyes are no longer what they were, Big Throat," Iron Shirt observed.

Bridger did not say anything for a moment but sat staring into the fire. The cold weather had begun to close in on them, and winter, they knew, would soon be throwing his icy blanket over the mountains and valleys of the Bighorns. Already the streams were becoming rimmed with ice, and each morning frost coated the ground. Bridger was leaning on one elbow, his long form spread out easily on a soft pile of buffalo robes. The toe of one boot tapped an errant stick into the central fire, which was the only light in the lodge's dim interior. In the dark recesses just beyond the feeble glow of the fire the lodge was a jumble of furs, weapons, parfleche boxes, and heaps of clothing. A leather-wrapped bundle of green arrow shafts, suspended from lodgepoles just below the vent, hung curing in the wispy column of smoke that curled lazily upward into the darkness above.

"Ye don't know what your talkin' about, Iron Shirt,"

Bridger grunted. "It's this blame green wood ye're burnin'. Makes my eyes water up."

"You think I'm a child who doesn't see the truth, Big Throat?" The old warrior shook his head and smiled. "It's not a thing which pleases me to say but you know it, too. We're both getting to be old men. I sit here huddled in my robes and don't want to get up in the morning to make water because it's so cold. When you come into my lodge you can barely straighten up your back. Bah, don't tell me stories about how young you feel. I've heard most of your stories as many times as I have seen the snow come. They're good stories but if I were to believe them all I would truly be the old fool some of the younger men think I am."

"Wagh!" Bridger said. "Ye're still an old fool and so am I, I expect. But I warn't talking about what you can see plain out but more like what you can see if you're looking with what's behind a man's eyeballs." He sat up stiffly and maneuvered a backrest of woven willow reeds behind him, groaning slightly with the effort. "My eyes may not be what they were but I'd have to be blind indeed to miss what Red Cloud is up to."

"Unnnh," Iron Shirt grunted. He was repairing the head of an arrow, a thin strand of sinew spinning out from between his compressed lips as his fingers deftly twisted the shaft to wind the moistened binding around it. He plucked the end of the sinew from his lips and worked it into the binding, where it would dry and shrink around the dogwood shaft to an iron-like hardness. He pointed the finished shaft at his white friend.

"That's so, Big Throat. There will be big trouble around here soon. Red Cloud will make a lot of trouble. He has convinced the Arapaho and some of the Cheyenne to take the Black Road with him. Dull Knife and Black Horse have refused but others are still angry from the fight at Sand Creek and will join anyone who will fight against the bluecoats. I think there will be much blood shed this winter."

*   *   *

J. B. GREGORY WAS SURPRISED TO SEE RIDGWAY GLOVER pushing his portable darkroom through the wood camp, his hat set purposefully at a rakish angle shading his eyes, a full haversack slung over his shoulder. Glover was whistling a tune that sounded suspiciously like "The Last Rose of Summer," although his pitch was so poor that Gregory couldn't be sure.

"Hey there, Brigham!" Gregory called. "What the deuce are you up to now? I thought you were going to wait for tomorrow's wood train?"

"Oh, hullo, J. B.," Glover said brightly. He stopped and let the cart gently to the ground before standing up and touching his fingers to the brim of his hat. "Just out for a bit of a stroll. Stretch my legs a bit, you know."

"Damnit, Glover," Gregory said, fists on his hips and his head shaking. "I thought we were plain on that score. I swear it's like talking to a damn mule. You twitch your ears, flick your tail, look intelligent and don't hear a damned word."

Glover grinned, "I don't have a tail, J. B."

"What the hell do you call this?" Gregory said, tugging lightly at the end of a lock of Glover's long, blond hair. "And if it ain't a tail, I'll tell you what it is and that's nothin' more than Sioux bait. I'm telling you, Ridgway, you go gallivantin' off all over to hell and back all by your lonesome and with that topknot of yours and you're likely to have it trimmed for you in a most ungentle way."

"Oh, don't worry about me, J. B.," Glover laughed easily. "I'm just going to wander on down to the lower cutting for the afternoon. A couple of the boys just drifted up from there a few minutes back and they say it's perfectly serene between here and there. If you're such a maid that it worries you then I'll wait for the train on Monday once I get there."

Gregory pursed his lips and scowled at his friend, who smiled back innocently. "All right then. But remember, keep your eyes skinned. First sign of trouble and you drop your rig and sell out as best you can."

"Right you are, J. B., I'll play the regular Molly Cottontail if it gets hot. Fair enough?"

Gregory gave a sharp nod and watched as Glover bent to

the handles of his rig. He straightened up balancing the whole easily on its front wheel and set off at a casual walk, looking no more concerned than a summer gardener moving a load of manure to a tilled plot in a neatly fenced yard. As he wandered down the hard-packed dirt of the Wood Road, the unevenly whistled strains of "The Last Rose of Summer" drifted over his shoulder and were swallowed by the hum of activity in the cutting. Gregory turned back to the blockhouse where he had been told a game of poker would be starting up in a few minutes. He rubbed his hands together and thought that he was feeling particularly lucky today.

GLOVER TRUDGED EASILY ALONG THE WOOD ROAD AS HE gloried in the peace of his surroundings. The sun had quickly melted off the light dusting of snow, and the temperature was low enough that the dirt on the road remained fairly firm underfoot. Squirrels scampered along pine boughs and darted up and down the ragged trunks hauling the smaller, more tender cones to their nests, which they were readying for winter. Woodpeckers tapped irregular tattoos that echoed through the trees, and a slight breeze had come up, bringing with it the scent of heavier snows in the mountains.

It was, to Ridgway Glover, an almost religious experience, and he felt that seldom, if ever, had he been as close to God as he was in these forests. Many men, he knew, were frightened of these spaces. They felt small and alone and vulnerable. Perhaps it was that in the absence of civilization, beyond the structures of buildings and banks, churches and railroads which circumscribed their lives, they felt naked in the eyes of God. Their sins and failings were exposed in column and rank with nowhere to hide. No countless mobs of other humans milling about in which their sins disappeared into the mass as a drop of water is swallowed by the sea. Ridgway Glover chose to see it differently. He felt not as if his sins were exposed but rather that they had been abandoned, left behind in the welter and bustle of civilization. Out here he felt clean and refreshed as if he had bathed his very soul in the clear streams that rushed in icy purity from the mountains. What few stains of sin he had were frozen and then swept clear to tumble and churn crazily over smooth pebbles, flashing past baffled trout as they were washed away out to sea.

If only I could capture this spirit in my plates, he thought. *If I could take the tranquillity and sense of renewal which a place like this exudes, distill it and lay it like collodion on a plate, what could I do for those suffering masses back East.* Those souls who lived in the dull brown, soot-stained jumbles of Philadelphia and New York, their only world a narrow slice of brick and tin framed by weathered, splintering sashes and viewed through the smoky glass of despair. Could his pictures, if he did them right, he wondered, if he put his whole being into them, could they perhaps lift the spirits, fuel the hopes of the despondent and dispirited? He bit his lip in eagerness and anticipation. It was as if he had been spoken to by God himself, like Joan of Arc or Saint Francis, given a mission in life. It was as if he were embarking on a great crusade of the human spirit. He picked up his pace and marched along humming to himself, shoulders straightened and head back as he followed the sharp bend of the road as it swung away from the lower cutting and slipped over a slight rise and down again in the direction of Fort Phil Kearny.

The sun had risen to its full height and the Wood Road was dappled and streaked with light and shadow as it stretched out ahead of him between ranks of pines that stood tall and ramrod-straight like serried ranks of soldiers in line of battle. He found himself humming "The Battle Hymn of the Republic" and composing new lines for it that described the glories of the country around him. The road ahead curved easily to the south and as he started into the bend his eye caught a hint of movement, which brought him to a halt. There, just on the verge of the road, not more than fifty yards ahead of him, was the most handsome buck he had ever in his life seen. It stood, legs splayed out, head bent to graze, fully as large as a horse and its thick, furry coat a radiant gold in the dazzling sunlight. He was mesmerized by the graceful bend of its long and pow-

erful neck, a rack of antlers, the tips polished and glinting in
the light.

Glover bent slowly, easing his cart to the ground, careful
not to make the slightest sound. He crouched behind his cart
in breathless wonder at the size and regal bearing of the beast
ahead of him. Moving his hands with painfully slow and deliberate patience, he raised them to form a sort of frame around
his left eye as if composing a picture. He had, to this point in
his travels, confined himself to taking views of people or vast
landscapes, and yet here, just before him, was a subject that
he had never yet considered. What a glorious specimen of
God's handiwork. Glover watched in bemused wonder for
what seemed like hours but was in fact but a few moments
before the antlered head came up suddenly alert, staring directly at the photographer and his odd little cart. Glover grimaced as the buck's muscles tensed and he bounded away into
the depths of the forest.

Ahh, well, Glover thought, *another time.* He shifted slightly
to grasp the handles of his cart and began to stand up when
he felt a sharp stabbing pain beneath his left shoulder blade.
Damn! He thought. *I've pulled a muscle.* And he grimaced
with the intense pain of it. *I must,* he thought, *have somehow
gotten into the wrong position. Damn muscle tightened up and
I pulled it good.* He went to straighten up slowly but found
that the pain, which had begun to radiate out from his shoulder
blade, was so intense that he could not move. He found that
he was having trouble breathing and his left arm seemed to
have gone numb from the shoulder down. He dropped to one
knee and tried to reach around to his back with his right hand.
It was incredible. The pain was so excruciating and he found
that he had become light-headed. The world began to swim
and blur in his vision. His mind began to race and he wondered if he were perhaps suffering a heart attack. *How odd,*
he thought. *I was feeling just fine not a moment ago.* He felt
his mouth filling with fluid, which seeped out from the corner
of his lips and trickled down his chin, and was puzzled to see
bright red drops dripping onto the handle of his cart and plash-
ing in the dirt of the road. How very odd, he thought as he

collapsed over the cart, tumbling it onto its side. He lay in the road a crumpled rag doll, one cart handle jammed uncomfortably under his armpit, the other extended like a ship's spar over him. His left check pressed into the dirt and his breath came now in short, strangled gasps. How very odd, he thought as the world tilted and rolled around him. Maybe if he rested here for a few minutes he could regain enough strength to go the last mile into the fort. Surgeon Hines likely had something that would put all this to rights. *I'll have to leave the pram here,* he thought. *Maybe Frank Fessenden and a couple of the boys could come out and get it for me before it starts snowing again tonight.* As the light faded all Ridgway Glover could hear was the thunderous rushing of his blood, like a mountain stream cascading over mossy boulders.

"DAMN COLD AGAIN THIS MORNING, LIEUTENANT."

Private John Ryan blew on his fingers and rubbed them together, trying to get the circulation going before reaching down to take up the reins from where he had placed them under his foot on the floor of the Dougherty. Ryan, who was not enthused about having pulled this duty, was at least grateful that he was driving the "avalanche" instead of having to hoof it or, worse yet, having to sit a saddle for what would probably be a long wild-goose chase. The badly sprung Dougherty would likely flatten the hell out of his backsides, but he'd still be able to walk the next morning and the canvas awning and top would help to break the chill of the wind. Lieutenant Bisbee, who was in charge of the detail, did not respond to Ryan's comment except to utter a noncommittal grunt and turn up the collar of his greatcoat.

Earlier that morning all had seemed quiet at the post. Although the sky had been overcast and threatening the night before, the expected snowfall had not materialized and the sun had risen bright and quickly burned off the morning mists that drifted up from the Pineys. But no sooner had the mist rolled off than the post's beef herd, which had been set to graze where the Little and Big Pineys forked, began to run. Shots

crackled in the crisp morning air and the sound of shouting
and whoops drifted over the palisaded walls of Fort Phil
Kearny. As fate would have it, Baldy Brown was the duty
officer that day and had insisted on having what he called a
"flying column" assembled just before first light with horses
saddled and carbines ready to hand. Lieutenant Brown had
become obsessed with the idea of Indian fighting. It provided
him a welcome relief from the tedium of being the regimental
quartermaster, a job that he loathed thoroughly.

Colonel Carrington had watched with interest from the
southeast blockhouse while Brown supervised the organization
of his pursuit party. Carrington had been about to return to the
headquarters when the rumpus began off to the east of the
Bozeman Trail and looking through his field glasses was surprised to see that the Indians mingled among the cattle were
brandishing revolvers. He glanced anxiously back at the enclosed lot between the quartermaster's office and half-
completed cavalry stables, where Brown's men were just
heaving themselves into their saddles. The pickets! Carrington
thought with a brief panic. Armed only with their muzzle-
loading Springfields and having already fired these weapons
they were entirely at the mercy of the Sioux who were bearing
down on them with six-shooters. Brown would never get there
in time. Someone had to act fast. One of the regiment's artillery pieces, a twelve-pounder, had been positioned in the quartermaster's yard just outside the main stockade. Carrington
rushed headlong down the ladder, snatching a friction fuse
from a box as he went and pushing out through the small,
nail-studded door into the yard beyond. Luckily, the fieldpiece
had been kept charged on his orders and it was but a split
second's work to run a pick down the touchhole to rupture the
powder bag and slip the "match" into position. Carrington
squinted against the newly risen sun, which gave a large advantage to the Sioux, and made a quick estimate of the range
to the charging knot of warriors. He bent over the gun's trail,
grabbed the iron staples, and jockeyed the piece quickly into
position. Sighting quickly over the gun tube, he gave the el-
evation wheel a quarter turn to the left and stood away, trailing

the fuse cord in his right fist. With one yank, the gun roared. Thick white smoke billowed out across the open ground as the gun rolled backward with the recoil. Several enlisted men came running up to join him, one snatching up the ramming staff while another grabbed a second charge from the caisson box parked a few yards to the rear.

Lieutenant Brown's pursuit party was just clearing the quartermaster stockade when the shell burst not fifty yards in front of the screaming Sioux. The warriors came to a stop, stunned by the explosion, and milled about just long enough for Carrington and the hastily assembled crew to load a second charge into the twelve-pounder. As Brown's party cleared the gate and spurred forward, the gun roared again. This time the shell burst within twenty yards of the Indians and sent a warrior tumbling from his saddle. The Indian ponies crow-hopped and reared, their hooves flailing at the air as the riders tried to control them. The Indians galloped over a low ridge and out of sight, now with Lieutenant Brown's party in hot pursuit, a large white smoke ring from the gun's discharge dissipating lazily in the air over the prairie.

NOW PRIVATE JOHN RYAN WAS STUCK OUT HERE ON BISBEE'S damned detail. They were to follow Brown's party, a thankless, nasty job that would have them jolting all over the countryside with damn Sioux lurking everywhere and probably take the better part of a day, which Ryan would much rather have spent safely inside the stockade. If they hadn't had to chase after damned Indians they'd at least have been able to stay out of the wind and maybe gotten a good strong mug of coffee every hour or two. Not that Ryan really needed the coffee. His bowels had been bothering him something fierce the last couple of days and the idea of staying close to the fort was more so that he could be close to the sinks rather than have to try to take a squat out here in the open in front of God and everyone and with some goddamn savage probably out there hoping to stick an arrow right up his ass in the process. John Ryan thanked God for small favors. As it was, if he had to take a squat he could hang his butt out over the wagon box and hope that any arrows launched his way would stick in the Dougherty and not the Ryan.

Thus far, Ryan thought, things had not gone too badly. The Sioux, after running off damn near most of the beeves, had swung about to the north and tried to skirt around the Sullivant Hills. The best thing about this was the fact that it gave Lieutenant Bisbee the option to follow Brown's movements by sticking to the Wood Road, a relatively smooth drive, which swung around the Sullivants in the direction of the pinery. Ryan much preferred this route to the alternative, which would have had them bouncing across the open country with every rut and rock slamming his tender hindquarters up and down on the box. Ryan settled in to the irregular rocking and jolting of the Dougherty and stared blankly ahead at the backs of the small detachment of mounted infantrymen who were jouncing along behind Lieutenant Bisbee. None of the men were very good riders. If they had been meant to be horsemen, Ryan thought grimly, they would have joined the damned cavalry in the first place. Private Burke, who had a reputation for being a bit of a Jonah, turned awkwardly in the saddle and grinned at Ryan just as his horse lifted its tail and began dropping its scourings in the road.

"There you go, Johnny," Burke chuckled. "Old Melonhead here thought you could do with a few horse apples. Careful you don't roll over 'em now. Maybe settle your stomach if'n you can get Cookie to bake 'em into a pie."

Ryan grinned back at his friend. "Who's to say them ain't the sort o' apples Cookie's been using all along, professor? It'd sure as hell explain why I've had the trots so bad."

Burke laughed and nearly lost his balance in the saddle, slipping precariously to the off side. His left hand scrabbled to get a grip on the cantle while his right fumbled awkwardly trying to manage both the reins and the long, ungainly Springfield that was half carried, half slung over the saddle.

"Burke!" Lieutenant Bisbee snarled. "Keep your sorry ass in that saddle and your mind on the business at hand! And if you drop that rifle . . ." Burke righted himself with an effort and braced himself for the coming tongue-lashing. Bisbee was in a particularly foul mood today and Burke felt sure that he was now in for it. But Bisbee's attentions were quickly diverted. The detachment had rounded a gentle curve just as the track passed into a heavily wooded area in the shadow of the Sullivants.

"Lieutenant!" one of the men at the head of the small column shouted over his shoulder.

Bisbee shot Burke a dark look, then wheeled his horse and trotted to the front of the detachment. His right hand immediately shot into the air, bringing everyone to a halt. Ahead of them the Wood Road was a scatter of wreckage, a splintered, ragged frame around a naked, white form sprawled facedown in the dirt. The body, a ghostly white, seemed even more pale for its highlights of crimson smeared as with a broad-bristled brush down the white of dead flesh. Blood had pooled in the dirt beneath the corpse and spread in a broad black stain. All about were scattered the shattered splinters of rosewood and mahogany, glittering bits of brass and shards of glass that flashed and sparkled in the sunlight. A single, smallish wheel lay tilted in the long grass at the verge of the road.

"Son of a bitch!" Bisbee spat. The lieutenant's head came up quickly, his eyes scanning the surrounding countryside, where they were greeted by the sight of several small groups of mounted Sioux, their ponies dancing on the slopes of the Sullivants, feathers fluttering in the breeze. The Indians were watching them closely but remained prudently out of rifle range. Behind Bisbee the troops pulled in tight on the reins of their horses. Inexperienced horsemen all, none of them wanted to risk the possibility of their mount breaking from their tight formation. Bisbee had already swung from the saddle and was down on one knee alongside the corpse, which he rolled over with relative ease.

"Glover!" Bisbee said. He noted the surprised look on the photographer's dead face and speculated that the end had come very quickly for Ridgway Glover. Bisbee had seen that expression many times before. *The poor bastard was probably lucky,* Bisbee thought. *He never really knew what hit him.* Bisbee let Glover's body roll back over and noted two wounds in the man's back. The larger of the two, inflicted by a hatchet, had been made after Glover was already dead. The smaller, less conspicuous wound, which had likely killed Glover, had been made by the steel head of an arrow that had entered just below the left shoulder blade and penetrated clean through to the heart. The shaft of the arrow had been snapped off when the killers stripped the body. Bisbee glanced around and saw the feathered shaft lying in the grass a couple of yards away. The photographer had been efficiently scalped, a large strip of skin peeled away from the center of his head, leaving the bloody skull open to the elements. Clots of blood were tangled in long strands of blond hair that still straggled from either side of the gaping strip. *So*, Bisbee thought grimly, *the goddamn Sioux finally gave you that trim we warned you about, Brigham, you poor, luckless son of a bitch.*

Lieutenant Bisbee glanced quickly around the site and noticed the smashed fragments of bottles that had held Glover's chemicals. He reached down and gingerly retrieved the remains of a shard of brown glass that retained a strip of paper label which read "potassium cyanide," then glanced up at a group of Sioux who were brandishing lances from a distant hillside. *I hope one of you stupid bastards tried to drink this stuff first*, he thought savagely. Bisbee flung the shard into the grass and stood up.

"Ryan! Bring up that ambulance!" he shouted as he swung back into the saddle.

The detachment shifted to left and right as the ambulance passed through and Ryan brought it to a halt alongside the lieutenant.

"Ryan, you and Burke load Glover into the back of the avalanche, then I want you to haul the body back to post."

What little color there was in Ryan's face quickly drained away. All that really registered on his mind were the scattered groups of Sioux warriors who still cantered along the slopes of the Sullivants yipping and waving weapons in the air a few hundred yards away.

"Beggin' your pardon, Lieutenant," he rasped out, his heart thumping wildly in his breast. "But Mr. Glover don't appear to be in no hurry to go nowhere. Don't you think he'll be just fine here until we come back around and we can pick him up on the way back to post, sir?"

The other men of the detachment said nothing but each secretly sympathized wholeheartedly with John Ryan. Here they were with Indians all over the damned countryside and the lieutenant expected Ryan to haul Glover's corpse back to post. Without an escort to run alongside there was no guarantee that the Sioux wouldn't sweep down and muster out Ryan and Burke along with the unfortunate Glover. Bisbee, however, was not open to argument. He glared at Private Burke, who quickly slid out of his saddle, handing the reins to a fellow trooper, and trotted over to where Glover lay in the road. Bisbee then turned on Ryan.

"Out of that wagon, Ryan," he barked. "Now, you listen to me, young man, for things'll go damn hard for you if you don't obey my orders this instant."

Ryan's face sank into a surly scowl as he wrapped the reins around the ambulance's brake lever and climbed down to the ground.

"You say so, sir," Ryan replied sullenly, "but things'll go a damn sight harder for me anyway if the Injuns catch up with me out there."

"Just do it, Ryan! And don't backtalk me!" Bisbee wheeled his mount around and looked at the rest of the detachment, who sat their horses quietly. "Burke, you and Private Harman will go along with Ryan. Don't delay but head straight back to post. The rest of you come with me." Lieutenant Bisbee unsnapped his holster and drew out a large revolver, then dug his spurs into the flanks of his mount and cantered off down the Wood Road. The rest of the detachment fell in behind him, bouncing uncomfortably in their saddles and leaving Burke, Harman, and Ryan to their grim task.

FRANCES GRUMMOND LEANED OUT FROM UNDER THE CANVAS covering of the ambulance, her gaze following the direction pointed by her husband's extended arm.

"Up there, Fanny," Lieutenant Grummond called out, a broad grin creasing his handsome face. "That must be Pilot Hill and the pickets are using signal flags to announce our arrival."

Frances Grummond could just barely make out the tiny figures on top of the hill mass to her left. One of the men was holding a small flag in his hand extended over his head and bringing it down repeatedly in a deliberate, sweeping motion. Her heart was fluttering with anticipation. They were nearing their new home. It would be their first real home together. They had been married a little over a year but this would be their first opportunity to establish themselves. To build a life and a home as a couple. No, that wasn't quite right. As a family. She had not yet told George but she was now convinced that she was pregnant. The very thought made her smile and at the same time brought tears welling to her eyes. As she watched her husband, Lieutenant George Washington Grummond, trot alongside the ambulance mounted on his magnificent Tennessee Walker, she felt her breath seizing up. He was so handsome, so dashing. Like a prince out of a child's book of fairy stories. Tall, slender, and erect, he sat his mount like one who had been born to the saddle. With his rakish dark looks and sweeping mustache she saw him more as a knight errant, or one of Napoleon's marshals. Their life together, she thought, was almost a fairy story in itself.

She gazed lovingly at her husband as he loped alongside the ambulance, the reins held loosely in his left hand, his gauntlet-clad right lying casually along the flank of his long, athletically shaped leg. He leaned forward in the saddle and cantered ahead just as the ambulance rolled slowly to a halt. The rest of the vehicles in the train, which included another ambulance, a baggage wagon, a mail escort, and a number of civilian freight wagons bringing supplies up from Fort Laramie, slowed to a stop behind them. The stockaded sides of Fort Phil Kearny were but a hundred yards distant and it seemed an odd place to stop. Frances leaned out from under the canvas to see what had occasioned the delay. Another ambulance, its canvas sides rolled up, had come up on the road from the opposite direction and was making the bend into the fort with two grim-faced young soldiers riding escort alongside. A young private, who was bent over almost double clutching at his stomach, rode the mule seat and handled the reins with his free hand. George suddenly wheeled his horse about and tried to bring it sideways to block her view into the Dougherty.

"Frances!" George called out in warning. "Don't look!"

But it was too late. Frances had caught a glimpse of the passing wagon's cargo, the pale white form of a young man stripped naked and butchered horribly. She felt the blood drain from her face and grabbed on to the struts of the ambulance to stop herself falling out onto the road. Her stomach turned over and she began to tremble violently. It was not that Frances had not seen death before, but this was so unexpected. It was like this was some terrible omen, that their arrival at their new home should be greeted by the mocking grin of a corpse. The towering mountains, which but a few moments before had seemed to hold their arms open beckoning her in, had now altered their appearance and loomed threateningly over them all. Suffused with menace, they stared unblinking and mercilessly down on the tiny party. She half expected a booming, disembodied voice to echo from the gray fastness of the crags, warning, *"Abandon all hope ye who enter here!"* Her hands dropped instinctively to her abdomen as if to shield the new life growing within her. *Oh God,* she thought, shuddering as the death cart rattled by, *just let us get within the gates.*

The ambulance jolted through the massive gates into the bustling interior of Fort Phil Kearny. Hardly anything was as Frances had expected it to be, for although the post was neatly laid out and almost unnaturally neat compared with the faded shabbiness of Laramie and Reno, Fort Phil Kearny was clearly a work in progress. With a few notable exceptions virtually every building was under some phase of construction. Some of the buildings lacked only roofs and supported a score of ladders up and down, which men clambered in a steady stream, like ants scaling freshly mounded dirt, carrying bundles of shake shingles that were tacked rapidly in place to the incessant staccato of hammers. Where some buildings were being fitted with window sashes and doorframes, others were but pale, skeletal structures open to the wind that blew down from the towering peaks and swept across the open parade, stirring small dust devils among the neatly stacked piles of lumber and clusters of tarpaulin-draped nail kegs. While the fact escaped Frances' eyes, George Grummond noted that near every work party a stand of weapons was stacked neatly within easy reach. It was but a few moments before the ambulance rolled to a stop before their new quarters, a tautly strung tent erected among a row of others. Lieutenant Alexander Wands, an old colleague, had come up to greet the new arrivals. He nodded to George.

"Hullo, Grummond. Welcome to Phil Kearny." He extended a hand to help Frances clamber down from the Dougherty.

"It's not much, Mrs. Grummond," he said softly. "But if it's any consolation, Colonel and Mrs. Carrington lived here until just last week. And Lucy and the children and I are just next door. Or would be," Wands grinned, "if we had a door."

"It will suit us just fine, Alex," she said, fighting down the panicked reaction she felt. "And the fact that we're among old friends is a true comfort to me."

That night Frances snuggled closely to George as they lay in the rough bed over which they had thrown a large buffalo robe, a gift from Alex and Lucy Wands. Frances nestled her head on George's chest, one bare leg twined around his, feeling the silky hair of his shins brushing softly against her toes. She lay awake listening to the beat of her husband's heart and riding the gentle rise and fall of his chest. Frances had not yet told him that she was carrying his child. Outside, the wind moaned and stirred their canvas home, which bellowed up heaving and straining against its hempen moorings. She listened for the faint calls of the sentries pacing their desolate posts and the mournful, yipping wail of a wolf as it was soon joined by other feral voices. She tried to sleep, but each time she closed her eyes the dream would come again unbidden. Over and over again the same scene replayed itself. They were halted in the road waiting for the ambulance to pass them by, the naked man's corpse shifting limply in the back. She saw him as the wagon rattled past and each time, as it passed through the gates, the corpse would sit up and stare directly at her. The dead man transfixed her with his dead eyes, looking as if he would speak but could not, before settling slowly back into the bouncing wagon bed as it disappeared behind the palisaded fort. What, she asked herself again and again, was the corpse trying to tell her? And why did he look only at her? Why did no one around her see the man rise as if to speak?

It was well past midnight before an exhausted Frances Grummond succumbed to a deep, dreamless sleep just as the first flakes of snow began to fall outside. They came more heavily and were driven by the rising wind slipping through every crack and crevice, swirling and sifting to settle on their robes and on every surface. Warmed by their shared heat, the Grummonds slept on, unaware that by morning nearly a foot of newly fallen snow would have drifted into their new home.

MARGARET CARRINGTON STOOPED IN FRONT OF THE OPEN fireplace and poked at the burning logs with the point of a bayonet that their man George had affixed to the end of a broomstick. It was rather an impromptu piece of equipment but served its purpose well, and she soon had a cheering fire roaring under the blackened pot suspended by its bail from the iron rod that swiveled out from the firebox. She, Henry, and the children had only just moved into their newly completed quarters. After months spent living out of a freight wagon or under mildewed canvas, the comfortable quarters were strangely antiseptic, almost hospital-like in their immaculate newness. It was a bit disconcerting to Margaret, although pleasantly so, for she had never before lived in a new house. The building still smelled strongly of the fresh-cut pine from which it had been fashioned, the new wood fairly glowing in the light from the fireplace in the evenings. After the months spent with but the thinnest of canvas sheeting between her and the wilderness, this simple structure had for her the solidity of the walls of Troy, a bastion against the cutting wind and a buffer to filter out the eerie howling of the wolves singing their despairing arias to a cold and gibbous moon.

We are here, Margaret thought, *not a minute too soon*. Winter would be upon them soon and the thought of keeping her household under canvas when the snow really started to fly had begun to worry her. Margaret rose slowly, smoothing the wrinkles from her plain brown dress and pushing a stray hair back from her brow. Exchanging the bayonet for a wooden spoon, she stirred at the porridge bubbling in the pot and slipped several slices of dried apple into the mixture—just a little bit of a treat for the boys. They had gone to Sunday services and as was their custom would eat upon their return. But Henry had been engaged in conversation with Reverend White, and Jimmy and Bobby, distracted by the turn in weather, were outside playing raucously in the newly fallen snow. They would have liked to hurl snowballs at one another had it been wet enough to scrape them together. But it was too cold, so the boys contented themselves with rolling in it, making snow angels and cupping both hands to scoop up enough to scatter over each other's heads with much screeching and giggling in the process.

Margaret glanced through the small, frost-glazed panes of her new windows and smiled to see her sons so happy and busily engaged in harmless mischief. This was their first real snow of the season, and Henry had advised her that it would likely be melted away by afternoon. The boys, he said, might as well enjoy the novelty while it lasted. The frozen parade ground looked to her as if some careless giant crossing the mountains with groceries in his arms had sprung a leak in a sack of confectioner's sugar and showered a fine powdery dust over the fort in his passing. It was a pleasant image and one that Margaret preferred to the reality that life at Fort Phil Kearny had become. The scenery was as beautiful, the mountains as majestic as they had been when she had first seen them, but now in a distant sort of way.

We're a bit like cousins who have come for a visit and overstayed our welcome, Margaret thought. The warmth of the family reunion had been replaced with polite but cold nods, strained smiles, and a studied avoidance of intimate contact. Everyone, hosts and guests alike, kept their distance, kept their silence. They interacted when necessary but no more than that. So it had been at Phil Kearny.

When first they arrived they had been filled with feelings of camaraderie and shared adventure. They had called to each other with clear voices exclaiming "Good morning, a fine day!" and "What beautiful weather!" Robust good health and a spring in the step seemed to be shared by all in a new and invigorating climate. In the evenings they had gathered to listen to the band, after which the officers and surgeons and some of the civilian contractors, men like J. B. Gregory and Leviticus Carter, gathered to play bridge and talk until late in the evening. They had discussed politics and the late war and philosophy and natural science. They had talked of literature and argued the merits of Herman Melville and James Fenimore Cooper against Charles Dickens and Washington Irving. Macaulay was held up against Whitman, who was found, despite his disregard for meter, to be more the popular. As the weeks passed and summer waned, the days of frolics and picnics on the Little Piney, merry games of croquet on the lush, green parade, and impromptu tea parties in canvas-roofed parlors grew fewer and more somber and finally ceased altogether. The festive mood of optimism that had colored the early weeks after their arrival had dulled and become gray and solemn to match the cold mist that rose in forbidding curtains off of the creeks and fogged the mountains early of a morning.

Jim Bridger had been a frequent and welcome visitor at the Carringtons' tent, although he tended to shun the larger gatherings. Margaret had continued their custom of reading Shakespeare to the old scout and she had grown accustomed to his wizened form folded comfortably into a rocking chair by the stove, his eyes closed, brow furrowed as he listened intently to the arcane rhythms of the plays. Bridger, she had noticed, was particularly fond of the comedies and would chortle with mirth at the antics of Puck and Benedick. He had taken especial delight in the exploits of Dogberry, and Margaret could not help but imagine that Old Gabe saw reflected in the poltroonish constable's bumbling a bit of the young officers' attempts at soldiering against the Sioux.

The unbidden memories washed over her and she could not suppress the sigh that slipped out and fogged the pane of cold glass, laying a soft, silvery sheen over her view of the outside world, blurring every object that lay beyond. The wispy, white one-dimensional cloud obscured her boys' frolic and she found her thoughts drifting back to her other children, obscured forever from her view. She felt the hot tears start at the corners of her eyes and tried to blink them away. Margaret placed her palm against the fogged glass and felt the warmth of her body melting the frost under her touch. She rubbed the window clean and thought, *If only life could be cleaned like this pane of glass. Note the dust and the smudge, the heartbreak and sorrow, and wipe them away with a passing of your hand.* Margaret gazed out and up at Cloud Peak's cold, impassive face, thinking, *If we were Greeks down here, surely that would be our Olympus. Zeus could dwell there as easily as anywhere else in the world.*

More and more of late she had felt a kinship to the doomed Tantalus. He had been Zeus' favorite but had sinned, giving ambrosia to his friends, offering the food of the Gods to mere mortals. For his punishment Zeus had cast him into Hades, where he thirsted for water in a clear, sylvan lake only to have it recede from under his cupped hands, where he hungered for ripe fruit that dangled, taunting him, just beyond reach.

Perhaps, she thought, *we have sinned by opening this land to the undeserving and for this we are punished like Tantalus.*

Their coming had seemed in such a noble and selfless cause, to open this country to emigrants who would build new lives in a distant paradise of their choosing. But so many of the people who had passed through seemed drawn by little more than the lure of gold and a lust for quick riches. Too many of them cared nothing for the land through which they passed, noting it only for what it could give them in their quest for wealth. An angered Zeus, she imagined, had charged Pluton to unleash his demonic hordes to torment and harass the interlopers. Margaret cupped her hands over her face and tried to drive the images from her thoughts. They were unworthy of a Christian-bred woman and especially so on the Sabbath.

She heard boots stomping on the boards of the porch followed by the rattle of the latch of the door behind her, felt the draught of cold air on her neck, and turned to see Henry shuffle in from his morning rounds, a rime of snow outlining the soles of his heavy boots against the wide, pine boards.

"Reverend White was in good form today I thought," he said brightly as he shrugged his greatcoat from shoulders that had become stooped with worry.

Margaret quickly brushed a tear from her cheek, affected a bright smile, and hurried over to help him with his coat.

"Oh, indeed, Henry," she said with more enthusiasm than she felt. She hung the coat on a wooden peg near the door, turned and gathered Henry's hands into her own, and was dismayed by their chill. "Your hands are blocks of ice, dear. Why didn't you wear gloves to church? You know how Mr. White loves to keep you engaged afterward."

It was true that the garrulous David White seemed to delight in bending the colonel's ear after Sunday services. He enjoyed Henry's company, seeing in him an intellectual equal and a particularly "moral" man, a man of principle and of reason. Nor was Henry put off by White's attentions, for even though their religious beliefs were sometimes at variance, both delighted in the gamesmanship of civilized debate and were frequently overheard sparring on topics as diverse as liturgical music and the prospects of the growing temperance movement back in "the States."

Margaret knew that her husband was a lonely man and was secretly thankful that the parson had taken on this one more duty. In addition to conducting church services, White had acquired stewardship of the education of the post's few children and frequently held classes of religious instruction for interested soldiers and civilians. While the reasons for it grieved her, Margaret could understand why White's "flock" seemed to have grown exponentially in the intervening months. The truth was that among his less happy duties White was called upon to minister to the souls of the departed. The demand for his services in this regard now seemed never-ending. Over the past two months not a single week had passed without at least one, and all too frequently more than one, body being laid in the earth. As the little graveyard had grown, so too had attendance at Chaplain White's Sunday services, and his classes swelled. If there was one remaining emotion shared in this community it was fear, a nameless, numbing frost on the soul, the icy clutch of an invisible hand at the vitals, squeezing the bowels, pushing the heart and stomach upward until they lodged in a person's gullet.

It was as if Death himself had taken up residence in the dark forests just beyond the white-shaved points of the stockade. He crept among the shadows along the base of the palisade. He crept among the pines half-concealed by the mountain mists, seeing all that passed through his domain, watching with studied disinterest for the unwary, the foolish, the distracted, the innocent. He was drawn especially to the dreamers, the enchanted, the beguiled, lured by the beauty of the land, seduced by its bounty and its promise. Stop to admire a flower, cup a hand in the clear water, stoop to pluck a berry, lay your sights upon a plump doe, and he would come for you. He would announce his presence with little more than a breeze in the pines overhead, a whisper of wind. But there was no wind, only his scythe sweeping with casual purpose and loosing another soul to drift upward threading through the needles, pinecones, and boughs, spiraling away from earth and all that was known with certainty.

"Yes," Henry said with a sigh. "The chaplain was rather talkative today. But this was a change from the usual. We talked about last night."

Margaret dropped her head and tried to contain her anxiety. She knew that something serious had transpired the evening before, had even heard shots fired, but Henry had seemed in no mood to discuss it when he finally returned to their quarters in the wee hours of the morning. Pretending disinterest, Margaret moved back to the fireplace and busied herself with the porridge, hoping that Henry would pour out the entire story.

*   *   *

THERE WAS A SMALL BAND OF CHEYENNE CAMPED ALONG the Little Piney, no more than nine or ten individuals, led by Dull Knife. Henry had taken Jack Stead along to translate and to see if he could find out anything to augment the fairly sketchy reports he had received from Jim Bridger of late. Dull Knife appeared pleased to see Carrington and asked for an allotment of provisions and permission to do some hunting along the Tongue River. Henry quickly agreed to both requests, though it didn't feel right to Stead.

"Somethin's up, Colonel," Stead said in a whisper. "These fellows have got something other than hunting on their minds or I miss my guess. The Cheyenne have already been huntin' up on the Tongue and it don't make a lick of sense for 'em to come all the way down here asking for permission to hunt that country after they've already done so." Carrington nodded. His lawyer's mind had already detected the contradiction in the Cheyenne's stated intentions and their description of their recent travels, but he had decided that he would approach the cross-examination with some circumspection.

After the allotments of coffee, bacon, sugar, and tobacco had been handed around, Stead and Carrington lingered in the Cheyenne camp and engaged Dull Knife in seemingly idle conversation. Over a period of several hours it had come out that Black Horse was ill and that "Big Throat" and "Medicine Calf," as most of the tribes referred to Bridger and Beckwourth, had been seen among Iron Shirt's band of Crows along the Tongue River. Beckwourth, Dull Knife said, was reported to be ailing, and some of the Arapaho told them that he had been poisoned by a jealous husband among his adopted Crows. What was more disturbing was Dull Knife's report that Red Cloud and Young Man Afraid Of His Horses were also camped along the Tongue and agitating for more warriors to join them in a proposed war against the whites. Iron Shirt, he said, had ignored the Sioux entirely, saying that winter was coming on quickly and that his people had better things to do than to get involved in a foolish war.

"Iron Shirt and Crooked Arm," Dull Knife said, "have still not forgiven the Lakota for stealing this country from them. I thought that they would have the two headcutters killed but they did not do it.

"I think it was because they had a white man with them that Iron Shirt did not kill them," Dull Knife said quietly, sipping at a mug of heavily sugared coffee.

"Ahh," Carrington said, "good for him. Jim Bridger is even more of a diplomat than I had expected."

When Stead had interpreted his words for the Cheyenne, Dull Knife looked at Carrington and shook his head.

"I'm not talking about Big Throat, Little White Chief," Dull Knife said. "The Lakota have a white man with them. He has no fingers on one of his hands and your friend kept saying he was North and a bad man. Big Throat said this white man hated all bluecoats and was trying to make a lot of trouble."

Carrington shot a puzzled look at Stead. "North?"

"Hell's bells, Colonel," Stead said spitting into the fire. "That'll be Bob North. He puts it across that he's a cousin to Frank and Luther who commanded the Pawnee at Kearney in Nebraska Territory but it's a lie for he's neither kith nor kin to 'em. He is a rough customer who claims to have been Secesh but even they wouldn't have him. He is bloody-minded and if Red Cloud has taken up with him it is indeed a strange world."

The hour had grown late and the two white men were headed back into the post when they were intercepted by a visibly agitated Chaplain White.

"SOME OF THE ENLISTED MEN," HENRY WENT ON AS MARgaret listened with growing curiosity, "were angry with David because he had been speaking well of the Cheyenne."

"But surely, that's a Christian gesture, Henry," Margaret said. "These Cheyenne have done nothing wrong that I know of. Why would the men have been angry with him for that?"

A charitable woman, kind and forgiving by her very nature, Margaret had always had difficulty accepting that most men were ill-disposed toward people who did not share their race or appearance. While she herself found the Indians to be exotic if smelly creatures, she could never find it in herself to deny their essential humanity. Christians they might not be, and some were capable of savagery, but they were not animals. Perhaps it was this uncritical charity, this gentleness, that Henry had found so attractive in her and that made her so worthy of his love and respect. This facet of her had never been so evident as during times of stress and hardship. When during the late war everyone had demonized the rebels she had refused steadfastly to condemn them and referred to them as if they were simply strayed relatives whose judgment, while faulty, had never forfeited their claim to unconditional love and forgiveness. Even now, Henry could see that her faith in humanity extended even to the Indians.

"It's not as simple as that, my dear," Henry said, moving across the room to warm his hands by the fireplace. "The private soldier does not easily distinguish between peaceful Cheyenne and warlike Sioux. An Indian is an Indian and a savage as far as they can see and they are in a murderous mood after the loss of their two companions last week." He pinched the bridge of his nose with long fingers, his eyes closed against the throbbing in his head. "David had heard rumblings among the men that a group of them would 'put paid to the savages' last night so he had borrowed Captain Marr's Henry and was on his way to stand guard against such an occurrence when he came across Mr. Stead and me."

Margaret's eyebrows arched in surprise. She knew that Chaplain White was not lacking in sand, his record in the war spoke for that, as did his exploits at Crazy Woman Fork. What did seem odd to her was that he would place himself in danger for the sake of the Cheyenne. Not that Margaret disapproved of this gesture; on the contrary, she thought it particularly noble. She knew that the Cheyenne had thus far had no hand in the attacks on the regiment. Jim Bridger had said as much before heading north. As far as she could see, the Cheyenne, as much as anyone, were unwilling pawns in Red Cloud's dangerous game. What made White's actions more noteworthy was the fact that he had to this point displayed little regard for distinguishing between the tribes. Margaret silently redressed herself, thinking that she should not be surprised. Why should the chaplain not be every bit as capable of making distinctions as she herself? She reached down a mug from a shelf built into the wall next to the fireplace, squatted down, and used the hem of her dress as a pot holder to pour coffee from the fire-blackened pot she had kept nestled in the hot coals. She handed the mug up to Henry, who took it gratefully, wrapping his chilled fingers around the warm ironstone.

"That was a noble gesture," she said simply. "He is an even better man than I had given him credit."

Henry nodded. "Yes, a good man, my dear. Well, he was right in his fears for a large body of men had slipped out of post with thoughts of malice and we just barely intercepted them. I had to fire my revolver to get their attention. Those were the shots you heard last night. And we managed to get them under control and turned away from the Cheyenne. But it was a close thing. A very close thing." His words drifted off, and Margaret sensed that whatever details he might have added were slipping quickly beyond her reach.

Henry held the mug up to his face and breathed in the soothing steam. Times like these, he thought, tended to bring out the extremes in men. So he had heard from those who had seen battle in its fiercest manifestations during the war. Every man carried within him the capacity for great good or great evil and until he was confronted by his own mortality there was hardly any way to know whether the spirit that animated him would be an angel or a demon. Henry had heard tales of men on the field of battle braving death to give water to a wounded enemy. But he had heard as well of men in battle from whom such tender sentiments had been stripped away like bark from a sapling. Men who would as soon put a bullet in the brain of another human helpless and prostrate, enemy or friend, as they would offer succor.

David White he could understand. A man of the cloth, educated and reflective. Mercy would come more readily to a man of his nature and breeding. But what of the other sort, the men White had faced down, there in the dark on the banks of the Little Piney? Were they of that dark breed which thirsted for revenge and took pleasure in meting out punishment even if those punished sinned simply in being of the same race of the transgressor? That such men might serve in his command worried Carrington. He had recognized some of his best soldiers among the mob last night. It upset his sense of equilibrium and set the world aslant when it should be level and plumb. Were they among the demons? That such men should exist he knew must fit into God's plan but it bothered him to think that he would be responsible for them and their actions. There were times when, as colonel of the regiment, he felt he must serve as a protector of demons. He wished for a moment that there were some way to root such men out of the Army, but then where would they go? Back into society, where their darker urges would have even fewer restraints on them? He had heard reports of former members of Quantrill's and Anderson's guerrilla bands having turned to lives of crime after their appetites for such pursuits were whetted by the war experience. It was a vexing question, for even he knew that such men were sometimes necessary for the dangerous, bloody work of the Army on the frontier. Had he the opportunity to rid himself of such men, could he, in truth, afford to avail himself of it? Would Red Cloud suffer any such pangs of conscience? An absurd notion.

Henry stood square in front of the fireplace, placing the heavy mug down alongside the ornate clock that had belonged to Margaret's father. It had been a gift to them from her parents, something to bind them to the ordered logic of civilization as they ventured into an untamed and unregulated wilderness. Henry had always liked the clock; its solid, dependable movements had in a way given him a measure of comfort, a sense that the world could be ordered and arranged in a comprehensible fashion. But now it had almost the opposite effect. It was as if the clock had taken on a spirit, one that looked on him with only lightly veiled disdain. It sat there, squat and complacent, smug in its command of the universe, as if to say, *"I do my part. I do my job to lend order to the world. This wilderness has not affected my ability to function. Every hour, every minute, every second is marshaled into its appointed place. I am as efficient in Wyoming Territory as I am in Ohio. Nothing has changed."*

Henry spread his hands wide on the mantel and stared at the impassive face of the clock, listening to the quiet whir of its small brass gears and the solid tock-tock-tock that seemed to echo in the room's silence. What was he to do? What did they expect of him?

There were barely men enough to do what they had been sent here to do. As it was his soldiers had barely a moment to spare for themselves. If they were not walking guard duty or serving as pickets, riding escort to emigrant trains and supply trains, or serving as couriers, they were splitting firewood and shake shingles, cutting hay or wood or guarding those who did. They guarded the horses, mules, and cattle, maintained their equipment, raised ridgepoles and set logs, hammered in sashes and laid stone for fireplaces. And they suffered and died. Most of them still lived under canvas and subsisted on wormy pilot bread and rancid bacon. Fruits and vegetables, beyond the dried bricks that the War Department called desiccated and the men called "desecrated" vegetables, were all but nonexistent. Already the surgeons had reported the first symptoms of scurvy among the soldiers.

It's criminal, Henry thought bitterly. Scurvy was a disease of sailors, of men who were thousands of miles from shore, adrift on an ocean, out of reach of gardens and orchards. Here they were in the midst of plenty and still the men's teeth rotted in their skulls. *We might as well be at sea*, Henry thought. *We've been cast adrift by the War Department. Washington sends us here telling us we're on a mission of peace and when we find ourselves besieged and bedeviled by a savage enemy they tell us we are being overly dramatic. They accuse me of lying. They accuse me of incompetence. They promise to send help and supplies and instead they rob me of my most seasoned officers and send me nothing to keep alive those who remain. When they made the maps of this country they should have labeled them in the style of the ancient cartographers. This was less Wyoming Territory than it was Terra Incognita and deserved the cautionary notation "Here there be dragons!"*

7

Canwepekasna wi
(Moon When The Wind Shakes Off The Leaves)

October 1866

Red Cloud watched impassively as the warriors slipped silently down the frost-rimed slopes below him. It had taken months of hard work and clever language to get to this point and now he would see just how well his words had worked. Lakota, Arapaho, Cheyenne were all represented here today, and he was anxious to see if he had been able to smooth relations sufficiently to let all of the parties involved cooperate without the petty squabbling and sniping that had become the usual custom among so many of these people. It had been a difficult process. Red Cloud knew that he was not a popular man among the tribes. He had accumulated a number of enemies even among his own people. Which made this moment even more appealing than it might otherwise have been. It seemed that he had always had to do everything better than everyone else.

He had seen but eight winters when his father had died of the *wasichus'* bad whiskey and he was left, in many ways, to fend for himself. Certainly there had been several older men who took an interest in the boy's early years but none of them was his father and the fact that his father had died of drinking rather than in battle or even from an accident in hunting cast a pall over him. He was the child who stood just outside the ring of light thrown by the *oceta*[1] listening in the darkness. Watching the other boys grow to manhood in a different society, a different world than was allowed to him. He had always felt separate and apart from the others and had always felt that he had to prove himself in every endeavor. So it was that he had grown up always going after the largest, meanest bull buffalo. He sought out the rogue bear in her den. In combat he dashed ahead of the others and when he killed a man he did it completely. He would go into a frenzy of slaughter and utterly destroy and dismember whatever enemy he came up against. Some of the older warriors had begun to look at him strangely. He had overheard some of them talking about him one night after a very successful raid against the Crow. Red Cloud had singled out his foe, a brave man with a fierce reputation, caught him unaware as he crossed a stream and brought him down with relative ease. But afterward he had leaped onto the Crow's body in the shallows and hacked it to pieces with his tomahawk. The stream ran red with the man's blood. It pooled in the shallows and then drifted into the current where it was sucked whirling downstream in a pink ribbon. The older warriors thought that the Crow, although well slain, was deserving of more respect than the young Red Cloud afforded him.

Red Cloud had been incensed by these comments and soon afterward had taken to hanging around the white man's Fort Laramie. Feeling he had been ostracized and unfairly criticized by his own tribe, he turned his face away from them. He was fascinated by the whites and soon had made a great many friends among the bluecoats. Or so he had thought. As he learned to understand more and more of their language he also came gradually to realize that the whites were no more fond of him than the older warriors had been. The whites smiled at him and asked him into their lodges and they gave him things. They acted as if he were their friend. But as the seasons passed he began to realize that there was something different about

[1]*oceta:* The central campfire in a lodge.

the way they treated him. They played jokes on him. This was not in itself bad, for all men play jokes on each other—but the way the whites did it was different. They did not have their fun with him as they would with each other but as if he were one of their pet animals. As if he were a dog or a bear kept on a chain for their amusement. And when they laughed they did not laugh with Red Cloud but at him. He saw that even the black-white men that some of the whites had to do women's work for them were treated with more respect than was he. He felt scorned and betrayed and a new sense of anger began to grow in him. But he was older now. He had learned something about men and he had learned how to hide his feelings from these people. There was nothing more that he would share with them. Instead he kept his own counsel, remained on openly friendly terms with them. He listened and he watched and he waited. Those who would demean him would someday pay for their arrogance and their disrespect. He would see to that if he did nothing else. They would come to fear and respect him as they feared and respected no other.

Now his patience would be rewarded manyfold. With this war he would be revenged on the whites for their treachery and arrogance. But better by far, he would be a great man among his own people, the ones who had rejected and scorned him as a child. It had been difficult to get all of these people to fight together instead of among themselves. Many of the older warriors, men like Spotted Tail and Old Man Afraid Of His Horses, had scolded and lectured him. They told him he was an ambitious fool who would bring destruction down on all of their heads. Others laughed at him or mocked him and so he had gone to the younger men. Once he had their trust and attention, speaking sweet words, he had fired their blood with hatred against the whites. Then he'd had to show them how the whites could be defeated. Hardly a day had been allowed to pass without some small strike against them.

They had started out cautiously. Killed a courier here, two prospectors there. Stolen a few cattle one week. Stolen horses the next. They killed the traders. They ambushed the small wagon trains of settlers. Then, as the tribes grew bolder and more confident, they took on the trains of the soldiers themselves and the parties of woodcutters and grass cutters. Always they had been careful to catch the soldiers and workers early in the mornings when they were still foggy with sleep or in the late afternoons when they were tired from a day of constant labor. And, whenever possible, had tried to strike them when they were away from the Buffalo Creek Fort or the little temporary forts they built with their wagons near where they worked. Now they would try something a little different. Now they would take the war to where the *wasichu* lived. This raid on the wood camp was a test. It would tell him if his goals were now truly within reach.

Hundreds of warriors had come forward to join this foray and thus far all had gone smoothly. As the men assembled that morning a feeling of general goodwill and eagerness prevailed as they readied their weapons and coated their bodies with paint and greased exposed limbs against the chill wind. There had been a bit of taunting and cajoling among the warriors but, to Red Cloud's relief, that which he had witnessed had been done in a lighthearted nature. Young Man Afraid Of His Horses had been in a particularly jocular mood. There had been a brief exchange of suspicious glances between Red Cloud and Crazy Horse, but Man Afraid had twirled a finger in front of his forehead.

"*Gnashkinyan!*"[2] Man Afraid quipped. "That Crazy Horse has always been a sour one. Sometimes I think he's truly touched up here. I doubt he would even enjoy his own wedding night."

Man Afraid had not noticed the sudden narrowing of Red Cloud's eyes at this comment, for at that moment Little Big Man, Crazy Horse's cousin, had come up and Man Afraid had trotted off to banter with him. Red Cloud clenched his teeth

[2]*Gnashkinyan:* Literally "Crazy Buffalo." The term usually refers to an evil spirit to whose influence and mischief the lovestruck are particularly susceptible but can also be used to say "He's crazy," or "He's just nuts." In this case Young Man Afraid Of His Horses may well be referring to the Black Buffalo Woman incident.

and silently cursed Man Afraid for his blathering bad manners. Everyone knew that Crazy Horse was still not over the affair with Black Buffalo Woman and held Red Cloud personally responsible for having had her married off to No Water behind his back. Trust Man Afraid to open old wounds with as little thought as he would give to kicking over an anthill. But it was perhaps not an entirely bad thing. It reminded him that this Crazy Horse bore careful watching. It was not unheard of for a man with rivals to die from a careless shot in battle. Red Cloud silently decided that he would keep a close eye on Crazy Horse. No Water would be well advised to do the same.

Beyond Man Afraid's careless remarks, however, everything had thus far gone with wonderful ease. He watched as scores of men, singly and in small groups—some on horseback, some on foot—flitted over low hillocks, down into and up out of ravines, darted from tree to tree with as little noise as a grasshopper makes crawling up a leaf. The breeze had shifted earlier and now carried what little noise the men made away from them—the quiet rattle of arrows shifting in their quivers, the clicking of bone hairpipe breastplates and tin cones, the stamp and snort of their ponies. Now the sun had drifted to a point where it would be in the eyes of those men who waited below them. The chunk-chunking sound of axes still echoed along the tree-covered slopes. The buzzing screech of the *wasichus'* large saw seemed to make the very air vibrate and made his teeth hurt.

The shrill screech of a war cry split the air. A loud boom echoed through the forest, followed by another. There was the sound of men yelling and the axes stopped. More shots cracked in the cold air and then came the screeching whistle that the whites' sawmill made. All around him the warriors had now abandoned stealth and were rushing headlong down the slopes, screaming and whooping, fitting arrows to bowstrings and cocking the hammers of rifles and pistols as they converged on the woodcutters' camp below. He could hear the distinct whoop of triumph as one warrior called out that he had counted coup.

Haiye! thought Red Cloud. *There's one less wasichu to cut trees!*

A smile cracked his face and he hurried downslope to join the others. This was something he did not want to miss. By the time he had gotten down into the fringe of trees that ringed the wood camp Red Cloud could see that the whites were hurrying into the blockhouses that had been placed there as little forts. A thin, ragged line of bluecoats had spread out across the camp's clearing and were firing and reloading their rifles as they moved slowly backward in an ever-narrowing circle converging on the blockhouses. A cloud of thick white gunsmoke hovered and rolled across the ground, drifting among the pines from behind which warriors poured a steady shower of arrows and bullets at the defenders. Scores of arrows soared into the smoke as braves screamed and yipped their war cries from every direction. The trilling of eagle-bone whistles cut through the thin air. Red Cloud watched as the last soldier, a large man with white stripes on his sleeve, fired his revolver straight into the chest of a young Arapaho before ducking through the doorway and slamming the heavy, nail-studded door shut behind him.

Red Cloud stood at the edge of the clearing watching critically as the muzzles of guns began poking from the small slits in the sides of the little forts. The guns would cough fire and smoke, then disappear into the slits only to reappear almost immediately afterward. A rolling cloud of gunsmoke billowed and eddied around the little forts and the firing of guns became an almost constant roar. He heard a clamor to his left and looked over in time to see a party of some twenty warriors led by Little Big Man burst from the trees and race screaming across the wood camp, all of them carrying muskets or pistols. The crowd of warriors surged on through the smoke and crashed bodily against the sides of a blockhouse, pushing and shoving as each vied to shove the muzzle of his weapon into one of the slits and fire it into the *wasichus* huddled within. Another group of braves rushed up to the door of the same blockhouse and began tearing chunks out of the wood with their hatchets. Sparks shot from the studded nails and splinters sheared away with every blow until a volley of gunfire from a second blockhouse cut down four of the young braves. Another volley followed, this one directed at the men who had pressed themselves up against the sides of the one blockhouse. Two more warriors were sent sprawling into the dirt. Another band of warriors rushed up and snatched up their fallen friends, dragging them off into the cover of the surrounding forest.

Enough, thought Red Cloud. *There is nothing more to be accomplished by this. It's time to call an end to this little fight.*

He was about to signal his wishes to the surrounding warriors when he caught a glimpse of a lone rider wheeling his pony in the middle of the camp. It was Crazy Horse. Both horse and rider were covered with tiny white hailstones painted on every naked bit of flesh. A desiccated red-tailed hawk bounced in the man's hair and a slash of blue paint in the jagged scrawl of a lightning bolt streaked down his cheek. Crazy Horse reined his pony up short in the center of the camp, lifted his arms into the air, and called out loudly, chanting a war song and then signaling for all of the warriors to break off the attack. The man's eyes glowed like blazing coals and his voice drowned every other sound. He sang the praises of the warriors and saluted their coups as he urged them back into the forest and out of the range of the *wasichu* guns. As the warriors rushed back across the open areas Crazy Horse turned his pony about to face the blockhouses, smoke still curling from the gun ports. He lifted both arms and screamed at the *wasichu*, calling them dogs and cowards. Finished he sat quietly on his pony, his cool gaze sweeping from one blockhouse to the next in the growing silence. The young Hunkpatila turned his pony's head and nudged the animal into a walk that carried him casually off into the brush. And then it was quiet.

Red Cloud saw that every warrior had slipped away and the wood camp lay silent and broken in the thinning fog of gunsmoke. He turned and made his way slowly back uphill, threading his way through the trees and thinking about this fight. He was irritated by Crazy Horse's performance. The boldness of

that last act of defiance was a masterstroke. For a man who
professed to have no interest in leadership Crazy Horse had a
flair for the grand gesture and one that in this case could easily
have thrown into shadow Red Cloud's role in forging the alliance that had made this attack possible. But there was much
to be learned from this raid. Even Crazy Horse's feat could
be turned to good use. The soldiers would certainly not forget
the Hunkpatila. Now Red Cloud would order these events in
his mind to see how best to use what he had learned, and
when.

"GOD DAMN THEM!"

Captain Tenedor Ten Eyck looked up from the morning
reports he was filling out. He had never known Henry Carrington to utter an oath of any sort, and he was genuinely
shocked to hear this outburst. He placed the pen carefully on
his desk and capped the inkwell, taking care not to brush the
freshly scribed figures with the sleeve of his uniform, and
waited calmly for Colonel Carrington's explanation. He was
plainly worried about the colonel, whose face had grown suddenly red against the stiff white collar of his shirt.

"Damn them!" Carrington spat out again. His eyes were cast
down on the small stack of papers just delivered by the courier. He fairly shook with rage. "Look at this, Ten Eyck! Just
look at this!" He held the small sheaf of papers out in a trembling hand.

Ten Eyck recognized the top two sheets for the small, rec-
tangular scraps used by telegraph operators. The nearest telegraph was located at Fort Laramie, which meant these had
probably originated at the War Department or Departmental
Headquarters in Omaha and were relayed through Laramie for
the commander of the Mountain District. A quick glance confirmed their origin with General St. George Cooke in Omaha.
Ten Eyck scanned their contents quickly and was stunned by
what could only be termed the errant stupidity of their instructions.

The first observed that the ninety-four horses carried on Fort

Phil Kearny's books were in excess of what was required by a single company of cavalry and instructed them to return all surplus horses to Fort Laramie immediately. Were it not so dangerously stupid, Ten Eyck thought, it would be perfectly laughable. For one thing, the promised company of cavalry had never arrived. Those horses which were still serviceable were being ridden by infantrymen who could never hope to catch up to the raiding Sioux on foot. More pointedly, they no longer had ninety-four horses left. Nearly half of them now belonged to the Sioux, along with nearly six hundred of the garrison's seven hundred beef cattle—all run off by Sioux raiding parties. The second telegram simply disbanded the newly formed Mountain District. Colonel Carrington's position had been eliminated. No longer was he commander of the Mountain District; now he was merely commander of the 18th Infantry Regiment. Not that it made much difference, for as far as Ten Eyck could tell, the 18th Infantry Regiment *was* the Mountain District. Ten Eyck shuffled through the rest of the papers. There was not a single item of good news to be had. Lieutenant Adair's petition to resign had been accepted, to be effective upon Lieutenant Bradley's return from escort duty with General Hazen. Lieutenant Fred Brown had been promoted to captain. It was a much deserved advancement. Brown was a good man and long overdue for promotion, but if the War Department worked in its usual fashion—and there was no reason to suspect it would not—it meant that Baldy Brown too would soon be receiving orders to report to Fort Laramie for reassignment to another regiment. Officers were already in such short supply and so terribly overworked that Lieutenant Grummond's arrival had been greeted with near jubilation. But lieutenants Adair and Brown had commanded most of the forays against the raiding Sioux and their experience was irreplaceable. Finally there was a complaint from the clerks at Departmental Headquarters whining that Phil Kearny's post returns for the month of June had not yet been forwarded to headquarters. Ten Eyck shook his head. *The idiots*, he thought. *Fort Phil Kearny did not even exist until July. Of course there are no post returns for June!* He handed the sheaf of papers back toward Colonel Carrington, who simply waved them away in disgust.

Carrington moved over to the window of the newly finished headquarters building, the wide pine boards squeaking quietly under his boots, and stared out at the parade ground, the grass now faded to a pale brown around the central flagpole. It was maddening. The Sioux seemed to become bolder and more aggressive with each passing day and by now hardly a man in the garrison had not seen some sort of combat. They had received some ammunition resupply but not nearly enough to cope with the Sioux. Medical supplies were short. Corn for the horses was gone and the local hay contained hardly enough nourishment to keep them on their feet let alone in shape to pursue the Indian raiders. Sometimes it seemed that the only thing in abundance here was criticism and inane orders from the War Department and Departmental Headquarters. They pulled valuable officers off for recruiting duty and detached them for escort duty with no hint of when they would ever get them back. How did they expect him to get anything accomplished out here in this wilderness? Henry Carrington was staring out across the parade when a light rapping came at the door. Private Archibald Sample, the colonel's new orderly, poked his head in cautiously.

"Begging the colonel's pardon," Private Sample said, "but there's a gentlemen to see the colonel."

Carrington looked over at Ten Eyck, who shrugged his shoulders in resignation. Ten Eyck was beyond hoping for any good news. The colonel nodded to Sample.

"Very well, Archibald," Carrington said with a sigh. "Show the gentleman in, if you please."

Moments later a rangy young man shuffled in through the door, a battered Stetson clutched in rough, weathered hands. He appeared to be in his late twenties with a firm jaw, and clear gray eyes that carried in them a glint of self-assurance and determination. The young man was dressed in the manner of a cowboy—heavy canvas coat, a simple canvas waistcoat, homespun shirt, and trousers of the material called jeans which was becoming so popular among cattlemen and miners. The trousers were tucked into a pair of well-scuffed, high-heeled boots onto which were strapped oversized Spanish spurs that rang lightly as he walked.

"How do you do, Colonel," the man said easily, holding his hand out. "Story, Nelson Story of Fort Worth, Texas."

Carrington took Story's hand and the two men shook briefly. The man's grip was firm and his hand rough and well callused. Carrington looked into the man's eyes, which gazed back unblinking. The man seemed to radiate a quiet confidence that saw no man as a superior. Story came quickly to the point of his visit.

"Colonel," Story said quietly. "I mean not to inconvenience you but decided to pay a courtesy call as I am passing through. I am driving some thousand head of longhorns through to Virginia City and intend to lay by here for but a day before pushing on if that's convenient for you."

"Convenient for me," Carrington said slowly. "I do not doubt that it's convenient for me, Mr. Story, but I'm afraid it may hardly be convenient for you. We have experienced some serious difficulties with our Sioux neighbors of late and the road through to Virginia City is hardly a healthy one at this time."

"I suspected as much, Colonel," Story said easily. "We had a brush with your neighbors down on the Dry Fork of the Powder. They tried to run off a few head. My longhorns do not bear the slightest resemblance to buffler so I'm afraid I took it rather personal."

Ten Eyck grinned at Carrington. This was a brash young fellow. Ten Eyck was amused by the nonchalant mention of a brush with the Sioux, which he knew was probably anything but casual. Carrington suppressed a smile and cleared his throat loudly.

"Well then, Mr. Story," Carrington began. "Can I assume that you remonstrated with the culprits?"

Nelson Story nodded. "Yessir, I b'lieve you could call it that. We remonstrated 'em straight to Kingdom, or wherever it is that a redskin goes when he has done what he could on this earth. We got our property back. Well, except for one heifer which they were about set to eat when we come on 'em. So I expect it all worked out happily in the end. Leastways, I'm fairly satisfied with the outcome although it cost us an extra day on the trail which I did not relish with winter fairly set to commence."

Both of the soldiers were somewhat surprised by Story's summary of the incident. Carrington frowned, his head cocked to one side.

"You did indeed?" Carrington asked. "If I may be so bold, sir, how many men in your party, Mr. Story?"

"Well, Colonel," Story scratched his head for a moment. "I had to leave a couple of the fellers at Reno as they were roughed up a bit in our scrape, which leaves twenty-five. I've got fifteen of the boys driving wagons which leaves me ten to ride point, drag, and flank. It tends to make for a long day."

"And you propose, Mr. Story," Carrington asked incredulously, "taking twenty-five men and pushing a herd of cattle through the entire Sioux nation?"

"Well, yessir, I b'lieve that's about right." Story's lip curled in a wry grin.

Carrington and Ten Eyck both shook their heads in disbelief. The Sioux had wreaked havoc on the regiment's beeves and here was an upstart of a young cattleman quietly announcing that he had made short work of a Sioux raiding party. Carrington felt his ears begin to redden. He took this cocky young man's success as a harsh comment on the colonel's inability to recover his own cattle. It was, Henry quickly reminded himself, an absurd thought. Story could have no idea of the travails borne by the regiment. But it was frustrating to think that an entire infantry regiment could not seem to accomplish what a few Texans would regard as a routine matter. A thousand head of Texas cattle, Carrington calculated. This might be a fortuitous turn of events.

"Mr. Story," Carrington said quickly. "The government is in a position to offer you a good price on your livestock which will obviate any necessity for you to venture further up the Bozeman Trail. Having already had one encounter with the Sioux I do not doubt that your men would welcome the opportunity to avoid yet another, possibly more fatal encounter with Red Cloud's warriors. The Indians notwithstanding, I am prepared to offer you fair market value on your beeves."

While his expression remained unchanged, Nelson Story's body stiffened almost imperceptibly. Henry Carrington perceived a slight hardening to the young cattleman's even gaze.

"Of that I am sure, Colonel," Story said quietly. "But I must decline your offer. I have contracted to move these beasts to Virginia City and do that I shall, Sioux or no Sioux. While I do not seek another encounter with Mr. Red Cloud, neither will I shrink from it. I am set in my purpose, sir."

"But what good will your purpose do you, Mr. Story, should you not reach Virginia City or, if you do, reach it with but a fraction of the cattle you have with you now? My offer is a fair one, sir, and I would hope that you would put it to a vote among your men. Perhaps they are not so willing to brave the Sioux nation as you."

"Colonel Carrington," Story said, "I will make Virginia City be it with but one heifer, of that I assure you. What you may have heard of Texans I do not know but we are more capable than the average man. As to a vote, sir, we are a cattle company and not a democracy. Leastways not while I command. That, sir, is something I expect you have experience of. I imagine that if you put it to a vote here most of your fellers would as soon head on back to the States as hole up in your fort. No, sir. I b'lieve we will push on soon as we can."

Carrington turned and walked to his desk. For a few moments, the only sound was the steady, tumbling click of the clock on the fireplace mantel. With his back still to Story and Ten Eyck, Carrington took a deep breath.

"I am sorry you see it that way, Mr. Story. As you know, I cannot compel you to sell your cattle, nor am I at present empowered to requisition your property." Carrington paused, hoping the implicit threat of requisition might soften Story's stance. "However," Carrington continued, "as the district commander I am responsible for the safety of transients through this region and empowered to set certain rules and regulations to insure that life and property of American citizens are afforded adequate protection. Captain Ten Eyck, will you acquaint Mr. Story with the standing orders regarding the strength of trains allowed to pass through the region?"

"Yes, sir." Ten Eyck turned to Story. "The current regulations require, sir, that a minimum of forty well-armed men should comprise any party which travels the road stretching between Fort Phil Kearny and Fort C. F. Smith."

"As you can see, Mr. Story," Carrington said quietly, "I cannot in good conscience permit your party to venture further until such time as it can be augmented with an additional fifteen men." The colonel spread his hands out wide as if to say that the thing was beyond his control. "Were I to make an exception in your case and anything were to happen to your men I would be answerable to Washington. It simply can't be done, Mr. Story."

"Colonel," Story said, his eyes hard-set and mouth tight. "Every one of my boys not only carries two revolvers but a brand-new Remington breech-loader. I wager that my crew is the equal of any regiment equipped with muzzle-feeding Springfields. I cannot afford to tarry hereabouts in the hope that some Montana-bound pilgrims'll wander through."

"Nevertheless, Mr. Story," Carrington went on quietly, "remain you shall. You are passing through my district and I am responsible for your welfare whatever your desires to the contrary."

Nelson Story fought down the urge to lash out at Carrington. He had dealt with red tape before, in its many guises, and learned that discretion was indeed the better course. If he made an issue out of it, Carrington, with a regiment of regulars to back him, could possibly do irreparable mischief to his venture. Best, he thought, to appear to cooperate. The young cattleman swallowed and nodded quietly. Carrington walked to a table cluttered with papers, ledgers, and rolls of maps piled in a loose stack. He shuffled through the maps for a moment, selected one, and rolled it out on the tabletop, gesturing for Story to join him.

"I should like you to picket your herd here, Mr. Story." Carrington pointed to a spot on the map. "You will, of course, be allowed full access to the facilities which the post can offer and can make your outfit comfortable until another train comes up. You can then join forces and continue on to Virginia City in relative security. If there is anything which we can do to make your stay more convenient you need only ask."

Nelson Story looked down at the map and quickly gauged the distances. "That's a good three miles off, Colonel," Story said, his voice low and carefully controlled to conceal the slow burn which was working its way up through his scalp. "If you are worried about what the Sioux are liable to do to our herd, sir, I find this rather a strange location. I don't yet know a hell of a lot about the Sioux," Story lied easily, "but am somewhat familiar with the Commanch and Kiowa and figure that any Injun worth his salt would see a herd laid in this far out as fairly easy pickings. I confess I don't figure how us stayin' way out there helps you any in keeping us safe from their deviltry."

Carrington glanced uneasily at Ten Eyck and then back down to the map. "Mr. Story," Carrington said quietly, "my primary job, you must understand, is maintaining the capability of this garrison to do its job and that means that I must look to the security of our rather diminished herd. I cannot have any of the government's cattle run off while mixed in with your livestock. I must reserve what grass we have close to the post exclusively for their use. My troops can respond quickly to any emergency you might experience but I cannot give the Sioux any more excuse to close on our own animals. I'm sure you see my dilemma."

"Yes, Colonel, I believe I understand your design to the letter."

Story extended his hand, which Carrington shook firmly, and then settled his slouch hat on his head, the brim pulled low over his eyes. "If you've nothing further, Colonel, I believe I'll get my outfit settled in before dusk. If what you tell me is true I expect we'll want to make sure we have some good pickets out tonight and I'll want the boys pulling guard well-rested and fed proper. Good day to you, Colonel." He nodded to Ten Eyck as he moved toward the door. "Cap'n."

Ten Eyck returned the nod and the door shut quietly behind Nelson Story.

Ten Eyck joined Henry Carrington, who was staring out the window at Nelson Story. One of Story's hands, an older man with a droopy mustache and weather-beaten face, was standing alongside two saddled horses, waiting for his boss. To Carrington's chagrin their mounts looked remarkably fit compared with most of the garrison's horseflesh. Carrington bristled to think that Nelson Story was probably right. His cowboys with rapid-fire breech-loaders were easily the equal of any party the Eighteenth could field with their antiquated Springfields. If put to the test Carrington did not doubt that the Texans could handle just about anything the Sioux might throw at them.

Henry Carrington hated what he had just done. It was unlike anything he had ever contemplated and he was not proud of it. Story's cattle outfit was, if anything, as exposed and vulnerable to the Sioux here at Phil Kearny as it was on the move north. But Carrington needed those cattle. Some supplies had begun to trickle in of late, including some corn for the horses, but with the 18th's own herds depleted by the Sioux, he would be hard-pressed to keep the garrison in meat over the long winter. If Nelson Story could be delayed for even a few days, the Indians would likely put enough pressure on the Texans to convince them to sell the herd at Army quartermaster prices. Ten weeks ago, Carrington reflected, he would never have considered playing such a dangerous and deceitful game, but then ten weeks ago he had had not lost so many cattle and men to Red Cloud's warriors. He thought back to the shouted threat of Young Man Afraid Of His Horses at the Laramie Conference. "In two moons you will not have a hoof left!"

"Well, Young Man Afraid," Carrington muttered under his breath, "you weren't exactly right, but not far from it."

"You thought him afraid, Colonel?" Ten Eyck ventured.

"Eh? Oh, no, Tenedor." Carrington waved his hand in the air as if dismissing a thought. "I was thinking of something else. Not Mr. Story. Quite the opposite I suspect." Carrington watched as the young cattleman and his companion swung easily into the saddle and turned their horses' heads toward the gate. "I wish I had a company of Nelson Storys."

"Mr. Story bears careful watching, Colonel."

"I don't know, Tenedor," Carrington said with a sigh, his thumb and forefinger pressed tight to the bridge of his nose. "Nearly everything and everybody here bears watching but I don't know that we've got the eyes or strength to watch all."

The pair watched Story and his companion disappear through the gate and Carrington turned back to his desk. "Well, we have lessons to impart on our colleagues at Department Headquarters, Captain Ten Eyck. Let us attend to that. We can worry about Mr. Story once we have dealt with General St. George Cooke."

"OH, FRANCES! THIS IS SIMPLY WONDERFUL NEWS!" MARgaret Carrington reached across the table and took Mrs. Grummond's hand in her own, squeezing it gently. Frances tried to smile but her eyes remained cast down at the delicate teacup that sat untouched before her. Margaret was genuinely delighted by Frances' announcement. It was the one bright spot in this place, which had become of late almost unbearably tense and uncertain. Frances was such a beautiful and charming girl and her husband, Lieutenant Grummond, was so much the picture of a dashing young officer, that this romantic and devoted couple had quickly become post favorites. To hear that they were to be blessed with a child was to Margaret the best news she could have wished.

Lord knew they needed some happy tidings. The Sioux had increased their harassing blows at the post as if hurrying to inflict every possible hurt before winter put a stop to their raids. So incessant had their attentions become in the past few weeks that Henry had taken to sleeping fully clad, his boots and revolver kept handy by their bed so that he might respond to any emergency. Every night, it seemed, he spent more and more time away from their bed as he checked each sentry post and supervised every change of guard. Margaret doubted he had slept more than three hours in any given night for the past two weeks. He had grown lean and haggard, his cheeks sunken and eyes underscored by dark circles. Margaret looked wistfully across the table at Frances and noticed the tears welling up in the younger woman's eyes.

"What is it, Frances? Surely this is something which you and George have hoped and prayed for. A child is the most wonderful gift which God can give you. This is a time for rejoicing and not tears, dear one. Truly it is."

Frances sniffed and nodded her head, choking back the sobs that threatened to burst forth unbidden at any moment. She pulled her hand gently from Margaret's and wiped the wetness from her eyes, taking a deep breath and gathering herself together. Margaret was right, this should be a happy time. Their first child. It would be a boy. Of that she was convinced, although there was no way to tell for certain.

"I haven't told him yet." Frances blurted it out and took a sip of tea, glancing over the rim of the cup for Margaret's reaction. Margaret managed a tight smile. She suddenly knew what was bothering her new friend and thought that the best course would be to get her to put her fears out in the open. Sometimes stating a fear went a long way toward making it manageable.

"That's understandable, dear," Margaret said with a nod. "The men are so consumed by their work these days that it is hard to know what to say to them. I have seen it in the colonel and it vexes me no end. They depend on us for a relief from the strain which this posting puts on them. They have worries enough with the Indians and the need to have the post finished before winter that we are loath to give them anything further to burden their thoughts." Frances nodded.

"You want to comfort your husband," Margaret went on. "You don't want him to worry and fret over something over which he truly has no control. The child will come no matter what he does or cannot do."

"Yes," Frances said. "You know it's so. He will fret and flutter and make a terrible fuss. He worries about my health now because we are living in a tent. If he knew I were with child he would go mad with worry. He would treat me like a child and spend every waking minute hovering about me, or thinking there was something he could or should do."

"Well, you must stay with us, Frances."

"No, I can't, Margaret," Frances insisted. "That's precisely what I must not do. Oh, don't you see? It is too kind of you to offer but it is so unfair."

"None of the other ladies is with child, dear," Margaret said, "and they all know too well how trying it is to be in your delicate condition in these circumstances. They'll not think it at all unfair."

"That's exactly what I'm worried about, Margaret," Frances said quickly. "I don't wish to be seen as delicate. George is so solicitous as it is that to present him with this now would be to distract him entirely from what he needs to do. Our circumstances are indeed ever on my mind but even more so because they must be uppermost in George's mind. He is a bold man, Margaret. I worry that he takes too many risks but if he must I wish him to think only of those risks."

"But you say he worries about you now," Margaret said. "If he knew that you were safe and warm in our quarters would that not ease his mind for your comfort and health knowing that you are with child?"

"That's why he can't know yet. I want desperately to tell him. You must know how hard it's been to keep this from him, but I feel I have no choice. If I can wait for but another week or so, our new quarters will be ready and I can tell him then. Once we are settled into our own home I am certain I can convince him that I am well and the baby is well and that he never had any cause to worry. I know it sounds irrational but somehow I just know that once we are in our own home it will be so much easier to give him the news."

Margaret looked at the younger woman across from her and considered Frances' reasoning. It was true that little would have changed for the young couple beyond having warmer, more secure lodgings, but in a way she could not fault Frances' appraisal of her husband's likely reaction. Men were strange creatures. They worried about things over which they had no real control or influence. Expectant wives and babies, she had found, unnerved most soldiers more than did the prospect of facing an enemy battery. They became flighty and overwrought. They took to fretting and daydreaming and mooning about. In most circumstances it would be amusing, but here a man who was baby-stricken was in mortal danger. A worried man did not sleep well, he was always tired. His mind tended to wander. At this post a man whose mind wandered was a danger to himself and others. The mere fact that they occupied their own quarters, that Frances was in a home of her own of which George was nominally master, might well make all the difference in how he received her announcement. *Well*, she thought, *the weather has moderated of late*. The first flurries of snow had now been succeeded by a period of glorious Indian summer. The days were bright and sunny, the sky a brilliant, cloudless blue, and construction was proceeding very quickly. With luck the Grummonds' new quarters would be ready in as little as a week or two and well before the winter closed in on them. More important, when the weather did change, when the snows finally began in earnest, the Indians would probably cease to be so great a threat as they now were. Henry had assured her that the tribes would have far too much on their minds throughout the winter to concern themselves with Fort Phil Kearny. By the time the spring came George Grummond would have become accustomed to his looming role of father. Reinforcements would have arrived at the post and, with any luck, Red Cloud would have realized the futility of opposing the march of progress. Lieutenant George Washington Grummond would be free to fret over Frances and the baby all he wished. She gave Frances a quick nod.

"All right then, dear," she said, reaching across to take her hand once again. "It'll be our secret for a few weeks more." Frances Grummond smiled easily for the first time that afternoon.

When Frances had left, Margaret found herself staring idly out the window at the snow-wreathed face of Cloud Peak. Never had she expected that she would so welcome the coming of winter. It was said that the winters here could be brutal but the prospect of snow was to her more of a promise of relief. Henry had assured her that construction on the post would be complete and he would have fewer demands on his time. The stream of emigrants passing up the trail, which had already slowed to a trickle, would cease altogether for the season. There would not be as many demands on the regiment for escort and courier duty. Patrols would become fewer and fewer as snow closed a ring around the post. The Sioux who depended upon game for their very survival would be far too occupied with keeping their families warm and fed to harass the soldiers and woodcutters.

Confined to post and quarters, the regiment could turn its attention to more pleasant pursuits. They would have parties and balls. The band would play and husbands would dance with their wives. Evenings would be devoted to bridge games and sewing bees. There would be conversation and funny stories and small theatrical efforts. They would read to the children and the women would bake cakes and cookies. They would sing ballads and hymns and jaunty ditties. And in the evenings the children would sleep snug in their beds and she would have Henry, sans boots and revolver, beside her once more. A few weeks would make all the difference in the world. Winter would be a blessing and December would bring Christmas and a reason for celebrating the birth of the Lord and peace on earth.

"WELL, BLAST IT ALL, NELSON. WHAT THE HELL'RE WE WAITin' on, Christmas?" Dutch Charley was irritated and did not feel the need to sugar-coat his frustrations for Nelson Story. He had known Story for years and while Nelson was in charge of the outfit, he was also a friend. Charley, who had at first enjoyed their extended stay at Phil Kearny, had quickly grown restless and was now anxious to get on to Virginia City. They had been camped here nearly a week and while everyone had been given the opportunity to sample the hospitality of the post—the most popular being Washington's pool hall, Judge Kinney's sutlery, and Liz Wheatley's kitchen—the novelty had paled quickly for Charley.

"Damn it all, Nelson," he said, "it won't be but a couple of weeks before it starts to really blow around here. We'll be in snow up to our asses and good-bye Virginia City."

"Fall back there, Charley," Nelson said easily. "You told me the casks were all filled up, canteens too. We've got full stores of everything I sent you over to Judge Kinney's for, right?"

"Well, you know that's a fact, Nelson and never any need to ask twice. But . . ."

"But nothin', Charley. You pull the boys in off of picket. Every one of them."

"What in the nation are you thinking, Nelson? Why those damned skulking redskins will just slaver away at the thought o' cuttin' out a few of the gals and . . ."

"Damnit, Charley," Nelson exhaled loudly, "we ain't gonna have a damned church social. I want 'em all in here now and it won't take but five minutes now get on an' get 'em in 'fore I throw a damned shoe."

Dutch Charley scowled at this and scratched his head but it was clear that Nelson had something gnawing at his brain and he'd best get on with it and see what sorted out. It didn't take more than a few minutes to have all twenty-five members of the outfit gathered in a tight circle around the chuck wagon. The boys Charley had drawn in from picket remained mounted at his instructions. He wanted a few of the boys ready to bounce out quickly if there was any sign of trouble while Nelson was holding his palaver. All of the men, most of whom were barely out of their teens, waited quietly for Story to say his piece. Story climbed onto the mule seat of the chuck wagon and stuck his thumbs into his pistol belt.

"Well, boys," he began, "we been sittin' here lollygaggin' for near a week now and I expect you're about as rested as you're gonna get. We put a couple of extra pounds on the herd and let their feet heal up some which should serve us well. Now, as you know, Colonel Carrington don't want us headin' up north without we got a full forty men to haul on through. He says the Sioux and Cheyenne're powerful trouble in these parts and you know that for a fact as we had to leave Jack and Benny back at Fort Reno to lick their wounds." He paused for a moment and studied the faces of his boys, all of them keen and alert.

"Now," Story went on, "we ain't about to get another fifteen boys any time soon and I don't know that I'd want 'em if they was offered. I know you fellows and I know what to expect if it gets hot for us. You got your Remingtons and you're comfortable with 'em and I'm comfortable with you. I propose we get on with this dance and do it right quick. I plan to move tonight. In fact I plan to move every night from now on til we get through Sioux country. Charley and me have spent some time up here before and we can tell you that the Sioux are a bit like the Commanch. They don't like to be out in the dark. Scares hell out of 'em and they think if they get kilt at night they won't make it to the Happy Place. Well, that's fine by me and I figure that's the best time to steal a march on 'em. We'll move at night and fort up somewheres during the day. If they try any of their deviltry, well, like I said, we got our Remingtons and we'll haul their freight for 'em like we done down on the Powder. Now I know you've all had a chance to talk to the soldier boys and the others who're over at Kearny and you know damn well that it's possible that the Sioux will try to make it hot for us. If any of you don't want to push through to Virginia City that's fine by me. I'll give you your wages and you're free to go and no hard feelings. But I need to know right now so speak up plain."

Story waited in the silence, scanning the faces of the cowboys, who seemed more interested in studying their own boots than anything else. One man only seemed uneasy with what Story proposed.

"George," Story said quietly, "you don't seem all that comfortable with the plan. If you've got a worry I'd appreciate to hear it."

George Dow rubbed his stubbled chin and shook his head slowly.

"Well, Nelson," Dow said, "you're right. I have my doubts about this venture and that's a fact. Jack and Benny got cut up pretty bad back there on the Powder and from what me and the boys heard, well, these soldier boys have had a real hard time of it out here. If the colonel says we ought to wait on a few more guns well, I wouldn't mind the wait. I'd just as soon get scalped at poker down at Washington's as get scalped for real on the trail. That's just the way I see it, Nelson, and no offense."

"None taken, George. Anyone else feel that way?" Story waited but heard nothing but a low mumbling and saw the shaking of heads. "All right then, we're a-going tonight. George, I'm sorry but you're outvoted. Now you understand that I can't leave you behind here. You'd have to get in to Kearny before we lit out and that would have the soldier boys out to foil us right off. Charley, Buster, you go on and tie George up and get him settled in one of the freight wagons. Make sure he's comfortable, I don't want him bounced around too bad. George, I apologize for this, I surely do, but it's gotta be this way. It'll only be for a day or so til we get clear of Kearny. We'll cut you loose then and you go on with us only as far as C. F. Smith and you can winter there. Like I said, you'll get your full wages up to there and I'll let you keep one horse and that Remington I bought you down at Laramie. C. F. Smith ain't got a Washington's pool hall but where there's soldiers cards can't be that far off and I imagine you'll be well enough til spring. No hard feelings, George, but that's the play of it."

"Well, by God, Nelson," George sputtered, "you just said I'd be free to go and no hard feelings. This is a damned raw deal, by God!"

"Hold on there, George," Story said quietly. "I just said there's no hard feelings and there ain't. And I said you'd be free to go and you will be. I just didn't say exactly where. C. F. Smith ain't but a few days up the trail and you'll be a damn sight safer there than if I left you hog-tied here or let you make your way back after being on the trail for a day or two. By God, George, but you ought to start using that head o' yours for more than a hat rack." Several of the other cowhands laughed.

George Dow was not particularly pleased. He had hoped on spending the winter comfortably ensconced at Washington's pool hall and enjoying the sight of Liz Wheatley as she served up her famous slapjacks. Now it looked like he would be stuck in some Godforsaken mudhole stick-fort with nothing but a bunch of blue bellies, Yankees all, to keep company with and not even a sight of a pretty woman, even if she was married with a couple of brats. Damn the luck!

"Well, George," Dutch Charley grinned at his old waddie, "just to show I'm the best-mannered jailer you ever had, I expect I'll let you take a piss and climb on up on the freighter yourself afore we hog-tie your ass."

"That ain't funny, Charley."

"Hell, no it ain't, George," Charley said with a grin. "It'd be funny if I had to brand your ass for being dumber'n owl shit." Buster McIlroy couldn't control himself and began to giggle. The image of Charley burning a large "D" on George's ass was just too much for him.

"Aww, shut your face, Buster," George growled, "or I'll commence to pissing on your boots."

"Hurry up there, boys," Story yelled. "If you ain't got your sougans rolled and pitched in the wagons get on 'er right quick. We got things to do and we're burning daylight. I ain't about to wait around here til Christmas."

"By God!" Carrington thundered, his fist slamming down on the desk with such force that papers swirled off to drift to the wide pine floorboards. Private Archie Sample stooped quickly and began gathering up the scattering sheets, which he hastily restacked on the colonel's desk. Captain Ten Eyck stepped forward, placed his fingers on Sample's sleeve, and with a nod of his head moved the young private quietly out of the door, leaving the two officers alone in the office.

"Captain Ten Eyck, I will not countenance such willful disobedience of my direct orders. It's an affront to the authority of the United States Army. I simply cannot allow it."

"With all respect, Colonel," Ten Eyck said quietly. "There's not much we can do about it. Had General Cooke declared the region under martial law . . ." Ten Eyck shrugged. "As it is Mr. Story is under no legal obligation to comply with our regulations."

Carrington glared at Ten Eyck for a moment but the fire quickly faded from his eyes. Ten Eyck was right, of course. If Carrington had kept the cattlemen within the confines of Phil Kearny it would have been another matter. The grounds of the post legally constituted Federal property and all who resided there were subject to the commander's directives. *I should have known better*, he thought bitterly.

"I should have seen it in the man's eyes, Tenedor. Leaving him out there away from the garrison, I might as well have turned Jimmy and Bobby loose in Judge Kinney's with coins in their pockets." Carrington sighed. "Well, I suppose there's nothing to be done at this point."

"Unless they are cut up by the Sioux."

"I know," Carrington said. "Mr. Story may be under no obligation to us but we are responsible for his safe passage. Have Lieutenant Adair assemble a detail and go after Mr. Story. He'll need fourteen men in addition to himself. Full field order, one hundred rounds of ammunition per man and rations for two weeks. I want them in pursuit this afternoon and they're to accompany Mr. Story as far as C. F. Smith."

"Ahem," Ten Eyck cleared his throat. "Sir, Mr. Adair has already submitted his resignation. Perhaps Sergeant Bowers or Corporal Phillips could serve as well?"

The colonel's head drooped. Ten Eyck was right again. It would be unfair to Adair knowing that he was liable to be released from all duties within the next few days. Carrington nodded.

"Yes, of course. Sergeant Bowers, I think, Tenedor, will do nicely." Carrington turned to stare out the window. "See to it immediately if you please."

He heard Ten Eyck's footsteps as he headed out the door to give out his instructions. There was a murmuring of voices in the outer office. Carrington gazed out the window toward the distant mass of the Bighorns. In a few hours he would be sending men up into those forests. Who, he wondered, is on those hills watching us, waiting? The voices ceased and somewhere a door closed. All was silent except for the regular chunk-chunking of the clock on the mantel. A breeze had come up and the Bighorns' lower slopes were alive with a shimmering, golden blanket of aspens. He stood, hands clasped behind his back, and watched in silence as the aspens shuddered and individual leaves shook themselves loose to pinwheel and soar in the wind that hushed through the trees.

8

Takiyuha wi
(Moon When The Deer Are In Rut)

November 1866

How about some coffee for an old man, Ten Eyck?" The
question came through the door pushed forward by a cold
draught of mountain air that carried with it the scent of woods-
smoke, stale sweat, and old leather.

" 'Y God it reeks of a pinery in here! But it appears to be
dry enough. I 'spect you boys got tired of livin' in Uncle
Samuel's tipis. At least it smells like you got some coffee in
this oversized coffin and I will take some of that if it's bein'
offered, which it ain't yet."

Captain Ten Eyck looked up from his desk with surprise. It
had been but a few weeks but those weeks had seemed such
a long time that he'd hardly expected to hear the familiar, gruff
voice again. He stood up quickly and moved around the desk
to take Bridger's hand in both of his and pump it vigorously.

"Good heavens, Major Bridger," he said eagerly. "But you
are certainly a sight for sore eyes." Bridger looked, if possible,
more frail and insubstantial than Ten Eyck remembered but
he could feel the man's raw strength in the roughness of
Bridger's hand.

"Don't mention sore eyes, Cap'n." Bridger snorted. "My
damned peepers is about to give up on me and this child does

not relish bein' reminded of it by some soldier boy who's playin' at office monkey."

The mountain man winked and grinned wickedly at Ten Eyck over the sleeve of his jacket as he wiped it across a nose that was red and raw from exposure. Ten Eyck grinned back at the old man whose performance, he saw, was a bit of melodrama enacted for the benefit of the gawking Private Sample.

"Wagh! This child is getting too damned old for such foolishness." The old man walked stiffly and rubbed at one hip in which the Blackfeet had left an arrowhead thirty years before. The arrowhead was long gone, removed years ago,[1] but the soreness lingered and acted up, particularly in cold weather. "Stove in with the rheumatiz, tired, cold, and hungry enough to eat my own damned mule. Which I would do did I not value his conversation so. The fact that I am fond of ye Ten Eyck's the only thing keeps me from eatin' your black heart raw."

Private Archibald Sample, who had never before laid eyes on Bridger but knew him only from tales spun around his exploits, was shocked by the language and baffled by the man's shabby appearance. Bridger's low-crowned slouch hat was well battered, discolored by the smoke of a thousand campfires, and greasy with fingerprints. The hat was tugged down over his eyes, allowing but a glimpse of the seamed, leathery face below. Prominent cheekbones tanned to the russet of an old saddle rose above gaunt cheeks covered with a stubble of dark whiskers flecked with gray. The man's throat

---

[1]The surgery had been performed by Dr. Marcus Whitman (1802–1847). Whitman, physician, missionary, and Oregon pioneer, first met Bridger in 1835 when looking for a suitable location to set up a mission among the Indians. He removed the arrowhead from Bridger's hip at the 1835 Green River rendezvous and earned the respect and admiration of the mountain man. The next year he brought his new wife, Narcissa, the first white woman to cross the Rocky Mountains, to establish a mission among the Cayuse near present day Walla-Walla. Relations with the Indians, however, grew ever more strained, and in 1847 Whitman, his wife, and twelve other members of the mission were massacred by the Cayuse.

appeared abnormally long and wattled like a turkey's and was marked by an odd swelling below his Adam's apple.[2] Bridger's only concession to his mountain-man reputation was a well-smoked and greasy buckskin jacket, in which several small rents had been stitched clumsily together with sinew and from which large chunks of fringe were missing—used as string to tie items to his saddle or playfully nibbled off by his mule. His heavy woolen trousers, the crotch area forked with buckskin against wear and blackened from contact with the saddle, were tucked loosely into the tops of stogy boots, the rough leather rock-scuffed and gouged with heavy travel. Sample wondered if this was indeed the famous mountain man and trapper who had opened the Oregon Trail and was said to have killed mountain lions with his bare hands. The man looked to him more like a tired old bullwhacker than the figure of popular legend, but his presence was nothing short of electrifying.

"Where's that coffee, boy?" Bridger turned on Sample, his glare galvanizing the young private into action. Sample grabbed up a tin cup and poured coffee into it from a pot that sat on the edge of a small stove in a corner of the room. The young private passed it to Bridger with a hand that shook noticeably.

Bridger grinned at Sample.

"Thankee, lad," he nodded. "Don't worry, boy, I shan't bite your arm off. Ain't truly my style no matter how peckish I be. I shall leave that to the tenderfeet and Californy-bound fools."[3] Bridger closed a clawlike hand around the crown of

---

[2]Bridger's thyroid was enlarged and goiterous, possibly the result of too little iodine in his diet. The swelling is likely why the Indians referred to him as "Big Throat."

[3]Bridger refers to the ill-fated Donner Party of 1846–47. In August of 1846 party of California-bound emigrants had, against all advice, swung off the main trail at Fort Bridger (in present-day southwestern Wyoming) to take the so-called Hastings Cutoff through Utah. It was a tragic decision which cost the train much valuable time and left the party stranded in the high Sierra in December of 1846. By the time aid reached the stranded travelers, forty-four of the eighty-nine persons who started had died and the survivors had resorted to cannibalism to survive.

his hat, tugged it off, and tossed it casually on a nearby table.

Captain Ten Eyck had meanwhile maneuvered a pair of ladder-backed chairs into position near the stove and invited Bridger to take a seat. The scout dropped his lean frame into the chair with a sigh, the tin mug clasped between weather-beaten, arthritic hands, the joints of which were swollen and cracked.

"Private Sample," Ten Eyck said, "run along to the dining hall and have someone broil up a large steak and some fixings for Major Bridger. Bring it back here as quick as you can and tell them not to skimp, that's a good lad. Off you go."

Sample jammed his kepi onto his head and rushed out the door as Ten Eyck turned back to Bridger. As the door closed it seemed that some of the rigidity melted from the mountain man's frame. Bridger's shoulders drooped and the muscles in his jaw relaxed ever so slightly.

"The colonel will be greatly relieved to see that you're back, Major," Ten Eyck said. "Things have been fairly quiet in the area for the last couple of weeks but I've got a bad feeling that we've not seen the end of Red Cloud's attentions."

Bridger closed his eyes and kept his head lowered over the mug letting the steam which rose from the coffee wash over his face. "Ummm. Where's the colonel at, Ten Eyck? I have a few tales to tell and I 'druther spit 'em out while they're all fresh in my head and before I get to feelin' too comfortable. Damn but I'm getting too old for this line of work." The old man flexed the stiffened fingers of one hand and grimaced with the effort.

"The colonel's out at the sinks." Ten Eyck nodded toward the rear of the building. "His bowels have been giving him trouble the last few days. He says he thinks he had a bad bit of meat but I suspect that it's more likely worry. I've seen it before in commanders who think they're coming into a big fight."

Bridger's head nodded. "Ummm," he grunted. "You will be right in your guess. Bad meat don't quicken your step for much more'n a day or two, even that salt horse you fellows

set so much stock by. And I say his instincts are good if he
thinks he's got a scrap coming on."

Ten Eyck looked away and out the window. "You know
the colonel has never been in a fight before."

"Well I do," Bridger said quietly. "But he'll soon have his
chance at a scrap, which is more the pity. I don't wish any
man a fight when it can be avoided and I like Henry Carrington more'n most. He is a decent man. And you can thank your
stars that he is no fool. It has been a hard thing not to try to
gut those red skunks but it has been the smart thing. The time
is not yet right."

The muffled slam of a door drifted through the headquarters
building and the two men looked up listening to measured
footsteps coming down the narrow hallway. The door opened
and a haggard and noticeably pale Henry Carrington moved
painfully into the room. While he maintained a stone face
Bridger was shocked by the appearance of the man who shuffled into the room. Between the massive structure of Fort Phil
Kearny that had sprung from the once-grassy meadow and the
aged appearance of his old friend it was as if Bridger had been
gone for years rather than a few short weeks. The old scout
felt a sudden empathy with the long-sleeping old Dutchman
in the story that he had heard Margaret Carrington relate to
the boys one night.[4] Carrington's shoulders were stooped as if
he bore a large weight on his back. Dark circles had formed
under his eyes and his mane of once dark hair now showed a
generous streaking of gray. *By damn!* Bridger thought. *It's like
I been asleep near twenty years!*

At the sight of Bridger, Carrington's face brightened and
the corners of his mouth twitched his whiskers as he broke
into a grin. Carrington came quickly over to Bridger as Ten
Eyck stood up and offered his own chair to his commander.

"Gabe!" Carrington said, eagerly shaking Bridger's hand.

---

[4]The "long-sleeping old Dutchman" would be Rip Van Winkle, from an old
folktale collected in a volume of such tales in 1819 by Carrington's former
employer, Washington Irving. A very popular story adapted many times, it
was well known throughout the country.

"It's good to see you. You don't know how much I've missed your counsel these last few weeks."

"Well met, Colonel," Bridger said warmly, "you're too kind to a crooked old man who has seen better days. How fares the colonel's lady and those two fine boys?"

"Fine, fine, Major. They've adjusted better than I to our situation and Margaret is more of a soldier than a soldier's wife. I'd be lost without her."

"I believe you at your word, Colonel. She is a fine woman and you are a fortunate man. Set down, sir. We've a bit of palaver to do and Ten Eyck here might as well stay so's you don't have to repeat it to him later."

Carrington waved Ten Eyck to bring another chair over to join them, which the captain did, bringing along with him a small notebook and a pencil. Bridger waited until he was satisfied that Ten Eyck was ready to take notes, and poured himself another cup of coffee.

"Did you get any of the news I sent down for ye earlier, Colonel? Good, that's good. I was worried that the fellas might not have won through. It's a fair rough piece of country up north of here right now." Bridger frowned thoughtfully. "Down below Clark's Fork I run across a young fellow pushing a passel of cattle toward Virginia City. Brash young Texican with more sand 'n sense if you ask me."

"Nelson Story!" Carrington and Ten Eyck said at once.

"That's the fellow. A lucky man that. He had a couple of scrapes with the Sioux and Arapaho but won through without too much trouble. Had some fancy fast-loading rifles and a set of rough young cobs with him." Bridger chuckled. "The Injuns were fairly riled by that last set-to. The Arapaho were leading the charge and Story's boys must have riddled 'em through. After the shootin' came the shoutin' between the Arapaho and the Sioux so I hear. The Arapaho accused Red Cloud of usin' the Arapaho to test the whites' new guns and spare his own bucks. It was a great hubaboo in council they say. Crooked Arm, he's the head of the Crow in these parts, he and Iron Shirt thought it was pretty durn amusing, the bunch of 'em squabbling over it. The Crow have no love for the headcutters,[5] you know. Red Cloud sorted it all out in the end, bad cess to him. He's a crafty one, that I will allow. He said the cowmen were always better armed than the soldiers and it weren't no proof that they'd fare likewise against the Buffalo Creek Fort. That's what they call your fort, you see. Nice piece of work you've done here, by the way, Colonel," Bridger added, jerking his head toward the window and indicating the fort beyond. "You should be snug enough for the winter, if your stock and vittles hold out."

"Yes," Carrington replied, glancing at Ten Eyck, "if indeed. We've laid in a fairly good set of provisions. With any luck we'll get another train in before too long and once the snow has started we can hopefully augment with some game. We should be comfortable enough."

Bridger shook his head. "Don't count on either, Colonel. I'll say it plain and not tell a lie. Red Cloud's got a powerful set of rascals collected up north. More damned lodges than I ever heared tell of along the Tongue and that's a fact. He's got the Arapaho and a passel of Cheyenne to come in with him, not to mention Sisseton, Hunkpapa, and Big Bellies. Big Mouth and Rotten Tail said it took 'em half a day to ride by all the Sioux and Arapaho lodges. A young Crow named Yellow Face said that up on the Tongue he had passed by camps strung out some forty miles or better. That's a heap of Injuns, Colonel."

"Are these men reliable informants, do you think?"

"Well, Colonel," Bridger grinned, "Yellow Face is over at Kinney's store right now and you can judge for yourself if you've a mind."

Carrington nodded. That Yellow Face was Bridger's traveling companion spoke volumes for his reliability. "How about Black Horse and Dull Knife?" The Cheyenne under these men

---

[5]"Headcutters": Derisive term used by Crow, Arikara, and Shoshoni tribes to describe the Sioux (Lakota). It is derived from ancient Lakota practice of taking the heads of their enemies. Although the practice was largely abandoned by this time the sign language of the plains tribes employed a finger drawn horizontally across the windpipe to signify "Lakota."

had once been favorably disposed toward Carrington's command but that did not mean that they had not, in the interim, been persuaded to join Red Cloud's alliance.

"No, Colonel, Black Horse and Dull Knife will not play his game. There is powerful bad blood between 'em right now." The scout ran his fingers back through his matted hair. "I never could get much to the root of it from the Crows. They are terrible gossips and tend to stretch a tale in the tellin' but it seems to hail back to when French Pete war kilt. There are maybe a hunnert Cheyenne have jined up that I can cipher. Young hotheads like Two Moons and a few cousins from over Colorady way and they are on the peck. These boys have a score to settle from Sand Creek and hearin' that Medicine Calf Beckwourth was among the soldiers probably helped 'em along in that idea."

"And the Crows?"

"No sir, you needn't worry on that score." Bridger shook his head. "The Crow will not plague you, of that I am certain. The Crow used to own all this land, as far as an Injun owns anything, and they are hard up on the Sioux for stealing it from 'em. Though Red Cloud was bold enough to ask 'em to jine up which did surprise me some. That's a brazen act after how they've dealt the Crow these long years. Red Cloud, the chiefs tell me, is waiting on the bad weather. Says he's going to cut the road and starve you out and then kill every bluecoat who ain't starved."

Carrington smiled grimly. "Well, Major Bridger, Red Cloud may think he can starve us out but he doesn't have any idea of just what we've laid by for the winter. I think that even come the worst we shall be able to get through the winter well enough and perhaps even into the spring as well."

Bridger raised a critical eyebrow and glanced at Ten Eyck, who avoided the old man's gaze. The veteran scout knew enough about the Army to know that Ten Eyck's job would have taken him through every inch of the commissary warehouses with Baldy Brown. Ten Eyck, if anyone, would know how accurate Colonel Carrington's boast was. The look on the captain's face told Bridger everything he needed to know. Although Ten Eyck would be reluctant to contradict his commander, the pained crinkle at the corner of the captain's eyes told Bridger that Carrington's assessment was optimistic at best and deluded at worst. *They'll be lucky*, Bridger thought, *to make it through midwinter*. Bridger elected to not pursue the issue but cached his impressions away for future use.

"As you say, Colonel," the scout said. "You know best your situation in that regard. But do not count on doing too much hunting this winter. It will prove a rum business I wager. Your younger officers will want to get out stalking a buck or two but the onliest kind of 'bucks' they're likely to find will shoot first."

"Fair enough," Carrington said. "I'll consider that fair warning. You mentioned Mr. Beckwourth. Did you see him while you were with the Crows? We've not had any word from him for several weeks now."

"Nor will you, Colonel." Bridger shook his head. "Old Medicine Calf has gone to what the Crows call the Other Side Camp. Took sick and went under while we were up among 'em. There was some loose talk he'd been pizened by a jealous husband."

"Dreadful thought," Carrington muttered, but Bridger waved it away with a bony hand.

"All talk and no cider, Colonel," Bridger announced firmly. "That pizen story I do not credit for it ain't a Crow's way, 'less a fellow like Shakespeare war spinning the yarn. A jealous buck would have stuck a 'hawk in his brainpan or a knife in his bowels. No, were there any truth to that, which I doubt, it'd be more like a squaw put him under with simple bad cookin'. Beckwourth never had much luck with women. A pretty face don't always stir the beans, but his eyes always got the better of his stomach. He did linger for a week or two and then passed on to Kingdom. Rest his untruthful soul." Bridger chuckled to himself.

"But ain't it just like Beckwourth to go under like that." Bridger's face creased with a half-smile and his eyes drifted away for a moment—to better times and old friends.

"Weren't ever but half what he said about his life which

war true in the first place and I wouldn't put it past the old
buzzard to have spun that tale about pizen his own self so's
he'd pass on with folks abuzz 'bout how he went. Count on
him to put a shine on most anything, even his own dying. I
imagine that he has near about talked the ears off all the Pow-
ers and Principalities by now and they are debating whether
to send him off to Perdition. But I 'spect they will deny Old
Nick the pleasure of his company for he is a rare diverting
fellow to have around once you get used to his blowing."

"Poor fellow," Carrington said, shaking his head. "He
seemed a good man and we'll miss his services. Seems a terrible waste after we've fought such a long war to free men
like James Beckwourth."

Bridger's eyes narrowed and the skin around his mouth
creased into deep wrinkles with the twist of his lips. "No sir,"
he objected quietly. "That you did not. That war had naught
to do with Jim Beckwourth. Black as the ace o' spades he was
but ne'er a slave nor would he think so. Jim Beckwourth was
freer than you or I will ever be, Colonel. I do not know my
letters, sir and am a slave to my ignorance. And you are a
slave to your duty. Medicine Calf never really belonged to
your world nor mine. Wouldn't neither accept him so he made
a world and a life of his own place and choosing. I allow most
of it was in his fanciful head but it was real and free enough
to him and that was well enough. No sir, you cannot free a
man who never b'lieved he was a slave."

Carrington shot the old scout a quizzical look. It was an
odd thing to hear. He had never considered so broad a definition of slavery and yet Bridger had put his finger on something. There were things which bound tighter than chains.
Held faster and weighed more than crude iron and stung
sharper than the lash. Ignorance was such a thing. He had seen
Bridger sit rapt as a child at Margaret's knee as she read to
him of people and places that were forever denied an unlet-
tered man except through the offices of another. Duty and
conscience were such things as well. He had himself often
looked out at Fort Phil Kearny and thought it no less a burden
than Ahab's great white whale dragging him relentlessly down

into the depths of despair. Carrington started to make reply but saw that Bridger knew his thoughts. No words were needed. A pained silence filled the room, a dark sea rising that threatened to drown the men who shared it.

"Well, that's neither here nor there," Bridger said, drawing himself up, his hands on his knees and blowing out through his nostrils as if to clear away irrelevant thoughts. "The last time this child saw James Beckwourth while he war still alive, Colonel, he said he'd recruited two hunnert fifty young Crow bucks who would ride against the Sioux and their friends."

"I've received authorization from General Cooke," Carrington said, nodding, "to employ Indian auxiliaries. I've already sent word back to Omaha to try to raise the Winnebago or some Pawnee. We are, in any event, only authorized to employ fifty and not the two hundred fifty Beckwourth said he recruited. But I would be interested to hear your thoughts on that."

Bridger sat quietly, his mouth working as if he were stroking a bad tooth with his tongue, then nodded.

"That's likely a better bargain than what Beckwourth come up with, Colonel. The Winnebago and Pawnee both have good guns and use 'em well. Crow are all pretty much still using bows and arrows. The Pawnee, once they sign on, will be bound to you. That's their style, for old Frank North[6] trained 'em right. If things get hot for the Crow you might expect to wake up one day and find 'em gone astray. They still have to live with the damned headcutters out here and they will think twice if it looks like the Sioux have a good day. Which they

[6]Frank North (1840–1885) grew up on a farm adjacent to the Pawnee Reservation in Nebraska Territory, learning the language and gaining the trust of the tribe's leadership. During the Civil War, Major North, along with his brother Captain Luther North, recruited and led Pawnee and Omaha Scout Battalions in combat against the Cheyenne, Sioux, and Arapaho. The Indian Scouts were devoted to the Norths and performed with great gallantry. Frank later joined his old friend William F. "Buffalo Bill" Cody's Wild West Show and performed with him until he died of injuries received in a horse accident. He was not related to the North rumored to be with the Sioux war parties.

likely will from time to time." Bridger nodded again. "No sir, I expect the Winnebago or Pawnee will work out well. If they get here on time. I do not expect that the Sioux will stop them but the winter well could."

"Will that be seen as an offense by Crooked Arm and the Crows, Gabe? That is, if we hire on Pawnees rather than Crows," Carrington asked.

"No, no, Colonel." Bridger gave a small smile and shook his head easily. "If anything Crooked Arm will be pleased, as it lets him off the hook. If the Sioux and Arapaho are on the peck then he'll have more cause to worry about his people if his youngsters are out ridin' against 'em. As long as his bucks aren't involved the Sioux will likely leave his people be in the hope that he'll want to join up sooner or later. This will let him sit easy and fat for the winter at least."

"Will Crooked Arm join up with Red Cloud?"

"No, Colonel. He will not. Nor will Iron Shirt, Medicine Crow, Wolf Chaser, Sees The Living Bull, nor none of 'em that I know. The Sioux will have to play this hand out with the cards they have. But with the Arapaho and some Cheyenne jined up I will allow that it's a pretty fair hand."

Carrington smiled grimly. "Fair hand or not, Major Bridger, we will see Red Cloud's ante and raise the stakes. The last civilian train of the season is ready to move north and we expect a detachment of cavalry any day now. At last report they had already departed Fort Laramie and are accompanied by some additional officers. We may yet strike a blow against Red Cloud and give him pause. At worst we should be able to convince his allies that a war with the United States government is ill advised."

Bridger gave Carrington a sidelong glance but said nothing. He got up to refill his mug, then moved to the window that looked out onto the parade ground. He stood there sipping his coffee, one hand stuffed casually into a pocket of his travel-stained jacket, his lanky frame silhouetted against the bright background of light reflected by the browned grass. The only sounds to break the silence were the quiet smacking of his lips and the steady ticking of the clock. Footsteps sounded on the boards of the porch and the figure of Private Sample moved past the window. Sample was carrying a large crate over which a towel had been draped. The footsteps stopped at the door and he could be heard fumbling with the latch. Ten Eyck moved to the door and opened it quickly. The young private was nearly sent sprawling but recovered himself and the crate he had balanced precariously on his forearms. The odor of cooked meat and warm bread set Bridger's mouth to watering and he lifted the towel to peer critically underneath it.

"That'll do for my supper, soldier boy," Bridger said loudly. "Well, don't let 'er cool in the breeze, haul it on in hyar and let's set to it." He turned and winked at Carrington, who smiled and waved him to a nearby table.

"Care to join me, Colonel? Do your bowels good to keep somethin' running through 'em."

"Thank you, no, Major. Please enjoy your meal."

Bridger retrieved his chair from its place by the stove as Sample carefully cleared maps and ledgers out of the way and replaced them with plates of food. The office was quickly filled with the heady aromas of broiled beefsteak, wild onions, and fresh biscuits. Bridger snatched up a biscuit and crammed it eagerly into his mouth.

"Injuns do a fair bit of meat, Colonel," Bridger mumbled as he swallowed the biscuit and washed it down with more coffee. "Mostly buffler. Dog is their favorite but that never did have much appeal to me. Musta got attached to one of the critters as a child. But they don't have the nariest idea of a good biscuit. Most Injuns figure that hardtack is a delicacy and won't drink coffee unless it's mostly sugar. Goes a long way to explaining why they are a savage and untrustworthy lot taken as a whole. Been with 'em many a year, even married one or two, but never could acquire much of a taste for their vittles. They'll do if you've a powerful hunger on but it's mostly pretty poor doin's.

"Say, where's your shadow catcher, Colonel?" Bridger said over his shoulder. "Beckwourth was queerly fond of the boy and I said I'd look after him when I got back."

"I'm afraid our Mr. Glover is dead," Carrington said quietly.

"A patrol found him about a mile from the post a few weeks past."

Bridger was not surprised. "Ummm-hmmm. Didn't figure that boy'd last out the year anyhow. Well, he'll be good company for Beckwourth, who'll have him taking pictures of himself with his arm draped over Saint Peter. Strange fellow. Reminded me of a damned Mormon with that handcart of his. Too much of an innocent. Mark me, Colonel," Bridger said, extending a bony finger to Heaven, "this country is particular. It does not forgive a man his innocence. The Good Book says that the meek shall inherit the earth but it does not say how. Most will inherit naught but a six-foot plot and a small heap o' rocks. If their carcass ain't found by wolves first."

No Water lifted a stray stick of wood from between the rocks ringing the central fire and placed it carefully into the small blaze that lit the interior of the council lodge. The lodge was crowded with men, mostly mature warriors, war leaders, and Shirt Wearers. The close air was redolent of tobacco and woodsmoke, sweat and body odors. Someone had tossed a braid of sweetgrass into the coals and the sweet, pungent aroma helped to scent the air. No Water's movements were maddeningly slow and meticulous and Red Cloud found himself wondering if he had been wise in matching him with his niece.

"I think we should forget about this war for now," No Water was saying as he poked idly at the fire. "We should concentrate on hunting while the deer are in rut. There will be time enough to fight once we have provided for our families for the winter."

Red Cloud suppressed the urge to criticize his nephew, for in truth it was pretty much what he would have expected to hear from the man. No Water was an acceptable husband for Black Buffalo Woman but not much more than that. He was a competent hunter but in no way remarkable. His family would not go hungry but neither would they grow fat. There was no fire in the man. He was capable at most everything and yet not gifted at anything.

Red Cloud had arranged No Water's marriage to spite Crazy Horse, who still loved Black Buffalo Woman and was not good at hiding his feelings. There would be trouble from this situation sooner or later, as most everyone in the camp acknowledged. Pretty Owl explained this to her husband with enough regularity and finger-wagging that Red Cloud had grown heartily sick of hearing about it. What Pretty Owl couldn't seem to grasp was the fact that No Water, whatever his faults, would never pose a threat to Red Cloud. Crazy Horse was another matter entirely.

"I suppose a man should concentrate on his hunting if that's what concerns him," Crazy Horse said with a hint of sarcasm in his voice. "When I spoke of hunting it was only to point out how we can better fight this war. I thought we were all here to talk about killing the whites, not filling our wives' bellies."

There was a low chuckling among the shadowy forms seated around the fire. No Water was unmoved and Red Cloud could only assume that the man was too dull-witted to get the crude joke, which was aimed at him.

"It's hard to fight on an empty stomach," No Water said slowly. "And the deer won't be in rut all winter."

"No they won't," Crazy Horse observed wryly. "We will leave that to you, No Water."

There was a ripple of laughter in the lodge. This time even No Water grasped the vulgar reference directed at him. He glared angrily across the lodge at his rival and half rose from his crouch near the fire. Crazy Horse ignored him but looked straight at Red Cloud, fixing him with an icy stare. Red Cloud read the challenge in the younger man's eyes but quickly decided that this was neither the time nor the place for personal squabbles. Red Cloud waved a dismissive hand at No Water, commanding him silently to sit down. The council lodge was no place for such bickering.

"You have something to say, Crazy Horse," he said evenly.

"As a Shirt Wearer[7] you are entitled to our attention in this
council. What is it about hunting that should change how we
fight the whites?"

Crazy Horse held his gaze at Red Cloud for a moment. He
seemed about to say something rude but apparently thought
better of it. There would be other times to deal with Red Cloud
and No Water. He looked to the other warriors assembled
around the floor of the lodge and addressed his words to them.

"When we hunt the buffalo or take new ponies from the
plains our grandfathers taught us to follow the herd quietly for
two or three sleeps. We ride along behind them, not chasing,
but following them."

The young warrior paused for a moment to see if the others
were with him. Several heads around the circle nodded. This
was not how it was always done but many of the older men
had used this method. Crazy Horse could tell that he had their
interest.

"After two or three sleeps," Crazy Horse went on, "we turn
our ponies about and go away from the herd and they become
curious and follow us. We do this for another two sleeps and
after a time we can lead them where we want them, into a
coulee or a box canyon. Ponies we capture. Buffalo we kill."
He closed the fingers of his hand slowly and made a violent
pounding motion with his fist. Grunts of agreement came from
several warriors.

"What does that have to do with the whites?" No Water
demanded. "You think we should follow them around like
dogs and then wander away and they will follow us? What a
stupid idea!"

"*Hetchetu!*"[8] Crazy Horse said with a smirk. "That truly

---

[7]Shirt Wearer: First established among the Hunkpapa around 1851, the office
of Shirt Wearer was a position of great responsibility in tribal affairs. The
institution, which spread throughout the Lakota nation, allowed for the selection of four warriors of exceptional merit to serve as intermediaries between
the tribal council and tribal leadership. With the aid of the *akicita* (a sort of
tribal police drawn from various warrior societies), the Shirt Wearers were
responsible for the implementation of tribal policy.

[8]*Hetchetu!*: "That is true!"

would be a stupid idea, I'm not surprised that you would think of such a thing." Several of the others chortled to themselves at this gibe.

No Water clenched his teeth, his jaw muscles tensing. He glanced quickly to Red Cloud, who shot a disapproving glare in his direction. No Water held his tongue.

"But that's not what I said," Crazy Horse said. "I have been watching the bluecoats. Whenever we fight them there are two ways the fight can end. If we stop the fight and are gone before they know it they are glad. They stay where they are or they go back to the fort or go on doing what they were doing before. But if we run from them and they see us run they chase us."

There was a brief moment of silence as he let this observation sink in, and then there was a low mumbling as the warriors talked among themselves. American Horse, who had kept his own counsel throughout the gathering, found himself smiling and nodding his head. It was true what the man said and he wondered why he had not seen it for himself before now.

"So," Crazy Horse went on. "We must convince the whites to chase us. Then we will lead them to the place where we can kill them." Red Cloud lifted his hand for silence and indicated that American Horse should have his say.

"How many warriors," American Horse asked, "should we use to let the whites chase after us, Crazy Horse? I too have been watching the bluecoats closely. If there are too many of us they are as likely to stop or go the other way as they are to come ahead. They are not like horses or buffalo. These *wasichu* are very unpredictable. They are a very strange people."

"*Nunwe!*"[9] Crazy Horse nodded. "Yes, that's true, brother. The trick will be to make them think that there are fewer of us than there actually are. Depending on how many bluecoats are in a party we can use as few as three braves but probably no more than five. It has to seem to them to be an easy fight."

[9]*Nunwe!*: Lakota equivalent of "Amen!"

"What about the bluecoats with the *maza wakan*, the fast-shooting guns?" Bad Wound interjected leaning forward with interest, his sharp features illuminated by the flickering fire. "The *Manpiyato* had a hard time with the cattle movers who had these new guns that shoot very quickly. A lot of our people were killed or badly hurt in that fight."

A low murmur of voices and a bobbing of heads punctuated his question. The Arapaho had indeed had a bad day of it with the cattle movers. Five of the Arapaho had been killed outright, one had died of his wounds later, and three others were still recovering from their wounds. There had been a nasty confrontation afterward with Tall Bear and Little Chief accusing Red Cloud of having tricked them into throwing their braves against the cattle movers just to see how well the whites' new guns worked. It had been a tense time and now several cold looks were cast furtively in Red Cloud's direction.

"Yes, Bad Wound," Crazy Horse nodded slowly. "The cattle movers had new guns that shoot quickly. Some of the pony soldiers have guns like that. But there are only a few of these at the Buffalo Creek Fort. I know it is hard to tell them apart but if you look closely you can see that the real pony soldiers sit on their horses more easily than the walk-a-heaps and they wear different clothes. If you look closely at their guns you can see that the guns that shoot fast are shorter than the guns the walk-a-heaps carry. We need to separate the pony soldiers from the walking soldiers. The *wasichu* are easier to deal with in smaller groups and they will not be as hard to kill."

Bad Wound listened intently, his brow furrowed and lips pursed in thought. His friend Red Leaf whispered in his ear and he nodded his approval to Crazy Horse.

"This is a good plan which Crazy Horse has," American Horse said to the entire assembly. "What he says about the bluecoats is true, I have seen it myself. But there are other things to remember. Especially with the fast-shooting guns. You have to get on top of these people quickly and kill them quickly. If they have too much time to see us coming they can be much more dangerous. And with the walking soldiers, their guns take a long time to reload but they kill at a great distance.

If we can remember this and get the two separated from each other we can kill them as Crazy Horse says. Yes, it might work. I think we should try the plan. As we kill these people we can take their guns and we will have an easier time when we fight the others."

The lodge hummed with the low tones of men's voices as the warriors talked eagerly among themselves. This was a new way of fighting whites that Crazy Horse and American Horse suggested, but it made sense. No Water sat quietly staring into the fire. He did not like Crazy Horse and knew that the man still looked at Black Buffalo Woman with lust. He would like to kill him but did not relish the thought of what would come afterward. So he sat still, watching the fire with eyes that did not see but were focused on other visions, visions of how he could get rid of this man and never have to look at him again. But whatever he did, he would have to be very careful. He looked at Red Cloud and saw that his uncle, too, seemed to be staring off into the future. He wondered how his uncle, who had himself once killed another Oglala, would take it if Crazy Horse failed to come home from a fight with the *wasichu*. It occurred to him that his uncle would not be overly grieved if the strange young man who still coveted Red Cloud's niece were to die in battle. A smile flickered across No Water's face. *"Sehanstuka!"* [10] No Water announced loudly, and stood to look across the central fire at his rival. "I am convinced that Crazy Horse indeed has a good plan. Let's try it and see how it works. I am for it." Crazy Horse looked up, puzzled. He had never expected No Water, of all people, to support him in anything.

"This idea you have of using decoys, Crazy Horse," No Water went on. "It is an interesting one. Do you think that you could show us how to use this successfully against the bluecoats?"

Crazy Horse nodded. He noticed the slight curl of No Water's lip and in that tiny fold of skin he saw what he thought was the truth of No Water's sudden enthusiasm. Perhaps No

---

[10]*Sehanstuka!*: "Most certainly!"

Water was hoping that the Hunkpatila would be a little too bold and find himself within the reach of one of the walking soldier's guns. Crazy Horse smiled thinly. Well, he could play No Water's game easily.

"Of course I can show how to do this. Why don't you come with me and have a very close look at how it's done, No Water? Why, even Red Cloud will be welcome on this hunt. You can't eat a white man but he is a much more interesting creature to hunt. As American Horse has said, you never know what they will do." Crazy Horse didn't say it but he knew that one could never really be sure of what any man might do, given the opportunity. That included No Water and Red Cloud. He decided that he would just have to wait and see.

SPOTTED TAIL TRIED TO FOCUS HIS EYES ON THE MOCCASIN through which he painstakingly drew a needle and sinew. The fire was getting low and he had to squint and lean far forward to see what he was doing. This was taking longer than he had hoped. Not that there weren't any number of women in the camp who would gladly have performed this menial task. He was still a handsome man and a well-respected one. But Spotted Tail didn't care to incur any of the implied obligations their assistance would levy on him. At least not yet. There would be time enough for that when the grass came up again in the spring.

Some of the people of the camp thought it was simple obstinacy on his part. Others whispered that he no longer had the wherewithal to be a proper husband to a woman. It was all nonsense. He still had an eye for a good-looking young woman and would get himself another wife. Maybe two if he wanted. But that could wait a little while. Spotted Tail didn't care for camp gossip. He let them chatter and went about his business. As far as he was concerned, his lodge was far from the empty shell it seemed. It was filled with ghosts. It was said that one could not talk to a ghost except in dreams, but he knew better.

"I can do this, woman," he mumbled quietly. "And don't

chide me about my eyes. If you had lived your eyes would not be as sharp as you let on. So leave me to my work. When the grass comes up in the spring I will find another woman to take care of these things." The needle slipped pricking his thumb and making him flinch. He stuck the thumb in his mouth and sucked away the blood.

"That was not necessary," he complained softly to the woman only he could see. "If you could do this I would let you. There is no need to be sharp about it."

The flap of the lodge opened and he peered closely to see whose figure had ducked in to join him. The dimness of the lodge made it difficult to determine who it was.

"I see your face, cousin." It was Red Cloud's voice. "I would like to talk."

"I see your face, cousin," Spotted Tail replied guardedly, and wondered what had brought the Oglala into the Brulé circle. This was unexpected. He had made no secret of his opposition to Red Cloud's plans and found it odd that the man should want to talk about anything. As far as Spotted Tail was concerned there was nothing left to talk about. Their differences notwithstanding, Spotted Tail had no intention of breaking with tradition and good manners. If a man came openly to talk with him he was of course welcome to do so and entitled to any hospitality which he could offer. He waved the younger man to the place of honor next to him.

"You are welcome in my lodge, *Mahkpia-Luta*. Do you wish something to eat?"

Red Cloud shook his head and thanked the older warrior. The two men sat quietly on the buffalo robes, side by side, both staring into the small blaze that glowed in the center of the lodge. Spotted Tail put aside the moccasins he was repairing and waited. Several minutes passed in silence. Finally Spotted Tail decided to prod his silent guest.

"I should tell you now, Red Cloud," he said quietly, "that if you have come to seek my approval for this war you will not get it. I am opposed to a fight with the *wasichu*. Whether I like them or not is beside the point. You have your Bad Faces with you, many of the Oglala, the Hunkpatila, the Sans

Arc, and the Shyela. You even have some of our Brulé who
will join you. But I am opposed to this fight and many of my
people have listened to my words and will not join you."

"I know that, *Sinté-Galeska*," the visitor responded without
heat. "I don't seek your approval in this matter. You say what
you believe and so it is. I do the same. I come tonight to put
a stop to the bad feelings between us for now."

Spotted Tail grunted and sat looking curiously at his guest.
The fire flared up briefly and died down, throwing the interior
of the lodge deeper into shadow. A wisp of smoke curled
lazily upward toward the cold and distant stars that had begun
to appear through the narrow vent at the peak of the lodge.
Spotted Tail reached behind him and retrieved his pipe from
its beaded bag. He assembled it carefully, mumbling a quiet
prayer as he did so. Then, as carefully, he prepared the mixture
of tobacco and red willow, sweetgrass and sage, cutting the
materials on a small board and then tamping them firmly into
the bowl with a pipe stick. Using a set of bone tongs he reached
into the fire and withdrew a single coal, blew on it gently, and
held the glowing ember to the bowl, puffing regularly. He offered the pipe to the four directions, the earth and the sky, then
handed the pipe to Red Cloud, who followed Spotted Tail's
lead. As Red Cloud smoked, his host reached onto the small
board and in turn picked up small pinches of sweetgrass and
sage, which he sprinkled onto the glowing coals in the fire, re-
leasing a thin but fragrant smoke into the lodge. Matters of importance were to be discussed and any evil spirits must be
chased from the lodge with the purifying smoke. A man who accepted the pipe and smoked knew he must tell the truth or he
would anger the Everywhere Spirit. The two men handed the
pipe back and forth between themselves, each taking two or
three puffs, until the contents of the bowl were consumed completely. Spotted Tail took the empty pipe and muttered another
prayer as he tapped the burned contents of the bowl gently into
the fire. He was careful to let not a single ash stray to the floor
of the lodge, for he did not want *Wakan Tanka* offended in any
way. When he had disassembled the pipe and returned it to its
bag he turned to Red Cloud.

"There is no hate in my heart against you, Red Cloud, whatever my words have been or how you have heard them from my own mouth, or the mouths of others. What I have opposed is your plan to fight against the whites right now. My arguments against your plan are just that—against your plan, not you personally. If anything I feel a great sorrow in my heart for you. You have won this argument between us but I think it will taste bitter to you in the end."

"So I have heard, but why do you think so, *Sinté-Galeska?*" Red Cloud asked quietly. "I know that with the tribes I have gathered in our cause we will defeat the whites and drive them out. I am sure of this. Why should a victory like this taste bitter to us? Why should we regret driving the whites from our home?"

"You still don't understand what I have been trying to say to you these many moons now. Yes, you may well drive out the whites, but at what cost to the people? How many lodges will be empty when winter comes again? How many children will grow up without their fathers? You of all people should understand, Red Cloud. You came to manhood without your father's hand to guide you. Yes, you've become a great warrior and you have a large following but it has not been any easy road. Would you make other boys walk this road?"

"I have walked this road," Red Cloud said. "Others may also. There are many who will be *Hunka*[11] to a boy of promise. It's not what I wish, but it may be necessary for some boys to grow up without fathers if they're to grow up at all."

Spotted Tail looked at the other man and shook his head.

"Grow up to do what? Do you really think that even if you drive these whites out this year that more won't come next year or the year after that? What if this fight doesn't end when these soldiers are dead or chased away, what then? What if the war goes on and on? Then those boys whose fathers and grandfathers have died in this war will not only have lost their past but their future as well. If you are the one who does this

---

[11]*Hunka*: A sort of adoptive father who takes a boy under his tutelage and helps to guide his steps to manhood.

to them they will hate you and you will live out your life as
a bitter man. Those who follow me will not be part of your
war. I will lead them away. Any others who wish to come
will be welcome."

Red Cloud sat silently for a moment, then rose to leave.

"We'll wait and see," Red Cloud said, "who is bitter in the
end. I'll leave that to *Wakan Tanka* to decide."

The younger man ducked under the lodge flap and was
gone. Spotted Tail's eyes remained on the space that Red
Cloud had left, staring at the emptiness. He nodded.

"Yes, woman," he said quietly. "I think you are right. I
think *Wakan Tanka* has already decided that." Spotted Tail
reached down for the moccasin he had been repairing and went
back to his work.

CAPTAIN TEN EYCK HAD AS MUCH REASON AS ANYONE AT
Fort Phil Kearny to be a bitter man. That he wasn't sometimes
surprised even him. He removed his wire-rimmed spectacles
and rubbed his eyes with the tips of ink-stained fingers. He
found that he needed the spectacles more and more for this
close work, and they gave him a fierce headache. He sat at his
desk in the headquarters building drumming his fingers on a
small stack of post returns, bills of lading, and official correspondence, which vied in vain for his attention. He should
leave it for Bisbee. Lieutenant Bisbee was now, after all, the
adjutant, and the handling of this administrative material was
really his job. But the lieutenant was an active young man
who preferred being out and about rather than chained to a
desk. Ten Eyck had, for his part, had more than his fill of
what the lieutenant classed as "active service." If given the
option, he had no qualms about filling in for Bisbee in the
office while the youngster was engaged in some more soldierly
pursuit. This usually involved chasing Indians with the newly
promoted Fred Brown. Ten Eyck had seen more than enough
of such nonsense to last him a lifetime. At least the headquarters building was a comfortable change from the tents they
had occupied for so long.

The old captain thought he'd best get on with the business at hand, especially since the infernal paper shufflers in Omaha were being so blockheaded these days, but his heart wasn't in it. Instead, Ten Eyck gazed in a dreamlike state towards the window against which drops of rain were being driven by a cold wind from the mountains. He sat there listening to the tink-tink of the large drops beating against the glass and the low moaning of the wind that rose and fell in waves. The ever-capricious weather had changed once again and these after-noon showers, always short in duration, had become frequent, sweeping down from the Bighorns with such regularity that one could almost set one's watch by them. Soon they would be replaced by snow. A single cottonwood leaf had been blown up from the groves along the Big Piney and was plas-tered to one of the panes of glass, its browned, heart-shaped silhouette looking like a Lilliputian buffalo hide stretched for tanning. This leaf had somehow fixed itself in Ten Eyck's gaze, mesmerizing him as the rivulets of water traced its out-line and streaked down the glass. The grayness of the day seemed to match his mood. Tenedor felt an odd kinship with the cottonwood leaf, blown far from home into an alien en-vironment and trapped against an immovable object. He looked down at the stack of reports that had been showering down upon them—a deluge of paper, red tape, and igno-rance—and thought for a moment that he would gladly exchange places with the cottonwood leaf. At least the leaf was not compelled to respond to the rain in writing.

The maddening torrent of ill-advised and ill-informed bu-reaucratic nonsense that flowed down from headquarters in Omaha had been matched by pressing internal problems, the hostile Sioux notwithstanding. An endless succession of mis-haps plagued every waking hour. He suspected that someone had been actively rifling through the supplies of corn and me-dicinal port. Doubtless, Ten Eyck thought wryly, the teamsters had more than their share of "medical emergencies" calling for a dose or two en route. Lieutenant Bradley had finally returned from escort duty after an absence of more than two months, bearing with him the unwelcome news that Jim Brannan, one of their most valued scouts and interpreters, had been jumped by a war party and killed. Two others from Bradley's escort detachment had slipped away in the night to seek their fortunes in the goldfields. Worse, the damned miscreants had taken their horses and weapons with them. Ten Eyck knew it would be far more difficult to replace the animals and equipment than the men themselves. Even Bradley's most welcome return was short-lived, for it released the resigning Lieutenant Adair from his duties without really replacing him. Bradley was promptly reassigned to the 3rd Battalion in Utah by those damned fools in Omaha. In quick succession five more enlisted men had "bounced" for the goldfields. The civilian master of transportation disappeared shortly thereafter, and with him the government funds allotted to pay for wood and hay supplies. Leviticus Carter swore he'd skin the man alive if he ever caught up with him. Colonel Henry Carrington was almost beside himself with rage and frustration, and Tenedor Ten Eyck was left to clean up the mess of paperwork that resulted.

With his zeal for attention to detail, Carrington had removed Ten Eyck from his position as commander of the garrison, taking over the duties himself. Tenedor, in addition to his duties at the headquarters, was left to look to the running of the regiment. There had been some straining of his relations with Henry Carrington over this apparent demotion but Ten Eyck attributed it to the immense pressure that Carrington felt he was under. Ten Eyck had to admit that his own growing fondness for Who-Shot-John, aggravated by the daily frustrations of life at Phil Kearny, hadn't helped matters any. Carrington tended to be a nervous man and having no affinity for the bottle himself simply did not appreciate another's recourse to that particular medicine for that particular affliction. After the disestablishment of the Mountain District, Ten Eyck found himself demoted from command of the garrison to command of the Second Battalion. Then that position too was lost with the arrival of Captain William Judd Fetterman. Fetterman had more time in service as a captain than did Ten Eyck and so the command of the battalion went automatically to him—as did Ten Eyck's quarters.[12] It was almost more than a man could bear.

Fetterman's arrival had occasioned a festive atmosphere at Phil Kearny, since he was accompanied by Captain Powell, Major Almstedt the paymaster, and Company C of the Second U.S. Cavalry under the command of Lieutenant Horatio Bingham. Colonel Carrington had been nearly delirious with joy at the arrival of this party. Here was the much-needed cavalry that had been promised them for months! The addition of Powell, Fetterman, and Bingham, combat veterans all, to the garrison rolls further improved Carrington's mood.

The new arrivals were greeted like long-lost friends, which, with Fetterman and Powell, was very much the case. Both had served with the 18th Regiment during the war, and they were greeted warmly by Lieutenant Bisbee and the newly promoted Captain Fred Brown, both of whom had served alongside them throughout the war. Now Fort Phil Kearny could be added to the store of shared memories of Corinth, Stones River, Jonesboro, New Hope, and Atlanta. There had been much good-natured ribbing, punching of arms, and slapping of backs as the old friends were reunited. A few of the older sergeants, like Bowers, looked on fondly, as they too had served with these men. They were comfortable with them and knew them more intimately in some cases than they knew their own kin, for the blood shared among these men was of a different and more compelling thickness. It was blood spilled and mingled in war.

Ten Eyck was not impressed. He had spilled his share of blood with the 18th and, after Chickamauga, spent months as a prisoner of the rebels. But it was almost as if his time as a prisoner had negated the value of the blood shed beforehand.

---

[12]A common feature of frontier army life was the practice of "ranking" or "bumping," in which a newly arrived officer, if more senior than those on post, took the best quarters. All other subordinate officers on down the line would then find themselves "bumped" down into the next most appropriate quarters. For the officers' wives this was a particular sore point. This practice remained in vogue as late as the 1970s.

At least that was the feeling he got from Fetterman and his friends. As auspicious as his arrival had seemed at the time, Captain Fetterman brought with him something that Ten Eyck could easily have done without. He wasn't sure what, particularly, but something about the man made him uneasy. Perhaps it was the man's cocksure arrogance.

Maybe the colonel's right, Ten Eyck thought. *Maybe I'm overreacting*. Well, there would be a small affair at the colonel's quarters tonight. Maybe he could get a better sense of the man in a less formal atmosphere.

COLONEL CARRINGTON, DELIGHTED TO HAVE MORE OFFICERS, especially with excellent combat records, added to Phil Kearny's post returns,[13] was anxious to welcome the newcomers to the command. Margaret Carrington, assisted by their manservant George, Ten Eyck's maid Black Susan, Mrs. Wands' cook Laura, and the winsome Elisabeth Wheatley, had spent the afternoon getting the commanding officer's quarters ready for the evening's festivities. The other officers' wives, delighted at any excuse for a social event, pitched in happily, lending silver, linen, candlesticks, china, and extra hands in an effort to make it an evening to be remembered.

The sun had long disappeared behind the Bighorns and the Carrington quarters were alight with the glow of candles that set every crystal goblet and piece of silver to sparkling. A cheering fire crackled on the hearth. The cozy parlor was a picture of good fellowship and homey comfort. Half a dozen conversations were going on in various parts of the room and a person drifting through would have caught snatches of small talk about children and horses, the relative gustatory merits of buffalo and elk, the latest comedic plays in New York and political power plays in Washington, the latest fashions in Mrs. Demarest's magazine and the most fascinating essays in *Frank*

[13]Post return: Daily official records of an Army post, including personnel rosters and status, activities, logistics, and other routine housekeeping affairs of running an Army garrison.

Leslie's Illustrated Weekly—which somebody said would be renamed *Frank Leslie's Illustrated Annual* if Ben Holladay had any say about it.[14] The officers were all in their dress uniforms. Brass buttons and epaulets added to the warm glow of the room. The women glided effortlessly from group to group with only the light rustling of silk, satin, and crinoline to whisper of their passage. After dinner several of the men had started out the front door to enjoy their cigars but were stopped by Margaret, who would have none of it.

"You gentlemen will do me a great kindness by enjoying your cigars right here in the warmth of our home. A woman who would choose quiet or the company of her own sex to the whiff of a cigar is a fool," Margaret announced firmly. "Besides, the scent of tobacco reminds me of my father and I am dearly homesick sometimes."

Henry Carrington could barely contain his pleasure and his pride. She was such a gracious and charming woman. Jim Bridger, who had settled in his favorite rocking chair near the fireplace, looked up at Carrington and gave him a sly wink. There was a clink of glasses and a burst of rough laughter from a small knot of officers gathered near the end of the fireplace opposite Bridger's chair. The dashing Captain William Judd Fetterman, his jet black hair combed neatly back and gleaming with pomade, was smiling broadly as the other officers, Fred Brown, William Bisbee, Horatio Bingham, and George Grummond, raised their glasses in toast to their friend. Fetterman cut a fine figure: slim and athletic with a confident

---

[14]Ben Holladay, of Weston, Missouri, also known as the Stagecoach King, operated the Holladay Overland Mail and Express Company, which was contracted for mail delivery to Fort Phil Kearny. A number of soldiers believed that to save on weight Holladay's employees deliberately discarded most of the periodicals to which they subscribed. While large quantities of such materials were likely damaged or lost en route, it is doubtful that this was deliberate, as overland travel did tend to be fairly rough on perishable commodities such as mail, newspapers, and periodicals. The complaints voiced can be easily attributed to the standard soldierly practice of griping about never having enough mail.

bearing. His muttonchop whiskers lent him the aspect of a hussar and Lucy Bisbee whispered to Frances Grummond that he resembled perfectly her image of what the literary Charles O'Malley would look like.[15] Elisabeth Wheatley, whose husband had been unusually moody and distant for the past three months, could not help but steal a few furtive looks in the direction of the handsome young captain surrounded by admiring junior officers. There was a mesmerizing, almost magnetic appeal about him, and Liz Wheatley felt herself blushing at the indecent thoughts that flitted through her mind.

"Hear, hear," Fred Brown said loudly. "That's the ticket, Bill. You'll show these blasted redskins a trick or two. The rascals have become too bold by half and it's high time that we showed 'em that we won't stand still for their devilment. Why, I suspect we've been waiting for you all along for a chance to lay Mr. Lo low!"[16]

The other soldiers laughed, and Mr. Bisbee quipped, "Lay low the noble savage! I say, Fred, you've got the makings of a low comedian if you keep writing lines like that! Why, you've been hiding your virtues under the Cincinnati Chicken."[17]

"Bisbee's right, Captain Brown," George Grummond added. "Why you've hidden out in the warehouses so long you've become hard to lo-cate!"

Lieutenant Bingham, who had imbibed a bit more Madame Clicquot than he was used to, broke into a stumbling parody of a sailor's hornpipe and began singing:

[15]A reference to "Charles O'Malley, the Irish Dragoon" (1841) by Victorian writer Charles James Lever. Lever was a prolific source of swashbuckling tales of knights, ladies, soldiers, and adventurers which appealed to young readers of the time. "Charles O'Malley" was a particular favorite of a young George Armstrong Custer.

[16]"Mr. Lo" was the frontier Army's nickname for the Indian. It was a cynical reference to French philosopher Jean Jacques Rosseau's romantic view of "natural man" epitomized in his descriptive line, "Lo, the noble savage!"

[17]Cincinnati Chicken: Slang for salt pork, a standard and unsavory staple of the Army's rations.

Blow the buck down, laddies
Blow the buck down!
Lay-Lo, blow the buck down!
Oh, Blast all those Sioux
And Arapahoes too!
With powder and ball
We'll whip one and all!

The others laughed and joined in on the chorus as Fetterman stood, one elbow resting easily on the mantel, a wineglass grasped lightly in slender fingers and a cigar chomped firmly between even white teeth. Jim Bridger took the entire show in with some evident amusement.

You'd think some of these boys woulda learned a thing or two 'bout Injuns by now, Bridger thought. "Good luck to you fellas," he said in his gruff wheeze. "This child expects you will have a belly full o' powder, ball 'n bucks soon enough afore this winter is through."

"Well, Mr. Bridger," Fetterman said with a wave of his cigar, "perhaps it'll be the other way 'round. All these savages have had to keep 'em amused around here have been a handful of whitewashed rebs who've had the tar kicked out of 'em already and that's hardly a challenge. The regulars are here now and we'll soon play 'em a new tune to dance by."

"Oh," Bridger said with eyebrows raised. "I should like to learn a new jig or two myself. But mebbe I'll just sit out the first set or two till I get the rhythm and the steps. I do not care to squander what little spry I got left."

Fetterman nodded and raised his glass. The room had grown quiet around them.

"You're entirely welcome to watch, Mr. Bridger," Fetterman said. "It's been all a game of blind man's bluff to this point. But now you've some real soldiers here. With eighty men I could ride through the Sioux nation."

Bridger rocked easily in his chair for a moment, then screwed up his lips and spat a large plug of tobacco into the fireplace. "Yessir," he said. "I expect that you could. The onliest trick I can see will be coming back out again."

*   *   *

WILLIAM JUDD FETTERMAN STOOD IN THE DARKNESS OUTSIDE of the commanding officer's quarters, one booted foot resting easily on the last tread of the steps leading up to the porch. His gaze swept the horizon as pale moonlight gave shadowy form to the rough-hewn structures of the fort. He leaned against the railing and stared up into the endless night sky. The smoke from his cigar curled lazily upward into the blackness and was drawn away by the invisible fingers of a light breeze.

Damn an ungrateful War Department! he thought bitterly.

It galled him to think that he had to stand in there and say "yes sir" and "no sir" to that bearded popinjay Carrington. *A colonel*, he thought, grinding his teeth. *The man is no more a real colonel than I am a goddamn Sioux!* Fetterman had been a lieutenant colonel during the war and been so often cited for bravery in action against the enemy that he had lost count. That a man like Carrington, a paper-shuffling bureaucrat of a lawyer, a man who spent the entire war raising recruits and socializing with politicians, should command this regiment while he, a real soldier, was left as a mere captain left him fairly quivering with rage. Well, this would not last long. Not if William Judd Fetterman had anything to say about it.

I'll have to watch my temper and my tongue in this godforsaken hole, he thought. *There'll be time enough to gloat once the promotion has come through.*

Before he'd come out to Fort Phil Kearny an old friend in Washington confided that he had heard the Army was to be expanded again shortly. It would not be a great expansion, a few thousand more troops at best. But, his friend assured him, he had heard from a very reliable informant that the 18th Regiment was to form the basis for part of the expansion. The 1st Battalion would be enlarged and renamed as the 27th Regiment of Infantry, and Fetterman was the natural choice for its new commander. He heard footsteps behind him and glanced over his shoulder to see his old friend Fred Brown coming heavily down the stairs.

"Evening, Fred," Fetterman said lightly. "Nice soiree, that. Mrs. Grummond and that young Wheatley girl make rather a pleasant treat for the eye, eh?"

Brown grinned. "They do indeed, Bill. Lovely ladies both. Mrs. Grummond is with child, you know."

"No, I didn't know. One would never guess. She will make a fine mother I should think. How has young Grummond been treating her? Well enough?"

"Considering he doesn't know either." He paused. "So you know about him then?"

"It's a small army, Fred."

"Yes, well. He seems to have come around quite a bit. To be honest, I don't think she knows a thing about his past. He's not touched a drop since they arrived here and is the very model of a proper young gentleman. No one's mentioned it out of deference to his wife and if he stays away from John Barleycorn he'll likely make a proper father. He's keen enough and one hell of a fighter."

"Well, Fred," Fetterman said with a tight smile, "I suppose I've learned a thing or two about your situation here." Fetterman paused and spat out a small bit of cigar. "Your Mr. Bridger is a rustic sort of a frontier character. Does Carrington actually depend on his advice?"

Brown nodded. "Bridger's just returned from a reconnaissance of the tribes up on the Tongue so he's not been around for some weeks now but yes, he does have Carrington's ear on most things."

"Ah well," Fetterman said. "That certainly explains why you're stuck sitting on your asses in this little pile of sticks out in the middle of nowhere."

"I don't follow you," Fred Brown said, a frown creasing his high forehead.

"Look, Fred, Bridger gets paid to be a guide and, if what you say is true, an advisor to Carrington. Now Carrington's a greenhorn if ever I saw one. The man's never been to see the

---

[18]"Natty Bumpkin" is an obvious, if unflattering, reference to James Fenimore Cooper's famous scout and frontiersman "Natty Bumppo," hero of his Leath-

elephant. If old Natty Bumpkin[18] in there wants to keep pulling in his pay then it's certain he'll put the worst possible light on everything out there." Fetterman waved his cigar in the direction of the Bighorns. "As long as he's got Carrington convinced that the Sioux is waiting out there ten feet tall and thirsting for fresh blood, why, you'll never do a damned thing the whole time we're stuck with the two of 'em."

"Well, hold on a minute." Brown was defensive. "We have seen a bit of action around here you know. Hell, not a week goes by that the damned devils ain't stealing our damned cattle or horses or runnin' off mules or sticking an arrow in some poor sod's back."

"Yes, and what've you done about it? Fired off a howitzer in their general direction? Hopped on a couple of those spavined beasts that pass for horses that you keep out there past the hay yard? Played Frog in the Middle[19] while you trotted around waving your Colt's around your head and swatting flies with it? For Christsake, Fred. Most of your stock's already gone and the damned cemetery stretches halfway up the hill over there. What the hell does Carrington plan to do with the damned Sioux? Take 'em to court? Charge 'em with criminal trespass and disturbing the peace? Well, that's not the kind of action I signed up for and I didn't think you had either!"

Brown stood there in the gloom grateful for the darkness that hid the flush of embarrassment coloring his entire face and bald scalp a bright crimson.

"See here, Bill," Brown sputtered. "I don't make the decisions around here. You know damn well I'd murder the whole bunch of 'em if given half a chance!"

Fetterman laughed easily.

"Hell, yes, I know that, Fred," he said, slapping his friend

---

erstocking tales and *The Last of the Mohicans*. "To see the elephant" was a common reference to having experienced combat.

[19]"Frog in the Middle": A popular children's game in which the "frog" stands in the middle of a group of children who run around in a circle calling "Frog in the middle, you can't catch me!" as the "frog" tries to leap out and catch one of them by surprise.

on the shoulder. "That's exactly my point! You ain't had half a chance to lam those devils." He laid his arm across Brown's shoulders and whispered conspiratorially into his ear.

"But we're going to change all that, old man. Just stay with me and we'll clean this mess up yet. I'm working on a plan that'll learn Mr. Lo a thing or two about dealing with real soldiers."

The two comrades started off together across the moonlit parade ground as Tenedor Ten Eyck peered out the window of Carrington's quarters.

"DAMNED BRAGGART," TEN EYCK MUMBLED UNDER HIS breath.

"How's that?" Henry Carrington asked.

"Oh, nothing, Colonel," Ten Eyck replied, turning back to the warmly lit room. "I am just not particularly taken with our gallant Captain Fetterman. I think he's too bold by half and he'll breed trouble."

"Oh, I don't know," Carrington ventured calmly. "Perhaps you're being a bit harsh on him. It's a hard thing, this postwar army. Men who were generals are now colonels and those who were colonels are now captains. Young firebrands like Fetterman find themselves in a smaller army where past glory seems to count for little and they're consigned to the frontier like guard dogs who've grown to be an embarrassment when company comes calling. I will admit that Captain Fetterman is a bit grating but it's only because he feels he needs to prove himself yet again."

Jim Bridger cleared his throat and rose from his place near the fire.

"Hell, Colonel," Bridger said, helping himself to glass of port. "I say Ten Eyck's right on his take. If'n you don't keep a sharp eye on that boy I'm thinkin' the only thing he'll prove is what a durn fool he is. And get a passel of your boys kilt in the proving it."

"Gabe," Carrington sighed, "not you too. You're both being too hard on the man. Besides, we need him. We've not got

half the men or officers we need to do our job out here and
we need every battle-hardened officer we can lay hands on.
He's new to this country and hasn't yet seen what the tribes
are capable of. Give him some time and he'll learn quickly
how different the Sioux are from the Secesh."

"Hmmpf," Bridger snorted. "Well sir. You are running
things here and I am not. Good night, Colonel. Cap'n Ten
Eyck. I'll head out the back way so's I can pay my respects
to the missus as I take my leave."

The two officers mumbled their good-nights as Bridger retrieved his battered slouch hat from the floor where he had
tossed it earlier and sought out his hostess. Margaret was bustling about in the kitchen along with Liz Wheatley, Laura, and
George, who were helping to organize the chaos left in the
wake of the evening's festivities.

"Don't worry about washing anything up, Laura," Margaret
said. "We'll tend to all of that in the morning and I want
Elisabeth to get home to her children."

"That's all right, Mrs. Carrington," Liz Wheatley said quietly. "The boys are long in their bed and James will certainly
not miss me for a few minutes longer. I'll be happy to stay a
bit longer to help put all to rights."

Margaret reached out and touched Liz Wheatley's slender
hand.

"No, dear. You get home to your husband and those boys.
Oh, hello Major Bridger, I did not see you standing there."

"Mrs. Carrington, ladies, George." Bridger nodded to all as
he twisted the brim of his slouch in gnarled hands. "I was just
wishing to say thankee for a pleasant evenin' and some wondrous good eating. Mighty fine doings and that's a fact."

"Well, you are quite welcome, Major, and always welcome
in our home." Margaret smiled brightly. "Major Bridger,
would you do me one last kindness this evening and escort
Mrs. Wheatley home? It is late and I would feel more comfortable knowing she was in your care."

"I will indeed, ma'am." He nodded to Liz Wheatley,
jammed his hat onto his head, and offered his arm to her.
"Well, then. Good night to you all."

"Good night, Major Bridger." Margaret Carrington smiled at the old man as she helped Liz Wheatley on with her threadbare wrap. She gave Liz a peck on the cheek. "Good night, Mrs. Wheatley. Thank you for all of your help. I simply couldn't have managed without you."

Elisabeth Wheatley, her eyes cast downward, smiled shyly as she took Bridger's arm and went out into the chill of the night with him. As they passed around the corner of the house the moonlight cast long shadows from a pair of dark shapes just visible at the other end of the parade ground.

"Oh look, Major," Liz Wheatley said. "Isn't that Captain Brown and Captain Fetterman over yonder?"

"Missus Wheatley, yer eyes're better'n mine but I b'lieve that's right."

Bridger squinted into the night. Brown was pointing to the mass of the Sullivant Hills and then down to a grove of cottonwoods which followed the course of the Big Piney. A small cloud of their steamed breath formed an irregular halo in the cold night air about their heads.

Now, what're them two soldier boys up to do you figger? Bridger wondered.

Bridger could not know what the two were about and would have liked to listen to their conversation, but his hearing was not so sharp as it once was and he was not inclined to go skulking about the shadows at this time of night. He would get Mrs. Wheatley safe home and then stop in the Judge's store and have a drink and leave the captains to their plotting.

"Hmmmpf," Bridger snorted. "Full o' fire and brimstone, the two of 'em, and up to some damn foolishness I will wager." He steered Mrs. Wheatley gently around the trail of a small howitzer and led her off toward her home.

"Sir, I must protest," Captain Ten Eyck said through clenched teeth. "This is utter lunacy. We have been dealing with the Sioux for months and not once have we been able to draw them into a trap of any sort. The only thing this plan will accomplish will be to deprive a good many of the men of some much needed sleep and have them shooting at shadows or each other."

William Fetterman smiled and leaned over the map spread out on the table in the headquarters building.

"Now, now, Tenedor," Fetterman said. "Don't be defeatist. It's high time we taught these scoundrels a bit of a lesson and this just might be the way. We need to beat them at their own game. Let's be realistic here, man. Whatever methods you've been using thus far, however hard you've tried, and I give you full credit for your efforts, the Sioux have still run off all but a small fraction of the stock. Whatever it is you've done to this point just hasn't worked and I propose a new approach."

Colonel Carrington looked from one man to the other, stroking his beard in thought as he weighed their arguments. Personally he was inclined to agree with Ten Eyck. The Sioux had been preternaturally adept at foiling every attempt thus far made to root them out and this plan did not seem to offer any revolutionary new strategy. On the other hand, he did not wish to be seen as timid by the newly arrived Fetterman. True, Fetterman was only a captain but he was a former lieutenant colonel and a man with a remarkable record of success in combat. The men who had served with Fetterman in the war hung on every word he uttered and were already quoting him to each other. The younger officers exhibited a sort of hero worship, which was understandable given Fetterman's record. Perhaps a small foray under Fetterman's leadership would be just the thing to boost morale. If the plan worked, then Carrington would be seen as a man with vision enough to take advantage of the talent available to him. If not, well, there had been any number of plans that had not worked. Carrington turned to Bridger, who stood nearby quietly taking everything in.

"Well, Major Bridger," Carrington said. "You've not said anything about Captain Fetterman's plan. What do you think his chances are?"

Bridger sucked his teeth for a moment and looked first to Ten Eyck, then Fetterman.

"Well, Colonel," Bridger said finally. "I would say that this

here is soldier business and you and these gentlemen here
know best how to do what needs doin'. It may be that Cap'n
Fetterman here needs to have a try at them devils and the
sooner the better. An' if a thievin' buck or two takes a tumble
from his saddle . . ." Bridger shrugged his shoulders. "Well,
this child will not mourn their passin'."

Ten Eyck's face flushed with anger. He had fully expected
that Bridger would support his view that this plan was a fool's
errand and was about to say something to that effect when he
caught a look from Bridger that gave him pause. He decided
to hold his tongue. Carrington too was somewhat surprised by
the old scout's acquiescence, but as he was halfway inclined
to give Fetterman his approval he dismissed his doubts and
nodded quickly.

"Very well, Captain Fetterman," Carrington said. "You have
my approval to try your plan. You may pick your own men
for this mission. I would urge you to have the officers personally inspect your party's arms as we have found a number
of pieces that are in dire need of repair or outright replacement.
I should remind you that Red Cloud does not fight like Robert
Lee. The Sioux are a crafty and vicious breed and you should
take care not to be drawn into an unwise position. I would
urge you to refrain from making a massed charge into the open
areas as that may give them the advantage. Now, I will have
Lieutenant Bisbee draw up the required forms to release a pair
of mules to you for service as your bait."

"I would prefer that we used more than two mules, sir,"
Fetterman said. "It would, I believe, look fairly suspicious to
the Sioux if we had but a pair of jacks out there and hardly a
tempting enough target. A half-dozen animals I think would
better serve our purpose. I do not intend to lose them in any
event so they should be safe enough."

"Very well, Captain. Six mules it shall be. Good luck to
you, sir."

Fetterman grinned and saluted before turning to stride out
of the room. Carrington, whose bowels were again giving him
trouble, excused himself and headed out back to the sinks,
leaving Ten Eyck alone with Bridger.

"Damnit, Bridger," Ten Eyck said with some heat. "Why the hell did you agree with that cocky little popinjay? This whole idea is a pipe dream and don't tell me that you don't know it."

Bridger snorted, gave a little smile, and walked to the stove, where he poured himself a mug of coffee before dropping into a chair. He stretched out his long legs and crossed his ankles in front of him.

"Hell yes, it's a load of nonsense, Ten Eyck," he said between sips of coffee. "Mr. Fetterman is not like to catch anything more dangerous than a cold out there and that is just the point. I say let the pup try it. The cottonwoods where he proposes to lay up ain't but a healthy spit away and if there be any hubbaboo, well you can deal with it right handy. I don't b'lieve that there'll be any need. The Injuns're watchin' this place like hawks an' they'll smell his little trap sure as a hog smells a snake. Yessir, I say let Jack Frost chaw on Fetterman's toes for a hour or two and mebbe it'll cool some of that fire afore it can get too many other folks burnt."

Ten Eyck stood stock-still, his eyes focused on a distant point as he turned this over and over in his brain. After a moment he glanced again at Bridger, then moved to the window and gazed in the direction of the cottonwood grove where Fetterman planned to conduct his operation. The surrounding palisade denied any view of the site but, in his mind's eye, he could see every detail, every fold of earth, every tangle of thicket, every ripple and moss-slick stone in the Big Piney's tumbling surface as easily as if the walls did not exist. He let out a long, slow breath.

"All right, Major," he said finally. "Let's just wait and see what happens. You may have judged right but even if what you say comes to pass I doubt it will have the desired effect. Some men have a peculiar ability not to learn that which they do not wish to know."

"Aye, that is so, Ten Eyck, that is truly so. I b'lieve I'll have me another cup of coffee."

*   *   *

BAD WOUND SNICKERED QUIETLY TO HIMSELF AS HE PEERED down into the valley below. He and Crazy Horse had been watching the bluecoats' activities with growing interest and wondering how they might take advantage of the situation.

"It looks like we'll get to try your plan sooner than I thought, brother. These *wasichu* are strange beings just like you and American Horse said."

Crazy Horse didn't say anything for a moment. He was fascinated by the scene unfolding below them. The soldiers had come out from the Buffalo Creek Fort just as the sun was going down behind the mountains. They had brought several mules with them and spent quite a bit of effort placing the animals just so and then hobbling them so they would not wander too far. The little soldier chief who was obviously in charge of this group strutted around like a bull elk in rut, tossing his head, making wide gestures with his hands and speaking in a voice so loud that it sometimes could be heard as far up as where he and Bad Wound were sitting. When the mules had been placed to the little soldier chief's satisfaction, he began moving all of his soldiers into the cottonwood thicket nearby. There was quite a bit of stumbling about in the dusk and Crazy Horse watched with amusement as the quivering of the few leaves that remained showed where the soldiers were getting themselves settled in. It seemed to take them an unusually long time to quiet down, but finally all the rustling and shaking stopped and the only movement to be detected was that of the mules as they cropped lazily at the grass in the small meadow. The steam of the animals' breath clouded the air around their heads and then drifted off as they pawed the ground and nibbled contentedly at the sparse vegetation.

"No, Bad Wound," Crazy Horse said finally. "Not tonight. Not yet. These bluecoats are very foolish. We must make them even more reckless and arrogant than they are already. To do this we must make them angry. Fighting them will make them angry, but not fighting them when they want to fight will make them angrier. The hotter the fire in their heads the more stupid they become. We'll let them be for now." Crazy Horse grinned. "We'll let them freeze a bit tonight and light a small fire tomorrow."

Bad Wound listened quietly to his companion and smiled. After a moment he nodded and the two men slipped silently away and headed off to join the small war party that had camped a little way off. Neither William Fetterman nor any of his men—already beginning to feel the biting chill of the November evening—noticed their going.

JIM BRIDGER SAT WITH ONE ARM RESTING COMFORTABLY ON the counter, his chair tipped back and leaning against the wall of Judge Kinney's store. His battered slouch hat was pulled low over eyes that moved restlessly over the dim interior of the sutler's store. He glanced over at Yellow Face, the young Crow who had come in with him and now squatted, as he did every night, in a dark corner with his back against the wall. Nearby a few civilians, the new wagonmaster, Breakenridge, the wheelwright, Leviticus Carter, and a couple of his hay-cutters, and the strange little fellow everyone called "Portu-gee" sat at the few blanket-covered tables munching on crackers and cheese and sipping whiskey or bitter coffee. Some of the men were playing cards, or pretending to play, while others talked quietly among themselves. Every once in a while someone would turn to Levi and ask the time. Each time Carter would fish the Hamilton out of his pocket, pop open the cover, and reply in a dull monotone. Bridger noticed that no one could resist the urge to glance in the direction of the unseen cottonwood thicket. At any moment they half ex-pected to hear the echoing crash of musketry from the sur-rounding night. All was silence. The only sounds that drifted in through the thick haze of pipe and cigar smoke were the random howl of a wolf and the plaintive call of the sentry.

"Eleven of the clock and all is well."

FRANCES GRUMMOND LISTENED ANXIOUSLY FOR THE CALL OF the sentry. She paced the floor of the small cabin that she and

George had only recently moved into. Now he lay somewhere out there in the dark, waiting as she waited. For a while she had kept a single candle burning in the window but the ghostly apparition of her own reflection staring back at her from the glass so unnerved her that she had finally extinguished the light with a shudder and resumed her pacing in the darkness. The few logs that had fueled the fire earlier in the evening were now but embers, and their red-orange glow, combined with the spare moonlight that filtered in through the rude curtains, was sufficient to keep her from stumbling into their scanty furniture. Frances had dressed for bed but, unable to sleep, had thrown an old Army blanket around her shoulders and shuffled barefoot across the floor, from window to fireplace and back, feeling the cold pine boards under her feet alternating with the rough burlap she had fashioned into a sort of carpet.

George had left behind his pocket watch and it lay on a small nightstand, its chain looped like the folds of a small, golden serpent, and Frances regarded it as if the oversized head were as venomous as a rattler. Every second that ticked by pumped the poison of fear coursing through her veins. What if he did not return? What if that watch were all that was left to her of him? What would she do? Where could she go? How could she raise their child? What would she tell him of his father? It was almost unbearable. She found herself with her hand on the door latch and did not know how she had come to lay her hand there. The latch rattled and she eased the creaking door open to slip silently out onto the porch, where the frigid air grabbed at her bare feet and crept over her ankles. In the stillness she could hear the distant, hushed roar of the falls on Big Piney Fork. Her eyes sought out the invisible cottonwood thicket and then drifted upward into the vast indigo of the heavens. She gazed out into eternity, mindless of the cold, and watched as a shooting star arced across the darkness and was gone.

A life brief and glorious, she thought, tugging the blanket more tightly about her shoulders. She looked at the stars that remained unmoved in their places, countless pinpoint diamonds in the dark expanse. *Did the others even notice your passing? Do they even know that you've gone? Is that how our lives will finally be measured? A tiny flash of light and then nothingness?* Somewhere in the mountains a wolf raised its mournful cry, a lament for the now dead star, and then came the echoing call of the sentry in his rounds.

"Twelve of the clock and all is well."

"INDIANS!"

Margaret looked up from her hymnal as the cry of alarm started other members of the congregation from their seats in the newly completed chapel. Captain Fetterman's party had spent a long, cold, and uneventful night concealed along the Big Piney. The ambush party had returned to the fort an hour after daybreak, cold and dispirited with nothing to show for their efforts. A gaggle of bleary-eyed soldiers had wended their way back to barracks snuffling, wheezing, hacking, and muttering curses under their breath as another Sabbath dawned. Some would find their way to the chapel for services but most made straight for their bunks and anything warm to drink. Some would go for coffee while others opted for something a bit stronger. Now these same men were dragging themselves back from sleep to the sound of the distant pop-popping of gunfire and the shouts of the officer of the day. The sounds of shooting came from the meadowland that lay to the east of the fort and on the side opposite of where Captain Fetterman had laid his ambitious ambuscade.

Well, Margaret thought grimly, *we've had our eye on the front door all night and here they come slipping in through the kitchen window!*

Were it not such a serious business it would have made her laugh. But she was not laughing. The shooting seemed to be coming from where she had just seen Liz Wheatley out driving with Mr. Reid. Liz frequently rode out that way to check on her husband's cattle about this time of day, but for some unknown reason Edwin Reid, one of the contract surgeons at the fort, had offered to drive her out there in his rig. The irregular popping of shots could only have come from Reid's new Henry rifle. A few moments later Reid's buckboard, with Liz Wheatley at the reins, lurched through the main gates just as a small party of horsemen followed. Lieutenant Bisbee passed them going the other way. Surgeon Reid, rifle in hand, was looking back at the Indians.

"They're running the Wheatleys' stock off, Lieutenant!" he shouted.

Bisbee nodded grimly, his fingers touched to the brim of his kepi in acknowledgment of Mrs. Wheatley, whose entire attention was focused on controlling her team. Bisbee waved the other soldiers on and galloped in the direction Reid indicated with the barrel of his rifle.

Captain William Fetterman, his uniform blouse unbuttoned and a revolver held loosely at his side, stood to one side as the buckboard passed through the gates. His eyes followed Bisbee's party as they dashed out across the valley toward a pale column of dust, which was already dissipating in the distance. Fetterman looked up to see Captain Ten Eyck standing opposite him also intent on Bisbee's pursuit. Ten Eyck eyed Fetterman briefly and then looked after the rapidly diminishing figures of Bisbee and his men. The two men said not a word to each other but Fetterman thought he caught the slightest twitch of a smile pass over Ten Eyck's face. The younger man snarled inwardly and resisted the temptation to fire a shot in the direction of the long-departed foe.

Damn them! Fetterman thought savagely. *And damn you, Ten Eyck! I see your gloating smirk, don't think I don't know what you're thinking, you self-righteous, sanctimonious son of a bitch! I'll show those damned savages yet and you and your spineless leader as well. You'll all be singing a different tune before long, I swear it!* The young captain turned and stalked off to his quarters, brushing past a bewildered Horatio Bingham, who was still trying to figure out what all the ruckus was about.

*   *   *

J. B. GREGORY SURVEYED THE SURROUNDING HILLS AND SPAT a stream of tobacco juice over the side of the wagon as it jolted steadily ahead over the rutted track that led back to Piney Island. The one thing he had come to detest about pine trees was the very thing which he had once found so appealing—the fact that they were never shed of their needles. It used to be that Gregory had found the constancy of the evergreen a comfort and a relief from the vagaries of life. At least one thing, he had thought, could be depended on, and that was the reassuring verdance of the pine. *Funny how your view tends to shift*, he thought idly. To J. B. Gregory's mind now, the only thing the evergreen's constancy represented was the guarantee of shelter and solace to the damned Sioux. He knew they were out there lurking in that forest, they were always there somewhere. Skulking and flitting about like damned mosquitoes waiting for a patch of bare skin. Now Gregory's fondest wish was to lay waste to every damned pine tree in the territory. The image he would conjure in his dreams was of the Bighorn range stripped bare.

I'll leave you nowhere to hide, you red bastards! he thought grimly as he looked over his shoulder at the line of wagons that stretched back along the wood road. It had become an obsession with Gregory, and now the hard work of logging could not proceed fast enough to suit him. Gregory turned back to the front and saw Lieutenant Bisbee, who, along with the recently arrived Captain Fetterman, was accompanying the wood party as escort today. Fetterman had not yet been out to the pinery and it was clear that Bisbee was eagerly pointing out to the captain every bend in the road, every fold of earth, every thicket that could possibly conceal a war party. The air was crisp and still and filled with the sounds of huffing horses and mules, creaking leather and wood, and the irregular clanking of logging chains vibrating in the beds of the heavy wagons.

The party had just rounded the last bend in the road before reaching their destination, the dark mass of Piney Island looming up ahead of them. A few yards in advance of the lead wagon, Bisbee and Fetterman halted at the stream and dis-

mounted to water their horses. Gregory noticed that Bisbee's
mount had lifted his head and his ears had suddenly pricked
up. The animal had begun to shy and back away from the
water while Lieutenant Bisbee yanked on the animal's reins
as he attempted to carry on a conversation with Fetterman.

The zip of a bullet passing overhead accompanied the echoing report of a rifle fired from behind a large log not fifty
yards away. The air was filled with the whooping and yipping
which left no doubt as to who had pulled the trigger. In seconds the loggers had drawn their wagons into a ragged stockade and were firing into the surrounding woods while the
Army escort moved to join their officers. Lieutenant Bisbee
and Captain Fetterman had dropped behind the overhanging
stream bank and were using their revolvers to add to the fire
now being poured into the underbrush. After a few moments
the crash of musketry ceased. The loggers and escort, who had
been through this experience time and again, were unable to
glimpse anyone at which to shoot and were unwilling to
squander ammunition that might be desperately needed at a
moment's notice. An uneasy silence settled in the woods as
gunsmoke drifted heavily among the wounded pines, gashed
by flying lead.

"Damned rascals," Bisbee whispered to Captain Fetterman.
"You'll get used to this sort of thing after a while, sir. The
skunks'll pop out of the brush and then disappear as quick as
they came."

"Not all of 'em," Fetterman muttered. "Look there, Bisbee."

Bisbee followed the captain's gaze and saw the figure of a
lone warrior who had leaped atop a fallen tree and was cap-
ering up and down its length, stopping only to flash his buttocks at the wood party and screech taunts at the top of his
lungs.

"Tuweska? Hokewin s'e? Watus'eks'e! We-we-we!"[20]

"The damned scamp!" Fetterman growled. "I'll settle his

[20]"Who is this? Women? Rubbish! Come!" The use of *"We-we-we"* is a
particularly derisive term, as this is used only as a call to dogs.

hash for him." The captain cocked his revolver and started up over the creek bank.

"Sir! Stop!" Bisbee hissed. "Wait! Wait! Hold on a second, Captain. Wait here a moment and I'll show you something."

Fetterman slid back down the embankment and watched as Bisbee splashed into the stream, threw one booted foot into the stirrup, and swung into the saddle. Gathering up the reins in one hand, he tapped the horse on the flank with his revolver and spurred up over the embankment with a yelp. As he sprang up out of the streambed the warrior hopped off the fallen tree and vanished in the undergrowth with Bisbee firing after him. The lieutenant had not gone more than ten yards when the thicket erupted with gunfire and several arrows streaked past him. But Bisbee had apparently anticipated this, for, lying low on his horse's neck, he wheeled the beast around and scrambled back into the streambed, where he threw himself down next to Fetterman, breathless and grinning.

"See there, old man?" he said with a chuckle. "It's a dodge they like to use lately. I thought that seemed just a bit too easy and sure enough it was."

"The low-life sons of bitches," Fetterman growled. "The bastards are mocking us using their own braves instead of mules as bait. They must have been watching us when we laid out that trap for 'em." The captain glared at the brush, then turned to Bisbee, a grudging grin on his face. "All right then, Bisbee. We'll give 'em this one. But we've got to figure out how to bring 'em out on our terms. Let 'em wave their asses at us one more time and we'll stick a bayonet up 'em."

As sophisticated as was the signaling system that Henry Carrington had arranged, there were times when the information forwarded was likely to be misinterpreted. This was one of those times. It was Barnes, the post's principle musician, who observed the frantic wigwagging of signal flags from the top of Pilot Hill. Being of an "artistic nature," as Captain Ten Eyck was wont to describe it, Barnes made a muddle of the business. A more sober man would likely have relayed precisely what the sentries on Pilot Hill had reported through the use of the flags—that the wood train was under attack by Indians. But John Barnes was an excitable man and the report he rendered breathlessly to Colonel Carrington was that the wood train had been attacked and all with it were killed. Mrs. Bisbee, who was within earshot, reeled against the side of a building and had to be held upright by Frances Grummond. Henry Carrington, a man already under enormous strain, felt his knees weaken. If true it was an unacceptable loss of men and material. But a few minutes were needed to mount a relief party, which Carrington led out the gates at a gallop.

The relief party had hardly proceeded a mile and were not even out of sight of the fort before they encountered the wood train's escort returning at a casual walk and decidedly more alive than dead. Fetterman and Bisbee, who were in the lead of the escort, were puzzled to see Carrington's party coming on at a gallop. Fetterman reined up and raised his hand to halt his party to await the colonel's arrival.

"Thank God, sir!" Carrington exclaimed with relief. "You were all reported killed by the Sioux."

"Not hardly, sir," Fetterman said, momentarily taken aback by the revelation.

"What's happened here then?" Carrington insisted. "You are reported under attack."

It was apparent that Carrington was flustered and unhinged by what he imagined had happened to the wood train. Fetterman's mind turned these thoughts over rapidly as he saw that the rest of the escort was gathering around listening intently. Glancing past the colonel's shoulder, he could see Fort Phil Kearny in the distance and noted that the flag had already been lowered to half-mast. A smile flickered across his face. Here was an unforeseen opportunity to add just a bit to his own reputation while at the same time taking a subtle bite out of Carrington's authority.

"More of an annoyance than an attack, Colonel," Fetterman replied coolly. "A few bucks tried to jump the wood train when we reached the pinery but they would not stand. Young

Bisbee here tried to run them off single-handedly. If anyone's been killed it's likely him." Fetterman turned to Bisbee, who was grinning broadly. "I say there, Bisbee. Are you killed or not?"

Bisbee looked down at the front of his uniform and made a display of feeling for holes. "Not that I can see, sir."

"Well, by God, neither am I," Fetterman said, feigning surprise. "I believe that Baldy Brown and George Grummond will be sore disappointed to hear all this. I imagine the vultures were already counting on their promotions and hounding Major Almstedt for that extra pay." A hushed chorus of chuckles and snorts erupted from the enlisted men gathered about.

"As you were," Carrington growled at the soldiers. "This is a serious business out here as you men should well know by now." He turned back to Fetterman. "Captain Fetterman, this may appear one big lark to you but I assure you that it is no such thing. A man can die just as easily at Big Piney as he can at Stones River and he is no less dead for who killed him. And you, Bisbee, for shame, sir! Mrs. Bisbee is in a terrible state with worry for your safety and you sit out here making crude jokes. And on the Sabbath! I expect better from you, sir."

Bisbee flushed a brilliant crimson and squirmed uncomfortably in his saddle. He had forgotten about Lucy and their son, Jean. Lucy would surely be frantic by now. A humbled Lieutenant Bisbee swallowed hard and averted his eyes from his commander.

"Yes, sir." Bisbee croaked. "Sorry, sir."

Carrington wheeled his horse about and headed back toward Phil Kearny with both parties now trailing in his wake. Behind the colonel and slightly to the right of the column rode a silent and grim-faced Captain Fetterman. Where William Henry Bisbee took his rebuke with a guilty conscience, William Judd Fetterman received the same dressing-down with anger and resentment. He was not a man to take criticism lightly or well.

                    *   *   *

"WHEN CAN I LOOK TO SEE YOU AGAIN, MAJOR?" CARRING-
ton asked.

"That I cannot say, Colonel," Bridger replied. "What I can
say is that it has been too quiet by half around here of late.
When you can't see any redskins you may be sure that is when
they are thickest and most likely up to devilment."

"That is precisely why you are most needed here now,"
Carrington insisted.

"No sir, that is not so and I'll say why," Bridger replied.
"Red Cloud has gathered up all his people up there on the
Tongue. There are a few bucks lurkin' about here but the big
show when it starts will surely start up yonder. I may be a
fair judge o' Injuns but I sure as hell cain't figger what they're
about from fifty mile away. I need to be on the Tongue where
I can get a closer look. C. F. Smith will suit my purpose
better'n Phil Kearny." Bridger paused and pointed toward a
lone, blanket-shrouded Indian who leaned casually against the
side of the commissary warehouse. "I'm leavin' Yellow Face
here with you just in case. He speaks passable English and
he'll know where to find me."

Carrington heard the jingle of bit and spurs behind him and
turned to look up at Lieutenant Horatio Bingham, who was in
charge of the escort detail that would accompany official dispatches and the mail on the trip to Fort C. F. Smith. Bingham
threw his gauntleted hand up in a sharp salute.

"Sir, the detail is ready," Bingham said.

"Very good, Lieutenant." Carrington returned the man's salute. He looked down the line of two dozen cavalrymen, who
had already formed into two ranks. Their carbines were the
old Starrs, badly in need of replacement but serviceable. *They
need Spencers*, Carrington thought.

"God speed to you sir. Keep your weapons always handy
and in good order. Stay alert and listen well to whatever Major
Bridger shares with you. When you reach C. F. Smith present
my compliments to Captain Kinney and take personal charge
of any dispatches which he provides. Make sure you rest your
command fully before you return, but then return without de-

lay. I'm not sure how much longer the road will remain passable. Have you any questions, sir?"

"No, sir!" Bingham responded with a final salute.

Carrington returned the salute and nodded to urge the detail
on its way. A piercing blast of chill air swept down from the
mountains as the small column passed out through the main
gates and wheeled left and to the north. Carrington stood just
outside the gates and watched as Bridger, mounted on his
mule, trotted easily alongside the column for a few minutes
and then drifted gradually up the slope and past the main body.
Carrington knew the man's methods. Bridger would draw farther and farther ahead until he was well out of sight and earshot of Bingham, the better to observe the country and provide
early warning of any ambuscades which lay in wait. Well,
Bingham was in good hands and there was nothing left to be
done.

It was late in the season, and although snow lay heavy on
the upper slopes of the Bighorns, Phil Kearny's meadows had
thus far been spared the full fury of the winter. But as Carrington watched the detachment grow smaller and finally disappear from sight, heavy clouds could be seen boiling up over
Cloud Peak, obscuring the pale disk of the afternoon sun. The
cottonwoods and aspen began to quake before a wind that
grew ever sharper and more insistent, and light flakes of snow
began to swirl about in the glowering half-light. Winter was
about to descend on all. Henry Carrington had a feeling that
when it arrived it would be with a vengeance.

9

Tahe 'caps 'un wi
(Moon When The Deer Shed Their Horns)

December 1866

Lieutenant Horatio Bingham clenched his jaw muscles together as tightly as he could manage. His teeth clicked rapidly together as he shivered uncontrollably in the bitter cold. Bingham hunkered down deeper into the collar of his overcoat and the hood improvised by inverting the short cape and fastening it over his head. The heavy wool cut the wind, but not nearly enough to be comfortable. The lieutenant, like all of the other men in the escort, had wrapped his scarf around his head to protect his ears. Viewed altogether the patrol, hunched over in their saddles and swaddled in every bit of clothing they could find, looked more like a gaggle of feeble grandmothers or tattered beggars than soldiers. In this country, martial style and the Army's uniform regulations quickly gave way to a man's innate sense of survival.

While no man of the escort party was a stranger to snow, winter in the Wyoming Territory was an experience unlike any they had ever known. Winds of incredible velocity and torturing cold roared down from the mountains, freezing a man to the marrow. Breath froze on mustaches and seared lungs. Tears were forced from wind-blasted eyes and froze and chapped the cheeks until they were rough and tender. Noses

were always red, raw, and runny, causing brittle stalactites to
form above blue, chapped lips and jaws sore with the effort
to control chattering teeth. Ears were in constant danger of
frostbite. For all the good it did, Bingham decided that his
overcoat might as well have been made of the lightest, sheerest
silk. The cold sliced through it as easily as a panther's claws
ripped flesh. He had never been so painfully cold and miserable in his life.

Damn this country, he thought bitterly. *The goddamned savages can have it and welcome to it. I wish to God I had never
laid eyes on Fort Phil Kearny or Henry-by-God-Carrington.
May they both rot in hell.* Bingham reflected sourly that hell
sounded damned inviting at the moment for it could not be
much worse than this godforsaken, frigid wasteland. At least
it was probably warmer.

Coming from the north, the wind pushed and prodded the
small party from the rear, urging them along as they clattered
down the road that had brought so much misery in its wake.
As they passed down the valley that opened onto Phil Kearny,
the wind began to drive icy needles in front of it. They ticked
against the frozen earth, stung exposed flesh, and coated every
surface with a glassy, surrealistic patina. Bingham had wasted
no time on the return trip from C. F. Smith and resisted every
temptation to turn and hurry back to its sheltering walls and
warming fires. It had taken his party seven days for the entire
trip up to Smith and back, a record time under any conditions,
but at no small cost. Bingham was sure that the quacks—
surgeons Horton, Hines, and Reid—would have more than
their share of trade from this little excursion. Some of their
patients would doubtless leave behind fingers and toes in pay-
ment for their efforts. If Horatio Bingham had his druthers he
would personally send an amputated digit to President Andrew
Johnson, every damned senator, and every damned congressman and have them served up at dinner on a silver platter.
The pompous, self-satisfied sons of bitches ought to know
what their idiotic policies cost the men who had to carry them
out. It was probably for the best that Lieutenant Horatio Bingham, commanding Company C, Second U.S. Cavalry, did not

know that, at the very moment he was leading his half-frozen men through the main gate at Fort Phil Kearny, his commander-in-chief was addressing the members of the 39th Congress.

"THE ARMY HAS BEEN PROMPTLY PAID, CAREFULLY PROVIDED with medical treatment, well sheltered and subsisted, and is to be furnished with breech-loading small arms." A smattering of polite applause greeted the President as he paused for effect. "Treaties have been concluded with the Indians who have un-conditionally submitted to our authority." Another burst of ap-plause, this one more enthusiastic, echoed through the House chambers as the speaker paused, nodding his head, and smiled as he waited for quiet to resume.

"And," he said, stretching his right hand out as if to grasp another hand offered in friendship. "And they have manifested an earnest desire for a renewal of friendly relations. Gentle-men, those purveyors of rumors of war are those who hope to profit by that war. They are but hopeful vultures who would feed on the flesh of men and leave their bones on the plains. They are unprincipled buccaneers who would plunder the pub-lic treasury and profit by the very strife they would incite. Cast them out, I say! Out into the darkness like the pariahs they should be and take no heed of these false prophets and vile profiteers. No, my esteemed friends and colleagues! I say to you, there will be no Indian war for we will not allow it, and peace, progress, and prosperity for all Americans, blue or gray, white, red or black are at hand!"

The response to this pronouncement was mixed. There was some enthusiastic applause on one side of the aisle complete with cheering and waving of hats. But a disturbingly large element either clapped politely or remained forbiddingly si-lent. The speaker's gaze was drawn almost involuntarily to senators Charles Sumner and Thaddeus Stevens, leaders of the Republicans' radical faction and his sworn enemies. They didn't care for his approach to Reconstruction and would likely do all they could to scotch any efforts he made to resolve the Indian question as well.

Think I'm too soft on the South, do you? Johnson thought bitterly. *Well, to hell with you! We've larger problems to solve than to indulge your petty thirst for retribution and vengeance on our prodigal brothers.*

Andrew Johnson looked out at the sea of faces and dark suits and smiled benignly. He had finished his first full year as President without the pall of a martyred predecessor hanging over his administration and he felt better than he had expected. The Radicals were a damned nuisance but they would be hard-pressed to find anything wrong to spoil the fast-approaching Christmas season and the start of a new year brimming with hope and opportunity for the nation. Johnson glanced down to see his Secretary of War, Edwin Stanton, a solitary figure sitting silently in the front row, arms crossed and eyes dark. Stanton was his usual brooding, malevolent presence—no change there. Johnson suspected that Stanton was in secret collusion with Sumner and Stevens, doing everything he could to stymie his policies. *Another damned fox in the henhouse*, Johnson thought. If only there were some way to get that scheming, bitter thorn of Stanton out of his side, maybe replace him with General Grant, he would be a much happier man.

"INDIANS!" PRIVATE SAMPLE GASPED AS HE CHARGED INTO the headquarters office. "Colonel Carrington, sir, the pickets are reporting that the wood train is under attack by large parties of hostiles, sir."

Carrington was instantly on his feet and out the door, pausing only long enough to snatch up his small brass telescope. Ten Eyck followed closely on his heels, reaching out to grab up his pistol belt as he passed through. Standing out on the frost-covered parade ground, Carrington snapped open the telescope and focused on the pickets on Pilot Hill. The bright red signal flags fluttered briskly as a young private waved them, repeating the wigwag pattern that signaled that an attack on the wood train was in progress. Carrington turned to Ten Eyck, who along with Private Sample was squinting up at the distant picket post.

"Captain Ten Eyck, have the post bugler sound the Assembly and To Arms immediately. I want two relief parties mounted and ready to depart in five minutes. Captain Fetterman will command the first, consisting of Bingham's cavalry and one squad of mounted infantry. I will command the other myself. Lieutenant Wands and Lieutenant Grummond will attend with a company of mounted infantry. Private Sample, fetch my revolvers and double-check the loads. Cap every chamber except the one under the hammer."

Ten Eyck and Sample scurried off to comply as Carrington turned and rushed in the opposite direction, cutting diagonally across the parade ground to reach the bastion at the northwest corner of the fort. Charging up the stairs and onto the sentry walk, he raised the telescope and quickly scanned the terrain in the vicinity of the pinery. There was some frantic movement discernible in that direction but nothing was clear enough to reveal the true nature of the attack. Judging by the volume of gunfire that drifted back to the post, an engagement of some size was under way.

The colonel leapt down from the bastion and sprinted toward the cavalry stables, where the relief parties were already forming up. Captain Fetterman and lieutenants Wand, Grummond, and Bingham emerged from between the barracks buildings leading their saddled horses and talking animatedly among themselves. Captain Fred Brown could be seen hurrying up to join his fellows, a pair of revolvers suspended in holsters from the belt that cinched his overcoat.

Trust Brown not to miss any chance at a fracas, Carrington thought irritably. *The man ought to stick with his duties.* He had half a mind to reprimand the overeager Brown, but his anger at yet another Indian attack overcame his usually strict adherence to regulations. *Let him ride with Fetterman*, he thought quickly. *Brown has had more experience at this sort of work. He may prove a useful brake on his friend's unguarded enthusiasm.*

"Gentlemen," Carrington said brusquely. "Captain Fetterman, you will take your command along with Lieutenant Bingham's cavalry. Captain Brown, you will accompany Captain Fetterman. Proceed due west at a gallop and relieve the wood train. Drive the hostiles ahead of you toward the Montana Road and the head of Peno Creek. I'm counting on you to drive them into us. Lieutenant Grummond and I will swing north along Lodge Trail Ridge and cut off their escape. Stay closed up and allow no stragglers. Gentlemen, form up your commands and let's go."

The officers scrambled into their saddles, wheeled about to gather their men, and trotted off to their respective gates. Fetterman's command hurried out the mill gate and onto the Wood Road. Carrington led his group out the main gate and in the opposite direction. Alexander Wands, confused about which group he had been assigned to, shrugged and hurried after Fetterman. The day was bitterly cold and vapor from horse and man alike trailed after the rapidly moving troops. In the distance the faint crackle of gunfire continued without letup.

Fetterman struck the first blow. As the command topped a small rise on the Wood Road the scene unfolded quickly below them. The loggers had managed to fort up in a small clearing, the men hunkered down behind and under their wagons firing steadily into the surrounding trees. A score of Sioux and Cheyenne warriors dodged and darted from tree to tree, firing pistols and rifles into the beleaguered men. Feathered flights of dogwood and willow shafts whistled through the cold air. Most passed harmlessly overhead but some drove their steel heads with solid thunks into wagon sides, logs, saddles, horses, and men. The arrival of Fetterman's command quickly shifted the balance of forces and the warriors began slipping away from the fresh troops. The warriors rushed for their ponies and fled with a chorus of whoops and shrieks.

"After 'em, boys!" Fetterman shouted, and kicked spurs into the flanks of his mount to leap off in pursuit. *They're headed right for the Montana Road*, Fetterman thought with grim satisfaction. *Exactly where we want you, you damned rascals!*

The entire party followed suit, kicking reluctant horses into a run as rifles and carbines were shoved forward and pistols came up spitting smoke and flame. Pursuers and pursued clattered over the rough terrain, dodging tree limbs and scrambling over rocky outcroppings. The cavalry, more comfortable in the saddle and mounted on fresher animals, quickly took the lead and drew ever farther ahead of the awkwardly mounted infantrymen. Lieutenant Bingham, with the veteran Sergeant Bowers alongside, raced ahead of the rest.

"Come on, boys," Bingham called out as he spurred forward. "Let's give 'em hell!"

The Sioux were the entire reason for Bingham to be here in this godforsaken place and he was now determined to make some of them pay for his discomfiture. He quickly emptied one revolver and tossed it aside in the heat of the chase. Private John Guthrie, who struggled to keep up with his commander, was shocked at this wasteful act, especially as he wished dearly for an extra revolver rather than the battered old carbine that banged painfully against his thigh. It was no wonder the troopers always seemed to have a bit of a limp after these little forays. The right thigh of every one of them was invariably bruised black from the pounding impact of the sling-suspended carbine that slammed into his leg with every step of the horse.

The party crashed through a dense thicket unmindful of a small group of warriors who launched themselves yipping and shrieking into the gap between Bingham and the rest of his command. Whirling their war clubs around their heads, they crashed headlong into the rest of the column, stopping them in midstride. Some of Bingham's stragglers, many of them raw recruits, faltered and began to fall back. Fetterman, Brown, and Wands, who had been urging the indifferently mounted infantry steadily along, were startled to see some of Bingham's troopers rushing back upon them. The suddenness of the encounter and the obvious terror of the retreating men started a panic among the other troops and soon a general rout threatened, with wild-eyed men dashing every which way as sergeants and corporals screamed out trying to reestablish order.

All three officers suddenly found themselves in the peculiar position of leveling their pistols at their own men.

"Halt, by God!" Brown shouted at the top of his lungs. "You damned skulkers! Turn, damn you! Turn and fight or I'll cut you down myself!"

Wheeling and crashing about in the underbrush, the three officers, along with the noncommissioned officers, screamed and cursed and waved their pistols until they had turned the rout around. Horses and men milled about in utter confusion until Fetterman, his dark eyes burning with fury, stood in his stirrups firing his pistol into the air.

"Rally on me, you yellow sons of bitches!" he screamed. "I swear to God I will kill the next man who so much as blinks without my order!"

Gradually they managed to get the panicked men under control. The sergeants cursed and kicked and swatted and forced the men and unruly animals into a ragged semblance of organization. Fetterman wheeled his horse in a tight circle and then bounded out in front of the troops. He turned in the saddle, waving his revolver and spurring his mount ahead.

"As skirmishers! Forward! Heeyaaahh!" The milling mob of blue-coated troopers struggled into line and surged forward yelling and firing into the warriors who had themselves now stopped and wheeled around to escape.

Hidden from view by the intervening Sullivant Hills, but closing fast on Fetterman's command, Henry Carrington was not faring much better than the brash young captain. Racing up the dirt track that paralleled the Big Piney, Carrington's party surged forward until they had drawn up opposite Lodge Trail Ridge just as the Big Piney began a gradual bend around to the west. Carrington hauled back on the reins and swiveled in the saddle, his eyes scanning the frigid terrain. The Piney's ford was completely iced over, a bad sign. *We've got to get across and this is as good a place as any.* Carrington urged his mount down onto the icy surface. With luck the crust would not yet be too thick. Horse and rider moved gingerly onto the ice, the horse pawing nervously at the unfamiliar surface. Grey Eagle's hooves scrambled for purchase. He skit-

tered across the glassy plane until his rear hooves slipped out
from under him, bringing the large animal rump-first down
onto the ice with a crash. Carrington's right foot slipped from
the hooded stirrup and the colonel was launched clumsily from
the saddle backward and down onto the surface of the Piney,
where he landed with a thump, the wind temporarily knocked
from him. Carrington struggled to his feet, his boots slipping
and sliding, spurs chinking with his ungainly movements.

"Son of a bitch!" Carrington cursed. He snatched up the
reins and began kicking viciously at the ice, jamming his spurs
deep into the now-fissured surface. Flushed and sweating, Carrington vented his fury on nature until he had kicked a large
hole in the ice. He stood up to his knees in the frigid water
glaring at the troops who had gathered above him on the bank.
"Come on, damnit! Don't dawdle!" he shouted. "Cross over!
Move! Move!"

The command scrambled down into the rushing stream and
splashed across as Carrington heaved himself panting back
into the saddle, then spurred ahead to overtake the lead of the
column. The column lurched forward and in a few minutes
had scrambled up the slopes of Lodge Trail Ridge heading
north. They moved rapidly along the ridgeline, looking always
to the northwest until tiny dark figures could be seen hurrying
across the broken country ahead. Indians! Carrington gauged
the distance to the fleeing figures below and realized that he
would have to move quickly to cut them off. He spurred forward, Grey Eagle breaking into a lope as they veered to the
left and down the slope on an intersecting course. A blur
flashed by Carrington's left and he looked up to see Grummond at a full gallop, pistol above his head, charging down
into the valley.

"Lieutenant Grummond! Hold up!" Carrington yelled.
"Hold up there, I say!"

Grummond appeared not to have heard but galloped on,
hunched low in the saddle and waving his revolver in front of
him.

"Private Harman!" Carrington screamed over his shoulder

at his orderly. "Overtake Lieutenant Grummond and slow him! He'll follow my orders or return to the post!"

Private Daniel Harman nodded and dashed after the figure of Grummond until both were lost from sight.

Damn the impudence! Carrington thought angrily. This was dangerous work and things were rapidly getting out of control. He wouldn't have it. If they didn't stick together the Sioux would cut them to pieces. The colonel scrambled down the slope and was suddenly startled and dismayed to stumble into a gaggle of Bingham's people, dismounted and milling about aimlessly in a small ravine at the base of the hill.

"What the hell is going on here!" he demanded. "Where's Bingham?"

Corporal James Kelly, a rail-thin Irishman with a florid complexion and a shock of red hair peeking out from under a dark blue kepi, pushed his way over to the colonel.

"Beggin' the colonel's pardon, sorr," he said, "but we dunno where he's at. There was a rumpus wi' the redskins an' Looten'nt Bingham an' Sarn't Bowers took off after 'em. The rest of the outfit got split up in the woods. Oi've got a bunch of 'em rounded up but thir's some still missin'. Then Looten'nt Grummond an' a man come by here but a momen' ago an' were spurrin fer the divil, sorr! They were away over yonder." Kelly pointed off to the north and around the base of a small hill. "There's a whole heap o' the red divils down there, sorr!"

"Damn them!" Carrington spat. "Where's your bugler, Corporal?"

Kelly reached behind him and pulled forward a dark-haired young man with piercing blue eyes. "That'll be Metzger, sorr."

"Metzger," Carrington bellowed. "Sound recall, son."

The young German nodded curtly, filled his lungs, and lifted his instrument to his lips. The brassy notes rang out through the frigid air and rolled echoing back on them from the surrounding hillsides. Colonel Carrington stood in his stirrups and strained to catch some glimpse of lieutenants Grummond or Bingham. He could feel the anger rising again in his chest. From the corner of his eye he caught sight of a slight movement off to the left and looked up to see a thin line of figures

moving steadily down the valley about two miles off. From
the dark uniformity of their appearance it must be Fetterman's
command. Well, that was something. At least Fetterman was
following his orders today. It was probably good that he had
allowed Brown to accompany him. Carrington turned back to
Corporal Kelly.

"All right then, Corporal, mount these men up and follow
me! You there, bugler. Stay by my side!" The colonel wheeled
to the north and galloped down the valley. Adolf Metzger
slung his bugle over his back, heaved himself into the saddle,
and scrambled after his commander, slapping the rump of his
horse violently to keep up the mad pace.

LIEUTENANT GEORGE WASHINGTON GRUMMOND DASHED
forward over the narrow, twisting track that wound along the
base of the hill and urged his mount to greater exertions when
he spied Bingham and two of his troopers galloping along just
a few yards ahead. The figures disappeared and reappeared as
they scrambled up and down through the deceptive terrain
folds. Private Harman, still unable to overtake Grummond,
scrambled along behind. Just beyond Bingham a lone warrior
could be seen hurrying off into the distance, his whoops echoing back through the frozen landscape as his nimble pony
scampered easily over the boulder-strewn trail.

CRAZY HORSE LOOKED BACK OVER HIS SHOULDER AT HIS PUR-
suers. These wasichu had to be some of the worst riders he
had ever seen. He thought he had been moving slowly enough
that even a young boy could follow him with ease but already
he could count only four of the bluecoats who had managed
to stay with him. He noticed that the little soldier chief had
tossed one of his pistols into the brush back near the island
and made a mental note of where the gun had landed so that
he could slip back there later and pick it up. *Stupid soldier,
throwing his gun away like that.* He had hoped to draw more
of the bluecoats in pursuit and shook his head in disgust. Well,

MOON OF BITTER COLD

they would have to do for now. He dashed past a plum thicket and caught a glimpse of Young Man Afraid Of His Horses and No Water peering out from concealment. Young Man was far too careless about such things and No Water was hardly a help. If they were too exposed to the whites No Water would never be the one to notice and insist that they do a better job of hiding.

Crazy Horse glanced over his shoulder again. The whites were still there and two more soldiers had joined in. He noticed that the little soldier chief was waving his long knife in the air. He must have lost his other pistol too. The young warrior made another note to look for this second pistol once they had dealt with these people and hoped that No Water at least had not seen where the man had dropped it.

Crazy Horse threaded his pony through a small stand of fir trees and down a slight incline, careened around a large boulder, and charged into a small, steep-sided ravine that ran twisting along the base of the hill. *Good enough*, he thought, and hauled back on the braided horsehair bridle clutched in his hand. His pony slid instantly to a halt and wheeled about under the touch of his rider's heels. The young Hunkpatila sat, rubbing his pony's flanks. He reached up behind his own left ear, growing numb with the cold, and felt for the smooth pebble that hung suspended there. He waited patiently for his pursuers. He had not long to wait. The clattering echo of horses' hooves rang through the ravine.

Washte! Good! Here they come.

He snatched up the leather-wrapped war club that hung suspended from his pony's flank and felt its reassuring heft. A thin-lipped smile twitched at the corners of his mouth. The little soldier chief was the first man around the slight bend and Crazy Horse shrieked and kicked his pony forward, whirling the club over his head.

Lieutenant Horatio Bingham gasped as he saw the young warrior rushing headlong at him. *What the hell!* Suddenly the air was filled with a thunderous roar of voices yipping, trilling, and shrieking. Warriors in every state of dress appeared from every direction. It was as if the very earth were spitting them up from the depths of hell. Rifles and pistols roared, horses reared, neighing and kicking in fear. Bingham swung wildly in the saddle and saw the panic-struck faces of the men who had followed him into the narrow, brush-choked ravine. His mind raced.

"Get out! Get out!" he screamed. "Go back! Run for it!"

LIEUTENANT GRUMMOND BARELY ESCAPED THE TRAP. He saw the warriors leap onto Bingham's group and reined up in time to avoid being overrun by the fleeing troopers. Grummond and the men with him wheeled their horses to flee but had to fight their way out as buckskin and blanket-clad warriors clawed and struck at them from all sides. Several of the braves were using their bows like hooks, attempting again and again to slip them over the heads of the soldiers and pull them from the saddle. The troopers swung their carbines like clubs and Grummond could hear the dull thumps and the grunts of the braves they managed to hit. A young Arapaho named Jumping Rabbit clambered over a boulder and leapt onto the saddle behind Private John Daniels only to have his head blown wide open by a slug from George Grummond's revolver. Jumping Rabbit tumbled heavily into the brush, a tangle of limp arms and legs. Lieutenant Grummond thumbed back the hammer again and sent a ball into the shoulder of Drags His Leg, who had grabbed on to one of the lieutenant's stirrups. Private Daniels dashed back past Grummond with Private John Guthrie close behind. Grummond turned and followed after them and nearly crashed into Private Harman, who stood in his stirrups, firing his carbine into the mass of warriors who were now swarming toward Lieutenant Bingham and Sergeant Bowers.

Lieutenant Horatio Bingham could not believe what was happening. He swung his saber wildly from side to side and felt it bite into flesh and bone at every swing. He glanced a few feet to his left where George Bowers, the old veteran, worked both of his revolvers with deadly accuracy.

Sweet Jesus! Bingham thought frantically. *Where did they all come from? My God we're all dead!*

"Come on, Bowers! Let's get out, man!"

They turned their horses in a tight circle and both men galloped back out of the ravine toward the small stand of firs beyond. Their friends were out there. Somewhere on the other side of those trees lay salvation if only they could reach it.

DEAFENED BY THE SCREAMING OF THE WARRIORS AND THE booming report of gunfire, George Grummond had no way of knowing that Carrington's command too was now hotly engaged with the Sioux and their allies. Carrington and Metzger had gone but a few yards when they ran headlong into another group of warriors, who stood boldly across the trail. Looking to his rear, Carrington was stunned to find that besides Metzger only a half dozen troopers had come forward with him. *Damn!*

"Dismount!" Carrington screamed, throwing up one gauntleted hand. "Form line as skirmishers! Fire at will!" The troopers tumbled out of their saddles and began working their carbines with deadly efficiency. The cold mountain air rang with the crack of carbines and pistols; bullets zipped overhead like manic, deadly bees, tearing away chips of pine bark, meat, and needles, and hurling them spinning through the thick clouds of gunsmoke onto sweating combatants, terrified and shying horses, and icy, rock-strewn earth. Private James McGuire, whose horse had lurched forward as he tried to dismount, was thrown to the ground midway between the line of troops and the charging mass of warriors. A lone Cheyenne brave leaped his pony over a fallen tree and swooped toward McGuire shrieking, his war club a gray blur whirling by his side. Carrington stepped forward, raised his pistol, and coolly shot the warrior directly between the eyes. The Cheyenne somersaulted backward over the rump of his pony and flopped heavily into the fallen pine needles.

The warriors, Sioux, Cheyenne, and Arapaho, whose numbers swelled with each passing moment, went quickly to ground and began firing back at the soldiers. Rifles, pistols, old trade muskets, bows, all were pressed into action. The maddening screech of eagle-bone whistles and war cries of every description added to the din. American Horse had taken an Army revolver from a hapless private a month earlier, leaving the man and the dispatches he carried scattered in pieces along the white man's road. It had taken him several days to get used to the heavy weapon but now he could fire and load it as easily and as quickly as any *wasichu*. He used the pistol with fierce joy now, standing boldly in the open and taking careful aim as he squeezed the trigger. He reveled in the heavy recoil as the gun bucked like a spirited pony in his hand. He was not a very good shot with it yet. But he loved the noise and the smoke and the kicking of the gun. It was a powerful medicine. The pistol roared and bucked in his hand again and he howled with glee to see one of the bluecoats drop his gun and clutch at his shoulder as he dropped to the ground screaming.

"*Haho!*" American Horse yelled to his friends. "Look at this! I have hit one of them! *Haiye!*" He looked to his right at Red Wolf, who grinned back at American Horse and whooped his encouragement to the older warrior, his mentor, his friend.

Red Wolf was a fine young man and his father, Tall Bear, had been one of American Horse's closest friends. A great warrior, a good husband, and a gentle father who was forever telling wonderful tales and funny stories. American Horse had loved him like a brother before he was killed by a Winnebago—a hawk-faced man with a scar that ran down the side of his face and a silver moon that dangled from his ear. American Horse had grieved for the loss of his friend and tried desperately to kill the Winnebago who had slain Tall Bear. But the Winnebago, who were working for the white soldiers, had returned to their homes and American Horse had never seen the man again. Instead American Horse had become Red Wolf's *Hunka*—brought him into manhood and taught him how to be a warrior and how to be a man. The whites were the ones who had brought the Winnebago to kill Red Wolf's father. American Horse would as soon kill a white as a Winnebago.

He dropped down behind a tree to reload his pistol and watched the boy he now considered a son work his bow with all the skill that a man could want. It filled the older warrior with pride to see how the boy drew the string tight against his ear with three fingers and breathed out as he released the arrow, just as American Horse had taught him. The older man watched as the boy sped an arrow straight through the cap of one of the soldiers. It tore the cap clean from the man's head and pinned it quivering to a tree just behind the horror-stricken bluecoat. Red Wolf was delighted and laughed out loud to see the bluecoat's hat pinned to a tree. He yelled to American Horse and made a funny face. The boy was so much like his father.

American Horse was just tamping home the loads in his pistol when Red Wolf leapt up to taunt the bluecoats. The boy turned his back on them and bent over, flipping the tail of his loincloth up to expose his buttocks and waggling it back and forth in their faces. He looked over at his *Hunka* and was grinning broadly when he was thrown headlong into a thicket by the impact of a bullet. The older warrior was stunned. *Hiya! Hiya! No!* his brain screamed out. *Not the boy! No!* American Horse dropped his pistol and rushed to the boy, where he crouched, lifting him in his arms and calling his name.

"Red Wolf! Red Wolf!"

But the boy's spirit had fled. A soldier's bullet had entered the boy's buttocks and torn through his small body exploding out through his chest. The veteran warrior, drenched in the boy's blood, cradled the lifeless form gently in his arms, sobbing and rocking back and forth, his tears dropping to mingle with Red Wolf's lifeblood already cooling in black pools on the frozen earth.

The forest reverberated with the chaos of battle until Fetterman's command hove into sight. The new arrivals slid thankfully from their mounts and hurried to take their places on the firing line. Rifles, carbines, and pistols roared into the rolling clouds of gunsmoke until Carrington realized that the enemy had melted quietly away from in front of them.

"Cease firing!" Carrington roared out as he stalked up and down the firing line. "Cease firing, men." Others along the line took up the cry and soon all was quiet but for the moaning of the wounded and the persistent ringing in everyone's ears. William Fetterman, with Fred Brown and Alexander Wands in tow, hurried over to Carrington.

"Where's Bingham?" Fetterman asked, shouting to hear over his own deafness.

"I would ask you the same question, Captain Fetterman," Carrington replied coldly. "He was assigned to your command. But then Grummond is gone as well, taken off after him down that way." He pointed off to the right and in the direction of the ravine.

"They may be in trouble, Colonel," Fetterman said quickly. "I suggest we follow after them."

Carrington did not like the man's tone but knew that they should push forward immediately. Silently he cursed the insolence of some of his junior officers. Arrogant young hotheads they were, insubordinate and willful. Dangerously so, he thought, for their precipitate actions had for a time split the two commands into smaller, disjointed and vulnerable fragments. They prided themselves on being combat veterans but this undisciplined madness would have been no more acceptable in action against Bedford Forrest than it was against Red Cloud. Carrington suppressed his anger and turned to order the now reunited command to horse when a thunder of hoofbeats came echoing through the trees to their front. Every head swiveled to see a hatless George Grummond and three troopers charging madly through the trees with a small mob of screaming, lance- and club-wielding Indians in hot pursuit. Fetterman and Brown leapt forward, their pistols blazing.

"Fire away, boys!" Brown shouted. "Cover 'em in! Ride, boys! Ride! Come on!"

A score of voices joined in, urging the fleeing soldiers to hurry into the ranks of their comrades. Carbines and rifles barked in a ragged volley. The Indians stopped in their tracks,

screeching and shaking their lances at the soldiers, then turned
and vanished into the trees.

"Mount up!" Carrington yelled. "Let's get after them!"

The soldiers scrambled for their mounts. Half of the now-
deafened command didn't even hear the order but took their
cues from their fellows. They stumbled over their own feet,
crashing into each other. Rifles clattered to the ground to be
snatched up again by stiffened fingers. Hats dropped rolling
and ignored into the underbrush. Terrified horses snorted and
turned in tight circles, dragging their reins through the pine
needles as riders struggled to snatch them up and clamber into
saddles that pitched and rolled under them. Through the confusion Lieutenant George Grummond spurred directly into
Carrington's path. His face was flushed, hair wild, and eyes
wide with terror and anger.

"Damn you, sir!" Grummond croaked nearly in tears. "Are
you a coward or only a fool leaving us out there to face those
savages? Where were you? Where was our support?"

Carrington's face grew black with rage and he exploded at
his accuser.

"No, damn you sir!" the colonel spat back. "You insubordinate whelp! You left your command, sir! You violated my
orders, sir! You endangered every man of this command with
your recklessness. And then you come running back like a
whipped dog with your tail between your legs. By God, consider yourself lucky that I don't shoot you down myself. Return to your command, Lieutenant Grummond, and by God
stay with it this time or I swear I will have you under arrest!"
Carrington turned back to the command and screamed out his
orders.

"By twos, forward at a trot. Forward!"

The command lunged forward, weapons at the ready, heads
swiveling to left and right as they moved cautiously down the
rough track and deeper into the trees. They had not far to go
to locate their missing comrades. A slight clearing bore mute
witness to the savage encounter that Grummond and three
troopers had only narrowly escaped. The clearing was carpeted
with browned pine needles now blackened by pools of blood.

A number of the trees were torn and splintered by gunfire and the cuts of saber and hatchet; a long smear of blood traced down the rough surface of a large pine and slumped over a lone stump was all that remained of Lieutenant Horatio Bingham. The corpse was stripped naked and casually butchered, scalp removed, arms and legs slashed open, head split and gray matter spilled out on the ground. The corpse was punctured with dozens of arrows, each slightly different in markings and fletching and representing every tribe and clan that had taken a hand in the day's grim work.

Several of the younger troopers vomited and staggered retching and gagging through the clearing. Within three feet of the lieutenant lay the body of Sergeant George Bowers. Bowers' skull was split and his scalp was gone, but he had been otherwise spared much of the violence done to Bingham. That the corpse had been so spared told an experienced frontiersman that the sergeant had died a brave man and was accorded this singular honor by his killers. Three overlarge pools of blood in a semicircle surrounding the body attested to the fact that at least three of his attackers had accompanied the sergeant into the realm from which no man returns.

Carrington looked about at the shambles his foray had become. Five men were wounded. Two were dead. A number of horses were bleeding profusely from their wounds. It was a debacle and they could only thank God that it had not turned out worse than it had. How many of the Indians had died that day he could not know. Not a single enemy corpse had been left behind. All had been borne off by their comrades and now they would do the same. The survivors gathered in silent, sullen knots, conversing in whispers, the steam of their breath mingling with that of the horses. The day had grown dark as clouds gathered thick and lowering above them, blotting out the sun. The wind began to whistle eerily through the pines and shards of ice began to fall pricking at faces and exposed hands. It had grown bitterly cold and dismal, a day that matched the mood of every man who straggled shivering and sober back down the rough track to Fort Phil Kearny.

*   *   *

"*AHAHE! HOJILA! HAIYE! HAIYE!* A GREAT DAY IS HERE!" announced Young Man Afraid Of His Horses, standing in council to have his say. "We whipped those *wasichu* all over the countryside. The party with the little soldier chiefs ran like rabbits when we jumped them. Oh, it was a great chase, my brothers. A great chase and better even than chasing buffalo."

Several of the younger warriors voiced their assent and shook their fists in the air, whooping. Everyone was speaking more loudly than usual because of the persistent ringing in their ears.

"Quiet! Quiet, I say!" Red Cloud shouted. "All of you youngsters be quiet."

He fixed Young Man Afraid with a stern gaze and indicated that he should sit down. "We are all glad that you so enjoyed this fight, Young Man Afraid Of His Horses, that is good. But it is not the reason for this council. We must look back at this fight in the most thoughtful way that we can to see what worked well and how we must change the things that did not work well. We cannot not make the same mistakes in our next fight. I will ask American Horse to tell us what he thinks of this fight. American Horse has lost his *mihunka*[1] to these whites and we will listen carefully to what he has to say."

All eyes drifted to the form of the mature warrior who sat grim-faced and silent staring into the dim glow of the coals of the central fire. A warrior much to be feared, he was a deadly fighter with many coups to his credit. For all his experience of war he was in a somber mood, still grieving the loss of his young friend Red Wolf. Everyone knew that he was the boy's *Hunka* and had loved him like his own son. It was because of this that Red Cloud had asked for American Horse's opinion, for he knew the older warrior would not be

---

[1]*Mihunka*: The purpose of the *Hunka* ritual, or *Hunkalowanpi*, is to create a bond that is stronger even than the tie of kinship, frequently between a mature warrior, the *Hunka ate* (*Hunka* father), and the *mihunka* (my *Hunka* or *Hunka* son).

distracted by foolish notions of glory and honors to be gotten from war. His loss fresh in his mind, he would provide a sober, serious view of the fight. That was badly needed right now.

Red Cloud glanced about the lodge and felt his heart rising in his throat. His efforts were finally beginning to show very real progress. A year ago he could not imagine seeing in this lodge the people he now saw gathered there. Not only were his own Oglala present but so were the fighters of the Minniconjou, the Gros Ventre. He knew them all: Pawnee Killer, Black Shield, White Bull, Crazy Horse, Sitting Bull, Soldier, He Has A Sword, Bad Heart Bull, Bad Wound, Red Leaf, Little Wound, Crow Dog, Afraid Of Bear, Short Bull, and Lone Bear. And then there were the Arapaho, Little Chief, Tall Bear, Spotted Wolf, Wounded Bear, and Black Crow, and the Cheyenne, Tall Bull, Two Crows, Little Wolf, Two Moon, Roman Nose, and Cloud Chief. Never before had so many of the people gathered together for one purpose and he, Red Cloud, had made this so.

Spotted Tail had said that it would never happen, that the tribes and clans were as trees in the forest, all were of the same large family but each stood separate and apart from all others and never to join together as one great tree. Spotted Tail was wrong. He had done it. He, Red Cloud, the orphan, the man shunned by so many. Hated, feared, mistrusted by all, he had put it all behind him, had suppressed his temper, softened his words. He had forced himself to smile where he would have snarled; laugh when he would have struck out; say nothing when he would have roared. He had talked to all as he might have talked to a beloved child, patient, knowing, gentle but firm, quiet but persuasive. And here they had all come to listen and to join. For how long the people would stay together no one could say, but with this single purpose in their minds, the driving out of these whites, it might be done for just a little longer. That was all that Red Cloud could hope for, a little while longer. American Horse rose to speak.

"Brothers," the veteran warrior said. "I will say that this was a good fight. Yellow Eagle led the fight and he acquitted himself well. *Ahahe!* He is a bold warrior and a good fighter.

I am saddened that we have lost brave men, good friends, in this fight but so is it always in war. When we take up the hatchet we must know that before it is laid down again that there will be sadness in some lodges. There is sadness in my lodge today since I have lost my *hoksicantkiye*, my beloved son. I will not keep his ghost but allow him to travel down the *Wanagi Tacanku*[2] to meet the old woman. Yes, this was a good fight because we drove back the enemy and those who have died have died as brave men." He paused and looked around him, his eyes lingering for a moment on Young Man Afraid. "It was a good day to die, but it was not a great day. For all of our fighting and our dead there were but two of the bluecoats who we know have been killed. More may have been killed but that we do not know for certain. We know only that six of our own will never again hunt or laugh with us and that cannot come from a great day." A number of heads nodded solemnly in agreement and Young Man Afraid and his companions cast their eyes downward with sheepish looks.

"Now," American Horse began again. "I do not say to the young warriors that they should not rejoice in this fight. They have done well. They have behaved as brave men and have been bold in their fighting. Yellow Eagle has led them well. That is as it should be. *Hetchetu! Washte!* Good! But now we should look at how we should make our next fight better. I think Crazy Horse's plan is a good one. We have now seen for certain how the whites can be led to where we want them to go. *Washte!* Let us do so again. But this time we must be patient and we must have more warriors in exactly the right places. This time too many of us were at the place where they cut the trees and we scattered out when the whites chased us. We never wanted to fight them at that place and so it was unwise to have so many people there. Instead, let us put all of our braves in one place, the place of killing, and let only those who are to lead them go off from the rest. This will be a very hard job. It is very cold and we will have to stay hidden

[2]*Wanagi Tacanku*: The "Ghost Road" along which the spirit, *wanagi*, travels after death until it meets the old woman who decides its fate.

for a long time waiting for them. The younger men find this a very hard thing to do when they smell battle coming but it must be so. No one may go by himself against the whites before it is time. This is what happened in this last fight. A few of the bluecoats came into our killing place but only a few. If this happens again I say that we must not kill them but let them pass through the killing place if we must. This too will be hard to do. It is hard to let an enemy pass without counting coup but we must be patient. If a few must get away so that we may kill many, then it must be."

There was a general grunting of approval which rumbled through the lodge. Many heads nodded in quiet agreement. What American Horse was saying made good sense. The older warriors saw this immediately but it was plain that many were worried about some of the younger men who were naturally eager to come to grips with the enemy. A number of critical eyes were turned toward Young Man Afraid and his friends, a fact that did not escape the brash warrior. Under their scrutiny he too found himself nodding in agreement. Red Cloud listened intently, studying the faces of those gathered in the council lodge. While there was general agreement that the whites should be driven out, he still sensed that not all of those present were likely to remain allies for long. When it was clear that American Horse had had his say, Red Cloud rose to address the assembly.

"Brothers," he said, holding out his open hands. "What American Horse has said is full of good sense. I think he's right and that the plan which Crazy Horse and others have suggested will serve to drive these whites from our land forever. The fight that Yellow Eagle led was not as successful as we had hoped but it was a good plan and it can work even better if all of us work together to make it so."

"What makes you think that this is the best plan, Red Cloud?" Little Chief of the Arapaho had risen to his feet. "We Arapaho have never fought in such a way. Why should we adopt this crazy plan that has already cost us dead? Who says that the Oglala are the ones who should say how the Arapaho

or the Cheyenne should make war? Especially when it is not
our way!"

A low chorus of grunts lent support to Little Chief's comments. There had been a serious altercation between Red
Cloud and Little Chief over the men killed in the fight against
the cow movers, and, while peace had been maintained, tensions were still high between the two men and their respective
followers. The fact that two more Arapaho had been killed
during Yellow Eagle's fight had done nothing to ease tensions.
Red Cloud fought down the natural urge to lash out at this
man and breathed deeply, collecting his thoughts. The others
gathered in the lodge waited breathlessly for the explosion that
was sure to come.

"Little Chief has a point," Red Cloud began quietly. "No
one can say that the way that Crazy Horse has suggested to
fight the whites is the only way that anyone should fight. I
grieve for the friends which Little Chief has lost. Who of us
has not lost friends and relations to these *wasichu?* But what
have we learned from those who died? If we go against the
whites as we have all done in the past, even the Oglala, then
we kill a few of the whites but always we lose too many of
our own warriors at the same time."

There was a grumbling of agreement among the gathered
warriors. None could deny that this war against the whites was
becoming a costly affair. Already there were more empty
lodges from this war than from any war against the Crow,
Shoshone, Nez Perce, Bannack, Pawnee, Arikara, or Winnebago.

"Now," Red Cloud went on, "many of us watched this fight
that Yellow Eagle led against the whites and it told us many
things about how these bluecoats fight. When we let them keep
far off where they can stay in one party and use their rifles
and the *maza wakan,* the fast-shooting guns, then they are very
dangerous. But when they get into smaller groups and we get
in close to them where we can count coup then they are not
so brave and they panic—especially the young ones—and they
are easier to kill. What this fight has shown us is how these
bluecoats move and fight when they come out of the Buffalo

Creek fort. It has shown us that some of their young chiefs
are like many of our young men." He glanced at Young Man
Afraid Of His Horses. "They get very excited and charge
ahead without thinking and they do not look where they
are being taken until it is too late. The longer the chase, the
more they shoot and the fewer bullets they have when they
come to the killing place. This is what we should try to do. If
only for this one fight." Red Cloud paused and spread his arms
out to the Arapaho and Cheyenne chiefs, who sat grouped
together in one segment of the council circle.

"Some say, 'Red Cloud wants to lead everyone in this war,'
but that is not so. I don't pretend to be a leader of all of the
tribes. I don't claim to lead the Lakota. I don't claim to lead
the Minniconjou, the Brulé, the Big Bellies. I do not claim
even to lead the Oglala; the *Tapis'lecas, Wagluhes, Payabyas,*
the *Kiyaksas.* I can speak only for the *Itesicas,* the Bad Faces
of the Oglala. The *Itesicas* will fight these *wasichu.* We will
fight them as Yellow Eagle and American Horse and Crazy
Horse have shown us how to fight them. I don't ask you to
fight under me, to fight under us. No, I ask you to join us, to
fight alongside of us as brothers, not as Hunkpatila, as Kiyaksas, as Lakota or Shyela or Arapaho but as Indians. That is
all I ask of any of you gathered here. To fight as an Indian.
To be an Indian!"

The lodge grew deathly silent. All that could be heard was
the brittle crackling of the low central fire and the soughing
of the wind beyond the hides that comprised the walls of the
lodge. It whistled through the blackened ends of the lodgepoles that towered bristling overhead. Little Chief, sitting
alongside his fellow chief Sorrel Horse, seemed nonplussed by
Red Cloud's pronouncement. He sat back thinking, his brow
furrowed and jaw jutting slightly forward as if he were chew-
ing Red Cloud's words. He looked to Sorrel Horse and then
across to where Roman Nose sat with Tall Bull. Roman Nose
nodded to him as did the others. Little Chief looked directly
at Red Cloud, then swept his eyes across the faces of the others
gathered around and leaning into the fire as if all awaited his

words. He turned slowly back to Red Cloud, looked deep into the man's eyes, and then nodded.

"Very well, Red Cloud," he said finally. "We'll do it. We'll fight alongside of you."

A rumbling of approval rippled through the assembly and voices could be heard muttering small side conversations as they considered the magnitude of what had just happened. Red Cloud stood and waited for the talking to die down of its own accord, which it would surely do. After a few moments it began to grow quiet again and all looked to the Oglala who stood waiting to speak.

"Very well," Red Cloud said. "It is decided. Now we must discuss exactly how it is that we will bring this great fight into being and where and how best we can bring the soldiers to the killing place."

LIEUTENANT GEORGE GRUMMOND GALLOPED FRANTICALLY down the valley. He was hunched over the saddlebow, leaning so far forward that his chin pressed into the lathered neck of his coal black charger. The horse's nostrils were flared, his eyes wide with terror, and flecks of white foam flew from his muzzle and disappeared into the blinding white brilliance of the snow that covered every surface. Grummond kept turning his head, looking back over his shoulder at the huge figure that bore down on him. A huge Cheyenne warrior, his face painted a brilliant red and black, and mounted on a fleet calico pony, surged effortlessly over the snowy landscape. Thousands of feathers seemed to flutter maddeningly in the windswept war bonnet that floated behind him, the tail feathers snapping over the rump of the pony, which moved as if it were merely an extension of the Cheyenne's own body. The Cheyenne's eyes glowed with the intensity of burning embers and an eagle-bone whistle clenched between the warrior's teeth screeched eerily above the pounding echoes of hoofbeats. But Grummond's widened eyes were focused on the cold, gleaming lance point that reached ever closer as his own horse plunged chest deep into a field of snow. Grummond's horse whinnied and the animal began plunging through the powdery white sea, pushing off of its rear haunches and leaping into the air to dive deep into the snowy waves. But the Cheyenne's pony seemed to float above the snow, skimming the surface, raising little more than a cloud of fine white dust as it passed over the frozen landscape. Grummond's horse moved slower and slower, struggling against the deepening drifts until it stopped entirely, mired to its chest in the icy white grip. The horse reared as the Cheyenne closed in from behind, thrusting with his lance and running the point clear through Grummond's back just as a fierce wind screamed through the valley and all dissolved in a blizzard of swirling whiteness.

Frances Grummond screamed and sat bolt upright in bed, her heart pounding wildly, eyes wide with horror and bedclothes drenched in sweat. She thrust wildly about the blankets and heavy comforter and felt the sleeping form of her husband under the mounded layers of fabric and batting.

"Whaa? Huh?" George Grummond stirred and sat up bewildered and disoriented, eyes still heavy with sleep. He blinked and looked around the spartan room, allowing his eyes to adjust to the darkness. He reached out to the small, upended nail keg that served as a nightstand and fumbled with a box of matches, breaking two before he got the stub of a candle lit. He looked at his wife, who stared back trembling and wide-eyed. Large tears rolled down her pale cheeks. She had dug her hands deeply into his shoulder and was gripping him so tightly that he had to place his hand over hers and gently work her fingers loose.

"What is it darling? What's the matter? Is it that damned dream again?"

Frances did not reply immediately but threw her arms around him and huddled close on his chest, sobbing into the nest of his shoulder. George could do nothing but hold her tightly to him, her small form enfolded in the cradle of his strong arms, his fingers smoothing her hair as he whispered soothingly to her.

"It's just a dream, darling," he whispered. "Only a dream.

I'm here with you. I'm fine. We're together and nothing and
no one can harm us."

"Oh, George, George," she sobbed. "It was horrible! So
horrible! It was so real I could feel the cold. I could hear the
hoofbeats. It was like I was looking into the future. Oh, dear
God!"

"Frances," George said quietly. "Fanny, it's all right. Everything will be all right, you'll see. It's just a foolish dream.
Nothing more. It's not a premonition. It's not a vision of the
future. You could feel the cold because you kicked off your
blankets and the hoofbeats were nothing more than your own
heart. Trust me darling. Nothing will happen to me. I won't
let it happen. Truly I won't."

"Oh, God, George. Oh, dear God, what would I do? Oh,
please swear to me that you'll be careful."

"Fanny! Sweet one, please don't cry. Please," George
pleaded softly. "It's only a dream. They're only phantoms. I
won't let them get me. I swear I won't. I'll be here for you.
I just know it. The fight we had was a close call but it was
only that. It was a warning to be cautious and I will. I swear
I will. Please don't cry, sweetheart. Come get back under the
covers and I'll hold you close. I'll get you warm again and
hold you closer than you've ever been held in your life. There,
there, my darling," he cooed. "There, there, go back to sleep.
I'm here for you. I'll always be here for you. Always."

Grummond smoothed her raven hair and rocked her gently
in his arms as she snuggled deeper and deeper into his chest,
her small chest still heaving as she struggled to fight down the
panic that welled up from deep inside of her. Outside in the
darkness a wolf sang its solitary, mournful song. His pitiful,
howling cry rose and fell through the pines that marched in
dark and silent rows down the slopes of the sleeping Bighorns.
Frances shuddered and pushed her face deeper into him and
George felt the warmth of her tears trickling down his chest.

COLONEL HENRY CARRINGTON TRUDGED WEARILY UP THE
steps of the headquarters building, his eyes downcast, hat

gripped tightly in gloved fingers. It had been an agonizing day
spent entirely in laying the dead to rest and there was work
yet to be done. Officers would have to be detailed to settle the
affairs of the dead men. Letters would have to be written to
their families. A few personal items would be shipped home,
the rest sold at auction, and the proceeds forwarded to the
Adjutant General in Washington. The grieving relatives would
have to apply to disinterested bureaucrats and work their way
through a labyrinthine series of clerks and red tape to recover
what piddling sums would result. The friends of the dead
would pile rocks on their graves to stave off the wolves and
it was the wolves who stood a better chance of achieving their
goal than did any widow or orphan.

Carrington had been trying in vain for months to squeeze
what he needed out of the Washington bureaucrats—a few
extra rounds of ammunition, rifles that were not falling apart,
medicines to treat the mounting rheumatic complaints, mittens
for men routinely in danger of losing their fingers to the cold,
horses and grain to feed them. All of his entreaties, it seemed,
had fallen on deaf ears and elicited no more than rebukes for
the tardiness of reports delayed by severe weather or the sudden deaths of the men who had tried to carry them.

"Colonel." A familiar voice jarred Carrington from his reverie.

"Eh? Oh, Ten Eyck," Carrington said. "I'm sorry, I'm still
a bit deaf from the gunfire and it's been a hard morning."

"Yes sir, that it has. Rest their souls." Ten Eyck glanced
across to the cemetery.

"The mail escort is ready to go, sir." An ambulance stood
waiting on the parade ground. He had been so distracted that
he had walked right by the ambulance and its mounted escort
without even noticing them. Lieutenant Bisbee, hardly recognizable as a human because of the bulky fur clothing he had
donned for the trip, was helping Lucy and their young son,
Jean, to get settled under layers of buffalo robes in the rear of
the ambulance. The day that Bingham and Bowers had been
killed, orders had arrived transferring Bisbee to duty in Omaha
with specific instructions that he accompany the next available

mail party. Carrington had thrown up his hands in dismay at the papers. To lose yet another officer when they were already shorthanded. It was, Carrington thought, a disgrace that in this beleaguered garrison he should be obliged to carry out all the responsibilities dropped on him with but a single officer to each company. It was a disgrace.

"Sir?"

"Oh, I'm sorry, Tenedor, I was just thinking."

"Yes, sir," Ten Eyck replied. "About the mails, sir. Are there any further instructions for Bisbee or the escort?"

Carrington looked over at Lieutenant Bisbee, now settling himself comfortably in the mule seat of the ambulance and tugging a Henry rifle from beneath the folds of the buffalo robes spread over his lap.

"No," Carrington breathed out quietly. "There's nothing more to be said." The colonel did not wait for a reply but continued up the steps and disappeared into the headquarters building.

Jim Bridger was waiting for him as he came through the door. The scout pushed a mug of coffee into Carrington's hands.

"Here ye go, Colonel," Bridger drawled. "Heat yer gullet and if this don't do it, I brung along a bit o' cheerwater what will take the chill off certain sure."

"Major Bridger!" Carrington exclaimed. "Good lord! I thought we'd seen the last of you for the winter. When did you come in? How are the roads up north? Is everything well at C. F. Smith? What's happened to bring you down here? If you've come to warn us about the Sioux risking a major attack I fear you are a bit late."

"Whoa, mule!" Bridger waved a bony hand and pushed the mug into Carrington's grasp. "Tain't much of a how-de-do, Colonel. What happened to 'How's yer rheumatiz, Gabe,' an' other such pleasantries?"

"Oh, I'm sorry, Major," Carrington said, tossing his hat on a table. "I've forgotten my manners. It is good to see you. How is your health, sir?"

"Wagh!" Bridger turned and dropped his lanky frame into

a ladder-back chair near the stove. "My health is a chancy business at the best of times, Colonel, but I guard my hair well enough. Which I see is more than some of yer boys're doin'. And no I did not come to warn you of that damned set of flea bites that ye've just been through." He nodded toward the window that faced the cemetery.

Carrington sighed and took a long sip of the coffee. "I would hardly call the deaths of two men 'flea bites.' It was a bad business and I confess I did not handle it well. We lost Bingham and Bowers to those rascals out there. It was a bad business."

"Yes, well," Bridger said easily. "So some of yer boys would have it thought but I do not agree."

"You weren't there, Major Bridger. You cannot know how badly the whole business was handled."

"Wagh!" Bridger snorted. "I'm no scholar but I kin read sign, Colonel. It is what you pay me for and you spend your dollar well. I saw whar that fight was and you may have been in it but I 'spect you don't know but half of what you seen. How many Injuns you figger ye stirred up out there where ye lost yer boys, Colonel?"

"Oh, lord, Major Bridger, I cannot say for sure but I expect that there were nearly a hundred warriors out there that day."

"A hunnert, eh?" Bridger cocked his head with a sly smile. "You'll be surprised, I wager, to know that it were more like three hunnert of the devils out there."

Carrington's eyebrows arched and he stared hard at the smiling scout.

"It's a fact," Bridger said, and refilled his mug. He turned his chair about to straddle it, leaning his elbows on the back and sipping at the hot coffee. "Colonel, it's like I have said all along, when you don't see no Injuns there you'll find 'em thickest! Where you thought ye saw a hunnert Injuns I will swear that there were more'n three times that number a-dancin' about. I have been over all that ground where ye fought 'em an' their scourings and leavings were plain and shiny as this here mug in my hand. I come across whar they'd camped the night afore yer scrap and it's plain as day that there were a helluva lot more of 'em than you think. And you paid 'em out fairly well for what they served you. From what I could see of the blood an' trailings yer boys kilt at least five of 'em, an' likely more, for their doctoring ain't what it should be. Thank the lord fer that much at least. Now, mebbe that don't seem like much to ye right now after putting two boys under but if I recall rightly it don't hold a candle to how the rebs done ye at Cold Harbor and Sharpsburg."[3]

Henry Carrington sighed deeply. Bridger was right, of course. But having just buried two men in a cemetery already filled with their comrades, only one of whom had died of what could be termed "natural" causes, Carrington found it was hard to keep these deaths in perspective. A mere two years earlier the loss of two men or even twenty would have hardly rated a mention in a commander's journal. But here the loss of a single man was enough to unnerve the most seasoned veteran and send the entire garrison into a deep gloom.

It was a curious thing. What was it about this war—this war that should never have happened in the first place—that made it so different from the terrible war they had just finished? Was it more terrible than brother killing brother? No, that was impossible, unthinkable! And yet there was something intrinsically horrific about this situation. For his part, Carrington knew that he had never felt so alone, isolated, and abandoned as he had here in this place. Perhaps that was it. The solitude of the place—its remoteness. Perhaps it was the fact that they were so far from home and civilization. No. Impossible. How could the mere proximity of civilization make any war more acceptable? Did the wanton destruction of so many homes in the Shenandoah, the razing of Vicksburg

[3]At Sharpsburg, Maryland (Antietam Creek), September 17, 1862, Union forces were thrown back by Lee's Army of Northern Virginia in the bloodiest single day of the Civil War. Union casualties for this one day were 12,400, while the Confederates lost 13,700. At Cold Harbor, Virginia, June 3–12, 1864, Union forces under U. S. Grant battered themselves against strong Confederate positions. One assault alone cost Grant over seven thousand men in less than thirty minutes.

and Atlanta, make that war any more tolerable? It did not obey
the rules of logic. Perhaps it was the very nature of the enemy.
Perhaps it was the fact that the Indians were so different from
any people he had ever known. And perhaps it was the very
nature of any war ever fought between two such very different
peoples. This was a war of stealth and ambush. Of skulking
and murder. Of unspeakable brutality. Of no mercy. That must
be it. Carrington thought about it for a moment and realized
suddenly that the only people he knew at Fort Phil Kearny
who seemed able to accept this kind of war, who seemed neither surprised nor entirely dispirited, were those who had either lived on the plains for years or who hailed from Kansas
and Missouri. People like Jim Bridger, a Missourian.

Yes, he thought. *The Missourians would know about this
kind of war. A war of utter savagery and no quarter. They
have seen this before—a war of vengeance and lust, of passion, and a complete lack of compassion and humanity.* It had
produced men like Quantrill and Anderson and massacres like
Lawrence and Centralia.[4] It was war stripped of any pretense
of chivalry or honor or civilized behavior. That was what this
war with Red Cloud had become, with no quarter expected
and none given. It was kill or be killed—horribly. For the
soldiers it was the thought of mutilation that was so unnerving.
A man alone, wounded or lost, was doomed. At best he would
die quickly, but all too often he was assured only of a painful
and lingering descent into Hell, knowing that even his remains
would be unrecognizable to the closest relative or dearest
friend.

---

[4]The Civil War on the Kansas-Missouri border was indeed the scene of some
of the most savage and indiscriminate slaughter during the entire war. Confederate guerrillas or "bushwhackers" under William Quantrill and "Bloody
Bill" Anderson cut a bloody swath through the region and were matched by
the depredations of the pro-Union "Jayhawkers" and "Red Legs." Along with
the Indian Wars, the Kansas-Missouri Border War was as close as this country
has ever come to the ethnic slaughters of Bosnia and Somalia in the late
twentieth century. The Civil War in Kansas and Missouri produced not only
Quantrill and Anderson but William F. "Buffalo Bill" Cody, "Wild Bill" Hick-
ock, and Frank and Jesse James.

"Colonel," Bridger said suddenly. "I hope you are listening to what I am telling you. It weren't a great victory but you were damned lucky you only lost two. From what I could read on the ground, you all got stretched out and busted up into little bunches for a time. If the redskins had come together at once they'd a et you up good, piece by piece. The fact that ye lost but two says ye pulled yourselves out in time and you need be thankful for that. Don't mourn the dead too long for it don't do 'em no good, nor you either. I liked young Bingham. I rode up to Smith with him and found him an honest young man. I do not doubt you shall miss him. But don't let his dyin' tempt you into foolishness, for the Injuns do count on that."

Carrington sipped his coffee, searching Bridger's eyes over the rim of the mug. The scout was speaking plainly and there was little argument with his case. It was sound, it was logical. Who knew these savages better than Bridger? Who knew better how they fought and how they schemed? What else did he know?

"Major," Carrington said. "You said you did not come down here to warn us of this trap, so what did bring you back so soon?"

"Aye, Colonel," Bridger replied. "Had it been my purpose to warn you of this scrap it's poor doin's, would'nt you say? No. This warn't the grand hoorah that worries me, Colonel. I'm thinkin' it be but a proof of how they mean to hustle up the swami in days to come. They mean to try what they tried on ye agin but the next time they'll do it up brown. Three hunnert bucks may sound a large party but when Red Cloud has more'n two thousand on the Tongue it may spell but one thing . . ."

"Two thousand!" Carrington interrupted. "You don't mean two thousand warriors, surely. You are counting families as well, are you not?"

"I am not or so I would have said, I b'lieve."

"What are they planning, Major Bridger? How might we strike first and foil their designs? What is their Achilles heel, sir?"

Bridger shot the colonel a puzzled look.

"What is their weakness?" Carrington restated his question.

"Colonel, as to what they are planning only Red Cloud knows for certain and he does not care to confide in me as you might expect. As to striking 'em first I would not do it, leastways not now. I'm thinkin' you have not the soldiers and your soldiers have not the skills they need to do naught but get themselves cut up an' kilt. I counsel patience, sir."

Bridger moved to the window and tapped on the glass with his tin mug.

"This weather has been bitter cold but there be no snow that you'd notice and you must wait for snow. When the snows come they'll come hard. Game'll go to ground. Forage'll be deep under an' the ponies will be chawin' bark afore too long. I'm thinkin' it'll be hard for Mr. Red Cloud to keep his rascals together up there once the weather turns. It'll be hard to feed families. Hard to feed ponies. Hard to move about. The tribes'll start to argue. They'll fight among themselves, paw and nip, then scatter an' look for hidey-holes till the spring comes. When the snows come you can likely do 'em a turn but not before then. Until that time keep a tight rein on your boys. Don't let 'em get flummoxed by their come-aheads, for that's what the devils want."

"Hmmm." Carrington scratched at his bearded chin and rubbed his fingers over his mouth as he considered Bridger's advice. "Yes, yes," he said finally. "We are sorely pressed for so many things. Men, ammunition, horses, weapons that are not falling apart." There was a twinge of anger in Carrington's voice. "But we'll do what we can while we bide our time. It's the one thing we are not wanting, time. We have the winter months ahead of us and we can use that time to sharpen our spears, so to speak. We should need to get the wood trains through, but two or three more trips and we shall finish construction of the barracks and lay up the last of the firewood. Once that's done we'll need to detach troops only for the mail escort and can concentrate our forces here."

"That's sound, colonel," Bridger said. "Injuns hail from a lot further south than Texas, colonel, if you take my meaning.

Take the time to break your fellas of their old habits from fightin' rebels and get 'em used to fightin' devils. Devils ain't near so frisky when it's cold. It ain't in their nature. When the deep snows come ye can bring your own kind of hell to the Tongue and be-damned to the lot of 'em."

PORTUGEE PHILLIPS USED THE HEEL OF HIS HAND TO RUB THE frost from the window of Washington's pool hall and watched as Private Thomas Maddeon hurried out the quartermaster's gate and cut across the meadow headed for the Wheatleys' boardinghouse. Maddeon had turned up his collar against the bitterly cold wind, and Jim Wheatley's rifle was gripped tightly in his mittened hand. Private Maddeon was the regimental armorer, and a handier man with firearms Phillips had never known.

A nice young man, Phillips thought. *Probably did a little work on Jim's rifle in exchange for some apple pie and a chance to steal a look at Liz Wheatley. Well, no harm in that.* Phillips turned back to his coffee and noticed that the wheelwright, George Breakenridge, was also watching Maddeon's progress and glancing wistfully in the direction of the Wheatleys' boardinghouse.

You too, eh Georgie? Phillips thought, shaking his head. *James Wheatley, you may be my partner and friend but it sure don't make you no less a fool. You got a beautiful and devoted young wife who has given you two fine sons and you treat 'er like she was no more account than them damned mules the Injuns run off.*

It was a remarkable thing, Phillips thought, that a man could have all he ever really needed—all that was of any real value—right under his nose and not know it till it was too late. He wondered how long Liz Wheatley would put up with it and quickly decided that she would likely put up with it forever. She seemed to be a devout Christian woman and did not encourage the men who hovered like bees round a honeysuckle. She did not flirt or banter or play the cat but treated them all with quiet good manners. You would think that this would put a damper on the attentions of the rough men who looked her way but in fact it was just the opposite. The less encouragement she gave the more alluring she became and men were drawn to her like horseshoe nails to a magnet.

Thomas Maddeon was one of her many admirers. Quiet and unassuming, he had a befreckled, fresh-faced innocence that made him appear as out of place in this rough country as some of the officers' wives. But his youth and apparent naiveté belied an uncanny mechanical aptitude. Maddeon's skills were such that he was considered indispensable and remained unassigned to any of the companies and excused all duties so that he could concentrate on keeping the regiment's weapons in a decent state of repair. The regiment's aged Springfields and Starrs were in such poor shape generally and repair parts were so rare that the innovative and industrious Maddeon found himself spending hours with the blacksmith casting, forging, and hand-shaping the parts which he needed and the government was loath to send west. So that while a small workspace had been set aside for him in the Quartermaster's office, Maddeon spent most of his time in a corner of the blacksmith's shop. Old Jose particularly enjoyed Maddeon's company and had helped the young private set up his operations. The interior door of the shop looked directly into Jose's forge so that during the cold winter months it was always clean, dry, and warm, and a perfect place for Maddeon and Jose or Maddeon's soldier colleagues to gossip or play cards and drink coffee. While this was an irregular arrangement, Colonel Carrington was impressed both by Maddeon's skill as an armorer and his penchant for keeping his shop orderly, and so actively encouraged the young soldier in his work. Maddeon spent hours hunched over his workbench cutting and bending springs, filing hammers, and reaming cap nipples while humming quietly to himself the cradle songs that as a youth he had heard only in Gaelic and now remembered but dimly.

Maddeon lifted the latch of the Wheatleys' door and slipped in from the cold, stamping his feet to restore the circulation and tugging off his mittens with his teeth. With the dim light of the early evening sifting through the calico-curtained windows he recognized every one of the dozen men who had already found their way in and were sitting in small clusters at three different tables. William Bailey and four of his miners were working diligently at their dinners, an aromatic stew that immediately set Maddeon's mouth to watering as their knives and forks tinked busily against the large tin plates set in front of them.

Bailey, a bear of a man with a curly brown beard, was an old hand on the frontier who had spent many years roaming this territory as a prospector and sometimes scout before settling at Phil Kearny for the winter with his fellow miners. An educated and well-bred man who still dressed neatly and spoke in low, cultured tones, his veneer of gentility had deluded many a rough customer who had assumed that William Bailey was a dude and a tenderfoot. They had assumed wrongly, for Bailey was not a man to be trifled with and suffered no fools. This likely explained why Bailey's group was sitting as far from James Wheatley and his partner as they could manage. Bailey, although he said nothing, did not think highly of either man. No one knew what it was about Wheatley and Fisher that Bailey found objectionable, nor did he ever volunteer to explain it. Instead he maintained a cordial, if distant, relationship with both as needed, but avoided social contact with either. Bailey looked up as Maddeon walked through the door and nodded a silent greeting to the young soldier.

Maddeon smiled a greeting to Bailey and nodded to a small group of haycutters who were drinking coffee and eating pie with Levi Carter. Jose waved a fork at his friend.

"Say, T-T-Thomas, have ye some o' this here p-p-pie an' wash 'er down with a mug o' mud, son. Levi's flush an' he will p-p-pay yer freight. Come on, don't be the shy one, come on over an' rest your chilly b-bones."

"I will indeed. Good evening, Mr. Carter. Pay no mind to Jose, sir, I will pay my own way."

Carter, his mouth full of apple pie, waved lightly at Maddeon as if to brush away his offer and motioned to a place on the bench alongside Jose. He swallowed his pie and waved at

Elisabeth Wheatley, who was pouring fresh coffee for the men sitting with her husband at a third table.

"Mrs. Wheatley, ma'am," Carter said. "Do me the honor of not accepting this young man's money. I will gladly entertain him as my guest." Carter turned to the other men gathered with him. "Now, boys, I don't recall having said as much about Jose but I don't see that it has affected his appetite in the slightest."

"Why, Levi y-y-you old skin . . . f-f-flint," Jose said with feigned shock. "After all I d-d-done fer you! Why for shame, for shame!"

Maddeon turned and left the old friends sparring good naturedly. The young soldier unbuttoned his overcoat as he approached James Wheatley holding the Henry rifle out in front of him. Elisabeth Wheatley nodded and said she would fetch him some pie and coffee directly. Maddeon averted his eyes and mumbled something which even he didn't quite understand while at the same time fumbling to remove his hat. He silently cursed his own treacherous ears which reddened involuntarily.

"By your leave, Captain Brown." Brown acknowledged the young private with an airy wave of the hand.

"Ahh, Maddeon," James Wheatley said casually. "I take it she's working properly again, eh?"

"B-beg pardon, sir?" Maddeon stuttered, his ears reddening even more, "Oh your rifle, yes sir. Right as two rabbits, sir. It was just a small burr in the action, sir. No trouble at all, sir."

Wheatley reached out and took the rifle while at the same time reaching into the pocket of his waistcoat for a coin. Maddeon shook his head.

"Oh, no sir," he said. "I couldn't possibly take money. It wasn't but a moment's work."

Wheatley nodded, dropped the coin back into his pocket then turned back to his conversation with his partner Issac Fisher and Captain Fred Brown. Maddeon stood there shifting uncomfortably from foot to foot and wondering what next to do. Wheatley, Fisher and Brown, however, seemed immediately oblivious of the young private.

"I'll just take this over to your friends' table, Mr. Maddeon."

Maddeon looked up suddenly at Mrs. Wheatley, who had fetched him out a generous slice of pie and a mug of coffee.

"Oh, uh, thank you ma'am. Here, I can get that."

"Nonsense, Mr. Maddeon," Liz said quietly. "You just take off your coat and hang your hat on that peg over there and it'll be waiting for you at Mr. Carter's table. Provided that Mr. Carter can keep an eye on Mr. Jose for you." She gave him the slightest of smiles and Maddeon felt his knees weaken as she turned and moved easily across the room to where Levi Carter and his friends were still eating.

Maddeon looked at Captain Brown and the two partners, then followed Liz Wheatley's advice. There was no sense letting a good piece of pie go to waste. It was also a sight more comfortable than talking to Mrs. Wheatley. Thomas had a fine touch with mechanical things, but women, especially when they were as pretty as Mrs. Wheatley, tended to make him nervous.

ELISABETH WHEATLEY LAY QUIETLY IN HER BED WAITING, wishing that sleep would come, but fearful of what it might bring. Would the dreams come again tonight? The moon had risen and its pale light poured easily into the small room, casting all in soft shadows of gray, blue, and indigo. The straw rustled softly in the ticking under her as she hitched the blankets and buffalo robe up to her chin. She did not look in the bed next to her. She didn't have to. James seldom came to bed anymore. At least not to be with her. She listened to the high, mournful wail of a wolf somewhere beyond the window and felt that she knew better than anybody why the wolf sang its lament in the pale moonlight. This had become her world over the past few months—cold shadows and emptiness. Too often she drifted in and out of fitful sleep, beset by dreams which came at first unbidden and then, as time passed, more frequently as welcome, if illicit friends.

She had felt guilty at first. It was sinful, the way she dreamed. But this feeling too deadened and passed as she told herself that God had paid no mind to her prayers so why should he pay any more heed to her dreams. If He wished her to stop dreaming then He would not give her mind cause to invent such tales which brewed up in the darkness of her loneliness. James, it seemed, had become more and more interested in anything that had naught to do with her. He and his friends sat up for hours talking about claims and stakes, pans and flumes, Indians, soldiers, mules, and gold. Anything, it seemed, which did not include her and their children. He drank. Not boisterously, but steadily. And he talked. But mostly to Zack Fisher, Portugee Phillips, and Fred Brown, not to her. On too many mornings Liz Wheatley slipped downstairs to find James stretched out on the floor in front of the fireplace, a buffalo robe draped over his snoring form. She had remained the same, sweet girl that he had once courted ardently, even recklessly.

She cast about in her mind for reasons why he no longer came to her bed and could find none, and so began to believe the only explanation she could accept: that once she had begat James' sons her only purposes in life were to raise those sons and cook for the men who would bring in more money to forward James' plans for his ventures in the goldfields. She carried out these duties willingly and cheerfully. What she could not bring herself to admit was that she still felt needs which neither children nor work could supplant. And so her nights had become peopled with other forms. Phantom lovers in many guises began to crowd the hours between dark and dawn. On some nights she could fashion these shades to fit her imaginings, weaving elaborate tapestries in which a handsome young officer was her most ardent suitor.

Of late, despite her feeble attempts to drive it from her mind, that phantom had assumed the features of the newly arrived Captain Fetterman. Perhaps it was because she knew so little about him that, in many ways, he remained a myste-

rious stranger. She liked him that way, for the less of reality
that intruded on her fantasies, the more freedom she had to
shape him into her ideal lover. In her fantasy the ever more
distant James Wheatley had vanished without a trace into the
Montana Territory. Left a young widow, she was free to entertain the attentions of her ghostly officer who insisted on
carrying her back to the dimly remembered states. He adopted
the boys as his own and dressed her in satin and crinolines.
He talked with her, asked her about herself, and delighted in
her company. He made them a home in a fine house in Washington with servants and a carriage. Together they attended
plays and cotillions, and even danced at the White House, after
which he embraced her passionately and made love to her
through the night.

But on other nights, when her needs were deeper, when her
fears were greatest, another phantom came for her. This was
a savage, faceless and fierce in his black and vermilion paint
and rustling feathers. She struggled beneath his grip, thrashing,
moaning, and helpless against the smothering weight of the
buffalo robes, her hands and feet tied by imagined strips of
rawhide as he ravished her again and again. Liz sat up suddenly, beads of sweat standing out on her brow. Her heart
thumped wildly in her breast. She felt drained and weak and
her hands trembled uncontrollably. The wolf gave voice again
to his lament and she listened intently. There was no echo.

"When ye kin hear no echo," Jim Bridger had once told her,
"they be real wolves and not Injuns and ye need have no fear.
When wolves are about Injuns are not, for they do not mix."
Thus, while some women dreaded the wolves' howlings, Liz
Wheatley had come to welcome them as kindred spirits. When
they were about, they sang to tell her that she need not face
her demons tonight. She blinked back the tears that welled up
in her eyes and turned on her side to stare out at the moon
and listen to the high, lonesome song of the wolf.

JIM BRIDGER SHIFTED SLOWLY IN THE ROCKING CHAIR, WHICH
by now the Carrington boys always referred to as "Major

Bridger's Chair." The boys had long since been hurried off to bed. Margaret Carrington sat in her chair opposite Bridger, a shawl draped over her shoulders, with Bridger's prized volume of Shakespeare open on her lap. The colonel had excused himself to make his rounds of the sentry posts. The fire had burned low. Bridger leaned forward to set another log carefully on the hearth and blew easily on the coals until the fire flared up and flames licked along the length of the log. Bridger sat back in his chair and rocked in time to the ticking of the clock on the mantle, his eyes closed in thought.

"I'm thinkin' I'd like to hear that part agin, ma'am," he said finally, his brow creased by a frown.

"Certainly, Gabe," Margaret said. "Where should I begin?"

"Where that feller Clarence are drowned in a bar'l of wine."

Bridger settled back into the rocker, his chin cradled in a gnarled hand which stroked thoughtfully at his stubbled growth of beard. Margaret found her place and began to read, her voice rising and falling as she assumed different personalities for each character. The floorboards creaked under the even rocking motion of Bridger's chair as Margaret read easily to her guest, her slender fingers slipping lightly down the page, pausing only to cover her mouth when the coughing spells came on her. She'd had this "chill" as she called it for nearly a month now and Bridger studied her face intently. *She has gaunted up some of late,* he thought. *If this be a chill then it has lingered too long.* Margaret coughed again, then resumed her reading.

"Hold a space, if you will," Bridger said suddenly one finger held aloft. "Could we double back a piece on the trail, if you please." He had a puzzled look on his face as if something had struck him wrong.

"Where should I start? From Clarence's death?"

"No, ma'am. Just a speech'r two back a-ways."

Margaret's finger slipped back up the page and began the scene again. Richard had ordered the murder of his young wards in the Tower.

"Enough!" Bridger said, holding his hands up to wave away the rest of the scene. "I'll have no more of his lies."

Margaret looked up to see the rangy Bridger standing in front of her.

"Lies?" she asked.

"Lies!" Bridger said, his eyes fierce and a bony hand held out for his book.

Margaret was baffled and slightly startled, but she placed the book in his outstretched hand. She had never seen him quite so disturbed since she had known him. It was unlike her Old Gabe to seem this distraught about anything.

"I'm curious, Major Bridger," she ventured softly. "You have always loved Master Shakespeare's tales. What is it about this one which has upset you so?" Her pure earnest face gazed up at him in the lamplight.

The mountain man sat back in the rocking chair, staring down at the book clutched in hands, on which the knuckles had begun to whiten. He looked at the leather-bound volume as if it were the snake he had drawn from under Margaret's camp stool many months before. He looked at Margaret and his face softened. Bridger stood slowly, his spare frame unfolding to its full height.

"I am no scholar, Mrs. Carrington," he said quietly. "But more'n forty-odd yar in the mountains has knowed me up some about man. Now, this child will tell a tale as tall as the next man and there be no harm in that. A man is expected to spin a good yarn funnin' himself or funnin' his pards. But there is something 'bout the way a man talks when his soul and his intentions're black as the pit. Ye kin hear it when a Sioux tells ye he's yer brother and there'll be peace 'tween his people and your'n forever. Ye kin hear it when a fat man in a shiny suit says that this here piece of paper'll keep the white man off'n Injun land long as the grass grows. When a feller tells you somethin' in a sartin way, ye'd best know to watch yerself fer he means ye no good. And this man," he held the book in the air, "this man is bloody-minded as a blamed Sioux. I kin tell from what he says an' how he says 'er that he is up to devilment."

Bridger flipped open the book to where Margaret had

marked her place with a scrap of paper. He stabbed the page with a bony finger.

"But Major Bridger," Margaret said, "I believe Richard was many years dead when this play was written."

"Don't make no never mind to me, Mrs. Carrington. Dead or alive he was ill-used by this Shakespeare and I'll not abide such lies. Injun or white, it's all the same to me."

Bridger's hand closed on a sheaf of pages and ripped them from the leather binding to hurl them into the fireplace. Margaret watched in wide-eyed wonder as the pages browned, blackened, and curled up before bursting into flames and peeling away to spiral up the chimney in spark-limned flakes of charred paper. Bridger continued to feed the flames until the entire book had been consumed. It was but a few moments before the last of the pages had been reduced to blackened ashes. He turned to Margaret, a look of sadness on his firelit features.

"Mrs. Carrington, I'm thinkin' we're livin' with the fruit of liars. Politicians an' Injuns, paper-pushin' bourgeways an' gold-hungry diggers all scurryin' about wagging their forked tongues and scheming how to cut up this here country. It's got so's it's all spiled by lies and liars. Many's the year I spent in these mountains with nary a soul to be seen for seasons on end. Now, ye can't spend a fortnight hereabouts without trippin' over a dead man. Mebbe it's a good thing this child's eyes are gettin' dim for I'm thinkin' I don't want to see no more." He put a finger to his head. "Mebbe it's what I see up hyar that's important. What I remember of what this country was like afore it got so dern crowded and bloody. But I am on the peck fer them what've spiled it and any who remind me of the same."

Bridger thought to go on. He thought to tell her how more than morning or meadows or craggy peaks at sunset he would miss the sight of Margaret's face. But he could not say it. The thought stuck in his throat and would not be dislodged. He considered waiting for the colonel's return but the silence between him and Margaret was deafening. A few moments later he was gone, and Margaret was left alone with her thoughts.

*   *   *

CAPTAIN JAMES POWELL REINED UP SHARPLY AND THREW one gauntleted hand into the air to bring the column to a halt. Some of the younger men had trouble controlling their horses, whose blood had been fired by the chase and were eager to run.

"Hold in those mounts!" Powell snapped. A carbine cracked somewhere along the line of troops.

"Cease firing, damnit!" Powell turned in the saddle and glowered at the detachment, which struggled to form up now, the troopers urging reluctant and skittish horses back into line. The smell of gunsmoke still lingered in the brisk air and mingled with the acrid stench of lathered horseflesh and sweating men. The horses blew heavily, the steam of their breath billowing around the mounted party in great white clouds. The whole affair had been fairly brief and thankfully bloodless. The wood train had again been attacked by a mob of mounted warriors, prompting a rapid response from the fort. Captain Powell, a stolid and cautious veteran, had led the relief party easily driving the attackers off and away from the crossing at the Piney. Leaving the infantry with the loggers, Powell had taken Lieutenant Grummond and his mounted detachment forward, pushing the fleeing warriors back through the trees and out into the open, across the frigid countryside and up the rock-strewn slopes of Lodge Trail Ridge. The brittle crack of gunfire had torn through the crisp air, echoed from the hillsides, and mingled with the shrill yips of the fleeing warriors, who managed to stay just out of rifle range. But when the troopers reached the crest of Lodge Trail Ridge, Powell called off the pursuit.

"Enough!" Powell shouted, and watched as the blanket-shrouded figures and their fleet ponies raced helter-skelter down the reverse slope. The fleeing warriors crossed Peno Creek and scampered up the slope of the next hillside, dodging among the large boulders that were scattered over the crest.

"Damn, Captain," Lieutenant Grummond hissed between

clenched teeth. "We almost had the bastards. We've missed another chance at 'em."

"Maybe, Mr. Grummond, maybe," Powell said calmly. "And then again, maybe not. Who's to say that we haven't simply denied them a chance at us?" He glanced over at the younger officer, his lips twisted into a tight smile. "Well, as long as I command this detail, we'll stick strictly to our orders. We've relieved the wood train and we've remained this side of Lodge Trail Ridge. I'll not exceed my instructions to chase a few ragged ruffians."

Powell clucked to his horse and nudged him about in a tight circle to head back towards Phil Kearny. Grummond remained behind for a moment, staring after the retreating Indians and gritting his teeth. In the thin, cold air sound traveled far and a slight breeze carried the trilling taunts of the warriors shrieking their derision at the soldiers, daring them to come on. There was a small puff of white on the far hillside and a few seconds later the anemic "whump" of an ancient trade musket drifted across the valley. Grummond ached to fire at the tiny figures, despite the fact that they were well out of range, but fought down the impulse and carefully lowered the Colt's hammer with his thumb. He spun the cylinder until the hammer came to rest on a capless nipple and thrust the weapon back into its holster. Grummond spit at the ground, then jerked on the reins, wheeling his horse about to rejoin the rest of the detachment, which was already picking its way gingerly back down the slope. Every foray, it seemed to the lieutenant, was destined to allow the Indians to play them as fools, and Grummond's patience for this game grew thinner with each succeeding day. It galled him the way they allowed these damned aborigines to toy with them like a cat with a mouse. Grummond glanced over his shoulder at the tiny figures now milling about idly on the next ridge and thought bitterly, *Just you wait, you damned savages! We'll give you a fight to remember yet.*

SNOW HAD FALLEN DURING THE NIGHT, A LIGHT, POWDERY dust, and Phil Kearny was blanketed entirely by a layer of pure, crystalline white that dazzled and blinded in the brilliance of the morning light. The white-shrouded flanks of the Bighorns glowed a shimmering roseate hue with the rising sun. As Henry Carrington stepped out onto the porch of the headquarters building he inhaled deeply, drawing the sharp cold into his lungs and letting it boil out in a wispy vapor which stung his nostrils. Everything appeared so clean and unspoiled, as if the world had been renewed and refreshed in the night. Christmas was less than a week away and for some reason he could sense a feeling of calm healing spreading throughout his chest.

Perhaps I worry too much, thought Carrington. *Things must work out well in the end. I must have more faith.* Provisions were adequate for the winter. The officers had already begun the regimen of intense training designed to hone the marksmanship and combat skills of the younger recruits. But two more loads of timber were required from the pinery to supply all of their needs for fuel and construction during the long winter months. There was precious little that could go wrong at this point. Virtually all that remained was for them to settle in for the winter, sharpen their skills, and await their opportunity. When the heavy snows fell, then would be the time to strike. It had been the Russian winter that had brought Napoleon to his knees and Red Cloud's Bad Faces, for all their daring, were amateurs when compared with Bonaparte's Old Guard.

We'll have to go for their home ground, Carrington thought. *We'll cut through the Valley of the Tongue like Sherman cut through the Shenandoah and lay it waste.*

General Sherman had made a Christmas gift to President Lincoln of the city of Savannah. Carrington gazed up at the face of Cloud Peak, sparkling and radiant in the sun's brilliant rays, and thought for a moment that were he not a more civilized man he would like to present President Johnson with the scalp of Red Cloud for his Christmas gift.

There was a bustle of activity from behind the quartermaster's buildings and overcoated soldiers were beginning to form ranks in front of Company E's barracks. They, along with twenty troopers of the 2nd Cavalry, were to accompany the wood train today and would be heading out for the pinery within the hour. The wood party would be unusually large today as the colonel had laid out plans to construct a bridge at the Piney Creek ford. If there was additional need for lumber throughout the winter this would make the crossing considerably easier and more efficient. It would also give him a chance to see if the Sioux were inclined to attack larger parties of troops. Carrington heard a door open and a slight scuffing on the porch of the adjacent quarters and looked up to see Lieutenant Grummond taking his leave of Frances. Grummond stood there and gazed down at his young wife as she fussed at his overcoat buttons and talked earnestly to him. While Carrington could not hear their conversation, from the look on Grummond's face it was fairly evident that Frances was pleading for him to take better care of himself. Carrington suppressed a smile as he watched the lieutenant's head bob up and down in silent agreement. Finally, with a quick kiss to her forehead, Grummond broke away like a young schoolboy anxious to be away from his mother. As Grummond trotted across the parade ground, Frances looked up and noticed the colonel watching her. She was biting her lower lip and Henry Carrington thought that she was close to tears. The poor girl was truly terrified. Henry smiled easily at her.

"Don't worry, Mrs. Grummond," he called out. "I'll keep him well out of any mischief today." Frances nodded, and a nervous smile crept across her trembling lips. The colonel smiled again in what he hoped was a reassuring manner. A moment later Private Sample appeared, leading Grey Eagle, the colonel's favorite horse, saddled and ready for the march out. Henry took the reins, swung into the saddle, doffed his hat to Mrs. Grummond, and turned his mount toward the quartermaster's office. Just beyond the large warehouses the heavy wagons of the wood train were already rumbling toward the gate that opened onto the Bighorn Road.

*   *   *

DESPITE HIS FOREBODINGS IT HAD BEEN A LONG AND THANKfully uneventful day. Henry Carrington leaned back into his chair and breathed out heavily, then stifled a yawn. He closed his eyes for a moment and pinched the bridge of his nose, fighting off the bone-deep weariness that threatened to drop him off to sleep at any moment. The trip to the pinery had come off flawlessly. The day's haul of timber had been collected in fairly short order; then, with both sawmills working feverishly, much of the lumber had been sawed into planking to facilitate construction of the bridge. Carrington was particularly pleased with the new bridge across the Piney Creek. In the brisk wintry air the soldiers had worked with an energy and spirit that surprised him. Peeling off their heavy woolen overcoats, the men had gone at the project with a will and much good-natured joshing and horseplay. Throughout the day there had not been the slightest hint of opposition from the Sioux. Jim Bridger and his now seemingly ever-present sidekick, Yellow Face, had arrived at the pinery in the midmorning. They had ridden out with the colonel, tracing a wide arc around the logging operations, looking for any indication that the Sioux might be lurking nearby. But the carpet of newfallen snow was smooth and unbroken by anything but the odd track of a deer or the feeble scratching of birds. Bridger and his Crow companion had poked cautiously among the pines.

"Yellow Face," Bridger had asked at one point. "Ye smell any Injuns?"

The Crow wrinkled up his nose and sniffed heavily, then shook his head.

"No smell headcutters, Big Throat," Yellow Face had said solemnly. "Smell snow. Big snow come soon. Son of a bitch, goddamn big, you bet."

Bridger had looked up at the sky and at the surrounding trees his head cocked to one side as he breathed in deeply. "Yep, 'spect you're right. Big snow, Yellow Face. Damn big snow."

By six in the evening, with the sun disappearing rapidly behind the mountains, the bridge was completed and the last

wagon was rumbling and jolting back through the gates at Phil
Kearny. All in all it had been a most satisfactory day. Now
that the animals had been cared for, the detachment dismissed,
the troops fed and returned to their barracks, Henry Carrington
was left to review the day's administrative details. Ten Eyck
had laid everything out on the colonel's desk for his review.
Morning report, inventory sheets from the commissariat, correspondence to be read, correspondence to be signed and sent
out—even out here in the wilderness the Army insisted on
reams of paperwork detailing every niggling facet of life.
There was a rapping at the door and Carrington looked up,
wondering what annoying little matter now needed his attention.

"Come," he barked at the closed door.

"Good evening, Colonel."

"Good evening, Colonel."

"Good evening, gentlemen." Henry replied, wondering what
could bring captains Fetterman and Brown to call at this hour.
Doubtless they had not come simply to pass the time or pay
their compliments. It occurred to him that Brown looked a bit
like a pirate with two heavy revolvers strapped on and his
spurs looped casually through one of the buttonholes of his
overcoat. "Please sit down, gentlemen. I am just reviewing the
day's correspondence. There is coffee on the stove although
probably a bit thick by now. What can I do for you?"

Fred Brown glanced over at Fetterman, who raised his eyebrows and nodded shortly.

"Well, Colonel," Brown began. "It's like this. Captain Fetterman and I have been thinking that with winter coming in
the time is right to pay out the redskins for their devilment.
We've already had a word with Mr. Bailey and his people and
he thinks he could raise fifty civilian volunteers easily. You
know Bailey's people, Colonel, veterans all. They're experienced men on the frontier, crack shots, and in most cases better
armed that we are. If we mount fifty veterans from the garrison
here we can join up with Bailey and cut right through to the
Tongue and raise the devil with Red Cloud's hooligans." A
light glowed in Brown's eyes as he warmed to his subject.

Brown was due to report to his new posting at Fort Laramie in a few days and he hoped to get one last shot at the Sioux before he had to pull up stakes. "Why, those red devils will never expect us to come after them and we'll sure bring fire and brimstone down on them. Colonel, I could take a dozen of them myself with these." Brown patted the butts of his pistols.

Carrington just looked at the two younger officers for a few moments. He knew Bailey, a veteran of the Civil War and a former captain; he was a formidable fighter and his miners—"Bailey's Boys"—had lent a welcome and expert hand on more than one occasion when it had come to a scrape with the Sioux. In some ways Brown was right—Bailey could field a formidable fighting force at need, and the winter was as good a time as any, in fact the best time, to strike a blow at the Sioux. But it was not yet right. Carrington leaned forward and shuffled through the papers on his desk, pulling out the most recent morning report. He scanned down the figures quickly, then handed the report to Fred Brown, who glanced up quizzically.

"Captain Brown, Captain Fetterman," Carrington began with a sigh. "I appreciate your efforts, gentlemen. I myself would welcome a chance to strike the Indians in their home, but it is not to be. Not yet, anyway. Look at those figures, Captain Brown. Certainly Mr. Bailey's aid will be most welcome. His men are, as you observe, good fighters. But were we to match his offer with fifty veteran soldiers it would strip away the core of our garrison. Most of the men are still green and untried. We need the veterans to stiffen them and train them. With the veterans all gone off on this raid which you propose we would be hard-pressed, indeed we would be unable to perform the duties required of us by Department Headquarters. As to the horses. Again, look at the numbers. You want fifty horses? As of this morning there are but forty-two animals fit for service in the entire post."

Brown looked down at the report and ran a finger down one of the columns, his lips moving silently as he tallied the numbers that marched down the page in Ten Eyck's fine, rounded hand. Carrington could see Brown's shoulders sag as it became evident that what the colonel told him was true. Brown looked over at Fetterman, a pained look on his face. Fetterman said nothing but the look on his face indicated that he had anticipated Carrington's argument and refusal.

"I'm sorry, Captain Brown, Captain Fetterman," Carrington said finally. "It just won't do. Not now at any rate. Perhaps in a month or two, given some more time to drill the men. Assuming that Department Headquarters provides us with the replacement arms and animals we so badly need. Should these factors shift then perhaps we shall have a better chance of staging the raid which you propose. I, as much as anyone in this regiment, am anxious to come to grips with Red Cloud and his minions but I am determined that we shall do so on our terms and not his. I applaud your show of initiative, gentlemen, but must deny your request."

Fred Brown shrugged, nodded, and handed the report back to Colonel Carrington.

"I imagine I should have thought that would be your answer, sir," Brown said shaking his head. "But I had hoped for one more go at those rascals."

Carrington nodded but said nothing.

"Come along, Fred," Fetterman said abruptly. "The colonel wants to finish this business up and get along to bed. We should not keep him from his duties." Fetterman turned to Carrington. "By your leave, sir."

Carrington nodded and wished the men good night as they left and headed out into the bitterly cold night air. Henry could feel the blast of winter swirl in and around his boots as the men pushed their way out onto the porch. The door closed and the colonel listened as heavy boots clumped down the steps and faded into the night. Carrington yawned and rubbed the back of his neck. Margaret would be waiting up for him. He wanted to tell her about the gifts he had arranged for the boys' Christmas. At his request Private Maddeon had cobbled together a beautiful little squirrel rifle for James and George Breakenridge had fashioned a perfect copy of it entirely out of wood for the younger Harry. The boys would be delighted and he hoped that Margaret would share their enthusiasm but thought it best that he apprise her of his intentions before the fact. He'd intended to do so long ago but the subject kept slipping his mind. He and Margaret had ordered some books for the boys months earlier, but as they had not yet arrived and with Christmas just days away Henry felt that they had best have a little something else put aside just in case.

Well, he thought, *Margaret will surely understand and, knowing the boys, they'd much prefer the little guns anyway.*

Henry sighed and bent his head over the desk, dutifully reaching for his stack of reports. Soon he would return to the warm hearth of his quarters, where he could talk with Margaret and find solace in her quiet voice and strong heart. He glanced once toward the window and wondered if Yellow Face and Bridger really could smell a snowstorm coming on.

LIEUTENANT ALEXANDER WANDS LOOKED UP AT THE BIG-horns and watched the heavy clouds that were building behind the white-shrouded peaks. It was as if they had been snagged by the rock and held in place like a woman's dress caught up on a thornbush. The valley itself lay bright and clear in the morning light, most of the previous day's snow having been blown off by the winds, the remainder melted by the sun's brilliant rays. Wands fumbled with the buttons of his overcoat, reaching inside to fish his watch out of a vest pocket. Nearly ten o'clock. He snapped the lid shut and tucked the watch away, shivering as the air slipped in through his open coat. As far as he could tell, whatever weather was moving in on them would likely hold off for the rest of the day.

"Well, Lieutenant?" J. B. Gregory was anxious to get his loggers out to the pinery and get one last load of timber in before the winter closed in.

"Well, sir," Wands said, shrugging his shoulders. "I would guess that the weather'll hold off a few hours yet. The colonel didn't want your party stranded out there if a big storm swept in."

"Yes, yes, I understand that, Lieutenant, but the longer we

dally the more likely that we'll get caught by it."

"Yes sir, I expect you're right. I'll just check with the colonel."

Wands turned and strode across the parade ground as Gregory stood stamping his feet and gritting his teeth with impatience. Gregory watched as the lieutenant scampered up the steps and disappeared into the building. A few moments later Wands reappeared and waved, nodding his head vigorously.

Good. It was about time. Gregory turned to untether his horse, gathered the reins in a thickly gloved fist, and hauled himself laboriously into the saddle, the bulky weight of his buffalo coat making the operation a bit more difficult than he had remembered. The horse sensed his awkwardness and skittered and shied as Gregory flung his right leg over the cantle and struggled to get his foot into the stirrup.

"Damnit, Buck! Steady up there! Stop fightin' me, boy, I've no patience for your shenanigans today. It's too damned cold."

Gregory nudged Buck around and headed for the quartermaster's yard, where the wood train had been waiting for the word to get started. As he started past the quartermaster's office, Corporal Legrow dashed up on foot and hailed him.

"Mr. Gregory!" Legrow called out. "Mr. Gregory, the colonel has assigned an additional squad as escort. Guess he wants to be ready in case the redskins try anything funny."

Gregory nodded quickly.

"All right, Legrow. The more the merrier. Have your boys hop up into the wagon beds and ride on out with us. Hell, it's cold enough as it is, no sense in working at bein' miserable."

Legrow grinned, tossed a careless salute in Gregory's direction, then hurried off to the wood train, a cloud of breath steaming in his wake. Watching from across the parade ground, Lieutenant Wands shivered and thanked his lucky stars that he had other work today. The paperwork that had piled up over the past couple of days was a terrible nuisance, but it would at least keep him indoors and near a warm stove. Wands watched as the last of the convoy rattled and jounced out of the gate, then turned and went into the headquarters building to warm up.

*   *   *

JUMPING BADGER QUIRTED HIS PONY, URGING HIM TO greater speed along the rock-strewn trail that was now ice-slick and treacherous. He was having a difficult time controlling his excitement and had to keep reminding himself to follow Lone Bear's strict instructions not to call out. Moments later he was in the midst of the friends who were waiting for him on the snow-covered slopes. More than a hundred warriors had gathered out here in the pines and were scattered about in groups of four and five, hunkered together under their robes and blankets, stomping their feet and fidgeting in the bitter cold.

"Hey, Jumping Badger!" called out his friend Weasel Bear. "Are they coming?"

Jumping Badger nodded vigorously and angled his pony over to join his friend. He slipped off onto the hard ground, shivering violently. Despite the heavy layer of bear grease he had slathered on his body earlier, the cold bit easily through both it and the woolen blanket that his mother had fashioned into a capote for him. Weasel Bear held open his heavy buffalo robe and motioned for Jumping Badger to join him. The two young warriors huddled together under the robe, the fur turned in to hold in their bodies' warmth.

A tall, powerfully muscled warrior, his face and upper body painted a bright crimson and charcoal black, stalked over to the group. Except for the paint and the notched feathers in his scalplock the warrior was naked from the waist up and seemed oblivious of the cold. Jumping Badger grimaced. He should have sought out Pawnee Killer immediately and immediately felt foolish. His ears flushed a deep red.

"Well, how many are they and where are they now?"

Jumping Badger tried to control the shuddering of his body as he eagerly soaked in his friend's shared warmth. The other warriors crowded around, anxious to hear his report.

"More than half a hundred, cousin. There are more soldiers with the woodcutters than usual. They are riding in the wagons. They will be at the bridge before the sun is straight up."

"*Washte!*" grunted Pawnee Killer, who immediately turned away from the little circle of men and strode off to inform the other groups of warriors.

Jumping Badger let out a sigh of relief. He felt sure that Pawnee Killer would have berated him for not going straight to him. He looked sheepishly at Weasel Bear, who just shrugged his shoulders and winked. Pawnee Killer had drawn the honor of leading this war party and everyone was especially careful to follow his orders even when he had forbidden that any fires be lit for warmth. He was a seasoned warrior and a man with an explosive temper, and none of the younger men would dare cross him. Especially now. Jumping Badger watched as the small groups began to break apart, shrugging off their robes and extra blankets, stringing their bows and fingering their arrows, checking the fletching and the binding of the points. A few men began to swing their clubs or hatchets in wide arches, limbering their cold muscles and getting the blood flowing again through their numbed bodies. It would be soon now.

"COLONEL, PILOT HILL SIGNALS THAT THE WOOD TRAIN IS under attack, sir."

"Very good, Mr. Wands. Have the bugler sound To Arms then present my compliments to Captain Powell. Have him report to me here. He will be taking out the relief party. Mr. Grummond will accompany him with the cavalry."

Alexander Wands saluted briskly and hurried out of the building to spread the word. When the young lieutenant had left the room, Henry Carrington moved quickly to the window and watched as the parade ground came alive with troops scurrying to respond to the sound of the bugle. It was no more than three minutes before Carrington caught sight of the stocky form of James Powell marching across the parade, a brace of pistols already buckled on. Powell was a solid, dependable man. No firebrand or glory hound, he could be relied on to do precisely as instructed. If Bridger was right about the weather closing in on them any time now, this should be the last occasion on which they would have to dispatch troops in reaction to an attack. This should be the last wood train of the season and the winter would soon confine the Sioux to their villages and campfires. All he needed to do now was to buy time. A few weeks should be enough. Enough time for him to get the recruits hammered into first-rate soldiers. Enough time to get in replacement horses for the mounted infantry and to fatten up those of the cavalry company. Enough time to get a shipment of replacement rifles in from Fort Laramie. Just a few more weeks and then let Red Cloud look to his laurels, for this dog would have his day. He watched absently as Powell stomped up the headquarters steps and came in through the door.

"Cry havoc, and let slip the dogs of war."

"Beg pardon, Colonel?"

"Eh? Oh, Captain Powell. Nothing, sir. Just mumbling to myself." Colonel Carrington ventured a thin smile and cleared his throat, then came straight to business.

"Well, James, I imagine you understand what needs to be done today, eh? Take Grummond and the cavalry along. I've transferred the band's Spencers to them so they should provide you a nice edge if they keep their wits about them. But keep 'em close and don't let them get out ahead of you. No heroics today, you understand. Relieve the wood train. If in your judgment you deem it necessary to remain while they complete the day's work, then do so and then bring them back in."

Captain Powell saluted and slipped out as quietly as he had come. Carrington stepped to a coatrack in the corner of the room and tugged on his overcoat and gloves, then jammed his hat firmly down onto his head. He turned up the collar of his coat and went out to make a final check of the relief force. Henry Carrington had no sooner stepped onto the porch of the headquarters building than William Judd Fetterman bounded up the steps, his kepi set low over his eyes and his jawline firm and unyielding. Fetterman drew himself to attention and saluted. Carrington returned his salute.

"Captain Fetterman."

"Colonel Carrington, sir." Fetterman jerked his head in the

direction of the parade ground. "I request permission to take out the relief force, sir."

"Captain Powell has already been assigned that duty, Captain Fetterman. I see no reason to alter that assignment."

"Respectfully sir, but I do," Fetterman persisted. "I have seniority to Captain Powell. By regulation the duty devolves to the senior company commander present." Fetterman looked at Captain Powell, who rolled his eyes and waved his hand dismissively.

"Colonel," Powell said laconically, "if Fetterman wants to freeze his ass off chasing phantoms, far be it from me to stand in his way. I'll be more than happy to settle in front of a warm stove and drink coffee."

Carrington disliked Fetterman's inclination to pull rank but Powell had led the last detachment out and in all fairness the man deserved a day off. It was bitterly cold and the assignment, however routine, would be harsh in this weather. In one regard he was almost glad that Fetterman was insisting on taking the relief party out. The very idea of letting him dash around for a few hours on what was likely a wild-goose chase was somewhat appealing. At the very worst the blowhard would catch a chill and mope around wiping his runny nose for weeks afterward.

"Very well, Captain Fetterman," Carrington said. "The command is yours. Captain Powell, you are relieved, sir. I thank you for your patience." Powell saluted and headed away to his quarters, a slight smile on his face.

Carrington turned back to Fetterman. "I will repeat the instructions I gave Captain Powell. You are to relieve the wood train and remain with it to provide additional security if it is deemed necessary. Do not pursue the Indians at its expense and under no circumstances are you to pursue the hostiles beyond Lodge Trail Ridge. Is that understood?"

Fetterman nodded curtly, saluted, and turned to join Company A, which he had already formed up in front of their barracks. Carrington watched him go, then turned to Lieutenant Wands, who had remained quietly in the background during the entire exchange.

"Mr. Wands, come with me. I want to inspect the relief party to insure that their weapons are in working order."

Wands shot the colonel a quizzical glance but followed along as Carrington headed across the parade. Fetterman came out as they approached and walked down the line of troops with Carrington checking the condition of the troops and their weapons. Fetterman himself dismissed three men who had but a few rounds of ammunition left in their cartridge boxes and two others on whose weapons the locks were so loose that they threatened to fall off if the hammers dropped on a cap. Carrington and Wands watched Fetterman's jaw muscles tighten as he sent the men packing but all three knew well that there was nothing to be done about shortages of ammunition or spare parts unless Department Headquarters chose to do so.

Five men whose coughing and hacking gave them away were sent off to report to the surgeon. Carrington conversed briefly with Fetterman and then sent Wands off to corral a small detachment of men from Company C to make up Company A's shortages. As these replacements were falling in with the rest of the party Captain Fred Brown strode up, pistols strapped on over his overcoat and his hat pulled down over his eyes. Brown saluted crisply.

"Good morning, Colonel."

"Captain Brown," Carrington sighed. "I take it you would like to accompany the relief party as well."

"Very much indeed, sir. I believe it'll be my last chance at those red devils before I'm off to Laramie. I'd hate to miss the fun."

"I doubt that it will be any fun, Captain, but go along if you wish. Have you a mount?"

"Yes sir," Brown grinned. "Your boy Jimmy lent me the use of his pony Calico provided I bring him back a bow and arrows."

Carrington shook his head and waved Brown away, then turned and headed back to the headquarters building. Brown sidled up to Fetterman, and the two stood there grinning conspiratorially at each other as if they were in on some great private joke. As the colonel reached the headquarters, two more men joined Fetterman's command. James Wheatley and Issac Fisher came up carrying their new Henry rifles.

"Say there, Captain Brown!" Wheatley boomed. "Thought we'd try these new toys out on the Injuns. Any objections to us tagging along?"

Brown looked over at Fetterman, who shook his head and smiled.

"The more the merrier, gentlemen," Fetterman quipped. "Let's get on with it."

Colonel Carrington and Lieutenant Wands watched from the porch of the headquarters building as the relief party came to attention, faced to the left, and trooped off toward the main gate. Captains Fetterman and Brown, along with Wheatley and Fisher on horseback, led, while the rest of the column was trudging steadily ahead in their rough leather brogans. The tap-tap-clicking of their hobnails and heelplates echoed from contact with the frozen ground. As Fetterman's command was passing out of the gate, Lieutenant Grummond reported to Colonel Carrington with his mounted unit. Again Carrington inspected the troops, dismissing several of the mounted infantrymen whose weapons were in poor repair. All of the cavalrymen—save one who was coughing up blood—passed muster easily. They were delighted to be carrying the band's Spencers and eager to try them out on the Sioux.

As the officers were finishing up the inspection, Private Thomas Maddeon trotted up, trailing his Springfield. Maddeon came to attention in front of the colonel and saluted.

"Begging the colonel's pardon, sir," Maddeon said. "But I'd like permission to go along, sir. The boys could always use an extra rifle and I've not had a chance at an Indian since we've been here."

Henry Carrington did not want Maddeon wandering off with Grummond. He liked the young fellow and depended on him to keep what weapons the regiment did have in some working order. It was a full-time job. But Maddeon's eyes pleaded with the colonel and Henry saw no reason to deny him at least one chance to do the job he'd signed up for. Carrington took Maddeon's rifle and looked it over carefully. The rifle was, of course, in perfect working order, spotless and lightly oiled. Carrington reached around and tugged Maddeon's cartridge box open.

"Forty rounds, sir!" Maddeon chirped happily.

"Very well, Maddeon," Carrington said with a wry smile. "If Lieutenant Grummond has no objections?"

"None, sir," Grummond said quickly.

Carrington nodded. The trooper dismissed for his coughing handed Maddeon the reins of his horse. The young soldier balanced his rifle over the crupper and swung up into the saddle. Gathering up the reins, he clucked to the animal and nudged it easily into line with the other soldiers. Carrington turned to Lieutenant Grummond.

"Mr. Grummond." Carrington said sternly. "The mission is to relieve the wood train. You are not to engage or pursue the hostiles for any other purpose. You will report to Captain Fetterman, obey his orders implicitly, and never leave him. Is that understood?"

"Perfectly, sir." Grummond saluted and turned to mount his horse.

Alexander Wands glanced back over his shoulder and caught a glimpse of Grummond's wife, Frances, standing on the porch of their quarters. As Grummond swung into the saddle Wands quickly moved up to him, reached up, and took him by the sleeve.

"Now for God's sake, George, don't do anything rash," Wands whispered urgently. "Think of your family. Think of Fanny."

Grummond smiled easily down at his friend.

"Don't worry, Alex," he said. "I'll watch myself. You just save me a cup of coffee." He looked up and blew a kiss to Frances, then turned and led his troopers off toward the gate. Henry Carrington watched for a few moments, then sprinted after them and leapt up onto the sentry walk that flanked the open gates.

"Lieutenant Grummond!" Carrington roared out. "Remember! Stay with Captain Fetterman! Don't let the commands get

separated! And under no circumstances must you go beyond
Lodge Trail Ridge! Is that clear?"

"Clear, sir." Grummond raised his hand in salute and then
ordered the column into a trot, quickly closing the gap between
himself and Fetterman's men. Alexander Wands climbed up
onto the sentry walk and stood there in silence, watching as
the cavalry trotted down the slope and caught up with Fetterman's infantry as they waded across the Big Piney.

"I would have thought they'd take the wagon road out, sir,"
Wands ventured.

Carrington looked at the young officer then back to the relief party where the infantry had stopped to remove brogans
and socks before splashing through the icy water then hastily
replaced their footwear on the other side.

"Well, Mr. Wands, normally I would agree but then you
see he's deploying them as skirmishers as they head up the
Montana Road. I rather suspect that Captain Fetterman is hoping to take the hostiles by surprise. They'll expect the relief
party to come up the wagon road. Who knows? Maybe he can
do it."

"I don't think so, sir," Wands said slowly.

Carrington frowned, then noticed that Wands' attention was
focused on the hills behind Phil Kearny. He followed the
lieutenant's gaze and squinted up to see what had caught his
attention. Carrington tugged out his collapsible telescope,
snapped the brass cylinder open, and peered up at the snow-
covered slopes. There! More than halfway up the hillside and
well out of rifle range sat a pair of small figures wrapped
tightly in red blankets. Sioux. Had to be.

"Damn!" Carrington rasped. "Now what are they up to?"

Lieutenant Wands said nothing but simply stared at the tiny
dots that sat above them. Watching.

IT WAS THE FLASH OF A MIRROR ON THE FAR SLOPES OF THE
Bighorns that told Pawnee Killer that his warriors had accomplished what they had set out to do. The tree cutters were still
huddled behind their wagons, which were almost hidden by

the gunsmoke. Whether they killed any of them was not important today. Pawnee Killer had moved off to a point where he could observe the fight and still see the Bighorns clearly and now he studied the mirror flashes. He watched closely, picking out the pattern. The soldiers had left the fort. They were coming. Wait. More flashes now. The soldiers had crossed the Buffalo Creek. They were coming the other way. Perfect! It could not be better. *Washte!* It was done. Now to get the young ones rounded up and away.

Quirting his pony into a run, Pawnee Killer dashed around behind the others and blew shrill blasts on his eagle-bone whistle, swinging his coup stick in a wide circle over his head. Jumping Badger leaned against a large tree as he nocked another arrow. He looked up at the older warrior with a puzzled look on his face. Pawnee Killer jerked his head to the rear.

"Get along, boy," he barked out. "Gather your brothers up and get back. Go to where the Shyela wait for us."

"But the *wasichu*," Jumping Badger protested. "They are still . . ."

"Hon! Don't argue with me, boy!" Pawnee Killer's face was hard and brutal with eyes that warned against argument. "There's important work to be done today, but not here. Not now. You do what I say and quickly. Go!"

Jumping Badger nodded dumbly and dashed off at a crouch through the snow, tapping his friends on the shoulder as he went and dragging them along in a rush back to where some of the younger boys had their ponies waiting. The other warriors too began to draw off, slipping back through the pines in twos and threes to clamber up onto their ponies and turn their heads away from where the tree cutters were shooting. Pawnee Killer was among the last to leave. He turned his pony in a tight circle and howled his derision at the whites before vanishing into the snow-shrouded wilderness. A scattering of shots sputtered from the corralled loggers before they realized that the woods around them were empty.

*   *   *

LESS THAN TWO ARROW FLIGHTS FROM WHERE THE CHEY-enne had gathered, Crazy Horse galloped over the slopes of Lodge Trail Ridge. The blood pounded in his ears and the air seared his nostrils. His blood was so hot that he did not feel the cold but was sweating as heavily as he would on a summer afternoon. He could feel the moisture dripping from the pits under his arms and soaking into the buckskin war shirt, where it froze almost instantly. He could feel it coming on, the red haze of battle swimming before his eyes. He could feel his heart pounding wildly as if it strained to leap up from his chest and the rusty taste of blood flowed around his tongue. His spirit was soaring above him, fluttering like a war bonnet in the chilling wind. This was it. The exhilarating, overpowering joy of battle, which he craved more than the old men craved the whites' crazy water. He clenched his teeth and tried to control the surging of emotion within his breast. It was nearly unbearable.

"Itok' eyas! Itok' eyas!" Again and again he snarled to him-self through tightly clenched teeth. *"Patience! Wait a little! Closer! We've got to get them closer!"*

He screeched and swung the bright red blanket in a whirling blur overhead. Glancing over his shoulder, he could see the thin line of soldiers stretched up and down the slopes moving steadily after him and his companions. Scattered among the frost-rimed boulders, the other warriors in his party weaved and danced their ponies back and forth, yipping and barking at the soldiers like so many dogs. As Crazy Horse watched, he heard one of the soldiers yell something. The blue line stopped for a moment and he could see the rifles come up as they were aimed at the warriors. Instantly the young braves quirted their ponies away just as a cloud of flame and smoke burst from the line of rifles. The crackling *pop-pop-pop* of the shots followed an instant later.

Crazy Horse heard the zip of a bullet as it sped harmlessly over his head. The cloud of smoke hid the bluecoats for but an instant before a stiff breeze blew it back through the ranks of the soldiers. He could hear the rattle of ramrods as they worked to ram home powder and ball. Now he and the other

warriors again turned their ponies toward the whites and
dashed forward screaming and yelping. One brave loosed an
arrow at the soldiers, another fired a pistol, while others simply
shrieked, waving blankets, brandishing hatchets, or whirling
clubs in the air. Before the whites could finish reloading the
warriors had wheeled about and dashed off again.

Again and again the warriors repeated this pattern, dodging
and weaving among the patches of ice and snow that lay between the bristling spears of brown, brittle grass. There were
no more than a dozen. But still the soldiers followed along.
Crazy Horse could see their reddened noses and ears in stark
contrast to the pale white of their faces and all wreathed by
the steamy vapor of their labored breathing as they slipped
and stumbled forward on the ice-slick hillside. And still they
followed closer, ever closer.

WILLIAM JUDD FETTERMAN WAS GROWING EVER MORE FRUS-
trated and angry with each step. Almost before they had completed their crossing of the Big Piney the damned rascals had
materialized out of the grass on their little ponies, darting this
way and that, screaming and taunting them at every step and
always remaining just out of reach. Time and again he had
halted the line to deliver a volley, and no sooner had the weapons dropped to present than the cowards sheered off and
dashed out of range. *Damn them!* Captain Fetterman heaved
himself back up into the saddle and waved the line forward
yet again. Sergeants and corporals barked their orders and the
ragged line of troops staggered forward, picking their way gingerly along the treacherous ground. Fetterman heard a grunt
and the clatter of a weapon hitting the frozen earth.

"Son of a bitch!"

"Damnit, Acherman, ye lunk-headed Dootchman! Git yorr
sorry ass up agin!"

Fetterman glanced over to see Private Acherman picking
himself slowly up off the ground and cursing as he examined
the hole ripped in the knee of his blue woolen trousers. A
smear of red discolored the dingy cloth of his long underwear.

Sergeant Murphy strode over to the young German, a black look on his face.

"Niver have I seen a sorrier, clumsier excuse fer a sojer as yerself, Acherman!" Murphy roared, and, grasping the collar of the private's overcoat, tugged the man to his feet with a jerk. "Don't be standin' thir gawkin' at yer precious trousers fer Chrissakes!" Murphy growled, his face within inches of Acherman's nose. "Git along wid ye! And wipe yer damned nose!"

Acherman sniffed and ran the sleeve of his overcoat along a nose already rubbed raw by repeated contact with the rough wool. He tucked his rifle up under his arm and loped unsteadily ahead to catch up with his comrades.

Captain Fetterman kicked the flanks of his mount and forced him forward. The beast was skittish and hard to control. Fetterman hauled on the reins and turned the animal's head upslope. The horse picked its way upward and to the right, passing in front of the line of troops as he moved ever closer to the top of the ridge. A hundred yards to the front the Indians scrambled ahead of them, were silhouetted against the skyline for a second, and then disappeared as they dropped down the other side. Fetterman kicked the horse again, forcing it upward. The captain reached up and pressed gloved fingers hard against his forehead, which was throbbing with a fierce headache now. He rubbed his forehead and his temple. He could feel the pounding thud of the blood in his veins like a steady, maddening drumbeat. The muscles of his neck were stiff and sore from the tension in his jaw.

"Damnit!" he snarled at the mount. "Move, you stubborn son of a bitch! Come on! Move!"

As they crested the ridge he reined up and squinted off into the distance. The barren landscape was empty. They were gone. *Damn!* Fetterman turned in the saddle and looked over his left shoulder. Further down the slope the infantry were laboring up the hillside, the entire line echeloned as it wheeled around to angle up the slope. He could hear the men coughing, sneezing, and snorting as they staggered up the ridge, their leg muscles straining and stiff in the bitterly cold air. At the farthest end of the line, Grummond's cavalry forced the wheeling motion around as the line swung like a door up and to the right. He recognized Wheatley and Fisher as they trotted along just beyond the cavalry, the bright metal of Wheatley's Henry rifle flashing in the pale winter light. Fetterman's horse began to shy and back. His hooves pawed the frigid earth, his ears straight up and twitching. The animal tossed its head, snorted and whinnied, fighting the reins.

"Easy, damnit! Whoa up, you stupid beast!"

Fred Brown came trotting up on Jimmy Carrington's little pony.

"What's wrong with that animal, William?" Brown asked.

"Just lazy. The son of a bitch wants to head back to the stables and eat."

Brown chuckled. "Well, I'm a little peckish myself. Can't say that I blame him."

Fetterman nodded toward the empty swale below them. "We catch one of those damned Sioux and you can have his liver for lunch."

"I don't want his liver," Brown snorted. "I'll settle for a scalp."

Fetterman looked over at his friend and grinned.

"Better take two, Baldy," he said wryly. "Then we'll see if the sawbones can stitch one on your pate."

"Very amusing, William. But I'll be damned if I can see a single scalplock fluttering in the breeze out there."

"What's the time?"

Fred Brown shoved a hand into his coat and pulled out his watch, flipping open the lid with the same motion.

"Just twelve o'clock. No wonder I'm hungry."

The two officers sat their horses and scanned the frozen landscape. Below them they could see the Montana Road, the trail John Bozeman had opened to Virginia City and the gold-fields not knowing he was also opening a Pandora's box. The dusty track ran across their front at the base of the hill, then climbed easily onto a long, narrow ridge covered with large boulders and flanked by outcroppings of jagged rock, a jumble of irregular gray forms. Among the boulders, long yellow needles of dry grass bristled and swayed in the freshening breeze. The clattering of hoofs brought both men to turn in their saddles to see First Sergeant Augustus Lang urging his mount up the hillside.

"Captain Fetterman!" Lang called out.

"Yes, First Sergeant."

"Sir," Lang said, calmly jerking a thumb over his shoulder. "The pickets are signaling to report that the Injuns have broken off the attack on the wood train."

Brown and Fetterman looked behind them to the gray bulk of Pilot Hill in the middle distance. Fred Brown reached down and drew a set of field glasses from a leather case slung over his saddlebow. He peered intently through the glasses.

"Lang's right," Brown breathed out from under the glasses. "They're wigwagging the message again. Care to have a look?" He held out the binoculars to Fetterman, who waved them away.

"I believe you." Fetterman turned back to look at his command, which had now come to a halt ranged along the crest of the ridge. Grummond's mounted unit was on the far left flank. He could see Lieutenant Grummond on his white horse looking eagerly up the hill in his direction. Waiting for instructions. With the attack on the wood train ended, the mission was in effect accomplished. The rascals had gotten away with it again. What to do now? Turn about and head back? A blur of distant movement caught his eye. There it was in the distance out beyond Grummond's people.

"Give me those glasses, Fred."

Brown handed the binoculars to Fetterman, who scanned the flats beyond Grummond's position.

"There!" he shouted. "There go the bastards now."

PAWNEE KILLER LASHED THE FLANK OF HIS PONY WITH HIS quirt. The animal snorted and surged ahead quickly, overtaking the other members of the war party. Pawnee Killer leaned forward over his pony's neck and led them at a run across the flats and behind the low ridges which shielded them

from the view of the *wasichu* pickets. The warriors splashed
across Peno Creek and veered to the north. As they crossed
the open flats, Pawnee Killer glanced off to the right, where
he could see a line of bluecoats stretched out along the length
of Lodge Trail Ridge. Pawnee Killer ignored them. The bluecoats would surely see them now, unless they were blind as
well as stupid. *Good*, he thought savagely. *Let them see us.*
The warrior leaned farther out over his pony's neck and urged
him on. Another arrow flight forward and they were again out
of sight. The entire party circled around to meet the Cheyenne,
who had gathered in a large group behind a low hill mass.

The Cheyenne were milling about in a great crowd, steam
rising from the mixed breath of men and animals. They huddled under their robes and blankets, each man standing beside
his pony and using the animal to shield him from the wind
that was sweeping down from the north. Pawnee Killer noticed
that their bows were strung and many clutched them in their
left hands along with a half-dozen shafts. He recognized Little
Wolf and Black Shield haranguing the other warriors. Doubtless giving them their final instructions. The Cheyenne were
ready. In the distance he could hear the yelping and barking
of the people who had gone out with Crazy Horse, the young
fool. They were making enough noise but would they be able
to bring the bluecoats close enough? Pawnee Killer brought
his pony up sharply and slid to the ground. Now he would do
all that he could do for the time. Wait.

"FIRST SERGEANT," FETTERMAN BARKED. "GO ON DOWN TO
Lieutenant Grummond. Tell him to move forward at a walk.
He's to keep moving forward. Swing out onto the Montana
Road and move to the north. Keep pushing the hostiles but
stay closed up with the infantry."

"Yes sir." Lang saluted and wheeled his horse around.

"And Augustus," Fetterman called out, "keep an eye on Mr.
Grummond. Don't let him get carried away."

Lang nodded and trotted down the ridgeline toward the
waiting lieutenant.

Fetterman felt his mood souring as they pushed forward. He wouldn't be able to keep the command out too much longer. With the wood train out of danger Carrington would expect him to return fairly shortly afterward and so went any chance at the hostiles today.

Well, he thought idly, *a few more minutes, another couple hundred yards won't make much difference.*

"Look there, William!" Fred Brown pointed to a tangle of brush among the boulders on the next ridgeline. There was a flurry of movement behind the brush. Suddenly half a dozen mounted warriors dashed out from behind the ridge and charged toward the soldiers. Their ponies splashed across a small creek and scampered up the near slope, their riders shrieking and brandishing weapons. The soldiers instinctively halted and checked their own weapons, ready for the expected order.

"Present!" Fetterman screamed out. There was a ragged rattle as rifles came up along the line, the clicking of locks crisp and clean in the thin air.

"Fire!"

A volley roared out across the valley, smoke rolling down the hillside. A pony screeched in agony and three of the yelping warriors tumbled to the ground. Immediately a dozen more warriors dashed out of concealment and rushed forward to scoop up their fallen comrades. Fetterman was amazed by the alacrity and ease with which the braves retrieved their friends. Two horsemen flanked the fallen man at a gallop, leaning over without apparent effort. Sergeants and corporals barked their orders. Ramrods rattled and scraped against metal as weapons were hastily reloaded. Fetterman watched in silence as the men reached into their cap boxes, fumbling for new caps. The tiny copper cylinders were becoming increasingly difficult for frozen fingers to grasp.

"As skirmishers," Fetterman yelled. "Forward!" He looked down the line for First Sergeant Alexander Smith and saw him about halfway down the ridgeline. If the attack on the wood train had sheared off then the Sioux were likely on the run to the north. If he could push the command ahead at a rapid pace he could close up on the fleeing savages just long enough to pour a couple of volleys into them. Then it would just be a matter of turning about and taking the road straight back to the post.

"First Sergeant Smith," Fetterman called out. "Move them down onto the road and form up in column facing to the north. We'll pursue just to the top that ridge and try to get a couple of volleys into their backsides. Make sure everyone stays closed up. We'll give 'em one last shot and then head back to station."

The line of troops surged ahead over and down the reverse slope, rifles thrust forward in white-knuckled fingers. Hobnails and heelplates clattered over rocks, and rough woolen trousers brushed through the brittle grass that stood in scattered clumps among the rocky soil. Sergeant Hugh Murphy dropped back a step and loped down along the line, checking on the men as they picked their way down the slope, their shoulders hunched against the chill wind, which had sprung up again and swept unchecked over the barren slope.

"Half-cock there, Kelley! If ye trip ye'll blow Burke to hell."

"Christ, Kelley," Burke cracked. "If it's warmer than this, you can fire away and fall back!" Kelley scowled at Burke and snorted back the snot that was clogging his head.

Privates Shannon and Buchanan laughed and hooted.

"Hey, don't be forgettin' yorr friends now, Kelley," Shannon quipped. "It's sure an' I'm colder'n a well digger's ass b'Jaysus."

"Shut up you lot," Sergeant Murphy growled. "Keep yer empty minds on the business to hand. The quicker we get this done, the quicker we'll get back in."

"Amen to that," Shannon muttered.

Captain Fetterman guided his horse down the rock-strewn hillside and out onto the Montana Road. He looked down the road to where it rose gradually up the rocky ridgeline and disappeared to the north. He waited as the infantry clambered down the slope and surged up onto the frozen wagon road, where First Sergeant Smith sorted them out by squad and company. A hundred yards to the front, George Grummond had put his cavalry out onto the road as well. The Indians had again disappeared and except for the rattle of equipment and the soft whining of the wind all had grown quiet. Fred Brown rode up alongside and sat shivering in the saddle.

"Damnit, William," Brown said, coughing into his gloved fist. "The bastards have slipped away again."

As the two officers watched, a solitary warrior appeared opposite them on the next hill—just where the Montana Road crested it. The Indian was naked from the waist up, his chest dotted with white spots as if large flakes of snow had frozen on him. A single, jagged blue streak of paint ran down the side of his face. The man slipped casually from his pony, a red blanket clutched in his fist, and slowly sat down in the middle of the road. With great deliberation he shook out the blanket and draped it around his shoulders. Well below the hillcrest the two miners, Fisher and Wheatley, pushed their mounts ahead bringing up their rifles as they moved. Pop-pop-pop. The rapid-firing rifles cracked again and again. Little spurts of dust began to kick up out of the ground near where the lone Indian sat, impassive and contemptuous of the whites' shooting.

"Cheeky son of a bitch!" Fetterman spat. "What the hell does that poxy bastard think he's doing?"

"Taunting us," Brown said.

"Not for long, I'll wager."

CRAZY HORSE COULD NOT KEEP FROM GRINNING AS HE SAT under his blanket in the middle of the road. After the first shots it was evident that the whites with the quick-shooting rifles could not control their horses very well. The animals danced about with every movement of their riders and unless the whites were very lucky there was little danger in sitting right where he was. He could see their red faces above bushy whiskers and saw that they were becoming ever more angry and frustrated. Just behind the shooters the pony soldiers had come up onto the road and were standing there watching. Farther up the road the walking soldiers were clumping together in a tight group, almost shoulder to shoulder. The whole party would be moving soon, but which way? Would they turn around and go back to the Buffalo Creek Fort? He waited another moment, then slowly stood up and turned his back on the soldiers, bent over, and dropped his buckskin leggings down, at the same time wiggling his ass at them. He pulled his leggings up casually, spat at the ground, and hopped lightly onto his pony.

"Cowards! Fools!" he screamed down at the whites, and spat again. He turned his pony to the north and rode slowly over the ridge and away from the whites. Ahead he could see more of his brothers dashing up the hill. Here came Big Nose and High Backbone with a number of younger men.

"Are they coming?" High Backbone yelled out.

"Patience, brother," Crazy Horse called back. "Give them another moment or two and we will go over and see if we can get them to move a little faster."

Farther to the north, where the road slipped down the end of the ridge and over a creek, the land flattened out in a broad expanse of scrub and grass-covered plain. Nothing moved but the brittle ends of the yellow grass as they bent to the ever-strengthening wind. The sky above began to grow gray with clouds as they broke free of the peaks on which they seemed to have been caught and straining for hours. Whirlwind, a hardened warrior, lay flat on the frozen earth, a blanket stretched out under him and a dusty buffalo robe thrown over his head. He heard a rustling to his left and peered out from under the robe to see Little Horse lifting his head and looking about with wide eyes. Whirlwind reached out with his bow and slapped the youngster on the rump.

"Get down, boy!" he growled. "When the time comes to get up I will tell you. Until then you keep your ears open and keep your head under that robe."

The boy disappeared back under his robe and Whirlwind peered anxiously about to see that none of the other younger warriors were becoming as impatient as Little Horse. His eyes scanned the expanse of grass and scrub. There was nothing. Not a movement. Not a sound. *Washte!*

WHEATLEY AND FISHER HAD HAD JUST ABOUT ENOUGH. Both men hastily reloaded their rifles and then started up the hill at a canter.

"Come on, Issac," Fisher growled. "Let's puncture a couple of hides. Any of you boys wanta come along?"

Several of the mounted infantry, all old veterans, grinned and kicked their horses into a trot. Lieutenant Grummond looked up and was about to call the men back. He glanced over his shoulder. Captain Fetterman hesitated a moment, then nodded curtly. Grummond turned to wave the rest of the cavalry forward. Sergeant James Baker edged his mount up alongside of First Sergeant Lang.

"First Sergeant." Baker leaned over the saddle. "I thought the colonel said we weren't to cross over that damned ridge back there. I tell you I don't like this."

"No more do I, Jimmy," Lang grunted. "No more do I. But Captain Fetterman is calling the tune and it's up to us to dance to it."

"As long as it ain't a scalp dance." Baker looked over his shoulder to where captains Fetterman and Brown were bringing up the rest of the outfit at a quickstep. "I hope to hell you know what you're about, Captain," Baker muttered under his breath.

CRAZY HORSE HAD JUST STARTED BACK UP THE SLOPE WHEN he looked up to see the first white men jogging over the rise. Two bearded men were leading a small party of soldiers on horseback. The whites shouted something and began shooting at Crazy Horse and his friends, who wheeled about and dashed back the way they had come, quirting their ponies savagely and yipping at the top of their lungs. They leaped off the ridge onto the flatlands and splashed through the small creek, the ponies scrambling up the far side and away.

Crazy Horse waved his arms and the warriors separated into two parties, one group following him, the other racing along behind High Backbone. The two groups sped up the opposite slope and away from each other as the whites hurried down the road. The two parties of warriors raced away from each other, turning a large circle as they swung around to look back at their pursuers. The pony soldiers were coming down toward the creek now and beyond them the walking soldiers were coming on quickly in a large, compact body. The walking soldiers had all crested the ridge, passed between the jumble of large boulders, and were coming rapidly down the road. Crazy Horse nodded and kicked his pony forward. The braves who had followed him now fell in to a file and headed back down the slope toward the whites. High Backbone, who had taken his party to the opposite side of the slope, watched Crazy Horse's group, then turned to the warriors who had gathered around him.

"*Haiye!*" he shouted. "My brothers, a great day is here!"

The warriors began to whoop and shout. High Backbone quirted the flank of his pony and raced back down the slope. The younger braves followed suit and now the two groups of warriors hurtled headlong toward each other back down towards the creek—and Fetterman's command.

FETTERMAN'S COMMAND HAD BARELY DEPARTED FORT PHIL Kearny when Henry Carrington realized that no medical personnel had gone along. Private Sample was sent off to fetch Assistant Surgeon Hines from the hospital. A few minutes later Sample returned with two saddled horses and a very cranky Hines, whose collar was turned up against the cold.

"Sorry to drag you out of a warm billet, Hines, but I want you to ride on out to the wood train in case they have need of your services. If not, continue on ahead and join up with Captain Fetterman's command. You can come back in with them. Private Sample will accompany you as your striker."

Hines said nothing but nodded and climbed painfully into the saddle. His joints had begun to bother him with the onset of cold weather and this was not the sort of thing he had planned for the day. He would have much preferred a quiet afternoon by the stove. Privately he cursed Carrington, Fetterman, Brown, and every other fool who insisted on mucking about in this god-awful weather. Private Sample, by contrast, was eager for the adventure and scrambled up onto his horse, a wide grin on his face and a Starr carbine clutched in his gloved fingers. When the two men had disappeared through the rear gate, Carrington and Wands walked slowly back to the headquarters building. It was unlikely that anything of much import would occur soon. The worst Henry Carrington expected was to have to listen to Hines' complaints when he got back in, chilled to the bone and in exceptionally bad temper.

"Dr. Hines didn't seem very enthused about his mission," Wands ventured.

"No, not very, Mr. Wands," Carrington said with a slight grin. "But then Dr. Hines has gotten rather vocal of late talking about how we ought to go out and thrash these damned savages. I thought perhaps an hour or two out in the brisk air might help to cool his ardor somewhat. Oh, don't worry, Mr. Wands, I rather suspect that this will be another of our wild-goose chases. Fetterman and Brown will skylark around out there for an hour or two and then come home with runny noses and saddle sores. Then they'll fume and fuss about the nefarious savages who run away from real soldiers."

Wands followed his commander up the steps. The colonel, he thought, was very likely right in his predictions. Nothing ever really came of these forays beyond a few chilblains, sore joints, and aching backsides. Even the Sioux, it seemed, were a little less vigorous in their efforts as the cold weather came on. The two officers pushed their way into the headquarters and peeled off their pistol belts, hats, gloves, scarves, and overcoats and hung them from pegs. Wands rubbed his fingers together briskly and blew on them to get the blood circulating again while Colonel Carrington moved directly to the small stove and poured out two mugs of coffee from the pot that was ever-present on the small, sheet-iron assemblage that was the sole source of heat for the office.

Carrington and Wands had barely had time to finish their coffee and have a cursory glance at the morning report before Assistant Surgeon Hines and Private Sample were stomping into the headquarters building, already back from their foray.

"What's going on out there, Hines?" Carrington demanded of the breathless surgeon.

"Goddamn, Colonel." Hines gasped out. "It's a mess out there. We couldn't get through. The wood train had gone on to the pinery so we swung east to join up with Fetterman but it was impossible. The whole valley is swarming with Indians. Hundreds of them, by God. I was certainly not about to try to ride through the whole Sioux nation."

JAMES WHEATLEY HAULED BACK ON THE REINS AND JERKED his horse to a complete halt.

"What the hell?"

The soldiers who had ridden forward with Wheatley and his partner reined up alongside and all stood staring at the two files of mounted warriors racing down the opposite slope on an apparent collision course. The men looked curiously at each other, hard-pressed to figure out what the Sioux were up to.

"Crazy bastards, ain't they?" Fisher chortled. "Hell, Jim, I say we give 'em a warm welcome when they get here." He slid out of the saddle and dropped onto a large boulder, throwing his Henry rifle to his shoulder and taking a slow careful aim. "Come on, you scamps," he said quietly. "Just a little closer now . . ."

The braves were closing fast. Two hundred yards away, and just on the other side of the small creek that separated them from the whites, the two files of warriors charged past each other, crisscrossing to their front and shrieking as they whirled their weapons over their heads. The noise of their shrieks was suddenly deafening as their voices were joined by those of thousands of their brothers. The grassy flats, which a moment before had seemed entirely empty, were now filled with warriors. They rose in a body from behind every clump of grass, every boulder, every small, twisted bush, throwing to the ground the buffalo and wolf-hide robes that had blended so perfectly with the surrounding landscape.

"Jesus Christ!" Wheatley swore as his horse reared and flailed its hooves in fear. Wheatley tumbled backward out of the saddle, barely retaining his grip on his rifle. The horse, free of its burden, whirled and dashed back through the following cavalry, its eyes and nostrils flared wide in abject terror. Wheatley rolled to a stop against a large boulder and scrambled quickly to his knees, his mouth open and gasping as he tried to recover the wind that had been knocked out of him by the fall. He came up next to Issac Fisher, who was already firing into the mass of warriors surging up at them. Gathered in a tight circle, Fisher and the soldiers all turned their horses loose and hunkered down in a jumble of large boulders that littered the slope. And all around them were thousands of shrieking warriors, their faces bright with crimson, black, and yellow paint, rushing screaming up the slopes toward them. The air around them buzzed with hundreds of arrows arcing in from three directions, clattering and splintering against the boulders, thudding into the frozen earth, chunking into human flesh.

"Jaysus!" screamed one of the soldiers, and crumpled to the ground, clawing helplessly at a shaft that had driven deep into his shoulder blade. Another soldier rolled onto his back, gurgling and staring sightlessly at the sky, an arrow transfixed in his throat and blood bubbling from his lips. Wheatley and Fisher and the three remaining soldiers crowded together in the slight shelter afforded by the large gray boulders and worked their weapons furiously. The miners' Henrys cracked again and again in rapid succession as the soldiers strained feverishly to work ramrods in the tight conditions. It was hard for them to miss at such close ranges. The Indians were within yards of their muzzles and the repeaters did such bloody work in the first few seconds that many of the warriors dropped back down the slope crouching behind bushes, grass, and boulders. The warriors had not expected such a firestorm from just a few men and the first wave of attackers faltered. For a few moments the Indians contented themselves to hunker down in the sparse cover and loose their arrows in a high arc against the whites.

Lieutenant George Grummond, who had also been watching intently the mounted warriors on the opposite slope, had no time to react to Wheatley and Fisher's problems. He had his own problems to deal with. Moments after the miners were attacked, hundreds of Sioux, Cheyenne, and Arapaho braves surged up on either side of the ridgeline along which his command was stretched. The troopers tried desperately to control their own mounts as the horses released by the men ahead of them came racing back through their ranks. The cavalry mounts reared and thrashed as the loose animals careered through them, empty stirrups and loose reins flailing wildly along their flanks and whipping them into a frenzy of fear.

"Control those horses!" Grummond screamed. "Rally on me! Rally!"

Grummond brought up his revolver and fired to send a Cheyenne rolling backward down the hill, half of the brave's face a mass of blood and gray matter. The warrior's place was immediately taken by two others, who rushed up to try to unseat the lieutenant. Grummond spurred his horse forward and bowled the warriors over at the same time, firing his heavy revolver into the side of a third who had leapt up onto the back of First Sergeant Lang's saddle. Lang tumbled to the ground alongside the mortally wounded Indian, losing his rifle in the process. Scrambling to his knees, the old veteran snatched up the Miniconjou's war club and swung it at another warrior. The weapon's solid stone head slammed into the man's shoulder and Lang heard the snap of bone and saw the look of anguish on the warrior's face as he dropped to his knees, clutching at his arm. Lang glanced up the hill toward where the infantry were now fighting for their lives as well. He could barely make out the struggling mass of blue-coated soldiers through the dense fog of gunsmoke that rolled and boiled along the length of the ridgeline. A moment later three dogwood shafts thudded into his back and he pitched forward

into the frozen earth. A young Oglala finished the work with
a large butcher knife before he too flopped into the dirt, slain
by an arrow from one of his brother warriors. In the confusion
and tumult Cheyenne killed Sioux, Miniconjou killed Brulé,
Arapaho killed Cheyenne. The frigid air was cut by the zip of
arrows and the whirring sound of war clubs swung in circles
overhead before smashing into bone and flesh. Above all was
a hellish chorus of shrieks and groans and the booming echo
of gunfire.

"TEN EYCK, WHAT THE HELL IS GOING ON OUT THERE?"

"Damned if I know, Colonel," Ten Eyck said in a half whisper. "Damned if I know."

The two officers stood side by side on the sentry walk,
staring out at the area from which the steady roar of gunfire
seemed to be coming. The firing had been sporadic at first. A
volley, then silence. A few minutes later another volley. But
that had since been replaced by the crashing of volleys as
somewhere beyond the Sullivant Hills Fetterman's force was
firing by files followed by the chaos of individual shots that
cracked and popped in the biting air.

The picket post on Pilot Hill had reported when Fetterman's
force disappeared from view, after which but a few minutes
had passed before Surgeon Hines and Private Sample returned
from their failed mission. The first faint shots were heard while
Hines was still making his report to Carrington and all had
immediately rushed out of the headquarters building to see
what was happening. Then the firing had begun in earnest.
Carrington immediately had Lieutenant Wands call out the
guard and began issuing weapons to all able-bodied men left
in garrison. While Wands was overseeing the issue of weapons
Captain Ten Eyck was at work in the quartermaster's yard,
having teams hitched to wagons and wagons loaded with medical supplies and cases of extra ammunition. Within minutes
a relief force had been assembled. They had managed to scrape
together seventy-five men. Most of them were civilians—
teamsters, miners, carpenters, and mechanics, anyone who

could handle a weapon—pressed hastily into service or who had stepped forward to volunteer. Ten Eyck and Wands hurried back to report to Colonel Carrington.

"Tenedor," Carrington said deliberately. "Take your command out and join up with Fetterman. Move as quickly as you can but keep your eyes open and don't let anyone slip around behind you. From the sounds of it you'll need to have medical people with you. Take Hines and Ould. I've given my horse to Private Sample. He will act as courier. If you need additional help do not hesitate. I've sent another courier out to retrieve the wood train, which should give us another fifty men as soon as we can get them gathered in. We've thirty or so of the cavalry left here, which I will hold in reserve." Ten Eyck and Wands nodded and Carrington went on. "I don't need to remind you that we are dangerously short of men. Do not take any unnecessary risks, gentlemen. Get through to Fetterman and bring him back in but do not act recklessly. Is that clear?"

"Clear, sir," Wands blurted out.

"Yes, sir," Ten Eyck said, and looked over at Captain Powell, who had just come up and stood alongside Carrington, his mouth set firmly, his eyes hooded and dark. Their eyes locked and Ten Eyck thought, *You're a damned pain in the ass, Powell. But I wish to God that it'd been you who'd taken that detail out instead of Fetterman. You'd not have been lured into a big fight and it would have saved us the trouble of sending more men out into this damned cold.* Powell said nothing but his jaw muscle twitched and Ten Eyck imagined that Powell was thinking much the same thing. Ten Eyck saluted and swung into the saddle. A few moments later the detail was moving quickly through the gate and out toward the Montana Road.

GEORGE GRUMMOND LOOKED DOWNHILL TO SEE JAMES Wheatley now standing alone among the boulders, a tangle of bodies surrounding his position. Wheatley was swinging his Henry rifle like a club and Grummond saw the jaw of a Sans Arc burst into a spray of blood and teeth as the butt struck him. Overbalanced by his own efforts, Wheatley staggered and then went down under four warriors. He disappeared screaming under the flashing blades of hatchets already dark with blood. Grummond was nearly deafened by the booming of his troopers' Spencers. The desperate and terrified men worked the loading levers frantically as expended cartridges clattered off of boulders and rolled underfoot. Unfortunately the repeaters had all been modified to permit loading only one round at a time—an economy-minded modification applied by a penny-pinching government. Although faster to feed than the muzzle-loading Springfields, they were not nearly fast enough.[5] The entire position was wreathed in a dense cloud of smoke punctuated by flashes of fire and through which dark figures loomed and a rain of steel-headed dogwood shafts cut like man-made sleet. The head of one of the shadowy forms was distorted by a fan of irregular shapes that Lieutenant Grummond rightly assumed was a war bonnet. He leveled his pistol at the shape and fired into it. The shadow's head exploded, sending the shades of feathers spiraling through the smoke.

The mounted infantrymen who had ridden with Grummond were in a particularly difficult position. The long Springfield rifles could be fired only once from horseback, after which they had to be reloaded. A difficult task in the saddle under normal circumstances, it was impossible with horses bucking and rearing in fear. Thus the infantry had swung or been pitched to the ground, where they bunched together, hunkered down behind whatever cover they could find—boulders,

[5]The "Stabler cut-off device" was little more than a small bit of steel, resembling a wing nut, screw-mounted just in front of the weapon's trigger. This retarded the movement of the Spencer's breech block so that ammunition in the feeding tube could not be pushed automatically into the breech when the loading lever was operated and requiring each round to be manually inserted into the breech. The U.S. government was concerned that soldiers would waste ammunition (and thus money) if allowed to fire too rapidly and ordered all Spencer repeaters so modified. Most veterans quickly "lost" the device but younger troops, unfamiliar with its function, were slow to undo the government's modifications.

brush, tangled bushes, the bodies of dead horses—firing and reloading as quickly as they could manage. It was not fast enough.

Thomas Maddeon realized this within seconds of the first onrush. It was his first action against the Indians, but even he could see that it would be his last. He'd never expected anything like this. His bowels had emptied into his trousers at the first onrush and what little breakfast he had taken had already been spewed out over the front of his overcoat. He was sobbing uncontrollably, the tears freezing on his face as they ran down toward his chin, cutting white rivulets through the smudge of gunpowder blacking. Some dribbled onto the paper cartridges he tore open with his teeth before jamming them down the smoking barrel of his rifle. He looked down in surprise to see that one of his fingers had been torn away by a razor-sharp arrowhead, but already the blood had frozen around the tiny stub and he felt no pain whatsoever, only numbness. Maddeon tucked his ramrod under his arm and squeezed off another shot, feeling the heavy thump of the recoil. Fishing into his cartridge box for another round, he reached down for the ramrod to reload and could not pull it loose. He looked down and realized that he had not grasped the ramrod but the shaft of an arrow that had sunk itself deep into his chest. His eyes widened in surprise and disbelief as he dropped to his knees, hugging his rifle for support, then crumpled over, the world white and swimming before his eyes.

Grummond saw Maddeon go down at the same time that he realized his revolver was jammed. A percussion cap had ruptured with the last shot and the tiny copper fragments were wedged firmly between the cylinder and the frame. The cylinder was frozen fast and there was no time to dig out the ruptured cap. As quickly as the Indians were swarming up over the ridge, they would be on him before he could get the cylinder freed and the first charge rammed home. He swung the heavy pistol like a small club, knocking over a young Brulé. Grummond thought the Indian could not be more than fifteen years old. He glimpsed another brave sighting down an arrow at him. Grummond ducked and hurled the useless pistol at the brave, which caused him to flinch long enough to allow the lieutenant to reach the saber strapped to his saddle. The bright steel arc came out of the scabbard with a sharp, metallic rasp, the brass knuckle guard flashing in the pale light.

It was hopeless. Even Grummond saw that now and re-solved to sell his life dearly. A knot of half a dozen warriors, their hands and forearms stained red with the blood of their enemies, scrambled out from behind the jumble of boulders among which Wheatley and Fisher had died and poured out onto the Montana Road. Grummond dug his spurs deep into the flanks of his horse and surged forward down the slope. From somewhere deep in his chest he brought up the half-remembered shriek which the Rebels had used to so unnerve him at Franklin. Animal, guttural, it was as savage and prim-itive as anything the Sioux or their friends could manage. It was the death song of the Berserker. He swung the saber wildly around his head, his mind a bloodred mist of anger and hatred. A lone brave leapt out from behind a rock. The saber swept along, cleaving the man's head cleanly off. Grum-mond's horse slammed bodily into the group of warriors, send-ing them sprawling across the rutted track. Grummond hauled on the reins, turning his mount in a tight circle and using his saber to slash and thrust at the shapes that now lunged up at him, knives and hatchet blades flashing, fingers grasping and clawing for a hold at his trousers and saddle as horse and man went down together.

CRAZY HORSE SLIPPED BACK FROM THE FIGHTING FOR A FEW moments and maneuvered his pony down the icy slope and out onto the flats, where he turned to look back on the chaos above. It was a curious sight, the rock-strewn ridgeline, which was now enveloped by a man-made fog of gunsmoke much like the peaks of the Bighorns ofttimes disappeared into real clouds. But these clouds were different. They echoed with the booming of gunfire and the shrieks and grunting of men tear-ing and blasting the life out of each other.

Hundreds of warriors kept streaming up the hill and disappearing into the smoke. Some tumbled out again, rolling and flopping lifeless and bloodied down the jagged hillside. Others jogged out leading the horses of the whites by their reins, the empty stirrups jerking and swinging under their bellies. It was all but done. The soldiers had never seen it coming. Surprise had been complete and overwhelming. What surprised him was how viciously the whites fought back. This would not be an easy fight. That much was already very clear. He had not counted closely but it seemed that dozens of his brother warriors had fallen. At this close range the whites' guns tore terrible holes in a man's body and with so many warriors pressing in so close it was hard for the whites to miss. Sometimes a single ball would pass through a man to hit a second and even a third.

Blood was everywhere. It spattered his face and hands and soaked his leggings so that they stuck to his legs. It flowed in small rivers down the hillside and froze in black sheets on which men slipped and fell. He heard a man chanting softly. From the wheezing and labored breathing it was obvious that the man was in terrible pain. He looked down to see a warrior sitting on the ground, propped up against a low boulder and half-hidden in the brittle grass. The upper half of the man's face was painted the yellow of the Kit Fox society, and a black stripe drawn across the man's cheekbones showed that he had killed an enemy. The man was clutching at his own bowels, which were spilling out between his fingers from an ugly gash. He was singing his death song as a dark pool of blood spread slowly out onto the ground.

"You have a bad wound, brother," Crazy Horse said quietly. "Shall I carry you back to the camp?"

The Kit Fox just shook his head and drew a shallow but painful breath.

"No, brother," he said through gritted teeth. "It is too late for that. It doesn't matter now so I will sit here and watch my brothers fight. *Hokahe*, brother. It is a good day to die."

"*Hokahe*, brother," Crazy Horse replied. "It is a good day to die."

Crazy Horse turned his pony back toward the fight and jabbed his heels into its flanks. As he headed back up the slope he could hear the Kit Fox singing his death song. He knew deep in his heart that the Kit Fox would have much company on the Ghost Road.

CORPORAL ADOLF METZGER SAW LIEUTENANT GRUMMOND go down, pulled from the saddle by a dozen shrieking fiends. The veteran bugler knew that there was now no point in remaining where he was and turned his horse uphill. Around him the remaining troopers of the cavalry detachment were likewise turning their mounts uphill. If they could just get up over the ridge it might be possible to break for the fort and safety. As the troopers floundered onto the crest of the ridge the wind picked up momentarily and blew clear some of the smoke that had obscured the fighting. Everywhere they looked hundreds of warriors scrambled over the rocky terrain. There were so many of them that even Metzger knew that reaching the position where captains Fetterman and Brown were fighting, a mere two hundred yards downslope, was impossible. They'd be cut down before they'd gone twenty yards. The infantry were withdrawing slowly toward a pair of large boulders that thrust upward into the smoke like twin monoliths.

They'll be your gravestones, boys, Metzger thought glumly. The cavalry troopers veered toward another collection of boulders that offered some shelter. The few remaining men galloped in among the boulders and swung out of the saddles, turning their mounts loose and driving them off into the masses of warriors who still streamed up at them. It was a minor diversion but at least it kept the attackers busy for a few moments as eager braves hesitated and then scrambled to try to grab the loose animals.

Even in the middle of a fight, Metzger thought, *a damned redskin can't pass by a chance to steal a horse.*

He got some slight satisfaction when a youngster with bright red paint splashed on his face, his braids wrapped in some sort of fur, reached up to catch hold of a bridle and was swung off his feet by the frantic horse. The horse then slipped on a patch of ice and crashed heavily to the ground, rolling over the young warrior and crushing him beneath. When the horse scrambled up again the Indian lay broken and still among the rocks.

Well, Metzger thought bitterly, *there's one less damned horse thief at least!*

Metzger looked around him. There weren't more than a dozen men of the company left now. They were kneeling or lying among the rocks, some cursing, some sobbing, some praying, all of them working the actions of their carbines furiously. Their faces blackened and smeared with powder, windburned and raw with tears, they blasted away at their tormentors for all they were worth, Metzger's own carbine had been lost in the retreat when a warrior slashed at him with a butcher knife. The knife had narrowly missed his ribs but had sliced through the carbine sling and sent the weapon clattering to the ground. Now Metzger's pistol was empty and there was no time to reload it. He scrabbled around on the ground, looking for another weapon, and spotted a Spencer under the body of Private Nathaniel Foreman, and noticed that Foreman had had enough sense to get rid of the small device that limited the weapon's rate of fire.

Smart lad, Nate! The hell with the damned bean counters. Metzger had always liked Nate, a cheerful young fellow always quick with a joke or a funny story. Foreman had taken so many arrows in his back and sides that the poor fellow looked like a porcupine. Metzger looked into the sightless eyes, which had once sparkled so with life and wit.

"Sorry, Nate," he whispered while prying the carbine from stiffened fingers. "But I need this damned thing more'n you do. I'll send a couple of the devils back to Hell for you."

Metzger worked the Spencer's loading lever, which doubled as the trigger guard, thumbed back the hammer, and threw the weapon to his shoulder. A warrior of the Brave Heart society loomed up out of the smoke at just that moment and took the slug square in the chest. With so many of them out there and so close it was hard to miss. Metzger fired again. An arrow snicked above his head and he ducked involuntarily as the missile splintered on a rock behind him. There was a loud *tonk* and Metzger looked down to see that another arrow had struck the bugle slung around his neck. The missile had glanced off but left a nasty dent in his instrument. Metzger was surprised to find that this little thing angered him. The German immigrant had spent eleven years in the army and been in many a tight scrape before but this was as bad a situation as he had ever seen. He crouched down behind a rock to reload. With a quick twist he tugged the loading tube from the Spencer's butt plate and shoved seven more rounds into the weapon. When things got this tight, he knew, the only thing to do was to dig in your heels and fight it out. With any luck at all the boys back at the fort, hearing all the shooting, would have figured something was wrong and started a relief party out this way. The only thing to do was to try to stay alive long enough to let 'em cut through. He squinted down the barrel and felt the thump of the weapon's recoil. Down on the flats a Cheyenne's pony collapsed and sent its rider cartwheeling into the dirt.

Take that, ye red bastard! Come on, boys, Metzger thought. *We're running short of time here!*

AS A CHILD HIS EYESIGHT HAD BEEN SUCH THAT THEY HAD named him Sees As Far As The Moon, and as a youth he had been a great hunter, skilled with bow and lance. But something had happened that robbed him of the clarity of his vision. Things began to appear cloudy and formless unless he held them close to his face and peered intently at them. His future as a warrior was thus limited and he had followed another path. The elders had all agreed that the *Wakan Tanka* had intended that the youth should be a prophet, a seer, for while his physical vision had grown weaker, his ability to see the things denied to others had become ever sharper and more uncannily accurate. Now he had served his people well in this role for well over fifty winters, and his counsel was ever sought after on matters of great import. Sees Far turned and

looked at Red Cloud, who sat wrapped in his red blanket staring intently down at the Buffalo Creek Fort. In the far distance
they could hear the booming echo of gunshots and the whoops
and yelps of the warriors. Another group of soldiers, this one
dragging wagons with them, had now left the fort and was
just moving behind the hills toward the fighting. A young warrior seeking counsel had once made a gift of a brass telescope
to Sees Far and he carried it with him always. The *Wicasa
Wakan* now used it to follow the bluecoats' progress.

"That is all that we will see of this fight for now," he said
half to himself. He was too old to enjoy sitting out in the cold
for such long periods and was hoping that Red Cloud would
take the hint that they should move on.

Red Cloud grunted and shifted his position. The blanket
offered little barrier from the cold and his buttocks too were
growing numb from his having sat in the snow for so long.
He watched as the last of the wagons disappeared behind the
hills, then got slowly to his feet and shook the snow from the
blanket.

"Let's go," he said simply.

Sees Far nodded and slipped the telescope back into its
beaded case, which was slung over his shoulder. The medicine
man walked beside Red Cloud as they trudged through the
snow toward where they had tethered the ponies. Neither man
said a word. Red Cloud seemed lost in his own thoughts and
Sees Far was too cold to want to get into any discussion with
his companion. As they maneuvered their mounts down the
hillside, the going became progressively easier as the snow
grew shallower until they came out onto the flats, where the
sun and wind had worked together to clear most all of it away.
The pair headed their ponies north and followed the tree cutters' road around the hills, taking the long way around to
where the killing place was. Once shielded by the hills they
could no longer hear the noise of the fighting.

"What," the old man asked, "do you think you will see
when we get to the killing place, Red Cloud? Will you have
the great victory that you are seeking?"

"You tell me, grandfather," the Oglala retorted. "You are

the one who can see what is brought by tomorrow's wind."

"Hunh," grunted the medicine man. Red Cloud had always had a way of him that reminded him of a porcupine or a cactus. He was a prickly man to be around. While worthwhile in some instances, he was generally more of an annoying person than one would care to spend much time with. Sees Far did not care to banter with the man, especially as he seemed in a particularly bad mood right now. He pulled the blanket tighter around his shoulders and felt the warmth of the pony's flanks seeping slowly into his legs. By the time they got to the killing place he would perhaps have thawed out enough to talk to Red Cloud about the things that were on his mind. He did not look forward to the talk, as Red Cloud would not want to hear what he had to say. But then a person seldom wanted to hear the things that he needed most to hear.

CRAZY HORSE WORKED HIS WAY BACK OUT OF THE FIGHTING once more, his war club dark with clotted blood and matted tufts of human hair stuck within the sinew binding. He was really beginning to feel the brutal cold now and found that he was shivering uncontrollably. The heat of his blood lust had now drained from his body and he felt cold and empty and a tremendous sadness. As his pony picked his careful way down the slope the young warrior was stunned by the carnage that surrounded him. This was not an easy fight. They had managed to divide the long knives from the walking soldiers, as he had suggested in the council, but they had not counted on the two men with the fast-shooting guns. Those two and the few soldiers with them had nearly spoiled everything. The bullets had come so fast and cut down so many warriors that the attack had faltered long enough to allow the rest of the soldiers to start shooting, and many fighters had been caught unawares as they came up on the *wasichu*. Dead and wounded men and boys lay everywhere in the yellow grass, among the brush and boulders, their blood spilling out onto the frozen earth and patches of snow and ice. With all the gunsmoke it had been hard for anyone to clearly see the ones they were fighting.

Warriors were killing each other in the confusion. The *wasichu* they hadn't already killed were not running but fighting like cornered beasts and they kept firing into the masses of people.

He heard a thunder of hooves and whooping and the shrill twitter of eagle-bone whistles. Now the Cheyenne were coming in on their ponies, their feathered lances, thunder bows, and crooked coup sticks bobbing above the gunsmoke. One brave carried the wheel lance and another had the Cheyennes' bundle of medicine arrows fastened to his bow lance. He recognized Little Wolf and Wooden Leg, Two Moons and Roman Nose with their followers. They were great fighters, but Crazy Horse wished now that they had thrown more of their braves into the fight earlier. They would have helped to break up the soldiers into smaller groups and made the fight go quicker. Well, that made no difference now. Now there was nothing left to do but to end this fight as quickly as possible.

"JESUS CHRIST, CAPTAIN!" LIEUTENANT WINFIELD SCOTT Matson's mouth dropped open in horror at the scene that was unfolding below them.

"As you were, Mr. Matson," Ten Eyck replied quietly. "Stay easy. Don't do anything foolish, boy. And for God's sake don't show any fear. We've got to bluff this one out. Now, I want you and Wands to ride slowly back down the line and steady the men. Make sure their weapons are charged and capped. But nobody does a damned thing without my leave. Clear?"

Matson gulped nervously. "Yes, sir."

Wands said nothing but gave a quick salute.

As the lieutenants turned their mounts away, Captain Ten Eyck sat back in the saddle and deliberately undid the snap of a leather case suspended from the pommel. He brought out his field glasses and surveyed the terrain below. Coming out of Phil Kearny, he had followed the Montana Road for a while and then turned to climb up a large hill mass that commanded views of both Lodge Trail Ridge and Fort Phil Kearny before turning back toward the sound of the heavy gunfire. He hoped to be able to see Fetterman's command while at the same time maintaining line-of-sight communications with the fort. If anything went wrong he wanted to be able to get word back to the colonel without delay. This route took a little longer and he felt sure he'd catch hell later from some of the others for lollygagging. Whatever happened, he wanted to make sure that they had the high ground, and the thought of pushing straight up the road through the valley not knowing precisely what was happening around the next bend was, as far as he was concerned, utter madness.

Let 'em squawk, Ten Eyck thought grimly. *They're not out here freezing their asses off and headed into God knows what kind of a mess.*

Peering through the field glasses, he now felt certain that he'd made the right decision about seeking the high ground. The valley below was literally filled with Indians. Hundreds of them. They were dashing about down there on their ponies, screaming and yelling up at them. Daring them to come down into the valley. Scores of the half-naked warriors were leaping from their ponies and slapping their own exposed buttocks, taunting them. Several of the braves were wearing blue uniform jackets, and through the glasses Ten Eyck could see yellow stripes on some the sleeves and brass buttons that indicated where they'd come from. In the distance he could still hear the firing from Fetterman's positions, but the staccato popping of gunfire was growing ever weaker and more scattered. The grim-faced captain turned to Private Sample, who sat astride the colonel's favorite horse, a well-muscled thoroughbred and probably the fastest one in garrison.

"It's hard to make anything out over there, Archie," Ten Eyck said quietly. "But I think that Fetterman's gone up along with his whole command." Ten Eyck mumbled something to himself that Sample could not quite make out but that he assumed was a bitter comment directed against Fetterman.

"Get back to Phil Kearny," Ten Eyck said quietly. "Don't stop for anything and keep your pistol handy. Present my compliments to Colonel Carrington and tell him that we can't see Fetterman's command but we expect the worst. The hostiles are challenging us to come after them but I'm not risking another seventy-five men without direct authority to do so. If there are any other forces available we'll need them straight away and as much ammunition as we can get. Also, if things have gone as badly as I think they have we'll need wagons to bring in the dead and wounded. If there are any wounded. Go on, son, and Godspeed."

Sample saluted, and tucked the chin strap of his kepi between his teeth, then tugged the revolver from his holster. He quickly checked the loads, then stuffed the weapon back into the holster. He would have liked to have kept it clutched in his fist, but the fact of the matter was that he wasn't all that good a rider, and he held on to the reins for dear life as he galloped back down toward the post. The young private felt like someone had driven a fist into his stomach and could feel a looseness in his bowels that threatened to have him glued to the saddle if anything went even slightly wrong.

I hope like hell you red bastards stay the hell down in that damned valley, Sample thought desperately.

If the Indians jumped him Archie Sample had already determined he would save one bullet in his revolver for himself. Powell and Bisbee and some of the others would likely start croaking about why Ten Eyck hadn't pushed straight on toward Fetterman, but Sample for one was in no rush to go down there among that mob of savages. If they'd already swallowed up Fetterman and his crew and were screaming for more they could count him out. Mother Sample had raised no fools.

CAPTAIN WILLIAM JUDD FETTERMAN HAD NEVER IN HIS worst nightmares imagined it could be anything like this. He'd gone up against the best that Bobby Lee could throw at them and never had things been so desperate. These people were not human, they were demons, fiends incarnate. Half-naked, screaming savages in paint, feathers, and fur. They didn't even have guns, for God's sake. But there were thousands of them, all screaming and scrambling in never-ending waves like an angry surf crashing against the shore. Fetterman slid to the ground, his back pressed tight against the rough surface of the boulder, and fumbled in his pockets for the small cardboard box of cartridges that he'd slipped in there at the last moment. There were more cartridges in his saddlebags but the damned horses were all gone now. Dragged off by Sioux and Cheyenne bucks in the melee. Fetterman looked down and saw that his hands were shaking and the flimsy paper cartridges went into the chambers of his revolver only with difficulty. Captain Fred Brown had somehow gotten hold of a Spencer and was trying to keep the damned savages at bay while Fetterman reloaded revolvers for both of them. *Son of a bitch! Son of a bitch! Son of a bitch!* He mumbled to himself as he used the loading lever to frantically tamp home the loads. He grasped the revolver between his knees so that with his free hand he could fish percussion caps out of the small leather box on his belt.

"Jesus, Bill!" Brown was screaming. "They're all over the goddamned place. They just keep on coming, for Christ's sake! Where the hell is Powell? Where the hell is Carrington? Can't the bastards hear this? Jesus Christ!"

The Spencer roared again and Fetterman heard the metallic clacking as Brown levered another round into the breech. The spent cartridge bounced off the boulder and caught on the collar of Fetterman's shirt, slipping down onto bare skin and searing it as it went. But Fetterman's numbed brain was too preoccupied to notice the pain. He stood up next to his friend and fired at a brave wearing a headdress consisting mostly of owl feathers. The slug caught the warrior in the left shoulder and sent him spiraling around, the buffalo-hide shield flying from his fingers as he tumbled backward.

"Whatever happens, Bill," Brown was shouting, "don't let the bastards take us alive!"

"You've got my word, Fred!" Fetterman yelled, and squeezed off a shot at a Cheyenne whose head had peeked out from under the neck of his running pony.

*   *   *

AMERICAN HORSE QUIRTED HIS PONY BRUTALLY, DRIVING IT faster up the slope and into the cluster of boulders where the last of the *wasichu* were cornered. The cursed bluecoats were fighting like badgers trapped in their den and too many of the people had already died in front of their guns.

We must end this quickly, he thought. *There are more soldiers already on the next ridge and more will be coming soon. This has gone on long enough.*

He looked to his left and saw a young soldier, the last standing in his small group, throw down his empty rifle and start swinging his brass horn as a weapon. He used it like a club, smashing it into the heads of two incautious braves and yelling abuse at the warriors who now circled him warily, two Lakota and an Arapaho. The little bluecoat shook the horn and screamed at the Lakota taunting them and daring them to come on. Then the Arapaho sped an arrow through the man's chest and the other braves rushed in to count coup. American Horse grunted. For a bluecoat he was a brave man. He turned his pony upslope and glanced up to see the soldier chief with the long whiskers cock his pistol and put it to the head of the other soldier chief who had no hair. The man fired the pistol into his friend's head, blood and brains spattered all over the boulders behind him.

They're killing each other now, he thought. *But this one is mine!*

He kicked his heels into the pony's flanks and the animal leaped over a large boulder, slamming into the soldier chief's shoulder and knocking him staggering backward. The *wasichu*'s eyes went wide and he brought the pistol up to his own head.

"Has!" screamed American Horse, leaping from the back of the pony and throwing himself onto the soldier's chest. The two men rolled on the ground grappling with each other. The soldier tried to bite American Horse's shoulder but the Lakota jerked away and struck the man across the face. He reached back for his butcher knife, the wooden handle studded with shiny brass tacks, and felt it in his grasp. It took only one quick swipe to sever the man's windpipe and watch the blood

gush out, spraying the ground and spurting up hot and wet in
his own face. American Horse thought of his friend Red Wolf
and deliberately bent over the soldier and drank his warm
blood as it jetted up into his mouth. He sat back on the soldier
chief's chest and smiled down at the man, whose eyes were
wide with horror as he looked up at his own blood smeared
and dripping from the contorted and screaming face above
him. The eyes rolled back in the man's head and American
Horse wrenched the pistol from the soldier chief's grip.

"You want a bullet, coward?" he screamed. "Here, take this
one!" He pressed the muzzle against the man's left temple,
where it exploded.

"Haiye! Haiye!" roared the frenzied American Horse. "A
great day is here!"

WHEN ARCHIE SAMPLE RACED BACK THROUGH THE MAIN
gate at Fort Phil Kearny with his report, he found dozens of
men and the few women residents of the post waiting anxiously for his words. Henry Carrington listened in horror and
then rounded up nearly every man left in garrison and rushed
them to the sentry walks that lined the stockade. Sample's
report raced through the entire garrison within minutes of his
arrival, moving from mouth to ear in urgent, unbelieving whispers. Was it possible? Could Ten Eyck be wrong? Maybe
Sample had just exaggerated it some. But what if the report
was true? What if the savages had killed them all? What if
they were even now headed this way flush with victory and
maddened with their blood lust? Every man, soldier or civilian,
grabbed a weapon. Even the guardhouse was emptied of pris-
oners, the padlocks tossed carelessly aside and tin cups kicked
into corners as the men rushed out, stopping at the armory to
grab weapons and fill their pockets with cartridges before
scrambling up onto the sentry walks. The shooting had now
stopped and the ensuing silence was all but unbearable in its
intensity. A hundred pairs of eyes strained and stared at the
distant hills. The waiting, the not knowing, that was the worst
part of it.

*   *   *

THE RIDE UP THE VALLEY HAD BEEN A SOLEMN AFFAIR. SEES Far had kept his counsel until they rounded the base of the last hill. Then he put his hand on Red Cloud's arm and leaned over to whisper to him.

"Even the best of plans has its cost, Red Cloud," the old man said. "Those things which cost the most need to be treasured and you must not dwell too long on what you have given for the prize. It does no good and makes the fruit bitter when it should taste sweet."

"Sees Far," Red Cloud said with a tone of exasperation. "What are you talking about?"

"You will see soon enough, Red Cloud. Just remember what I've said."

Red Cloud shook his head and nudged his pony forward, the *Wicasa Wakan* following along a few paces behind. The sight that greeted them was more and less than what Red Cloud had hoped for this day. The fight was over and the warriors were coming back from the killing place, pushing through the long, brittle grass in groups of two and three. Some warriors walked by alone, carrying their weapons at their sides. Many carried guns and equipment taken from the bluecoats. Fresh scalps, already stiffened in the cold, hung from many a lance or bow. Red Cloud stopped a Miniconjou who wandered up, his eyes distant and unfocused.

"How many of the *wasichu* got away, brother?" Red Cloud asked.

"None," replied the Miniconjou without enthusiasm. "We killed them all." The man then pushed by and continued on his way.

Red Cloud was puzzled. What was wrong with these people? This was a great victory. Why did they pass by so sullen and quiet? They should be frantic with joy and yet he heard no songs of victory. No recounting of coups. There should have been singing. There should have been boasting. But instead there was silence. Then he heard the singing. The wind had been carrying the sound away but now he heard it as the others returned from the killing place. But all he could hear was the wailing of the death songs of the warriors. Then he saw them coming up from the valley and down from the ridges carrying their brothers with them.

They limped and staggered back through the biting wind, worn and battered, streaming blood that had frozen in their wounds. They carried their dead, lifeless limbs trailing limp in the grass. Others led ponies across which bodies had been slung. The animals themselves were covered with caked and frozen blood and limping from bullet wounds. Arrows projected from the rumps and withers of some of the animals. Red Cloud watched in grim resignation as he counted up the cost of this fight. He heard the warriors mumbling among themselves as they passed by. Yes, it had been a good day to die. And many had. Too many. It was as American Horse had once said—a day when so many lodges are made empty cannot be called a great day.

IT WAS DARK BEFORE TEN EYCK'S COMMAND STUMBLED EX-hausted and ashen-faced through the main gate. The wagons that Carrington had sent out full of ammunition rumbled and jolted along behind the silent column. Men crowded around the returning command anxious for word of Fetterman and their colleagues. The returning men said nothing and their eyes were downcast, avoiding the stares and questioning glances of eir friends. Colonel Henry Carrington rushed down the head-quarters steps and reached up to grab Ten Eyck's bridle as the weary captain reined to a halt.

"What of Fetterman, Tenedor?" Carrington whispered urgently. "Is he coming in?"

"He's already in," Ten Eyck said sullenly, and jerked a thumb over his shoulder. "Second wagon in line. At least we think it's Fetterman. Brown too. What we could find of him."

Henry Carrington walked unsteadily back toward the wagons, where men had already crowded around in silence and horror. As he pushed his way through the knot of onlookers, some of whom were vomiting, he could see what looked like cordwood, bleached white in the sun and stacked carelessly in the wagons beds. It was not wood but human limbs, naked, frozen solid, torn from sockets, smeared with blood, slashed and crushed and broken.

Oh my God, my God! Carrington thought as he steadied himself against the side of the first wagon. He turned to Lieutenant Wands, who had pushed up next to him.

"How many, Alex? How many?" he asked quietly.

"We don't know for sure, sir," Wands whispered hoarsely. "We think we have fifty in these wagons but the dark was coming quickly and we thought it best not to risk a longer stay. There were thousands of hostiles out there, Colonel, thousands. But we resolved to bring as many of our people in as we could manage. We couldn't leave them all for the wolves."

"We'll leave none of them," Carrington said deliberately, drawing himself erect. "First thing in the morning I'll take a party out myself. We'll bring them all home. All of them."

"Yes sir," Wands said.

"Grummond?"

Wands shook his head and both men found that they were staring toward the dim light of a candle flickering weakly behind the oiled paper covering of the windows of the Grummonds' quarters. She was in there. Waiting. Waiting for word of her husband. Praying that at any moment he might walk through the door. Dreading the thought of what lay before her if he did not. She was in there wondering. Wondering if he would hold her ever again. If ever he would run his fingers through her hair. If ever he would clutch her to his breast. If ever he would see the child she now carried in her. Henry Carrington felt the moisture welling up in his eyes, the lump forming in his throat. It was his duty to tell her. It fell to him to bring the news that would crush her world and maybe destroy her utterly. For the first time since he had taken command of the regiment Henry Carrington truly hated his job.

As darkness closed over the valley the temperature began to fall rapidly. It had been bitterly cold all day, well below freezing, but now the air was turning arctic. The mercury began dropping slowly and then, as full dark settled in, plummeted below zero. The residents of Fort Phil Kearny, shaken by the grisly cargo brought back in Ten Eyck's wagons, retreated into their homes and barracks. But however large they stoked the fires to fight off the chill, however much they sought the company of others, never had any of them felt colder or more alone than on this grim, this most dreadful of nights.

"It's a dark day, Margaret," Henry Carrington whispered as he held his wife tighter. It was as if he would pull her physically into him, melding their bodies as their souls had melded long years before. They stood before the fireplace in silent embrace. They listened to the sounds that threatened to overwhelm them—the ticking of the mantel clock, the low rumble of the fire, the rasping wheeze that wracked Margaret's thin frame, and outside the roaring of the wind that set the windows rattling in their frames. Upstairs the boys slept together under heavy buffalo robes, and in another room Frances Grummond slept. At least they hoped she slept. Surgeon Horton had administered a sleeping draught and Margaret had sat with her until dreamless sleep took the widowed Frances in its embrace. Now Margaret pulled back from her husband and looked up into his eyes.

"You told her everything, Henry?"

Carrington said nothing but nodded slowly.

"Is there no hope at all?"

"No, my love, no," Henry said gently. "The only hope is that he died quickly. That he was not taken alive by them. The alternative cannot be endured."

"Frances doesn't suspect that he, I mean, that they might have . . . ?" She left the question unfinished, afraid even to consider what it meant.

"No," Carrington said firmly. "I told her that he died instantly and bravely. And even if it should be proven otherwise, that lie will stand forever as the truth. The only truth that need ever be known. I have talked to my officers and they agree that it must be so."

"But what if she sees his body when he is recovered? Will she not know or at least wonder?"

"No, dear," Henry assured her. "Some of the carpenters are working tonight and we shall at least take some coffins with us in the morning. His remains, at the very least, will come home as they will go to their final rest." Henry paused. "I have a favor to ask of you, Margaret, and it is a hard task to set."

"Anything," she said readily.

"I will bring back Grummond's remains but we absolutely must prevail on her not to view them. We can't know what hideous acts they've performed on his remains but I have little hope that he will appear as she remembers him and that I would not have on my conscience."

Margaret pressed her fingers to his lips.

"Shhhh," she whispered. "Say no more. I'll talk to her. I'll make it right."

"If only we could, my love. But there is too much here that will never be made right."

"She's not the only widow here tonight," Margaret said quietly. "They tell me that James Wheatley was with Captain Fetterman's command. If that's true then Elisabeth Wheatley and her little boys are left alone in this world."

Margaret pulled herself into his chest and tried to stifle the fit of coughing that she felt rising from her lungs. She thought of the young woman sleeping in the room above and of Liz Wheatley alone with her children in this wilderness. What if it had been Henry instead of George Grummond out there? What then of her and the boys? She imagined what Liz Wheatley must be going through this terrible night and felt the hot tears streaming down her face.

Henry too was thinking of Frances Grummond and Elisabeth Wheatley. In his heart he was trying hard not to curse the memory of William Judd Fetterman, who had brought them to this misery and snuffed out the lives of so many good men. So many men gone. That fool Fetterman could not wait. A vain, arrogant glory hound charging in recklessly to his death. And nearly a third of the command dead with him. Now they would never be able to strike a blow at the Sioux in their winter camps. Red Cloud had lured that fool into making the first move. They were playing a deadly game out here and Red Cloud had won this round. And maybe won the game.

THE GRIM WORK OF RECOVERY WAS DONE THE NEXT DAY UN-der skies that were nearly black with the promise of a winter storm building beyond the mountains. The temperature hovered at fifteen degrees below zero and was driven by a wind that sliced through even the heaviest clothing, burning ears and noses raw. The cold left a man's face numb and his forehead pounding. As he had promised, Henry Carrington took personal charge of the detail. Jim Bridger, suffering badly from his arthritis, insisted on coming along to keep company with his haggard and haunted friend.

"Your lads need have no fear on this day, Colonel," Bridger said between sniffles. "The devils won't be back this day or the next. I b'lieve they've had their fill for a piece."

"What makes you say that, Gabe?" Henry asked quietly, his face a mask of anguish at the sights which assaulted him on every side.

"Too many ghosts, Colonel," Bridger said, jerking his head toward the battlefield. "Fettermen and these boys weren't the onliest ones had a rough time of it out here. Lookee yonder and ever'where the boys fit, ye can see they fit well. The Sioux and their friends'll never leave a dead friend behind if they can help it and from all the blood what they left here there's many a corpse they had to haul away."

"Not nearly enough to suit me."

"Well, mebbe not, Colonel. Nor me neither but there's a whole heap o' dead bucks out there in them hills this day I'll wager." Bridger jabbed a thumb over one nostril and blew a stream of mucus out onto the ground. "Wagh!"

"Colonel!" Corporal Frank Fessenden's voice rang out in the eerie silence that had settled over the ridgeline. "We've found Lieutenant Grummond down here, sir."

Carrington nodded and he and Bridger picked their way down the ridgeline, stepping carefully to avoid treading on the entrails and other body parts of soldiers that had been scattered liberally across the frozen landscape. The ritual mutilations that the Sioux and their allies had meted out were hideous in the extreme, and Carrington was grateful for the cold, which at least served to mitigate the pervasive smell of death. The Indians, Bridger told him, were not about to face their enemies whole in the afterlife and so they gouged out eyes, sheared off genitalia, slashed tendons and ripped off trigger fingers. Skulls were split and brains scooped out onto rocks and smashed into jelly. It was impossible in many instances to tell which parts belonged to which corpse and so the soldiers stopped trying. It was enough, they decided, to keep their friends' remains from the scavengers, which had prowled the ground last night and would come back tonight to try to pick the bones clean. Carrington and Bridger looked down at the mortal remains of Lieutenant George Washington Grummond. Bridger squatted down alongside the corpse and turned him over. Henry Carrington was immediately glad that they'd brought several coffins along with them. He did not want Frances to remember him like this. No woman should endure such a thing.

"Lord, Lord!" exclaimed Bridger. "Well, here be one good thing, Colonel. The thievin' rascals have done left the lieutenant's weddin' ring. Grummond had his own guts tangled 'round that hand and the devils plumb missed it." The old mountain man carefully worked the ring off the stiffened finger and wiped it clean on the remnants of Grummond's own clothing.

"Here ye go, Colonel," Bridger said quietly, holding the ring out in his clawlike fingers. "It be not much at all but it may bring some small comfort to his missus. Tell 'er ye found it in his pocket or hung round his neck. It seems an odd deception but in this one case I will allow that a lie is not so sinful a thing."

Carrington nodded quietly and slipped the ring carefully into a handkerchief as Corporal Fessenden and Private Murphy carefully placed Grummond's corpse in a simple pine box. The colonel borrowed Bridger's hunting knife, leaned over the corpse, and deftly cut a small lock of what little hair had been left by the Sioux's scalping knives. He wrapped the lock of hair in the handkerchief with the ring and slipped the mementos carefully into his pocket. He and the scout then turned and walked a few yards up the ridgeline to a group of large boulders. Bridger squatted down by a soldier's corpse that had inexplicably been covered by a buffalo robe and spared the mutilations dealt out to so many of his colleagues.

"By God!" Bridger exclaimed. "It be that little Dutch feller. The bugler. What whar his name, Colonel?"

"Metzger, I believe," Carrington said slowly. "Corporal Adolf Metzger. Had a slight German accent I recall. A decent young man. Why was he not so ill treated as the others?"

"Colonel," Bridger said, standing up next to his friend. "There lies a brave man. Even them red devils had to 'low him that. He must've took a passel with him and I 'spect it were one buck what stood over him afterward and waved the rest away. I'm thinkin' this buck had lost him a good friend and wanted his pard to have a servant on the Ghost Road. Another Injun wouldn't do but a brave enemy would. Whoever this Metzger was, he was a brave man."

"They were all brave men, Major," Carrington said quietly. "Some were just not very smart."

"Wagh!" Bridger spat. "It don't take a scholar to get a heap o' men killed." He looked up at the darkening sky. "And it don't take a scholar to know when to get in out of the weather. Colonel, we need to finish up this day's work and get along or this country'll kill what the Injuns ain't."

THE FIRST REAL STORM OF THE SEASON FOLLOWED CLOSE ON the heels of the recovery party's return to Fort Phil Kearny. Barely had the gates swung shut behind them when the wind began to whistle, sweeping down from the mountains with ever-growing intensity. Individual flakes of white skittered out ahead of the wind, flitting through the yellow grass that bent over double in the icy wind. These were followed by flurries that swirled and eddied around trees and boulders. The whistle grew to a howl, then an earsplitting roar, driving before it clouds of snow that ticked against windows and flattened onto the vertical walls of the stockade, where it began to pile up in drifts that sloped up toward the ragged parapets. In the quartermaster's yard the animals huddled together in whatever thin shelter they could find in the lee of the warehouses and scattered sheds.

Hunched over against the blast, Portugee Phillips struggled across the parade ground toward the Carringtons' quarters. He was wrapped in an oversized bearskin coat that bulged out where he had a bundle stuffed under it. Phillips staggered up the steps of the colonel's quarters and pushed through the door, which Lieutenant Wands, who had been watching for his arrival, held open for him.

"Good evening, Phillips," Wands said quickly. "They're waiting for you in the parlor."

"Thankee, Mr. Wands, I'll go straight in."

The group gathered in the parlor was a grim-faced and solemn one. In addition to Colonel Carrington and Lieutenant Wands he recognized Captain Powell and Captain Ten Eyck. Mrs. Carrington sat on a small sofa, her arm draped around the shoulders of a bereaved Frances Grummond. Phillips did not remove his coat but walked quietly up to Mrs. Grummond.

"Beg pardon, missus," he said. The odd cadences of his Portuguese accent added a soft, surreal quality to his rough, frontier English. "I am sorry your husband is gone under by them savages. I will bring help to you. Here." He reached under his coat and produced a wolf robe, which he presented shyly to the young widow. "This keeps you warm in this bad weather, please."

Frances Grummond looked up with tear-rimmed eyes and smiled her thanks to the little miner who had never before said so much as a word to her. Phillips looked away, embarrassed, and then turned to Colonel Carrington.

"I'm ready, Colonel," Phillips said simply.

Carrington nodded to Captain Ten Eyck, who produced a small, oilskin packet containing the colonel's written reports of the battle that had taken so many lives. The situation was

indeed desperate with so many men dead and the distinct
threat that the Sioux would quickly press their advantage and
move to wipe out the remaining garrison. They needed reinforcements, they needed better weapons and more ammunition, and they needed all this quickly. Phillips tucked the
packet deep into the recesses of his coat. Lieutenant Wands
then produced a Spencer carbine and two leather cases containing extra ammunition for the weapon.

"Here you go, Mr. Phillips," Wands said solemnly. "It's not
much but it may be of some comfort."

Phillips nodded his thanks and slung the ammunition cases
over his shoulder just as Colonel Carrington was putting on
his overcoat and a bearskin cap.

"Come, Mr. Phillips," the colonel said. "You'll use my
horse. It's the least I can do for you on this very hazardous
duty."

The two men headed out into the storm and made their way
to the stables, where Carrington's horse was waiting. Private
Sample had slung a sack of oats across the cantle and, when
no one was looking, slipped a flask of whiskey into the saddlebags along with some food for Phillips. Sample had also
loaded two of the colonel's heavy revolvers and slung them
across the pommel of the saddle in their holsters. As Carrington and Phillips slipped into the stall, Phillips handed the two
oversized cartridge boxes to the young private.

"Archie," Phillips said quietly. "Once I get in the saddle,
you strap them boxes to my ankles, okay? Help my feet keep
in the stirrups ifn I get sleepy."

"Mr. Phillips," Carrington said finally. "We'll let you out
down by the water gate. It's the farthest away from the hostiles
and closest to decent cover. Hopefully the weather will keep
them all in their lodges and away from the trail."

Phillips nodded then swung up into the saddle, his slight
form almost dwarfed by the huge animal. Sample reached up
and shortened the stirrup straps, then lashed the cartridge
boxes to the legs of Phillips' heavy buffalo-hide boots. Carrington picked up a lantern and took hold of Grey Eagle's
bridle with his other hand while Archie Sample swung the

stable doors open. The colonel then led horse and rider out into the swirling clouds of blowing snow. As the men approached the gate a voice came out of the darkness.

"Halt! Who comes there?" It was Private John Brough, who had been on duty for a while and was understandably anxious. Brough threw his rifle to the "on guard" position, bayonet thrust forward and trembling slightly. The sergeant of the guard, Sam Gibson, looked over at Brough and shook his head.

"Fer Chrissake, Brough, ye great lunk," Gibson said. "When's the last time ye seen a damned Injun come at ye from the stables carryin' a lantern?" Gibson squinted at the shadowy figures illuminated only dimly by the candlelit lantern.

"Come to attention, Brough!" Gibson barked. "It's the commanding officer!"

"Never mind, Sergeant," Carrington said. "Open the gate for Mr. Phillips."

Sergeant Gibson fumbled with the keys, his fingers inept in the frigid air, but finally managed to open the padlocks and slide out the heavy bars. He and Brough then shoved their shoulders into the large wooden panels and the gates creaked open, snow swirling through the yawning gap in the stockade. Carrington reached up to Phillips and extended his hand.

"Good luck, Mr. Phillips," the colonel said. "Our prayers are with you, sir. God go with you."

Phillips' mittened hand came up in a sort of salute. He clucked to the horse and nudged him with his heels, starting the animal out through the gate. Man and rider quickly disappeared into the purling snow. Carrington and the guard detail stared into the night after him, listening intently, anxiously for the whoop of a human predator or the crack of rifle or pistol shot. They waited there together, mindless of the cold and peering into the darkness until it was pointless to remain any longer. Colonel Carrington turned and headed back to the headquarters building, the new snow squeaking under his boots, as the guard detail swung the gate shut and slid home the bolts.

"Sarge," asked Private Brough. "Where's Portugee headed?"

"Fort Laramie, Brough," answered the sergeant. "Nearest telegraph."

"Fort Laramie! Good lord, Sarge!"

John Brough shook his head in disbelief and thought that it was a fool's errand if ever there was one. Fort Laramie was over two hundred miles away. Indians everywhere and the worst damned blizzard he'd ever seen in his life. Portugee Phillips, Brough quickly decided, was probably a dead man.

Hell, he thought bitterly. *We're all probably dead men.*

PRETTY OWL BUSIED HERSELF WITH A SOUP, DROPPING white-hot stones hissing into the pot and letting the steam wash over her face. The wispy smoke from the small fire eddied uncertainly in the lodge, at the mercy of the wind, which howled in the lodgepoles above, first drawing the smoke straight up then shoving it back down into the lodge, where it swirled erratically only to be pulled suddenly up again and out into the night. She fanned the smoke from her face and looked up at her husband, who sat slumped against a willow backrest, a robe thrown over his shoulders, staring blankly into the glowing coals. She was not sure if he saw her or was even aware of her presence here, so lost was he in himself. His mind was far away, in another place, another time. If there was one thing she appreciated about the weather tonight it was the unceasing roar of the wind, for it blocked out the wailing and sobbing that had followed the fight with the *wasichu*.

No circle had been spared the effects of that day, for the men had returned bearing with them the dead and hurt ones, which numbered in the scores. For a week one could not leave one's lodge without hearing the Death Song—for many died of their wounds after lingering in agony for days afterward. Already the people were calling it the Fight of One Hundred Dead, and she knew not if they were talking about how many whites had been killed or how many of the Lakota, Cheyenne, and Arapaho had traveled down the Ghost Road because of that fight. That it had been a victory was not in doubt, but as *Sinté-Galeska,* the Brulé who had counseled against this war, kept saying, the people could not afford to win many more such fights.

Perhaps he was right, Red Cloud thought bitterly. *Perhaps Spotted Tail spoke the truth when he warned us against this war. Already the clans are moving away and leaving the fruit of this fight in the trees as they go.*

He had chanced upon Spotted Tail out in the forest the day after their return from the fight, and Spotted Tail had pointed up to the low branches of several trees where families had placed the wrapped bodies of their dead.

"So, Red Cloud," Spotted Tail had said quietly. "You have made the impossible happen. You have made the trees bear fruit in the winter. But it is a fruit the people cannot swallow without choking."

Red Cloud had said nothing in reply. He had simply turned and walked away, but it was not so easy to walk away from the truth of Spotted Tail's words. The words hung in his mind and broke his sleep.

"Don't brood so," Pretty Owl said to him, bringing him back from his thoughts. "Yes there are many dead but the whites have been driven back into their fort. That's what you wanted. The winter is here and there will be no more fighting until the grass is up in the spring. The people will survive and we will have more children, more warriors to finish the work you've started. You've done what no other Lakota has ever done before. Even the *wasichu* must now know this and fear you, fear the wrath of the people. Maybe when the grass is up they will realize that we mean to keep our land. Maybe they will see that there is not enough room for us and them and that we will fight them for every pine needle and every shoot of grass that they have trod on. You have showed them this. You and no other. Maybe they will listen to the weeping of their own women and young ones and leave us here forever."

"Maybe," Red Could said absently. "Maybe."

Pretty Owl threw her arms around her husband and pulled him tight to her breast, rocking him gently and humming the song he had used to court her so many years before. She looked at the sleeping form of their little son wrapped in the furs of the buffalo and the wolf, then closed her eyes and dreamed about the next child, which she so longed to have. Above them the wind howled and keened in the lodgepoles, and Red Cloud sat there staring into the coals, and felt the tears running down his face. For him this time would always be known as the Moon of Bitter Cold.

July 1908

The old gentleman sat quietly by the window, staring out at countryside that streamed past in an endless panorama of brown grass, rolling hills, and the purple smear of chokecherry and wild plum in the hollows. The car swayed gently and echoed to the hypnotic clacka-chuck, clacka-chuck of the rails that passed briefly underneath before slipping back out into the fierce prairie sunlight where they stretched in shiny ribbons to the distant horizon. The air in the car would have been stifling had not the windows been slid down to admit the breeze of the train's forward movement to waft through the compartment, tousling the male passengers' hair or cooling their bald pates and toying gently with the fringe on the women's shawls.

The man's snowy beard rustled lightly in the breeze as he gazed out at a land he had not seen in forty years but which in all those years had never been far from his thoughts. He felt delicate fingers wrapping themselves around his hand, squeezing it gently. Henry Carrington looked up into the eyes of his wife, who sat quietly in the seat next to him.

"The last time we saw this country," she said softly, "it was forty below zero and I thought we'd never get through the snowdrifts. Remember?"

"How could I forget," he said, turning back to the window. As he watched, every now and again a pronghorn would look up from his grazing and stare dumbly at the passing train or run startled, bounding through the grass. It was strange to see the fences that seemed to parse so much of the land now. It didn't look right to him when he remembered how, when not mounded with snow, this country had once been covered with great herds of buffalo. The huge, slow-moving masses of dusty fur and dull eyes had taken days to pass by.

"I felt sure," she said to him, "that we had come to the end of the road then. But you got us through, Henry. You never doubted for a moment that we would win through."

Henry looked at her and smiled. He squeezed her hand, now wrinkled and covered with the spots that come with age.

"Oh, I had my doubts, but I was afraid to show them. Too much depended on it. You were a brave little trooper then and you've never faltered once in all these years."

It felt strange to him in the swaying warmth of an enclosed railcar to pass over in a few minutes country that had re-uired days of backbreaking, freezing agony to cross. He looked around at some of his fellow passengers. A prosperous merchant fidgeted with his watch chain. A fashionably dressed young lady adjusted a hat pin and smoothed a wisp of wind-ruffled hair back into place. A young man—probably a reporter, judging from the telltale smudge of ink on his cheek—adjusted his spectacles and scribbled something in a small notebook. A banker, beads of sweat on his high forehead, snoozed comfortably, his head thrown back and mouth open in a most unbankerly pose. They had no idea what it had been like to cross these plains in rough wagons in the dead of winter. They had no real concept of what this land had once been like. How could they know?

"If you hadn't written, my dear," he said to the old woman sitting next to him, "I do not know how I would have survived what was yet to come. Whatever I did for you on that terrible trip to Casper is as nothing compared to what you did for me. You are the one who saved my life."

"Nonsense!" Frances patted his hand. "Henry Carrington, I loved you and Margaret more than anyone on earth. You were both so kind to me when I lost George. You took me in as a part of your family. When I heard that Margaret had died I was devastated. A kinder, more beautiful woman never lived."

"No," Henry said, "two kinder and more beautiful women never lived. That I have been fortunate enough to be married to each of you makes me the most blessed of men."

"We'll be in Sheridan soon," Frances said. "Have you finished your speech?"

"I think so. I'm just afraid that I will forget to mention someone. There were so many brave men and women there with us. They deserve to be remembered."

"We remember them all in our hearts, Henry. In the end that's the only thing that counts."

THE OLD MAN SQUINTED THROUGH THE GREEN GLASS GOGGLES that he wore to ward off the burning rays of the July sun. He didn't think that they helped all that much, for in truth he was nearly blind now anyway, the weakened eyes now filmy and sunken in a face deeply seamed and furrowed by the years. He could not so much as step up into a wagon without his son's help. A strong man, Jack was his pride and joy, his legacy. A wild boy, he had grown into a mature and gentle man who sacrificed much for his father, for his people. Red Cloud was justly proud of him. It was hard to believe that Jack had now seen more than fifty winters.

It was a thing of wonder to the old man that time seemed to have slipped away so quickly. He remembered how when he was young he and his people had never given much thought to time. The days came and went. The sun rose and set. One season passed into another and so life had flowed like a river. But it had all changed here. Here in these hills, here among the boulders and the brown grass, time had caught them as the wind catches a tumbleweed and sends it spinning along over the prairie. Somehow it all seemed to have started here, and so he knew that he had to return one last time before it was time to travel down the Ghost Road.

That the white men had chosen this day to dedicate a monument to their fallen friends on this spot was something he had not expected. Jack Red Cloud had been surprised when they topped the ridgeline and he saw the collection of buggies and horses gathered around a large stone monument a few hundred yards away. He reined up the team and sat watching, his father sitting next to him in the bright stillness. The two men sat there quietly and waited. Jack was not particularly concerned about whites. After all these years he was used to them. But today he just didn't feel like having to deal with them. He was also worried that his father might be a little uncomfortable riding up to this group of whites if they were indeed the ones from the days of the old Buffalo Creek Fort.

"Father," Jack said finally. "It looks like the ceremonies are over. They're all getting into their buggies. They'll be gone in a little while and then we can go over to the hill."

Red Cloud grunted and nodded his head. He knew what his son was thinking and thought it was a little silly. He had a great many white friends now. But he was pleased that his son was concerned for how he might feel. He was a thoughtful son. Red Cloud didn't mind the wait, as he was in no hurry to go anywhere right now. It was good just to sit here and feel the sun on his face, the warmth soaking into his old bones. He sat on the wagon seat and listened to the soft whistling of the wind in the long grass and thought back over the years. That he was nearly blind didn't seem to matter. The things he needed to see were as sharp and clear before him as they had been nearly a half century before. So much time had passed one might think that the ghosts would be gone, that they would have moved down the Ghost Road long ago. But that was not so. They were still here. He could feel their presence. He closed his failing eyes and listened. Yes, they were still here. He could still hear their singing. Could hear the death songs. They floated up through the years on the wind. They knew he was here too. They were waiting for him, here where they had fought the whites so hard for what had been theirs but was no longer.

The Fight of the One Hundred Dead was not the last time they had fought the whites for this land. He had been afraid after that fight that all the tribes would abandon the war. There were so many empty lodges that winter. But they had some-how hung on. Somehow he had convinced them to carry on

the fight. When the grass had come up in the spring they had
started again to harass the tree cutters and the soldiers who
guarded them. When the late summer came they had fought
two great battles against them. Thousands of warriors had ridden with him against the *wasichu*. Ahhh, the things they had
done together!

But the whites had whipped them badly at the two great
battles.[1] Too many of the young men had gone down the Ghost
Road. The bluecoats had replaced their old rifles with new
ones that shot faster and farther. The people had not expected
this and had paid dearly for it. Red Cloud had thought that
they had lost the war. But they had not. The whites never knew
how badly they had beaten the people and the Great Father in
Washington and his chiefs had had enough. A road was not
worth so much trouble, so much death.

No one was more surprised than Red Cloud when the whites
asked him for peace. He had thought it was a trick but the
Great Father had sent his people out to talk and beg him to
touch the pen. The whites abandoned all the forts along the
road and Red Cloud himself had watched as Little Wolf took
his people into the empty Buffalo Creek Fort and burned it to
the ground before the bluecoats were even out of sight. The
tribes and clans had all celebrated and rejoiced. It should have
been a glorious time for him.

But something had made it hard for Red Cloud to share the
joy of his people. The dreams had started after the Fight of
the One Hundred Dead, after Spotted Tail had shown him the

[1]These battles, known as the Hayfield Fight and Wagon Box Fight, occurred
on 1 and 2 August 1867 respectively. The first pitted some eight hundred
Lakota and Cheyenne warriors against nineteen soldiers and six civilian hay-
cutters in a field about two miles northeast of Fort C. F. Smith. The second,
known to the Lakota as the Medicine Fight, took place about a mile southeast
of Piney Island near Fort Phil Kearny and pitted twenty-seven soldiers and
civilians against an attack by some three thousand Sioux, Cheyenne, and
Arapaho. The soldiers' use of the newly issued Trapdoor Springfield, a
breech-loading, rapid-fire rifle, negated the tribes' numerical superiority. The
combined casualties for the whites were thirteen killed, while the tribes' combined losses have been estimated at nearly three hundred killed.

trees used as burial scaffolds for so many of the young ones. Thereafter it was as if *Wakan Tanka* came to him every night and showed him again this "bitter fruit," as Spotted Tail had called it. And in these dreams the dead rose up from their burial scaffolds. They looked at him with sightless eyes and called to him, begging him to watch after their widows and their orphan children. After the Medicine Fight even more joined the numbers of the dead who called out to him. On too many nights he had awakened sweating and breathless. Tormented by the dead, the ultimate victory seemed to him empty and bitter.

When the treaties had been signed, when he had touched the pen, he'd gone home to Pretty Owl, looked down at his small son playing outside the lodge and the infant daughter that Pretty Owl now cradled in her arms, and made a silent vow that he would never again follow the Black Road. The others could fight if they would but he would look for other ways to help his people, help his children. Over the years he had become more like Spotted Tail than he'd ever imagined possible, and when others called for war he counseled peace. He had retained many followers and had led them well through the years. He'd learned how to live with the whites. But the old feuds between the Smoke people and the Bear people had been rekindled and the people had begun to fight among themselves. Too many had followed the calls of the firebrands and the so-called messiahs. Even his son had for a time rebelled and gone with the young warriors. Many of the people thought he'd grown old and soft and had come to hate him. Some criticized him for not fighting on even longer. Some held him responsible for all the dead. The dead were not like the grass. They did not come up again in the spring. None of them knew what was in his heart. None of them knew the dreams he had to live with. It was a hard thing to bear.

All the young warriors, Red Cloud thought. They were all gone now. All traveled down the Ghost Road before him, where he must soon follow, for he knew his time in this world was growing short. But in his mind's eye he could see them still, strong and defiant—Roman Nose and Wooden Leg,

Crazy Horse, Kicking Bear, American Horse, Gall and Sitting
Bull, Red Leaf and Little Wolf—their faces and bodies painted
for war, feathered bonnets rustling in the breeze. They danced,
they boasted, they sang. They rode and they fought, thundering
into battle shrieking and calling out *"Hokahe! Hokahe!* It is a
good day to die!" He could hear the whoops and yells, the
shrilling of the eagle-bone whistles, the crack of the rifles, the
rumble of hooves, the twanging of the bowstrings. And then
there was nothing—silence. All was still but for the rustling
of the grass and the high, distant shrill cry of a hawk circling
lazily above on the warm, rising air.

"Father, someone's coming this way," Jack said quietly. "A
white man. He walks with a stick. An old man with a white
beard."

"Wicasa kin le washte ca slolwaye." The old man was nodding.

"How do you know he is a good man, Father?"

"I know who this man is," Red Cloud said quietly. A sad
smile creased his ancient face. "He is wearing a soldier's suit."

"How do you know this, Father? He is still farther than you
can see."

"I don't know how I know this. Maybe the Everywhere
Spirit has told me. He talks to me much more now that I am
an old man, you know." Red Cloud's face creased with an
enigmatic smile.

The old white man stopped a few feet from Red Cloud and
his son. The white man was bent with age but straightened himself with difficulty and shifted the cane to his left hand and
leaned on it. He raised his right hand and held it palm open in
front of him.

"Hau, kola!"

Jack Red Cloud repeated the greeting loudly in his father's
ear. Red Cloud nodded. He removed his goggles, folded them,
and set them carefully on the seat, then motioned to his son
to help him down from the wagon. The old man grasped the
wheel of the wagon with a clawlike hand as he climbed painfully to the ground, then gently brushed Jack's hand off of his

arm and walked a few paces forward, raising his right hand as he went.

"*Cannako, kola,*" he said. "It has been many years has it not? The sun feels good to us old men. You have to speak loudly. I do not hear so well anymore."

"Do you know me?" the old man in the soldier's uniform asked.

"How could I not know you, Little White Chief? Just as you surely know that I am *Mahkpia-Luta*, you would say Red Cloud. I coveted your horse. He was a fine animal and I would have taken him if I could. You had a good eye for a fine animal."

Henry Carrington smiled.

"Yes, he was a good horse," Carrington said, a distant look in his eyes. "I thought you were going to steal him that day in Laramie. I had almost forgotten."

"Well, I thought I would wait and let you bring him to me."

Carrington walked over to Red Cloud and extended his hand. Red Cloud took it and they shook hands then stood next to each other and looked out over the country that lay below them, the wind blowing into their faces, bringing memories tumbling along with it. For a long time neither said a word, each alone with his own memories.

"They tell me your woman wrote a book about this place and those times," Red Cloud said. "Is this so?"

Carrington stared out over the countryside and nodded.

"Yes," Henry said softly, his head nodding. "She wrote a book."

"Hunh. That's good." The old warrior grunted his approval. "It is good that we remember those days. We have lost our Winter Count many years ago. Is your woman well?"

"She died many years ago."

Red Cloud said nothing but simply nodded, his weak eyes blinking in the sunlight.

"It was a hard time," Henry said.

"They were brave men. Good fighters," Red Cloud said. "I've always told the white men that we only lost eleven braves on that day but it was a lie."

Carrington looked at the old Indian and cocked his head. The old chief's eyes were clouded and wet as he squinted off into the distance.

"There were many empty lodges that winter," the old chief went on. "Many women cried and the little ones were hungry. It was hard to listen to them crying. It was worse when the grass was long again. Young men are not like the grass. They do not come up again in the spring. You were gone when we fought again. They tell me that we won that war but I think we lost more than we won. I would not fight again. It was too hard. Too hard to listen to the little ones crying."

Carrington put his hand on the old warrior's shoulder. He too could feel the tears welling up in his eyes. He'd thought he would not feel the hurt so badly anymore but it was still there, deep in his breast.

"I'm sorry for what happened here," Henry said. "I did not want a war."

Red Cloud nodded but said nothing. He had been the one who wanted war. He had been the one who had sent so many young men to travel the Ghost Road. It was something he had lived with for many seasons and it had never gotten easier.

"In the end, perhaps you were more fortunate than we," Carrington said. "You lost many warriors in these fights, good men all I am sure, and eventually you lost this land too. I fear that we whites may have lost our souls. How this turned out is not how I had hoped it would be. It all went wrong."

Red Cloud turned to the old soldier and brought his hand up to the old man's sleeve. He looked into the eyes that had once been so clear, now rheumy, squinted with age and wet with tears.

"Do not think so, old friend," the warrior said. "I used to think the same. I used to ask myself if the things I had done had been done differently would it have been better. But this is a foolish question to ask. Something to keep old men awake at night. Maybe things could have been worse. It's not for us to know. It is part of the circle of life. This land was Absaroka, home of the Crow. And we took it from them. You took it from us. Maybe one day someone else will take it from you.

It is the way of the Everywhere Spirit. We cannot know his plan. It's not for us to say that this is right and this is wrong. It is enough that it is. He moves us through life and we do the best that we know how. Maybe we were enemies so that the children of our children's children can be brothers. We should give thanks for what *Wakan Tanka* gives us."

Carrington nodded and pinched back the tears that blinded him.

"Ahh, your new woman comes, Little White Chief."

"Henry. Please, call me Henry."

"Yes, it is a good thing, Henry," the old warrior said solemnly. "Does your new woman know of the things that happened here? Have you brought her here to tell of the things that once were?"

"No," Carrington said, shaking his head. "She knows too well what happened here. She was here with us and saw all that we saw. Her first husband died over there on that hill many years ago. He commanded the cavalry at the fight."

Red Cloud watched her quietly as she approached. He looked again at the windswept ridgeline where the fight had happened so many years before, and Carrington could almost see the memories washing over the old man.

"*Has!* A brave man, the little chief of the pony soldiers." Red Cloud grunted and nodded his head. "Our young men talked of him for many years. He rode a white horse and charged the warriors like a Braveheart! He counted coup on many men that day. He was a very brave man and died like a warrior."

"Many brave men died that day," Carrington said. "On both sides."

"It is a good thing that you took the Braveheart's widow into your lodge. It is what a Lakota would do. I can hear it in your voice that she has been a good wife to you. We say *Tuwa tawicu kin washte can he lila tanyan wokini*. He who has a good wife is lucky."

"Yes," Henry said, smiling. "She brightened my heart when I thought all was lost."

"*Washte!* This is as it should be. It is the circle of life. The Everywhere Spirit has smiled upon you."

The two men stood in silence and waited as Frances moved steadily up the hill toward them, her black skirt trailing through the brown grass and buffeted by the breeze that was blowing steadily down from the north. She was still a handsome woman and Red Cloud was surprised to see that she seemed able to climb the hill without difficulty. She crested the rise and stood for a moment looking at them before moving to join the two old men.

"Henry," she said. "Are you all right, dear? That is a long climb up here."

"I'm just fine, dear," Henry replied, taking her outstretched hand. "I want you to meet an old friend of mine. His name is *Mahkpia-Luta*. We would say Red Cloud."

Frances looked sharply at the old warrior, her eyes narrowing as she took in the figure of a frail old man dressed simply in white man's clothing and dusty moccasins, his braided hair now white and brittle with age. She looked into Henry's eyes and saw something there that told her that the time had come to let the hurts of the past fade back into that time and place so very long ago. She slipped her arm into his and nodded at Red Cloud, her eyes growing soft.

"I never thought to meet you, sir," she said quietly. "I hope you are well."

The old warrior smiled at her.

"An old man is never well except that he is alive and has his memories. You too have your memories and I am sorry for the ones that give you pain." He nodded toward the distant ridgeline where a stone monument had been raised among the boulders.

"Thank you," she said. Frances held her husband's arm tighter and reached up to finger a small object suspended from a black satin ribbon around her neck.

Red Cloud saw the glint of gold and realized that it must be the wedding ring that had belonged to her long-dead husband. He reached out and laid his hand gently on hers. She noticed that it was a withered hand, veined, bony, and burned to a dark brown by the sun.

"You are lucky," the old warrior said. "The Everywhere Spirit has touched you. Your first husband was a brave man. And this husband," he nodded to Henry Carrington, "he is a good man."

The old warrior turned and motioned to his son, who came forward and took his father by the arm to guide him back to the wagon that waited nearby. When he had settled onto the wagon seat, Red Cloud looked down at the couple who stood watching him in silence. Henry Carrington stepped forward and reached up to take the old warrior's hand in a final clasp.

"*Nape ciyuze*, old friend," Carrington said to him. Red Cloud smiled.

"*Nape ciyuze*, Henry."

Henry Carrington then turned to the warrior's son. "*Wicasa wan lila ksapa kin heca!*"

"Yes, Colonel," Jack Red Cloud said quietly. "He is a man of great wisdom. But I think he fears that it came too late to help our people."

"Maybe," Carrington said slowly. "Maybe it comes too late for any of us. Maybe it's why we insist on making the same mistakes again and again. Wisdom is wasted on us old men. We make our mistakes when we're young and by the time we've learned from them the young people don't trust us anymore. And perhaps they have reason to be wary of us, for we've fared so badly."

"*Hetchetu! Sehanska!*" the old warrior said. "The Little White Chief has it right, my son. It is the way of things. Maybe you can change what we could not, but we were blinded by our times as you may be blinded by yours. Try not to judge us too harshly. We leave this country to you young ones," Red Cloud said. "It is up to you to use it wisely. My friend Henry and I, we have too many ghosts."

He reached down and picked up a handful of the dusty, dry earth that had collected in the wagon and stood looking at the lengthening shadows. He held out his fist and let the sandy soil sift out. It was caught by the wind and blown in a fine spray over the countryside.

"This is what we have left," he said. "Shadows and dust. This is our world. I will go and talk to my ghosts now, Henry Carrington, and I will leave you with yours. Live well, brother."

"Live well, brother," Carrington said.

Jack Red Cloud climbed up onto the wagon and settled onto the seat next to his father. He picked up the reins and shook them, giving a cluck to the team. The old wagon lurched forward and headed slowly toward the far ridge, the oversized wheels rumbling and creaking to the jingle of the harness. In a few moments the sound was lost to Henry and Frances, who stood alone on the hill, looking after the departing men. They stood for a long time listening to the wind in the long grass and to their ghosts.

The Ghost Road

John "Portugee" Phillips completed his ride for help, traveling over two hundred miles in some of the most grueling blizzard conditions imaginable. Phillips, carrying Carrington's dispatches, arrived at Fort Laramie at midnight on Christmas night of 1866. Wrapped in heavy buffalo coat, leggings, cap, and mittens, he staggered exhausted and nearly snow-blind into the midst of the garrison's annual Christmas Ball, a full-dress, fancy cotillion, which was in full swing at the time. Portugee Phillips' Ride has since gone down in the history of the West as one of the most incredible feats ever performed. After the Fetterman Fight he continued to work for the government as a freight contractor and later became a successful rancher and hotel owner. He died in Cheyenne, Wyoming, in November 1883.

Captain Tenedor Ten Eyck never really recovered from his experiences at Fort Phil Kearny. After the Fetterman Fight he became increasingly morose and distant and soon turned to drink. Ten Eyck quickly sank into an alcoholic haze and was court-martialed for "conduct unbecoming an officer." The judgment was set aside by General U. S. Grant and Ten Eyck ordered back to duty, but within five years Ten Eyck had left the Army and disappeared into history.

Elisabeth Wheatley turned out to be a tough young woman and perfectly suited for the territory. After the death of her husband she remained at Fort Phil Kearny to raise her two sons and carry on her business. The few records remaining indicate that she filed several unsuccessful suits against the government in attempts to recover losses incurred when the Army abandoned Fort Phil Kearny. But Elisabeth was not a quitter; she stayed on in the Territory and held her own. She later married the post's blacksmith, George Breakenridge, who, it seems, was a good stepfather to the boys, as he and the boys were later co-owners of one of the first livery stables in Billings, Montana.

Margaret Irvin McDowell Sullivant Carrington made the hazardous trek with her husband and two young sons first to Fort Casper, where they were turned about and headed for Fort McPherson in the dead of winter. She then busied herself with transforming her journal into a book of her experiences at Fort Phil Kearny, which was published as *Ab' Sa' Ra' Ka': Home of the Crows* in 1868 (it remains in print to this day). In 1870, Margaret and Henry returned to Indiana, where he assumed a professorship at Wabash College, but she had contracted tuberculosis, and died on 11 May 1870. Her son Jimmy grew up to become a well-respected journalist, establishing the Chicago office of *Scribner's Magazine*, and was one of the nation's foremost commentators on art and architecture.

Taschunka-Witko **(Crazy Horse)** went on to become one of the most legendary of all American Indians. An inspired warrior and strangely charismatic figure, he would help to lead his people to victory against General George Crook at the Rosebud and, one week later, against George Armstrong Custer and the 7th Cavalry at the Little Bighorn. After surrendering to the U.S. Army in 1877, he was resettled at the Red Cloud Agency near Fort Robinson, Nebraska. The U.S. Army attempted to recruit Crazy Horse to lead Sioux scouts against Chief Joseph's Nez Perces. During the negotiations a scuffle broke out, apparently instigated by his cousin Little Big Man, who had grown resentful of Crazy Horse's reputation and prestige. Crazy Horse received a bayonet thrust and died of his wounds. His grieving followers spirited away his body and interred it in an unmarked grave.

Wasicun Taschunka (**American Horse**) remained for years a staunch opponent of the whites and fought at the battle of the Little Bighorn in 1876. An eloquent speaker, he found himself a frequent visitor to Washington, D.C., where he became a spokesman for his people and over time a shrewd negotiator. For a time he traveled the world with Buffalo Bill's Wild West Show and became convinced of the futility of armed resistance to "progress." In later life he was a strong advocate for peace and reconciliation between Indians and whites but grew to dislike Red Cloud, and political and personal feuds marred their relations. When the Ghost Dance phenomenon swept the northern plains, American Horse feared that young firebrands among the movement's leadership would turn the new religion to catastrophe for the Lakota, and on several occasions risked his life in attempts to counsel caution and restraint. His intercession was not appreciated by the Ghost Dancers, who destroyed American Horse's home and threatened to murder him. American Horse died in 1902.

Tamela Pashme (**Dull Knife**), also known as Morning Star (*Wahiev*), could not keep his Cheyenne people forever from conflict with the whites, and he himself joined his friend Little Wolf in opposition to white expansion. While there is no evidence that he fought at the Little Bighorn, many of his followers did, and he himself conducted a stubborn fighting retreat in an attempt to lead his people to safety in Canada. Pursued relentlessly by the Army, he and Little Wolf surrendered in the spring of 1878. But conditions at Fort Robinson, Nebraska, became intolerable, and in January 1879 he led a daring escape attempt in which almost one-third of his followers died. Dull Knife and his remaining people made it to Red Cloud's reservation on the Rosebud, where they were sheltered. He died and was buried there in 1883.

Sinté-Galeska (**Spotted Tail**) eventually remarried—four times—and remained a respected but controversial figure among the Lakota. A frequent visitor to Washington, D.C., he negotiated personally with presidents Grant and Hayes and Secretary of the Interior Carl Schurz. He personally selected the location of Rosebud Agency and became deeply embroiled in Indian-White political wrangling. He strongly opposed armed resistance to the whites, which resulted in the Little Bighorn fight and the subsequent breakup of the Lakota nation, preferring to employ his considerable political wiles to better the lot of his people. He made a number of enemies within his own tribe, and on 5 August 1881, while returning from a tribal council meeting, was assassinated by Crow Dog, a fellow Brulé and former Chief of Indian Police at Rosebud Agency.

Frances Grummond Carrington took the remains of her husband back to Franklin, Tennessee, where she soon discovered that her tribulations were not at an end. George Washington Grummond, it turned out, had been married previously, and the divorce had not been final when he had married Frances, making him, in fact, a bigamist. There followed a lengthy legal battle in an attempt to obtain the pension benefits to which Frances had thought she was entitled. The case was eventually settled and Frances' status recognized but not without considerable heartbreak. When Frances learned that her old friend Margaret Carrington had died she wrote a letter of condolence to Henry Carrington, which began a correspondence. Within a year the two were married. In addition to the children of previous marriages the Carringtons had three more children. Frances died of tuberculosis on 17 October 1911.

Henry Beebe Carrington spent most of the rest of his life defending his reputation as a soldier. While the Army's official investigation into the Fetterman Fight fully exonerated Carrington's actions, the impact of the massacre on the nation's psyche was so great that the government and the military scrambled to find a scapegoat. The findings of the Army's Sanborn Commission were quietly filed away in obscurity and Carrington bore the brunt of the nation's anger. Henry left the service in 1870 and taught military science and mathematics at Wabash College in Indiana. He went on to write a number of books and articles on American history, earning him a well-deserved reputation for superb scholarship. It was not until 1890 that General Philip St. George Cooke, Carrington's superior during the Phil Kearny days, admitted that Henry Carrington was blameless in the Fetterman affair. Henry Carrington died on 26 October 1912 and is buried alongside Frances in Hyde Park, Massachusetts.

Jim Bridger remained in the Bighorns for but a few more months following the Fetterman Fight. With his eyesight growing weaker and saddened by the passing of his way of life, Bridger quietly packed up his mule and headed back toward Kansas City. The old mountain man, explorer, raconteur, and scout retired to a quiet life on his farm in Westport, Missouri, where he died in 1881.

Nelson Story completed his cattle drive, arriving in Virginia City on 9 December 1866. It was the culmination of an amazing feat. Having started the drive in Texas with the intention of selling the herd in Kansas City, Story's crew made it as far as Kansas before being turned back by local cattlemen. Not to be deterred, Story turned the herd about and headed for Montana in one of the longest cattle drives in history. Story remained in Montana, where he became a successful rancher and entrepreneur with interests in commerce, banking, and even real estate. He died in 1926, a wealthy and well-respected man.

Mahkpia-Luta (**Red Cloud**) won his war against the United States, a fact that is often overlooked. While the Lakota would enjoy the fruits of Red Cloud's victory for a few years, all would come to a catastrophic end in the late 1870s. Sobered by the cost of his victory and the scope of the United States' power—which he observed firsthand while traveling the East Coast—Red Cloud fought hard to preserve his people's way of life and to stave off further conflict between red and white. Thus in a note of supreme irony he found himself assuming much the same stance for which he had previously held Spotted Tail in contempt. A strong advocate for peace, Red Cloud strove to mediate between his people and the whites and as a result was very much caught in the middle of warring and irreconcilable cultures. Toward the end of his life Red Cloud was visited at his Pine Ridge home by the anthropologist Warren Moorehead. Red Cloud said to him:

"You see this barren waste? Washington took our lands and promised to feed and support us. Now I, who used to control five thousand warriors, must tell Washington when I am hungry. I must beg for that which I own. If I beg hard they put me in the guardhouse. We have trouble. Our girls are getting bad. Coughing sickness every winter carries away our best people. My heart is heavy, I am old, I cannot do much more."

Red Cloud died on 10 December 1909 and was buried on a hill overlooking the agency.

Absaroka

The word "Absaroka" is an adaptation of "Ab' Sa' Ra' Ka," which means literally "Home of the Crows" and refers to the Crow Indian tribe, which claimed as its home the portion of the Wyoming Territory in which the story is set. The word was originally used by Mrs. Margaret Carrington in her memoirs, *Ab' Sa' Ra' Ka,' Home of the Crows: Being the Experience of an Officer's Wife on the Plains.* Margaret was the wife of Colonel Henry Carrington, commander of the 18th Regiment of Infantry, and a pivotal character in this tale. By the time Margaret arrived in Wyoming Territory, in 1866, the Crow had been dispossessed by the Lakota and Arapaho, who were in turn about to be challenged for possession of the land and its resources. Margaret Carrington's reminiscences were first published in 1868 by J. B. Lippincott and Co., Philadelphia, and remain in print to this day. For those who wish to read more on the events and people described herein I cannot recommend it too highly.

Unlike Margaret's memoirs, this book is first and foremost a work of fiction. While I have taken pains to keep the story as true to the known facts as possible, one liberty that I have taken is in moving forward in time the spectacular feat of

Portugee Phillips. I leave it to the historians to delight in dis-
covering the other discrepancies—real and imagined—and to
agonize over the things they missed. One of the great delights
of the historical novelist is the license to hang flesh on the
bones of the actors and set the blood pumping through their
veins. While the purist may decry this practice, others will
find it useful and perhaps informative. There is a sense in
which fiction can reveal to us more of the truth than history
in that historians are frequently constrained by their reliance
on relics, some written, which are in themselves the products
of imperfect and differently motivated human beings. So while
the historian can at best provide an objective account of the
facts (however incomplete or imperfect), it is the province of
the novelist to address not only the objective facts of a period
and a people but their passions as well. To paraphrase Macaulay, it can be the difference between a topographical map
and a painted landscape.